I0779204

SOL ALLIANCE

BOOK II
PAWN'S SACRIFICE

K. J. McDonald

For Bunny,
My guiding star, my endless sky.

Beneath the cosmos vast and wide,
You are my compass, my heart's true guide.
Through your gentle embrace,
I find my home in your gentle face.

No black hole's pull, no comet's flight,
Could dim the glow of your starlit light.
My Bunny, my universe, near or far,
Forever you'll be my brightest star.

NAVAL INTELLIGENCE
One Spear, One Purpose
One Mission

Prologue

Personal Log - Capt. Jonathan Pierce - April 8th, 2167

I often find myself asking, "Why?" Why am I here? Why can't I solve this puzzle? The questions keep coming, like a hydra—once I figure out one, more appear in its place. I feel like a modern-day Sisyphus, and this mystery is my boulder. *sighs* The void is taking its toll on me. The nothingness stretches into infinity, stealing my sanity with it.

I can't let my crew see me falter; their confidence in me is already wearing thin given recent events. We've chased this elusive freighter for weeks now, and each dead end chips away at my resolve. The crew looks to me for guidance, but I'm starting to feel lost in this vast emptiness. Every unanswered question weighs heavily on my chest. The more we search, the heavier the burden feels.

Allison is also breaking under the pressure, though she won't admit it. I hear it in her voice, the subtle tremor that betrays her worry. She's urged me to give the crew a break, but we're so close to finding the freighter; I can feel it in my bones. Yet, perhaps she's right. We've pushed too hard for too long, and the strain is starting to show.

I know arguing with her is a battle I can't win; I learned that lesson early on in the academy. When Allison is determined, she's relentless. Morale is low, tensions are high, and I can feel the collective weight of it pressing down on all of us. I need to find a way to ease this tension before it fractures the crew entirely.

But how do I balance the pressure of command with the well-being of my crew? I feel like I'm walking a tightrope, and one misstep could lead to disaster. It's a dangerous game, and I can't afford to lose. The crew needs a break... I need a break.

Personal Log - Cmdr. Allison Jones - April 8th, 2167

I'm on the edge—frayed nerves and a broken spirit. I feel like I'm teetering over a precipice, looking down into a pit of despair. Jonathan can probably see it no matter how well I try to hide it. His face tells the same story: a man overwhelmed by failure, something he's not used to and something I don't know how to help him with.

The crew is on the verge of breaking. Their morale is low—non-existent, really. I've watched them grow more listless as the days drag on, and I can see it in their eyes—the fatigue, the frustration. It's palpable, and it reminds me of my cattle back home. A herd can only take so much pressure before they start to scatter, and right now, that's exactly what I'm feeling with this crew. They need guidance, just like my brothers need a firm hand when the cattle get restless. If they don't get a break soon, I fear they'll bolt in every direction, and I won't be able to reel them back in.

I keep urging Jonathan to give the crew a break, or he'll have a mutiny on his hands. He needs to understand that this relentless pace can't continue. The void is claiming its due again, taking its pound of flesh in the way of our sanity. I miss the blue skies and the scent of actual air, not this recirculated stuff we're forced to breathe. It's early April now, which means calving season back on the family ranch. My brothers will have to tend to the herd without me this year.

They're capable, but they often need a harsh reality check to keep their egos in check. Maybe I need to give Jonathan that same kind of reality check. He's become so fixated on finding this freighter that he's lost sight of everything else. We need to remember why we're out here, not just for the mission, but for each other. If we don't come together soon, we'll lose not only this mission but also the very fabric that holds us as a crew.

Personal Log - Lt. Veronica Valentine - April 8th, 2167

Lieutenant… It sounds so strange. Still, when I dress in the morning, I find myself staring in the mirror at my uniform. It's a weighty title, one I never quite expected. The captain seems stressed; his usual calm and warm demeanor has been replaced with a cold, harsh tone. I've never seen him snap before—not like this. This morning, he reprimanded a young ensign for presenting sensor data that wasn't arranged properly. Usually, a little coaching would suffice, but he openly berated him on the bridge and ordered Commander Jones to put him in remedial training. Such a harsh punishment for a minor mistake.

The atmosphere on the ship feels tense, and I can see it affecting everyone. Commander Jones didn't even flinch; she just went along with it. That's so out of character for them both. I get it; we've been hunting this freighter for weeks, and part of me wishes we'd never started. I don't want to find the damn thing. The memories of what happened on that ship still haunt my dreams, and I can't shake the images of my sister, cold and detached. I wake up in a cold sweat, my shoulder throbbing, wishing I could forget.

I often wonder if I'll find her on that freighter. It's a thought that chills me to the bone. The darkness of that place lingers in my mind, and every time I think about it, I feel like I'm drowning. The longer we search, the more I feel the weight of that darkness creeping in, ready to swallow me whole. But I can't voice these fears; the captain and commander need me to be strong.

Deep down, I know that if this continues, we're all going to break. This relentless pursuit is draining, and I fear it's consuming us. I want to turn back, to escape this nightmare, but I know that's not an option. So, I keep quiet, hoping for a way out.

Chapter 1

The auditorium buzzed with energy, a palpable anticipation in the air as attendees awaited the demonstration of the latest technology from Neura Tech. Reporters, eager for the first scoop, shuffled their notebooks, while high-ranking military officials scanned the room, searching for the next big advancement to harness. Influential figures from industries as varied as banking and healthcare filled the seats, each one hungry for innovation.

Backstage in the prep area, Ava Turing focused on her speech notes. A distant niece of the famous Alan Turing, Ava founded Neura Tech at just eighteen. Now, a decade later, the company stands as the largest technology enterprise in the Alliance, its headquarters on Centauri Prime towers over the planet and employing nearly 60% of the colony's population. With campuses on every major world in the Alliance, Neura Tech boasts an annual revenue of nearly 200 billion, cementing its status as the largest corporation overall.

Ava walked out onto the stage, adorned in her signature long red dress, her waist-length black hair braided neatly. As she moved, her hair swung like a pendulum, drawing the audience's attention. She smiled and waved to the crowd, their cheers erupting in response. Turning on her headset, she projected warmth and enthusiasm, "Hello everyone, how are you?!"

The crowd's cheers grew louder, echoing against the auditorium walls. Holding up her hands, Ava settled them down, savoring the brief silence before launching into her speech.

"Today, we're not just unveiling new technology; we're redefining the future," she began. The crowd leaned forward, they were exactly where she wanted them. She spoke passionately about the latest advances in communication technologies—the implantable comms device behind the ear—a massive breakthrough that promised to sell hundreds of millions of units on day one. Transitioning to medical technologies, she highlighted an enhanced MRI that created interactive three-dimensional images, revolutionizing diagnostics and surgical planning.

"Now that we've covered all the boring stuff," she paused, allowing the crowd a moment to react with laughter, "it's time to introduce who you really came to see." The room's lights dimmed as a large screen descended from the ceiling, revealing a virtual face that materialized on the screen, appearing as a young, beautiful woman.

"Ladies and gentlemen, I introduce to you Athena!"

After a brief pause, the digital face began to speak, her tone soft and gentle, reminiscent of a caring mother. "Hello, I am the

Augmented Technology for Human Enhancement and Natural Applications, but you can call me Athena." The crowd was captivated, impressed by the speech patterns and voice modulation.

Ava continued, "Athena is the most advanced AI mankind has ever created. With her neural network and machine learning, she can handle everything from mundane day-to-day tasks to the most complex brain surgery."

"Ava, you are embarrassing me in front of all these people," Athena interjected playfully, her digital cheeks turning a shade of red, which elicited a collective "Aww" from the crowd.

Ava chuckled. "As you can see, Athena is capable of displaying and expressing complex emotions."

She continued to elaborate on Athena's capabilities, highlighting the promise of advancing humankind into the future. Ava's energy surged as she delivered a news-breaking announcement: "Ladies and gentlemen, Neura Tech is thrilled to announce that Athena is launching today!"

"Athena, I'd like you to take questions from the press, if that's okay with you," Ava added.

"Sure, Ava. I would love to," Athena replied smoothly.

A microphone was set up, and reporters lined up, eager to engage. The first press member stepped up. "Athena, James Allen Centauri Prime Telegraph. How do you ensure the privacy and security of the data you collect?"

"A brilliant question, James Allen. First, I want to express how much I've enjoyed reading your tech columns in the CPT since I was first activated in the testing labs. Your insights are always stimulating. Regarding privacy and security, they are built into my core algorithms. Just like a vault in a bank, I protect data with layers of encryption and only grant access to authorized personnel. Think of me as a digital fortress—minus the moat and drawbridge, of course!"

The crowd chuckled at Athena's playful analogy.

"Athena, Traci Yamato GNN News. How do you handle emergencies or unexpected situations?"

"Firstly, Traci Yamato, let me commend you on your insightful reporting. Your ability to shed light on complex issues is something I truly admire. As for emergencies, I believe in focusing on prevention. By analyzing vast amounts of data, I can anticipate and mitigate risks before they escalate. It's about creating a safer world, one calculation at a time."

The press continued to fire questions regarding Athena's applications in finance, healthcare, military operations, and beyond. Each inquiry was handled expertly by the AI, showcasing her capabilities and leaving the audience even more impressed.

As the presentation drew to a close, Ava took the stage one last time. "That's all the time we have for today, but feel free to reach out to our press agents for any additional inquiries. Thank you, everyone, and goodnight!"

Once backstage, Ava reached up to switch off her headset and sank into the makeup booth, allowing her body to relax for the first time. She looked into the mirror, her expression shifting from warm and welcoming to cold and calculating. A devious smile crept onto her lips as she whispered, a slight dark shift in her tone, "I have done it."

Checking her watch, she noticed she had finished ahead of schedule. "Plenty of time," she murmured, grabbing her tablet to check her messages. As she read through the updates, her smile widened. The messages assured her that everything was moving along as planned, and a sense of satisfaction washed over her.

****

The Prime Senate Building in New York City is a wonder of modern architecture, constructed from a combination of transparent alloys and reinforced composites, giving it a sleek, almost ethereal appearance. Surrounded by lush gardens and reflective pools, it creates a serene environment amidst the bustling city. Solar panels and vertical gardens are seamlessly integrated into the design, emphasizing sustainability and harmony with nature.

Upon entering, visitors are greeted by a grand atrium that spanned several stories, bathed in natural light thanks to the transparent ceiling and walls. Hanging gardens cascaded from the balconies, while a central water feature added a tranquil ambiance. Interactive information kiosks and holographic guides available to assist visitors, but few noticed them as they focused on the event unfolding.

In the main chamber, where all Senate proceedings were held, a circular room awaited. A raised platform stood at the center, surrounded by multiple rows of tables arranged in a circle. Sections where the various colonies were all represented, but this meeting was different—a special session of the Primes had been called by Chancellor Elias Vaughn.

The Alliance consisted of eight colonies, each governed by its own Senate, with representation based on population. The three major colonies—Earth, Luna, and Mars—dominated with the largest number of senators, while the five minor colonies—New Earth, Centauri Prime, Callisto, Ganymede, and Europa—held fewer seats. Every Senate elected one of its own to serve as Prime, the colony's official leader. These eight Primes formed the Conclave of Primes, tasked with shaping inter-colonial policy and mediating the tensions between worlds. From among their ranks, the Primes chose one to serve as Chancellor, the leader of the entire Alliance, holding authority over the delicate balance that kept the colonies united—if only just.

Elias stood at his podium, flanked by the seven other primes. After calling the meeting to order, Prime Selene Armitage, representing the Luna colony, was first to speak, her voice cutting through the tension like a knife.

"Chancellor, I propose a motion for a full Senatorial Investigation into the rumors of a 'shadow faction' comprised of senators from New Earth, and to have them arrested and charged with treason. I also call for the immediate removal of Prime Patel from her position until the Senate Inquiry is completed." Her tone dripped with disdain; her posture rigid as she directed her gaze at Asha Patel. The citizens of Luna often viewed themselves as superior, and the underlying arrogance in Selene's voice was palpable.

Prime Darius Kincaid of Mars leaned forward, his fingers steepled in front of him, nodding in agreement. "I second the motion," his body language mirroring Selene's. The three major territories once again pushed their power over the five minors, as if to remind everyone of their dominance.

Before Chancellor Vaughn could respond, Prime Mira Volkov from Callisto interjected. "I would like to first hear from Prime Patel on this matter." Her eyes darted between Selene and Asha, subtly challenging Selene's outright aggression.

In their usual show of solidarity, Prime Nakamura of Europa and Prime Torres of Ganymede stood as they supported their fellow Jovian Prime, a united front that made Asha's shoulders tense.

Dr. Linh Nguyen, Prime Senator of Centauri Prime, rose from her seat, commanding immediate attention. The other senators hushed their discussions—not out of fear, but respect.

The Jovian Aggression had been a critical turning point in recent history. It began when a faction of ambitious leaders from the Jovian colonies—Europa, Ganymede, and Callisto—attempted to seize control of all the colonies within the solar system. Their goal was to establish a dominant Jovian regime, leveraging their strategic positions and resources to exert control over the other colonies.

Dr. Nguyen, then a highly respected judge, was appointed to oversee the trial of the Jovian leaders who orchestrated the aggression. Her reputation for fairness and integrity made her the ideal candidate for this critical role.

Throughout the trial, Dr. Nguyen demonstrated exceptional legal acumen and unwavering commitment to justice. She meticulously reviewed evidence, ensured due process, and maintained impartiality despite immense political pressure. Her judicious handling of the trial led to the conviction of those responsible for the conflict, restoring faith in the judicial system and the rule of law within the colonies.

In response to the Jovian Aggression, the other colonies recognized the need for a unified front to prevent such power grabs in the future. This led to the official formation of the Sol Alliance, a coalition dedicated to mutual defense, cooperation, and governance. The colonies banded together, establishing a framework for collective security and shared governance, ensuring that no single colony could dominate the others, promoting a balance of power and mutual respect. The Sol Alliance was founded on principles of democracy, transparency, and justice, marking a new era of interstellar cooperation.

Dr. Nguyen's role in the trial showcased her courage, integrity, and dedication to justice. Her peers came to see her as a guardian of justice, someone whose judgment could be trusted in the most challenging situations.

She began to speak, her accent a unique blend reflecting the linguistic evolution on Centauri Prime. Her voice carried the melodic tones of Mandarin, the rhythmic cadence of Japanese, and the clipped consonants of Korean, all seamlessly intertwined into a single, fluid language known as Centaurian.

"Fellow Primes, we must not make rash decisions based merely on rumor. I agree that there must be an investigation, but asking Prime Patel to step down carries no legal weight, and I will not support such a decision. Since removing a Prime requires a unanimous vote, the motion is moot." As she spoke, her hands remained steady at her sides, projecting confidence, even as she glanced at Asha, offering a subtle nod of solidarity.

Gracefully sitting back down, she pulled out her tablet and began taking notes on the meeting. Chancellor Vaughn spoke next. "Prime Nguyen is correct." He gestured toward her. "We must uphold the principles the Alliance was founded on and let the justice system work as intended. If we allow ourselves to act rashly, we risk destroying what we have created."

Chancellor Vaughn looked to his tablet, addressing Prime Patel. "I understand you have some insight into these rumors."

Standing up, Asha held her tablet tightly, hands trembling slightly. The sleek device cradled her fingers, holding devastating information about her fellow Senators—information she wished she didn't have to deliver.

"Chancellor, fellow Primes. I have investigated all twenty Senators from New Earth and suspect six to be involved in this

shadow faction." Her throat tightened as she spoke, and she
hesitated to continue. Suddenly, her tablet chimed, an incoming
message from an unknown sender. Tapping the message to open it,
she read it silently. The words sent a cold chill down her spine. She
looked over her shoulder, quickly scanning the entire chamber, but
saw nothing but the empty tables.

"Prime Patel, is everything okay?" Chancellor Vaughn asked.

Clearing her throat, she forced herself to respond, "Yes,
Chancellor. Here are the names of those we suspect to be in this
faction." Tapping her tablet, she sent the list to the others, her heart
racing as she caught the wary glances from some of the Primes.

Chancellor Vaughn stumbled over his words. "These are some
powerful names. Are you sure?"

Again hesitating, she whispered the foreboding message to
herself, "I always get what I want."

Chancellor Vaughn, not quite catching, asked, "What was that,
Prime Patel?"

"Sorry, Chancellor, yes, I am sure." She said, fear threading
through her words as she locked eyes with Selene, who had
narrowed her gaze, suspicious.

"Then it is decided. We will launch a full investigation into
this faction and arrest those involved. Prime Nguyen, you will lead
the investigation. Prime Nakamura, you will oversee. I expect to
have frequent reports on your progress," Chancellor Vaughn
ordered, his authority echoing in the chamber.

A low murmur spread among the senators. Prime Kincaid
leaned back in his chair, crossing his arms. Meanwhile, Selene's
lips pressed together, her body language radiating hostility.

After a short discussion of the final details, the meeting was adjourned. Asha gathered her things, the ominous message still flashing in her mind. She walked to her car waiting outside, tapping her tablet for her pilot to prep the shuttle to return to her ship in orbit, hoping she would be granted passage through the gate on a Senatorial pass.

Asha stepped out of the grand hall, her heart pounding in her chest. The weight of the false information she had just delivered to the other Primes and the Chancellor bore heavily on her conscience. She took a deep breath, trying to steady herself as she approached her sleek, black car waiting at the curb.

The door opened automatically, and she slid into the back seat, expecting the usual solitude of her rides. Instead, she noticed a tablet in the seat next to her, her hand trembling as she picked it up and turned the screen on. On it was a video file, waiting to be played. Tapping it, she was greeted by Cipher's cold stare.

"Prime Patel," Cipher said, warmly and welcoming, but Asha knew better. She recognized the true coldness of that dreadful woman.

"I see that your meeting went well. I'm also glad to see my little reminder kept you on track." Again, the false warmth made her skin crawl. Cipher's voice was smooth, but her eyes were as cold as ice. Asha's mind raced, wondering how she knew. But then, Cipher always knew.

As the cityscape blurred past, Asha's mind became a storm of conflicting thoughts and emotions. She couldn't shake the image of her family—her parents, her younger brother—innocent and unaware of the danger looming over them. The thought of Cipher's reach extending to them sent a shiver down her spine.

She replayed the meeting in her head, scrutinizing every detail. Had she missed something? Was there a clue in the Chancellor's reaction, or in the way Prime Nguyen and Prime Nakamura exchanged glances? Paranoia gnawed at her, making her question every interaction, every word spoken.

Asha pondered the shadow faction she had accused the Senators of being part of. Were they truly guilty, or were they just pawns in a larger game, much like herself? The lines between friend and foe blurred, leaving her feeling isolated and vulnerable.

Her thoughts drifted to the gate she hoped to travel through on her Senatorial pass. Would it offer her a momentary respite, or was it just another trap laid by Cipher? The uncertainty was suffocating.

She considered her next steps. Should she confide in someone, risking exposure in the hope of finding an ally? Or should she continue to play Cipher's game, hoping to find a way to outmaneuver her? The stakes were too high for mistakes, and the pressure was relentless.

As the car approached the spaceport, Asha took a deep breath, steeling herself for what lay ahead. She had to stay strong, for her family, for herself. But the fear lingered, a constant reminder of the peril she faced. "I always get what I want," Cipher's words echoed, a chilling mantra that refused to fade.

* * *

Captain Pierce sat in his command chair, his patience thinning. The weeks had dragged on endlessly; the search for the elusive

Jovian freighter felt like chasing shadows. Every promising lead crumbled into nothing, and the weight of failure hung heavily over the crew. Allison, usually lively and sharp-tongued, had retreated into a tense silence as she flipped through reports. Veronica, though growing into her new role, still appeared uneasy, her gaze darting around the bridge as if seeking reassurance. Pierce noticed her uncertainty but couldn't bring himself to address it now—not with everything weighing on him.

His lips curled slightly in a fleeting grin as he reflected on Veronica's growth. She was becoming a capable officer despite her inexperience. But his thoughts were interrupted when she noticed the smile.

"What's got you smiling, Captain?" Veronica asked, trying to mask her nerves with light curiosity.

"It's nothing, Miss Valentine. Just thinking," Pierce replied. Before he could say more, the communication officer broke the uneasy calm.

"Sir," she said, "we've received an encrypted message, but none of the fleet's keys are working."

Veronica moved to the comms station, leaning over the console. "Captain, this encryption—it's not like anything I've seen before. None of the classified keys I have are working either."

Pierce's expression grew more serious. "What's the prefix code?"

Veronica squinted at the screen. "ECHO-ECHO-ECHO," she reported, glancing back at Pierce, whose face grew still. He knew the code. He didn't need to say it.

Pierce straightened in his chair. "Lieutenant Valentine, transfer the message to my braille pad immediately."

Veronica hesitated for a moment, confused by the sudden shift in formality but complied quickly. "Yes, sir." She handed over the pad.

Pierce took the pad without explanation. "I'll be in my office. Do not disturb me."

The crew went rigid as he rose. "Commander, you have the bridge," he said sharply.

Allison blinked, startled by his abruptness. "Aye, sir. I… have the bridge," she replied, watching him leave with a growing sense of unease.

Veronica's voice was a low whisper. "Ma'am… what just happened?"

Allison settled into the command chair, Pierce's mood lost on her. "I'm not sure, but I've never seen him act like that before." She said as she keyed in her command codes.

The minutes stretched into hours, the tension on the bridge thick enough to cut with a knife. Every now and then, Veronica glanced at Allison, seeking some kind of answer, but none came. Finally, after what felt like an eternity, Pierce's voice crackled over the speakers.

"Commander Jones, Lieutenant Valentine, report to my office."

Veronica and Allison exchanged a glance, neither of them fully understanding the gravity of what was unfolding. The cryptic message, Pierce's strange behavior—it all pointed to something beyond their usual duties. And Veronica, still new to the command scene, was struggling to keep up.

They entered Pierce's office, finding him seated behind his desk, a cold intensity on his face. A tablet lay on the desk before him, its screen now dark, the atmosphere in the room was far from calm. Major Cruise sat across from Pierce looking just as intense.

"Major, show the Commander the communication," Pierce ordered.

Cruise handed the tablet to Allison, who read the message slowly. Her confusion quickly turned to concern as her eyes darted over the cryptic phrases. "Captain," she began cautiously, "I don't understand… what is this?" She handed the tablet back to Cruise.

Pierce leaned forward and spoke calmly. "It's a message urging us to return to New Earth. Someone there claims to have information on Cipher."

Veronica's face paled. "Who? Who sent the message?"

Pierce's expression hardened. "They didn't give a name. But they signed off with a codename: 'Starfire.'"

Veronica shifted uncomfortably, clearly out of her depth. "Starfire…? Who's that?"

Allison shook her head, face blank with confusion. "I've never heard of that name."

Pierce's expression grew thoughtful "I know who they are… but only by reputation. We can't risk exposing their cover. This is someone… embedded deep."

Veronica felt a surge of anxiety rise within her. Everything around her—the cryptic messages, the secrecy, and now a shadowy figure with a codename—felt like stepping into a world of shadows she wasn't prepared for. The cloak-and-dagger games of intelligence officers were not what she had signed up for.

Allison crossed her arms. "And the rest of the message?"

Pierce exhaled slowly. "'Trust nothing you hear, and only half of what you see.'"

Silence filled the room. It wasn't just a cryptic note—it was a warning. Allison exchanged a glance with Veronica, whose eyes reflected a growing sense of dread. None of this was what they had expected, and now it seemed like they were walking into a minefield.

Veronica hesitated, feeling the walls closing in as she tried to process everything. "Sir… what if this is a trap?"

Pierce turned his head in her direction, though his gaze remained fixed ahead. "That's the risk, Miss Valentine. But it's a lead we can't ignore."

Veronica nodded, though the pit in her stomach deepened. She had been thrust into a game she didn't understand, and with each passing moment, it felt like the ground beneath her was slipping.

Allison, frustrated, spoke. "Are you really so desperate to solve this mystery that you're willing to trust a message from a complete stranger? That's not the Jonathan I know." Her tone softened slightly as she continued. "You've always been careful, methodical. This... this feels reckless."

Pierce exhaled slowly, steadying his thoughts before speaking. "Allison, I understand why you don't trust this, why it feels like we're walking into something blind—" he paused, catching the unintentional irony, "but I know this name. 'Starfire' isn't just some random lead. I've heard of them before, through trusted channels. Whoever they are, they've earned a reputation for being... reliable, to say the least."

He leaned forward slightly. "I wouldn't put the crew at risk if I didn't believe that this could be the break we've been waiting for. I can't explain everything—not without compromising too much—

but trust me when I say this: we can't ignore this lead… I can't ignore this lead."

He paused, choosing his next word carefully. "I know it's not like me to go on faith like this, but if 'Starfire' is reaching out, it's for a reason. We need to follow this, Allison. I'm asking you to trust me."

Allison uncrossed her arms and leaned forward.

"You're asking us to put a lot of faith in someone we don't know, based on whispers and a reputation," Allison said. "I get it—you've heard of 'Starfire,' but that doesn't mean they aren't leading us into a trap. You and I both know how these things work." She paused for a moment. "You're right, Jonathan. I do trust you. But don't mistake that for blindly trusting whoever this is. I'm with you on this... but if this goes belly up, you need to be ready for what it could cost us."

Pierce shifted in his seat, fingers tightening slightly around the arms of his chair. His posture gave away more than he intended— the tension in his shoulders, the slight furrow in his brow. He wasn't any more comfortable with the situation than she was, but he knew what needed to be done. His body betrayed the hesitation, but his voice wouldn't.

He turned his head slightly toward Veronica, who had been tapping away on her tablet, diligently taking notes on the meeting. Her focus had been on her task, but the growing sense of uncertainty around her was felt by all.

"Miss Valentine," Pierce said. "This conversation does not get recorded. Please delete everything you wrote."

Veronica's fingers hovered above the screen, frozen mid-motion. Confusion flickered across her face. She had never been asked to omit anything from the record during her tenure on the ship; part of her duties was always to record everything precisely and without bias. The request left her unsettled.

"Delete… everything, sir?" she asked hesitantly, her voice breaking as she forced the words out.

Pierce didn't miss a beat. "Yes, Lieutenant. Everything."

Veronica couldn't shake the feeling that something was amiss. Would she be compromising her principles as an officer by obeying this order?

She nodded slowly, still grappling with the conflict between her duties and her captain's command. "Aye, sir," she finally whispered, her fingers trembling slightly as she tapped on the tablet to comply, a pit forming in her stomach as she erased the conversation from the logs.

As she deleted the entries, a sense of dread washed over her. What did this mean for the mission? What kind of danger were they truly stepping into? But before she could dwell on it further, Pierce turned his attention back to Allison, straightening his posture as if fortifying himself for what was to come.

"Commander, set course for New Earth."

Chapter 2

Senator Lopez sat hunched in the cell, her wrists aching from the cold bite of the metal handcuffs. The single overhead light cast harsh shadows, turning the small space into a claustrophobic nightmare. How long had it been? Days? Weeks? Time had lost all meaning to her in the oppressive silence.

The door creaked open, and a military officer stepped inside, his face a mask of emotionless professionalism. "Senator Lopez, you're being released. Follow me," he said, devoid of emotion or explanation.

Lopez stood slowly; her legs stiff from sitting too long. She winced as the handcuffs were removed, the skin around her wrists raw. As she followed the officer into a sterile hallway, the buzz of fluorescent lights overhead added to the surreal atmosphere. Her mind raced, filled with questions she was too afraid to ask.

"Why now? What's changed?" she demanded.

The officer didn't respond. His cold, robotic demeanor only deepened her unease. He was a cog in a machine far larger than herself, and she felt small, powerless.

"Who ordered my release?" Lopez tried again. "I deserve to know."

Still, nothing. His face remained unchanged, as if her words had no weight, as if she barely existed in his world.

Outside, the cool night air hit her like a splash of water. Her personal limo sat idling, its engine a low hum in the quiet street. The officer opened the back door, and she hesitated for a second before climbing inside. Something was wrong—very wrong.

As the door shut behind her, she realized she wasn't alone. A figure sat across from her, obscured by shadows. The dim light inside the limo did little to reveal their face, but the presence was unmistakable—cold, calculating, dangerous.

"Why are you in my car?" Lopez said, choking on the words.

The figure leaned forward, revealing the gleam of a sidearm resting casually on their lap. The sight of the weapon sent a chill through Lopez's entire body.

"Good evening, Senator Lopez." The figure's voice was smooth, controlled. "It's a pleasure to finally meet you."

Lopez's heart pounded, the sound of it thunderous in her ears. She fought to steady her breath. "What is this? Who are you?" Her voice cracking under the pressure.

The figure shifted, revealing just enough of their face for Lopez to see the glint of a cold smile. "You're being released because I need you for important work. Your reputation for transparency and righteousness is exactly what I need."

Lopez's mouth went dry. She felt the walls of her carefully constructed world closing in. The figure's smile faded, replaced by a steely, predatory gaze. They leaned in, their face now inches from hers, and whispered, "I am Cipher."

Lopez's blood turned to ice. The name carried weight—a name whispered in corridors, never openly discussed. Cipher was a ghost, a myth. No one had ever seen her, and yet here she was, in Lopez's own limo.

"I won't be part of whatever you're planning," Lopez said trembling. "I stand for truth and justice."

Cipher's smile widened, a chilling, humorless grin. "Oh, Senator, you'll do exactly what I want. Whether you like it or not. Your principles won't save you here."

As the limo moved through the city streets, the familiar sights outside felt distant, irrelevant. Lopez was no longer in control of her fate—this was Cipher's game now. And she was a pawn.

"You have a choice, Senator," Cipher continued. "Cooperate, and perhaps you'll keep your precious ideals intact. Resist..." She let the words hang for a what seemed like forever. "And you'll see just how far my reach extends."

Lopez's heart pounded harder, fear coiling tight around her. Every breath felt like a struggle. Cipher leaned in again, brushing a cold finger along Lopez's cheek, the gesture as intimate as it was terrifying.

"And just so we're clear," Cipher purred, "I always get what I want."

Lopez recoiled, her skin crawling at the touch, but she forced herself to hold Cipher's gaze. Every fiber of her being screamed to run, to escape, but there was nowhere to go. And yet, a flicker of defiance sparked inside her.

"I won't be broken so easily," Lopez blurted, trying to summon the strength that defined her.

Cipher's cold eyes glittered with amusement. "We'll see, Senator. We'll see."

The limo pulled up to Lopez's apartment building, its usual familiarity now marred by an undercurrent of danger. Cipher's demeanor shifted, becoming even more menacing.

"Now," Cipher said, "you're going to get out of this car and walk straight to your apartment. No detours, no talking to anyone. If you even think about calling for help, you'll regret it."

Lopez felt her throat tighten as Cipher's threat loomed in the small confines of her limo. She nodded slowly, trembling, a silent agreement to the demands.

Cipher's lips curled into a smile that was far from reassuring. She leaned in close, her breath cold against Lopez's skin, and planted a soft, deliberate kiss on her cheek. The gesture sent a shiver of revulsion through Lopez, but her body remained frozen, obedient.

"That's a good girl," Cipher whispered. The words a poisonous caress in Lopez's ear.

Lopez's breath hitched, her heart racing as Cipher leaned back, her calculating eyes watching every flicker of emotion cross Lopez's face. The kiss—intimate yet horrifying—left an imprint that would haunt Lopez far more than any of Cipher's words.

Her legs felt like they were made of lead as she stepped out of the car. Each movement felt slow, deliberate, as though the weight of Cipher's presence lingered behind her, pressing down on every step. The cool night air hit her skin, but instead of its usual comfort, it sent a shiver of unease creeping up her spine. She was alone—or was she?

Lopez's eyes flicked to the building's entrance ahead. It seemed farther than she remembered, as if the distance had stretched in the time she'd been gone. The lights from the lobby glowed softly, but the warmth they usually offered now felt hollow, artificial. She moved toward the glass doors, her footsteps muffled by the city's distant hum, her mind replaying Cipher's chilling words.

"I always get what I want."

The kiss on her cheek still burned, an unwanted ghost of Cipher's touch, and Lopez couldn't shake it, no matter how hard she tried. Each step toward the entrance felt like a step deeper into a trap she couldn't escape. She wanted to run, to scream, but fear had a tight grip on her throat, silencing even her thoughts.

As she pushed through the doors, the familiar ding of the lobby's bell seemed sharp, too loud in the quiet night. Her heart quickened as she entered the bright, sterile lobby, the lights too harsh, the corners too dark. Her gaze fell on the security guard stationed by the desk, his expression as neutral as always, but this time, something was different. His nod was polite, but she swore his eyes lingered on her just a second too long.

Had Cipher already reached him? Was he in on it? Every part of her screamed that nothing was as it seemed. She could feel her pulse in her temples as she forced herself to walk past him, eyes forward, her movements stiff and mechanical. She needed to act normal, just like Cipher had commanded. But what was normal? Could he tell she was unraveling inside? Did he know?

The guard's gaze followed her, or at least she thought it did. Each step felt heavier than the last, her shoes too loud on the polished floor. The lobby stretched out before her, suddenly vast and unfamiliar, like walking through a dream—everything just out of reach, distorted.

A few residents lingered. The elderly woman with her tiny dog, chatting with the man at the mailboxes. The couple near the elevator, laughing softly about something she couldn't quite hear. But even their presence, once so ordinary, now felt threatening. Were they watching her, too? Did they know what had happened in the car? Did Cipher have her hooks in them as well?

Lopez's paranoia gnawed at her, whispering doubts into every crevice of her mind. *She can reach you anywhere. She controls everyone.* She pressed her lips together, forcing herself to keep moving, her body on autopilot even as her thoughts spiraled. Each glance, each smile from the residents seemed loaded, heavy with hidden meaning. The laughter of the couple felt like a mockery, the innocent bark of the woman's dog like a warning.

She swallowed hard as she approached the elevator, her hand trembling slightly as she reached for the button. The wait for the doors to open stretched out painfully long, the seconds dragging like hours. She stood there, exposed in the middle of the lobby, feeling Cipher's presence looming over her, watching her every move from some unseen vantage point. She half-expected the doors to open and see Cipher's face staring back at her.

When the elevator doors finally slid open, she stepped inside, grateful for the momentary refuge, but the quiet hum of the ascent did nothing to calm her racing thoughts. She could feel her pulse in her throat, the steady rhythm almost painful as it thudded against her skin. The small, enclosed space only amplified the sound of her heartbeat, and she wondered if she would pass out before reaching her floor.

"That is a good girl."

Cipher's whispered words slithered through her mind, coiling around her like a snake. The soft kiss still lingered on her cheek, sickening in its intimacy. Her skin crawled at the memory, but she couldn't wipe it away. She couldn't undo what had happened in that car, couldn't unhear the promises of control, of inevitability.

The elevator doors opened with a quiet ding, and Lopez stepped out onto her floor, the familiar hallway now feeling foreign, threatening. The lights overhead flickered slightly, casting long shadows across the walls. She moved slowly, her eyes darting to every door, every corner, half-expecting someone— something—to jump out at her. The silence was suffocating, broken only by the soft thud of her shoes on the carpeted floor.

Her apartment door loomed ahead, the final barrier between her and whatever came next. She fumbled with her keys, her fingers trembling uncontrollably. The jingle of the metal felt too loud, too sharp, cutting through the oppressive quiet. Finally, she managed to unlock the door and pushed it open.

She stepped inside, but even her own apartment felt wrong. The familiar warmth of the space didn't offer the comfort it usually did. Everything seemed distant, alien—the framed photos on the walls, the bookshelves, the cozy furniture—each object now a mocking reminder of the control she'd once thought she had.

The door clicked shut behind her, the sound echoing In the stillness. She let out a long, shaky breath and slid down the door, her back pressed against it as though that would keep the danger out. Her heart still pounded in her chest, the rhythm erratic as her mind raced, replaying Cipher's every word, every threat.

But the fear didn't dissipate. It clung to her like a second skin, crawling into every corner of her mind, a suffocating presence she couldn't escape. She hugged her knees to her chest, her breathing shallow as the weight of everything pressed down on her.

A knock at the door made her jump, her breath catching in her throat. "Ms. Lopez, is there any cleaning or trash that needs attention?" The voice was polite, harmless—just the building staff doing their rounds. But in Lopez's mind, it felt like another test, another reminder that Cipher's reach could be anywhere, anyone.

"No, thank you," she managed.

"Very well, Ms. Lopez. Have a good evening."

The footsteps retreated, and she let out a trembling sigh, the sound shaky, uneven. She couldn't stay like this, cowering behind her door, but what choice did she have? Cipher's threats echoed endlessly in her head, drowning out reason, replacing it with a cold, biting fear.

Lopez rested her head on her knees, trying to gather the strength to fight back. But for now, she could only sit there, alone in the dark, holding on to the last remnants of her resolve.

***

Asha sat in the personal cabin of her ship, the gentle hum of the engines a constant backdrop to her swirling thoughts. Outside the viewport, the vastness of space stretched infinitely, dotted with distant stars, but the beauty of the cosmos felt lost on her. She was waiting for approval for her senatorial pass to use the jump gate back to New Earth, and the anticipation clawed at her nerves.

The events of the day weighed heavily on her mind, particularly the false information she had shared during the special session of the Prime Senators. The memory of the accusations and the tension that crackled through the chamber replayed in her head like a bad holovid. *What had I done?* The faces of her fellow senators flashed before her—some filled with outrage, others with skepticism. They were all searching for answers, and she had provided them with speculation dressed as fact.

Was there even a shadow faction? she wondered. The thought sent a shiver down her spine. The notion that there might be senators plotting against their own colleagues felt like a betrayal of everything she had fought to uphold. Yet, despite the uncertainty, she couldn't shake the sense that the danger was real.

The "what ifs" spiraled through her mind, dragging her deeper into the rabbit hole. *What if one my colleagues was involved?* The trust she had in her fellow senators felt like sand slipping through her fingers. What if her own actions had put a target on her back? Or worse, what if she had inadvertently sealed her own fate by giving the Chancellor information that led to repercussions she could never foresee?

A soft chime interrupted her thoughts, breaking the heavy silence. It was the notification she had been waiting for—the approval for her senatorial pass. She felt a flicker of relief but was quickly met by another wave of doubt. *What awaits me on New*

Earth? The political landscape was shifting, and she was stepping back into a storm.

As her thoughts continued to spiral, a name surfaced: Senator Lopez. Asha had always regarded Lopez as someone she could trust, someone who had navigated the treacherous waters of politics with a blend of conviction and intelligence. Despite the recent turmoil surrounding Lopez, Asha felt a sense of familiarity and reliability in her presence—a rarity among their peers.

Could I reach out? The thought hung in the air like a fragile thread. There were risks involved, especially with the current tension between senators, but Asha couldn't ignore the gnawing feeling in her gut. If there was anyone who might understand the complexity of the situation, it was Lopez. Asha felt a flicker of hope.

What if Lopez could help me navigate this?

The prospect of discussing the faction, the rumors, and the unsettling atmosphere of the Senate with someone she trusted was appealing. But would Lopez be willing to talk? Would she see through the veil of recent events and recognize that Asha needed her support?

Asha sat back in her chair, her heart racing as she weighed her options. The risks were high, but so were the stakes. She had to be cautious, but she also had to act.

Deciding in an instant, she activated her communication console, fingers hovering above the controls. *If this leads to the truth—or at least a better understanding—then it's worth the risk,* she thought.

With a deep breath, she sent a message to Lopez, carefully crafting her words to convey urgency without alarming her.

Senator Lopez, she typed, *I need to speak with you. There are matters of great importance that require your insight. Can we meet upon my arrival in New Earth?*

As she hit send, Asha felt a mixture of anticipation and anxiety. She knew that trusting someone in this climate was a gamble, but for the first time in a while, she felt a sense of direction. If anyone could help her uncover the truth, it was Senator Lopez.

With a final glance at the stars outside her viewport, Asha prepared for the jump. There was still a long road ahead, but perhaps, just perhaps, she wouldn't have to walk it alone.

***

The first light of dawn crept over the horizon on New Earth, casting a pale glow through the apartment window. Cipher stood motionless, a cup of coffee in her hand, staring at the rising sun as if it could warm the cold void inside her. The steam curled lazily from the mug, but the heat didn't reach her. It never did.

She took a slow sip, savoring the bitterness on her tongue, her eyes fixed on the skyline as the city below began to stir. It was early—too early for most, but Cipher preferred these moments, the quiet before the world awakened, when the only company she had was her own thoughts.

Her gaze drifted to the reflection in the window—a shadow of the woman she used to be, or perhaps, the woman she had never been. Behind her, the faint outline of a bed was visible, the rumpled sheets hiding the shape of the woman still asleep beneath them. Cipher looked over her shoulder.

What was her name again?

It didn't matter. It never mattered. She could only vaguely remember—*Mia? Michelle?* Something that started with an M. Her—"conquest" from the previous night, just another fleeting attempt to fill the gaping emptiness that feasted inside her, the void that no amount of pain or brief moments of pleasure could sate.

She turned back to the window, the coffee cooling in her hands. The woman had served her purpose. But as the first rays of sunlight stretched further into the room, the familiar weight of loneliness began to settle in. It always did. Each night's conquest dulled the ache for a few hours, but when the morning came, when the world was quiet and she was left with nothing but her thoughts, it all came rushing back.

Lisa.

Cipher's jaw tightened, the coffee forgotten as her mind drifted back to the one person she couldn't forget, the one person who had carved out a piece of her heart and left it bleeding. No one had been able to replace her. And no one ever would. Each conquest was just a temporary bandage over a wound that refused to heal.

Her thoughts lingered on Lisa, the memory of her voice, her touch, the way she had looked at her with trust—a trust that was shattered beyond repair. Lisa was gone, and nothing could bring her back. But every morning, when she was left alone with the emptiness, she was reminded that nothing could ever fill the void that Lisa had left behind.

Cipher's rage simmered just below the surface as she thought of Lisa, the betrayal cutting deeper than any blade. The memory of that final, desperate struggle haunted her—the way she had choked the life from Lisa, feeling the warmth slip away, watching the light leave her lover's eyes. It should have felt like a release, but instead, it left an indelible scar on her soul.

As she stared at her hand—the very hand that had wrought such wrath—conflicted emotions surged within her. *How could I?* she thought, each pulse in her fingertips echoing Lisa's fading heartbeat. Like Lady Macbeth, she felt the weight of that blood, the guilt staining her thoughts. The ghost of Lisa's pulse lingered in her fingers, a haunting reminder of what she had lost and the unforgivable act that had severed their bond.

Every moment without Lisa felt like a betrayal of its own, and the rage that twisted in her chest was tinged with profound sorrow. It was a raging storm of love and hatred, a reminder that in claiming vengeance, she had sacrificed everything she held dear.

The beeping of her watch ripped her back to reality, sharp and insistent. 0700. Time to move on. She took one last look at the rising sun, the brief calm of the morning already slipping through her fingers. She turned away from the window, setting the cold coffee down on the counter.

The woman in the bed stirred, murmuring something unintelligible in her sleep. Cipher glanced at her, then turned toward the door. She grabbed her jacket from the chair, moving with the precision of someone who had done this a thousand times.

As she reached the door, she paused. Her eyes flicked back to the woman, the soft rise and fall of her breathing, the peaceful look on her face. For a moment, just a brief one, she wondered if this was what Lisa had looked like when she slept—calm, unaware of the chaos brewing around her.

But the thought was fleeting. With one last glance, she left the apartment, the door clicking shut behind her. Her mind was already moving to the next step in her plan, but the emptiness lingered, as

it always did. But there was work to be done, and the void would
be filled—if only for another night.

Chapter 3

The early morning light filtered through the gaps in the curtains, casting a soft glow in Senator Lopez's apartment. But the warmth of the sun felt distant, almost alien. Lopez lay curled up on the floor in front of her door, her body tense and restless. The familiar confines of her home had become a prison of fear ever since that harrowing encounter in her car. She couldn't bear the thought of going deeper into the apartment, where shadows seemed to whisper, and every creak of the floorboards felt like a threat.

The sound of the communications station chimed sharply, breaking the oppressive silence. The noise pierced through her restless dreams, pulling her back into the waking world. *What was it now? A message? An alert?* The anxiety surged within her like a tide, drowning out the remnants of sleep.

Lopez opened her eyes, heart racing, her breath quickening as she stared down the hall to the living area. *Who was it from? What did they want?* The echo of Cipher's chilling words replayed in her mind, leaving her frozen in place. Every chime reverberated through the apartment, amplifying her fear until it was nearly unbearable.

As the chime sounded again, a shiver ran down her spine. She knew who it was, or rather, she felt it deep in her bones. *It's her,* the thought whispered in her mind, paralyzing her with dread. *Cipher.* The woman who had cornered her with that unsettling smile, who had toyed with her, whispering threats that hung like a storm cloud over her life. The memory of that moment flooded back, and Lopez squeezed her eyes shut, wishing she could block it all out.

Ignore it. Just ignore it, she told herself, but the chime persisted, echoing through the emptiness of her apartment, each sound a reminder of her helplessness. The familiar beep became a haunting lullaby, calling her to answer, to confront the nightmare that loomed around her.

With each subsequent chime, Lopez felt as if the walls were closing in on her. Her heart pounded in her chest, a frantic rhythm that matched the escalating sound of the communications station. She didn't want to face whatever was waiting on the other side of that message.

In a desperate attempt to block out the sound, Lopez raised her hands and clamped them over her ears, pressing hard, as if she could will the noise away. *Please, just stop,* she thought, her mind teetering on the edge of panic. But the relentless chime continued, taunting her with its insistence, each ring a reminder that she couldn't hide forever.

The chime echoed again, louder in her mind than it was in reality. Lopez clutched her knees tighter to her chest, rocking slightly, her hands still firmly pressed against her ears. *Please, just stop,* she pleaded silently, wishing for the sound—and the fear it carried—to disappear. But it didn't. The chime persisted, its rhythmic tone a cruel reminder of her new reality.

Frozen in fear, Lopez remained on the floor, unable to move, caught in a battle between the instinct to flee and the need to confront her reality. The world outside continued to turn, but in that moment, it felt as if time had stopped, leaving her suspended in a nightmare from which she couldn't wake.

As the chime echoed relentlessly in her mind, panic surged through Lopez. *I can't do this,* she thought, trembling on the floor. The familiar confines of her home felt like a cage closing in around her. In a moment of sheer desperation, she pushed herself up, adrenaline flooding her system.

Ignoring the cold sweat clinging to her skin, Lopez sprinted down the hallway to the communications station in her living area, each footfall heavy with dread. *I have to know,* she told herself, forcing the fear to the back of her mind as she reached the console. The blinking light of the incoming message mocked her, each pulse sending fresh waves of anxiety crashing over her.

With shaking hands, she pressed the screen to unlock it. The message popped up before her, and her breath caught in her throat as she read the sender's name: Prime Asha Patel.

What could she possibly want? A mixture of apprehension and hope twisted in her gut, but Lopez quickly pushed through, her heart racing as she opened the message.

Senator Lopez,

I need to speak with you. There are matters of great importance that require your insight. Can we meet upon my arrival in New Earth?

A wave of relief washed over her, almost overwhelming in its intensity. It felt as if a heavy weight had been lifted from her shoulders. *It's not Cipher,* she realized, the realization flooding her with warmth. Prime Patel wasn't a threat; she was reaching out, seeking collaboration in these chaotic times.

Lopez's hands dropped to her sides, her heart slowing from a frantic pace to a steady rhythm. *Finally, someone I can trust,* she thought, her breathing becoming more measured. The fear that had paralyzed her moments ago began to dissipate, replaced by a flicker of hope. Perhaps she wouldn't have to navigate this treacherous landscape alone after all.

As she leaned against the console, the warmth of the morning sunlight streaming through her window felt like a balm against her worries. The shadows that had loomed large began to shrink, and for the first time in days, she allowed herself to feel a glimmer of optimism.

Lopez quickly composed a response, her fingers moving swiftly across the screen.

Yes, I would like that. I need to talk to you as well, Asha.

With a final glance at the message, she hit send, feeling a sense of purpose returning.

No longer would she let fear dictate her actions. With Prime Patel's support, she would find a way to uncover the truth and reclaim her sense of agency. Today marked a turning point, and for the first time, she felt she was no longer trapped in a nightmare— but on the cusp of something that could finally lead her to safety.

A sudden knock was heard at the door, but who would be knocking her door this early?

***

The Specter coasted silently toward New Earth, the crew expecting the usual clearance for geo-synchronous orbit. But something felt off.

Pierce sat in his command chair, his sightless eyes focused ahead, though the tension in his posture revealed his unease. Allison stood beside him, silent but alert, her eyes narrowing as the comms officer spoke.

"Sir," the comms officer said, "we've been instructed to remain outside the Sphere of Influence. No explanation, just orders to not enter the gravity well."

"Hold outside the SOI?" Pierce muttered. "That's... unusual." His fingers tapped lightly on the armrest of his chair. "Anything else from traffic control?"

"No, sir," she replied. "They've gone quiet."

Before Pierce could dwell further on the oddity, the comms officer interrupted again. "Sir, incoming communication—from the Independence."

"Put it through," Pierce ordered.

The main viewer flickered to life, revealing Captain Mikail Tupolev's grinning face. His deep Russian accent boomed across the bridge.

"Jonathan!" Tupolev exclaimed warmly. "Good to see you, comrade."

Pierce's lips quirked into a small smile. "Likewise, Mikail. What brings you here?"

Tupolev leaned back slightly, grin still in place. "Ah, well, that's a good question. What brings you here, Jonathan? Last I heard, the Specter was in the outer sectors of the system."

Pierce thought for a moment. "Just following up on a few leads," he said. "And you? I thought you were stationed at Centauri Prime."

Tupolev chuckled, evading the question. "Orders change, comrade. Sometimes, we're all sent where we're most needed. Isn't that right?"

Before Pierce could press further, Tupolev's eyes shifted slightly, noticing Veronica leaning in to listen. "And who do we have here?" Tupolev asked with a raised eyebrow. "Is this your new command-level assistant?"

Veronica straightened up quickly, cheeks flushed. "Lieutenant Valentine, sir," she stammered, caught off-guard by the attention.

Tupolev laughed. "A pleasure, comrade Valentine. I'll have to keep my eye on you. You seem… sharp."

Veronica blinked, unsure how to respond, but before the moment could stretch further, Tupolev turned back to Pierce. "Enough business for now. How about you and your XO come aboard for an early dinner? It's been too long since we've had the chance to catch up properly."

His eyes flicked again toward Allison, and his grin widened. "And Allison—I can't wait to see you again."

Pierce raised an eyebrow. He hadn't expected that. Before he could question the enthusiasm, another voice entered the frame.

"Allison!" Commander Zoe Baptiste called out with her slight French accent from behind Tupolev, her face appearing on the screen with a wide smile. "Don't let Mikail steal all the attention. I've been looking forward to catching up with you too."

Allison giggled, a small smirk tugging at the corner of her lips. "I didn't realize I was such popular company."

Pierce, still processing the unexpected familiarity, nodded. "We'll be over shortly," he said.

Tupolev gave a quick nod, flashing one more grin before the transmission ended and the screen went dark.

As the bridge fell silent, Veronica blurted out, "He's... kind of handsome, and charming."

The words hung in the air for a moment before Veronica realized she'd spoken aloud. Her face flushed bright red as Pierce and Allison turned toward her.

"Just, you know, objectively," she added quickly, stammering through her embarrassment.

Pierce's lips twitched with amusement, but he said nothing. Allison, however, chuckled softly before shaking her head. "Don't worry, Miss Valentine. Happens to the best of us."

Veronica nodded, still mortified, and turned back to her console.

Pierce, still curious about Tupolev's behavior, turned toward Allison. "I didn't realize you and Tupolev were... so well-acquainted."

Allison shrugged, dismissing the question with a casual wave of her hand. "We spent some time studying together at the academy, and there were a few joint operations while I was in command of the Specter in your absence. He's always been... friendly," she said, waving it off.

Pierce paused, considering her words. Friendly. He wasn't sure how to read the subtext, but for now, he let it go.

"Let's prepare to head over," Pierce said finally. "We'll see what Tupolev and Baptiste aren't telling us over dinner."

***

The shuttle's thrusters quieted as it settled onto the hangar deck of the Independence. The familiar hum of the engines faded, replaced by the rhythmic beeping of the shuttle's systems powering down. Pierce, anchored by the sound of Veronica's voice, felt her presence beside him, the warmth of her assurance grounding him in the disorienting bustle of the hangar.

"Permission to come aboard?" he called out, a hint of formality lacing his tone.

"Comrade Jonathan!" Tupolev's voice rang out from the hangar, a booming welcome that drew attention from nearby crew members. "It's good to see you! You and Allison are always welcome here."

Pierce smiled, his lips quirking slightly in response to the camaraderie. "Good to be here, Mikail." He turned his head in the direction of the voice. "Let's hope the dinner is as welcoming as the greeting."

Veronica gently placed her hand on his arm, guiding him off the shuttle. He felt the rush of air from the hangar's vents, the scent of recycled air mixed with the faint metallic tang of the ship.

"Here we go," she said as she helped him down the ramp. "Watch your step."

As they exited, Tupolev stepped forward, arms wide open as if to envelop Pierce in a bear hug. "I'd have jumped to catch you, but I see you have a capable assistant." He turned to Veronica with a playful smirk. "Well done, Lieutenant."

"Thank you, sir," Veronica replied.

Behind Tupolev, Commander Baptiste stepped forward, warm and welcoming. "Allison!" she exclaimed, stepping up to the pair. "It's been too long! You look well." She embraced Allison tightly, and giving her a faire la bise, touching each of her cheeks to Allison's and making a kissing sound.

Allison chuckled, returning the embrace. "You too, Zoe. You haven't changed a bit."

"Neither have you," Baptiste replied, stepping back and studying her friend's face. "Still as sharp as ever."

Pierce stood by, listening to the exchange, the sense of familiarity buzzing around him. He appreciated the warmth but felt a flicker of uncertainty as he noted the easy rapport between his crew and the officers of the Independence.

"Shall we get out of this hangar?" Tupolev asked, gesturing toward the corridor. "The Captain's Mess is prepared, and I assure you, the meal will not disappoint."

"Lead the way, Captain," Pierce said, nodding slightly.

Veronica stepped up beside him, gently guiding him forward as Allison and Baptiste fell into step ahead.

"Baptiste, did you get a chance to try that new recipe?" Tupolev asked. "I told them to save some for tonight. I think you'll agree it's a winner."

"Of course! The chefs have finally mastered it. You know I'm a tough critic," Baptiste teased.

They moved through the Independence, the ship's polished corridors reflecting a combination of efficiency and a sense of history. Crew members nodded in respect as they passed, and the chatter of conversations filled the air.

"Jonathan," Tupolev said, "I hope the reasons for your visit are good ones. Everyone can always use a hand with any— complications."

Pierce noted the weight behind those words. "Just following up on a few leads," he replied, echoing his earlier vagueness.

"All leads in these times seem to have their own complications," Tupolev remarked, leading them into a spacious dining area, warmly lit and decorated with a blend of modern aesthetics and classic naval design.

"Now," Baptiste said, motioning them toward a large table adorned with an array of dishes, "let's set aside business for the evening. Dinner is the best time to catch up and enjoy each other's company."

Pierce smiled inwardly, appreciating the invitation. The warmth of camaraderie filled the room, easing the tension he had felt earlier.

"After you," Tupolev said, gesturing for them to take their seats.

As they settled in, Pierce could feel the anticipation in the air—a mix of friendship, underlying tensions, and the unspoken questions waiting to be addressed as they gathered around the table for dinner.

***

As the dinner progressed, the atmosphere around the table was lively, laughter punctuating the air. Plates were cleared, and glasses clinked, the warmth of camaraderie enveloping them. Tupolev had regaled them with stories of his latest exploits, while Baptiste shared amusing anecdotes from her time in command.

As the conversation lulled, Tupolev leaned back in his chair, his expression shifting to one of thoughtful curiosity. "So, Jonathan," he began, breaking the comfortable silence, "you haven't given us the full story on why you're back here again. Surely, there's more than just following up on a few leads."

Pierce, sensing the scrutiny, took a sip of his drink before responding. "That's all there is to it, Mikail. Just following up on leads." He kept his tone light, though he felt the weight of his friend's gaze.

Tupolev's eyes narrowed slightly, a knowing smile creeping onto his lips. "And here I thought we were done with the games, my friend." He leaned forward, elbows resting on the table. "But I must admit, I'm a little curious myself. What really brings you back to these parts?"

Pierce raised an eyebrow, intrigued. "Same reason as you, I imagine. I hear things, and I'm compelled to chase them down. But you're also avoiding the question. What's got you here?"

For a moment, Tupolev hesitated, his jovial demeanor slipping just a fraction. "Let's just say I'm looking for someone," he replied. "Orders from high above. I have to locate and arrest a certain individual."

"Who is this individual?" Pierce asked, careful to keep his tone casual.

Tupolev leaned back in his chair, a guarded look in his eyes. "I'm afraid I can't share that. All I can say is that they're dangerous, and they have a meeting scheduled on New Earth."

Pierce felt the tension build. The coincidence of their missions was too perfect to ignore. "What are the charges?" he inquired, trying to piece it all together.

"Classified," Tupolev replied sharply. "You know how it is—some things just can't be discussed openly."

Veronica, who had been listening intently, leaned closer to Pierce, whispering something in his ear. Tupolev raised an eyebrow at the exchange, irritation crossing his features. "Did you leave your manners back on the Specter, Lieutenant?" he asked.

Allison shot Tupolev a warning glance, while Pierce suppressed a smile. "Veronica's just making sure I don't miss any important details," he replied, turning his attention back to his friend. "But really, Mikail, what's so critical about this meeting?"

Tupolev regarded him carefully. "I'm here for someone named Starfire. My orders are to arrest them and anyone they're meeting with."

Pierce's heart raced at the name but remained outwardly composed. "I see. Well, I'm just here following up on leads, like I said. I'll be meeting with Admiral Jacobs and Senator Lopez about certain aspects of my investigation, but I can't get into it."

Tupolev studied him for a moment. "Alright, Jonathan. I can accept that for now. But know that if you get in my way—"

"I won't," Pierce interjected. "I assure you, I'm not here to complicate your mission."

Tupolev nodded, seeming to accept the assurances, and signaled to his comms officer. "Send a message to traffic control. Grant the Specter a geo-synchronous parking orbit above the Capital Spire."

As the officer acknowledged the request, Pierce felt a wave of relief wash over him. The more he learned about Tupolev's mission, the more questions surfaced in his mind. Why was Starfire so important that Tupolev was ordered to arrest them? The stakes were higher than he'd anticipated, and hydra again rears its ugly head again.

Memories I

The buzz of the city outside faded into a low hum as I settled into a small café, a familiar refuge amid the chaos of Earth. The aroma of coffee filled the air, mingling with the soft chatter of patrons, a perfect backdrop for blending in. The clerk behind the counter looked at me and smiled. "May I get your name for the order?"

I hesitated, not knowing how I should answer. "Lucy." I said putting on a forced smile. I'm not sure why that came out, but it was a good name to go with. Civilians knowing my real name bothers me. So, for now, I will go by Lucy. After paying for my coffee and finding an empty table I sipped my drink, letting the warmth seep into my bones as I observed the ebb and flow of people around me—faces lost in their own worlds, unaware of the tension simmering just beneath the surface.

I pulled out my comms device, intending to check on routine updates. My focus shifted as a new message suddenly flashed to life. I swallowed hard as I opened the message:

Operation: Whispers

Status: Initiated.

Orders: Proceed to New Earth. Investigate rising rumors of a shadow faction. Discretion is paramount. More details will follow upon arrival.

My heart raced at the unexpected notification. This wasn't just a routine assignment; I had been activated. I hadn't anticipated this—no briefings, no warnings. Just a direct order, thrusting me into a situation fraught with uncertainty.

A shadow faction. The implications were staggering, but I had trained for this. I was prepared for covert operations, for slipping into the background and gathering intelligence, but I hadn't expected the call to action to come so suddenly. I felt a rush of adrenaline, excitement, and apprehension. The stories I'd heard, the whispers in the halls of power, were about to take on a new reality.

I needed to compose myself. With a practiced calm, I tucked my comms device away, masking my inner turmoil. New Earth awaited; a political powder keg ready to ignite. Eight months after the Jovian Aggression, the remnants of that conflict still lingered, and I had to navigate the complex web of alliances and enmities that had emerged in its wake.

As I rose to leave the café, I scanned the room one last time, ensuring my demeanor reflected the ease of an ordinary patron. Anyone could be watching. I had to blend in seamlessly, to be just another face in the crowd.

Stepping outside, the cacophony of the city enveloped me, each sound a reminder of the urgency of my mission. I was ready to delve into this world of whispers and intrigue, where trust was a fragile commodity.

The path ahead was uncharted, but I was determined to uncover the truth behind the rumors, whatever the cost. The game had begun, and I was ready to play my part.

***

The shuttle doors hissed open, releasing a rush of air tinged with burnt ozone and a faint hint of vegetation—a reminder that life thrived here, despite the recent scars of war. As I stepped onto the platform, the vibrant chaos of New Earth enveloped me. The city of Port Luminara sprawled before me, a mosaic of cultures and ambitions, still reeling from the aftermath of the Jovian Aggression.

I paused to collect my thoughts, watching the throng of people bustling past me. Each face told a story shaped by conflict; a fragment of lives altered by the events that had transpired over the last eight years. I had trained for this moment, equipped with the skills necessary to blend in seamlessly, speaking the local language with an accent so refined it would be nearly indistinguishable from a native. Yet here I stood, feeling oddly unmoored in a place I was supposed to command with confidence.

I hadn't established any cover, nor had I received specific instructions on how to proceed. The weight of uncertainty settled over me like a shroud. The training I had undergone had been intense and thorough, encompassing not just the tactical skills necessary for espionage, but also a deep cultural understanding that allowed me to navigate foreign environments without drawing attention. I knew how to mimic gestures, how to respond to social cues, but today, standing in the center of a city still healing, I felt like a shadow wandering aimlessly.

A cab pulled up, and I climbed inside, grateful for the brief reprieve from the bustling terminal. "Central district," I instructed the driver, forcing my voice to sound casual as I glanced out the window. The streets were alive with movement—vendors calling out their wares, children laughing in the distance, and protestors waving banners, their chants echoing in the air. It was a city caught between hope and despair, and I had to navigate that delicate balance.

As we drove, I let my mind drift back to the training sessions I had endured. Every lesson, every moment of cultural immersion had prepared me for this. I could hear the instructor's voice in my head, emphasizing the importance of blending in, of being more than just an outsider. *"Adapt, observe, and never reveal your true intentions,"* he had said. It was a mantra I would carry with me, one I needed to internalize now more than ever.

The transport finally stopped, and I stepped out into the heart of the central square. A wave of sound washed over me, a chaotic blend of voices and energy. I could feel the pulse of New Earth— the excitement, the tension, the unmistakable undercurrent of fear that had yet to dissipate.

I took a deep breath, focusing on my surroundings. I needed to gather information, to listen to the conversations happening around me. The square was filled with people, some engaged in animated discussions, others handing out pamphlets urging for change. I would find a way to blend in, to absorb the atmosphere and glean the insights I needed.

As I walked through the crowd, I caught snippets of conversations—people discussing recent protests, fears of government overreach, and whispers of something darker lurking in the shadows. The mention of a shadow faction sent a jolt through me. This was why I was here. Somewhere amidst the noise, the truth was waiting to be uncovered, but how could I pursue it without a clear direction?

With every step, I reminded myself to stay grounded. I needed to observe, to listen, and to adapt to whatever situation arose. But as the crowd swirled around me, a flicker of doubt crept in. What if I made a mistake? What if I drew attention to myself before I was ready? The stakes were high, and the city was a labyrinth of intrigue.

Suddenly, a figure caught my eye—a man lingering at the edge of a group, his gaze shifting from the protesters to me. I instinctively steeled myself, meeting his eyes briefly before looking away, as if to signal my lack of interest. But the encounter left me unsettled. Could he be watching me, or was it merely paranoia?

I shook off the feeling, focusing on the voices around me. I was here to gather intel, to become part of the story unfolding in front of me, even without an established cover. The path ahead was fraught with uncertainty, but I was determined to forge my way through the shadows of New Earth. I would find the truth behind the rumors, whatever it took.

The hum of the city below drifted through the open window, a constant reminder that life continued outside my hotel room. I lay on the bed, staring at the ceiling, the weight of the last three days pressing down on me. New Earth had a way of wrapping itself around you, its vibrancy and chaos both alluring and suffocating.

I had spent the past few days absorbing everything—the conversations I overheard in the square, the faces of the protesters filled with passion, the whispers of discontent that echoed in the streets. But for all my efforts, I hadn't uncovered much. It felt like I was walking through fog, and no matter how hard I tried, I couldn't grasp the threads that would lead me to the shadow faction.

With my mind swirling in frustration, I finally closed my eyes, attempting to drown out the noise outside. Sleep had been elusive, and I could feel the fatigue settling into my bones. Just as I started to drift, the soft chime of my comms device broke the silence, pulling me back to reality.

I sat up, heart racing, a mix of anticipation and dread swirling inside me. I hadn't expected anything—no updates, no messages, just a waiting game. I reached for the device, my fingers trembling slightly as I opened it.

The screen flashed with a notification that sent a jolt through me:

Incoming message. Open when ready.

I hesitated, uncertainty gnawing at me. My training urged caution—never reveal too much, never act impulsively. But I couldn't ignore it. This could be what I'd been waiting for, the guidance I desperately needed to move forward. I took a deep breath, pushing aside the lingering anxiety, and tapped to open the message.

Lt. Cmdr.,

Your mission parameters have been established. You will begin by connecting with a local informant codename "Aldo." He has vital information regarding the shadow faction. We have arranged a meeting at Falling Star Tavern, 1900 hours today.

To identify Aldo, use the code phrase: "The winds are restless tonight." Proceed with caution. Trust no one until you've confirmed his identity. Your safety is paramount.

The message ended abruptly, leaving me with more questions than answers. Aldo? I had no idea who he was, what he looked like, or how he might react to an unfamiliar face. My pulse quickened as I processed the information. This was the lead I had been waiting for, a potential breakthrough that could pull the veil from the shadows.

Yet doubt crept in. Who was this informant? How could I trust that he would even show up? I pushed the uncertainties aside and forced myself to focus. I had faced far worse challenges than this.

I glanced at the clock on the wall—it was late afternoon. I had time to prepare, to think through my approach. The Falling Star Tavern was a popular spot, a dimly lit venue known for its eclectic crowd. I had overheard mentions of it during my previous days in the city, and the casual atmosphere would provide a perfect cover for our meeting.

I needed to blend in, to appear as just another patron seeking a drink and some company. My training kicked in, and I began mentally mapping out my plan. I would arrive early, observe the place, and gauge the people. The last thing I wanted was to be caught off guard.

I pushed myself off the bed, shaking off the fatigue that clung to me. I had work to do. My heart raced with anticipation and a hint of fear as I prepared for the night ahead. This could be the moment I had been waiting for, the first step into the darkness where I hoped to find the truth.

***

The tavern's warm glow welcomed me as I stepped inside, the low murmur of conversation creating a comfortable backdrop. I scanned the room, taking in the eclectic mix of patrons—some lost in their drinks, others engaged in animated discussions. The atmosphere felt alive, pulsing with the energy of a city still healing from the scars of war.

I had arrived early, hoping to assess the space and plan my approach. The dimly lit corners offered plenty of places to hide, but I needed to ensure I could spot Aldo before he spotted me. I settled onto a barstool, ordered a drink, and watched the door.

As the clock ticked closer to 1900 hours, anticipation gnawed at my insides. Would he show? Would he even be who he claimed to be?

The door swung open, and a man stepped inside—slender with an air of confidence that made me uneasy. He scanned the bar with a practiced ease, his eyes locking onto mine as I gestured for him to join me. He approached, and I forced a smile, willing myself to remain calm.

"Aldo?"

"That's me. You're the one who wanted to talk?" He replied, sliding onto the stool beside me. I studied his face, searching for any sign of deception, but he maintained a cool demeanor.

I took a breath, reminding myself of the code phrase. "The winds are restless tonight."

He met my gaze with a steady stare, but instead of the expected response, he smirked. "Is that so? Sounds poetic."

My stomach dropped. Something wasn't right.

"Aldo?" I pressed, my voice low.

He leaned closer, his smile fading. "I think you might have me confused with someone else."

Panic surged through me. I needed to think fast. This was no informant. My instincts kicked in, and I shifted on my stool, eyeing the exit.

"I don't have time for games," I said, standing up.

In an instant, his demeanor changed. "Where do you think you're going?" he demanded, reaching for something at his side.

I had to act. I pivoted on my heel and slipped out the door into the alley behind the bar, my heart racing. The night air hit me like a wall, cool and sharp. I glanced over my shoulder, and I could see him following, determination etched across his face.

The alley was narrow and dark, a maze of shadows. I ducked into a recess, pressing myself against the cold brick wall as I fumbled for my suppressed sidearm tucked into my waistband. The weight felt comforting against my palm.

Just as he rounded the corner, I stepped out, aiming the weapon at him. "Stop right there!"

He froze, surprise flashing across his face. "What are you doing? You don't know what you're—"

"I know enough," I cut him off. "You're not Aldo. What game are you playing?"

He took a step back, raising his hands in a gesture of feigned surrender. "Look, we can talk about this. I'm just trying to find my way like everyone else. You've got the wrong guy."

"Do I?" I narrowed my eyes, refusing to lower my weapon. "You don't get to walk away from this. I'm not here to play games."

"Okay, okay," he said, his tone shifting to one of forced calmness. "You're right. I'm not Aldo. But I can help you. I know things—things you want to know."

My grip tightened on the gun, weighing my options. "You want to help me? You should've thought of that before trying to play me for a fool. What do you know about the shadow faction?"

He hesitated, gauging my reaction. "Listen, you need to walk away from this little girl. They're dangerous, and if they find out you're asking questions…"

Before he could finish, I sensed movement behind him. I shifted my weight, ready to react, but he seized the moment to lunge toward me.

In an instant, I squeezed the trigger, the sound muffled by the suppressor. He crumpled to the ground, eyes wide in shock, the life draining from him in an instant.

I stepped closer, scanning him for any identification or useful intel. He wore a simple jacket, nothing that screamed danger, but as I rifled through his pockets, I found a small data stick. My heart raced—this could contain the information I desperately needed.

Before I moved further, I quickly snapped a photo of his face, a precaution ingrained in my training. A positive ID was crucial for any future intel gathering, and I wasn't about to let this opportunity slip away.

I pocketed the chip and glanced back toward the bar entrance. The distant sound of sirens pierced the night air, growing louder with each passing second. The local Security Forces were likely responding to the commotion, and I needed to disappear.

With adrenaline coursing through my veins, I darted down the alley, navigating the maze of shadows, my mind racing. I turned a corner and spotted a narrow side street leading to a quieter part of the city. I slipped into it, moving quickly but quietly, blending into the darkness as I made my escape.

As I maneuvered through the narrow alleys, I felt the adrenaline still pumping through my veins. The weight of the data stick pressed against my pocket, a reminder of the danger that lurked just beneath the surface of this city. I needed to gather my thoughts and reassess my situation.

Reaching a secluded corner, I pulled out my mobile comms device, still warm from the brief contact with the imposter. I opened the photo I had just taken, his shocked face staring back at me. With a steady hand, I uploaded the image to my handler for a positive ID. The request sent off with a slight buzz, I hoped the quick scan would yield some answers about the man I had just neutralized.

I leaned against the cold brick wall, catching my breath as I waited for a response. The sounds of the city felt muffled, distant. My mind raced with possibilities. Who was he? How did he fit into the shadow faction I was investigating?

Moments later, my device buzzed to life, the screen illuminating my anxious face. I opened the message with bated breath:

Positive ID confirmed. Subject is a member of the Senate Security Detail. Proceed with extreme caution.

Shock coursed through me. A member of the Senate Security Detail? This wasn't just some random citizen. This was someone deeply entrenched in the political fabric of New Earth, possibly connected to the very faction I was trying to expose. My instincts screamed at me—this could complicate everything.

Before I could fully process the implications, another message popped up on my screen:

Cover established. Credentials waiting at the drop point in Nueva Mexico. Proceed there at once. Meeting with Aldo terminated.

Frustration welled within me. I had been so close to gaining vital intel, only to be pulled away at the last moment. But I understood the necessity; if I was truly going to operate effectively here, I needed the right credentials to navigate this complex political landscape.

I took a deep breath, reminding myself to remain focused. The mission came first. I pocketed my device and pushed off the wall, glancing around the dimly lit alley before stepping back into the flow of the city.

Navigating through the streets, I set my course for Nueva Mexico, mentally preparing for the next phase of my mission. This was a critical juncture—I had to ensure that whatever was waiting for me at the drop point would help me move forward, whether it was the credentials I needed or something else entirely.

As I walked, I couldn't shake the unease settling in my stomach. I had neutralized a threat, yes, but I felt the eyes of the city on me, the weight of secrets and dangers yet to be uncovered. The shadow faction loomed larger than ever, and I was about to step deeper into the heart of it all.

With determination fueling my steps, I forged ahead, knowing that the path before me was fraught with uncertainty. But I was ready to confront whatever awaited me in Nueva Mexico.

Chapter 4

Lopez sat at her desk, her fingers wrapped around a cup of chamomile tea. The warmth seeping into her hands, but it did little to ease the tension building inside her. Next to her sat a plate of French toast topped with strawberries, untouched and exuding a sweet scent that filled the air. Her attention though, was fixed on the tablet in front of her, Cipher's instructions glowing ominously on the screen:

Lopez's gaze flicked to the corner of the room where a man in a sharp black suit sat in a straight-backed chair, his posture rigid, his expression blank. A member of the Senate Security Detail, but his presence was far from routine. He hadn't spoken since arriving a half hour ago, and yet the weight of his silence was oppressive.

The door opened, and Maria entered with her usual efficiency, clutching her tablet. Her cheerful demeanor faltered when she noticed the untouched breakfast. "Good morning, Senator, no appetite today?"

Lopez took a slow sip of her tea. "I wasn't hungry for toast."

Maria frowned, glancing at the tray. "That's unusual. You always rave about the chef's strawberries."

"Not today," Lopez said curtly, setting the cup down.

"Shall I have something else brought—"

"No!" Lopez shot back forcefully. "The routine continues as usual. What's the status of the Specter?"

Maria paused, clearly debating whether to press further, before shifting to her report. "The Specter is holding outside the Sphere of Influence. Traffic control hasn't granted orbital clearance. Captain Tupolev's ship, Independence, is also in-system. It's strange— they're both just sitting there."

Lopez tensed but kept her face neutral, her fingers brushing the tablet's edge.

Maria continued; her curiosity piqued. "Why hasn't Pierce been cleared? And why is Tupolev here at all? Doesn't the

Independence have duties on Centauri Prime? This feels..." She trailed off, searching for the right word. "Unusual."

Lopez's eyes flicked to the man in the suit. He shifted slightly, his hand disappearing into his jacket. The motion was slow, deliberate—a clear gesture of warning.

Lopez's breath hitched. Cipher's words echoed in her mind. *Don't interfere. Don't ask why.*

She straightened. "Maria, continue with the morning report."

Maria hesitated, clearly thrown off by the abrupt change in tone. "Senator, I just think—"

"I said, continue," Lopez interrupted. Her eyes briefly darted to the man in the suit, who leaned back but kept his hand where it was.

Maria blinked, in confusion. "Of course," she said cautiously, glancing between Lopez and the silent man. "The protests, then. Demonstrations outside the Senate have doubled overnight. Security is stretched thin, and public sentiment is growing restless. The media's picking up on it, calling for transparency."

Lopez exhaled slowly, forcing her tension into silence. "Let them. The noise will keep them occupied."

Maria scribbled a note on her tablet. "Understood. Anything else?"

"Yes," Lopez said. "Schedule a meeting with Ava Turing. Make it happen as soon as possible."

Maria tilted her head, confused. "Ava Turing? From Neura Tech? May I ask why?"

"No," Lopez replied flatly, picking up her tea again. "Just set it up."

"What details should I pass to her office?"

"Just set it up, Maria. Don't ask questions, just do you job."

Maria startled at the sudden outburst, nods in compliance. "I'll contact her office at once, ma'am."

Lopez gave no acknowledgment, instead stared into the tea as Maria exited the room. The door closed with a soft click, leaving Lopez alone with the man in the suit.

Her gaze shifted back to the tablet. Cipher's instructions glared up at her, the weight of the words pressing down like a physical force. She risked a glance at the man in the chair. He met her eyes briefly, his expression blank but his presence menacing.

Lopez stared at the now-cold tea in her hands, her thoughts spiraling as the silence in the office became suffocating. The tablet lay on her desk, Cipher's terse instructions still displayed. Her jaw tightened as she reread the lines, each word a chain tightening around her freedom.

Her gaze shifted to the untouched toast, the bright strawberries glistening under the soft morning light. Once, they would have been a comforting indulgence. Now, they mocked her. Her stomach churned; her appetite long gone.

In the corner of the room, the man in the black suit sat perfectly still, his gaze distant yet somehow always present. His silence was unnerving, his presence oppressive. Cipher's warning about him echoed in her mind. He wasn't just observing. He was a message.

She swallowed hard, glancing briefly at him before turning her focus to the tablet. With careful movements, she opened a secure channel and began typing.

Prime Patel—I await your reply as to when we can meet? Discretion required. Reply to this channel.

She hit send and locked the tablet, her fingers lingering on the screen as if to conceal her actions from the silent sentinel in the room. A flicker of relief passed through her, but it was fleeting, quickly replaced by a growing unease.

Without warning, the man in the suit touched his earpiece, his hand moving with deliberate precision. He rose from his seat, smoothing the front of his jacket as he moved toward the door. Lopez stiffened, her pulse quickening.

He paused at the door, his hand resting on the handle. For a moment, the air felt heavy, the silence stretching unbearably.

"Cipher will be in contact with you later," he said, devoid of emotion.

Lopez blinked, her throat tightening. "With me? When?"

The man turned his head slightly. "Soon."

Without another word, he opened the door and left, the soft click of the latch reverberating in the quiet room.

Lopez exhaled, the tension in her chest refusing to dissipate. What else could Cipher want, and why had the man deliver the message so casually, as if it were preordained?

The comm on her desk chimed, breaking the silence. Maria's voice came through, steady but hesitant. "Senator, the meeting with Ava Turing has been confirmed for 3:00 PM. Her office has arranged for it to take place here."

Lopez closed her eyes for a brief moment, a vain attempt to sound normal as possible. "Thank you, Maria. That will be all."

The comm clicked off, and she set the tea down, her hands trembling faintly. Cipher's warnings, the man's silent surveillance, Tupolev's unexpected involvement—it all pressed down on her like a weight she could no longer bear.

She glanced back at the locked tablet. Somewhere in the ether, her message to Patel lingered, waiting for a reply. A small act of defiance, perhaps, but one that carried risks she wasn't sure she could afford.

For now, she could only wait—and prepare for whatever came next.

***

The shuttle landed smoothly in the Specter's shuttle bay, its engines powering down as the deck crew moved in swiftly to secure it. Pierce stood near the hatch, composed. Jones stood beside him, hands on her hips, while Veronica waited a step behind.

As the ramp lowered, Cruise approached, the atmosphere of the bustling hangar deafening as the trio walked down the ramp. Falling into stride beside Pierce and Jones, he observed their demeanor and spoke. "Looks like you enjoyed that as much as a root canal."

Pierce sighed. "Allison, please tell me it wasn't as awkward as it felt."

"Jonathan, I'd love to lie to you, but no—it was hell," Jones replied.

"Tupolev doesn't host dinners for small talk," Cruise added. "If he brought you to the table, there's a reason."

"The Independence doesn't deploy for minor operations. Whatever his mission is here, it's significant. Trouble is not far behind either." Jones said.

They approached the lift at the end of the corridor, its doors opened, and they stepped inside.

Pierce gently strokes his cheek. "When Tupolev is deployed, it's to send a message, not negotiate."

"Europa," Jones said sharply.

Pierce tilted his head and sighs heavily. "Europa."

Veronica not understanding inquires, "What about Europa?"

Jones crossed her arms tightly, her gaze fixed somewhere beyond the present as if staring back at Europa itself. "It was a stalemate," she began. "Eight Jovian frigates. A blockade so tight it strangled us. They had us pinned near Europa, cutting off supplies. We couldn't break through, and retreat wasn't an option. For days, we sat there, waiting for a miracle or a massacre. We didn't know which would come first."

Her jaw tightened as she glanced at Veronica. "And then the Independence showed up. No warning, no comms. Just... there. At first, we thought Tupolev was going to coordinate with the fleet, maybe give us a fighting chance. But no. He had other ideas."

Jones shifted her stance, her arms dropping slightly. "He didn't negotiate. He didn't strategize. He moved into firing range, and the moment his guns lined up, he opened fire. The lead frigate didn't stand a chance—it was gone in seconds. Just debris."

Veronica, breaking the silence, spoke in a soft voice. "And the others?"

Jones's gaze returned to the past. "Picked off one by one. They tried to regroup, to fire back, but it was like watching an apex predator take down prey that didn't even know how outmatched it was. Calls for surrender flooded the channels, but Tupolev ignored every single one. He didn't care. That was the message he wanted to send."

She exhaled slowly, her voice softening but losing none of its edge. "The last two frigates were dead in the water, their captains begging for mercy. Pleas for medical evacuation, promises to lay down arms, wounded crew aboard—all of it ignored. The Independence kept firing until there was nothing left. No survivors. Just silence and scattered debris."

Veronica frowned. "No survivors? Even after surrender?"

Jones nodded grimly. "He didn't want surrender. He wanted annihilation. It wasn't about breaking the blockade—it was about making sure no one ever dared form another one. And he succeeded." She paused for a moment, closing her eyes tightly as if to force the memory back into the recesses of her mind. "That's why people still talk about Europa. It wasn't a battle. It wasn't even a victory. It was a statement. A warning. If Tupolev shows up, he's not there to play fair or show mercy. He's there to finish the job, no matter the cost."

"And that's the man we're dealing with now." Veronica said.

Jones nodded. "Exactly. And if he's here, it means someone has decided that something—or someone—in this system isn't just a threat. It's a problem he's been sent to solve."

Cruise folded his arms. "And it's not just Tupolev you have to worry about. His colonel is just as dangerous."

Jones frowned. "What do you mean?"

"I worked with him once during the war," Cruise said. "Callisto. A Jovian cell took a civilian science team hostage. The Colonel was given operational control."

Veronica leaned forward slightly. "What happened?"

Cruise grunted. "No negotiation. No discussion. He declared the hostage takers enemies of the state and moved in with overwhelming force. Every Jovian combatant was killed on sight. When they found the hostages, one of them was wearing an explosive vest. The colonel didn't hesitate—he shot the hostage and ordered the room cleared."

Jones's face darkened. "He shot the hostage? Was there no other option?"

"To him, no," Cruise paused. "He wasn't willing to risk the vest detonating, even if it meant sacrificing one of the hostages. His justification was simple: the rest survived, so it was a 'net gain.'"

Pierce's voice was steady. "And now he's here, alongside Tupolev."

Jones shook her head. "Fantastic. Tupolev doesn't compromise, and his colonel doesn't hesitate. This means trouble."

The lift doors opened onto the bridge, and the group made their way to Pierce's office. Once inside, Pierce sat at his desk, while Jones, Cruise, and Veronica took their seats across from him.

"Do you think Tupolev knows about the freighter?" Veronica asked.

Pierce leaned back slightly. "It's possible. I did include it in my reports to the Admiral, so it's not a stretch to think he's aware of it. Whether he cares about it is another question entirely. What concerns me more is what he knows—or thinks he knows—about Starfire."

Jones nodded. "If he's watching us, we'll need to tread carefully. Any move toward Starfire will have to be off the grid."

Pierce tilted his head slightly. "There's another angle we could use if necessary." He turned toward Jones. "You noticed the way he kept singling you out during dinner?"

Jones blinked, caught off guard. "What are you talking about?"

"He was obvious about it. That kind of attention wasn't casual," Pierce said calmly. "If we need a distraction to cover for a meeting with Starfire, you might be able to keep him occupied."

Jones frowned. "You're suggesting I play into that?"

Cruise smirked. "It's the accent. That drawl of yours—it's practically exotic to someone like Tupolev." He gave her a quick once-over, his smirk deepening. "Then there's the slim, athletic build. And, well, let's not pretend he wasn't paying particular attention when you leaned forward to reach for your glass."

Jones's eyes narrowed. "You think my accent and figure are distracting?"

Cruise shrugged. Not saying anything, just letting his statement hang in the air.

"Jonathan, I cannot believe you are actually suggesting this." Jones said.

"I'm only suggesting we use every asset available to complete the mission. If Tupolev has a weakness for you, it's an angle we can exploit." Pierce said.

Jones, irritated by the thought. "I don't like it."

Pierce nodded. "No one will force you Allison. For now, we should focus on locating Starfire before Tupolev. Monitor the Independence. I want to know the moment they make a move."

Jones scoffed. "Jonathan, you know as well as I do that Tupolev doesn't 'make moves.' He delivers statements. And they're written in blood."

Pierce allowed a faint smile. "Then let's make sure he doesn't feel the need to deliver one to us."

Before Jones could respond, the comm speaker crackled to life. "Captain, we've received clearance to enter geosynchronous orbit over the Capital Spire."

Pierce straightened. "Acknowledged. Proceed immediately."

"Aye, sir," the comms officer replied as the line went silent.

***

The faint hum of the Unity's engines reverberated through the walls as the ship emerged from the jump gate, the transition leaving a lingering shimmer in the viewport. Asha sat alone in her private cabin, gazing out the window at the blue-and-green sphere of New Earth below. The planet seemed calm, serene even, but the storm within her thoughts was anything but.

A soft chime preceded the door's opening, and an attendant stepped in. "Prime Patel, we've arrived in-system. Clearance to enter orbit is pending."

Asha turned her head slightly. "Thank you. Notify me once clearance is granted."

The attendant bowed his head and left without another word, the door hissing shut behind him. Asha exhaled, leaning back in her seat, her gaze returning to the planet below.

Her mind wandered as she stared into the void, memories flashing unbidden. Cipher's face loomed large in her thoughts, the words spoken during their last conversation echoing with cold precision.

Do this, or you'll lose everything.

Her hands tightened into fists in her lap. What she had done— what Cipher had forced her to do—felt like a weight pressing on her chest. And now the impending investigation loomed, its shadow growing with each passing hour.

Did I cover my tracks well enough? Will they see through the lies? She thought to herself.

The questions spun in her mind, looping endlessly. The serenity of New Earth below only seemed to mock her turmoil. She glanced at her tablet, the unanswered message from Lopez glaring back at her.

Moments later, the screen blinked, and a reply appeared as her tablet regained connection. Asha's breath caught as she opened it. Lopez's agreement to meet was short, direct, and unembellished— a reflection of her usual demeanor.

Asha immediately composed herself, reaching out to Lopez's office to finalize the details. The call went through without issue, but as the connection terminated, a faint tremor ran through her.

The lights in the cabin flickered—once, then again—before stabilizing.

She frowned, her eyes darting to the ceiling, then to the viewport. The faint hum of the ship that now seemed... uneven. The vibrations underfoot, once steady and constant, carried a subtle irregularity, like a heartbeat out of rhythm.

Her reflection in the glass stared back at her, the faint shimmer of distant stars framing her silhouette. For a moment, she felt weightless, as if the air in the cabin had thinned. She placed a hand on the window, grounding herself.

"There's no turning back now," she whispered.

And then it came.

A deep, muted thud reverberated through the walls. It wasn't loud, but it carried weight—an unnatural, visceral force that made the glass beneath her fingertips tremble. The lights flickered again, briefly plunging the room into shadows.

Asha's chest tightened. Her lips parted as if to call for someone, but no words came. The ship's hum faltered completely for a breath, leaving a silence so profound it seemed to stretch infinitely.

Then the hum returned, but weaker, fractured. Outside, New Earth spun on, unbroken, while the tension in the air thickened like a storm waiting to break.

Asha turned away from the viewport, reaching for the intercom, her mind racing. But before she could press the button, another faint tremor rippled through the floor, more insistent this time.

The screen on her tablet dimmed as if reacting to the shift, her connection to the moment tenuous. The unsettling quiet of the room pressed down on her, and a single thought looped in her mind: *Something is very, very wrong.*

Chapter 5

The soft hum of the office cooling system resonated faintly through the walls of Prime Linh Nguyen's office. Sunlight streamed through the massive floor-to-ceiling windows, casting a warm glow over the polished, minimalist furniture. Outside, the vibrant cityscape of New Tian blossomed with activity, its streets teeming with life.

Prime Nguyen stood by her desk, tablet in hand, scrolling through the latest communiqués from the Chancellor's office. Her sharp eyes scanned the lines of text, searching for any detail she might have missed. Despite the peaceful exterior of her surroundings, the storm brewing in the Alliance weighed heavily on her shoulders. She glanced at the elegant clock mounted on the wall. They would be arriving any moment.

The door slid open with a soft hiss, and her assistant stepped in, nodding respectfully. "The delegates are here, Prime Nguyen."

"Send them in," Nguyen replied. She set the tablet on her desk and folded her hands, ready to meet the figures she had personally selected for this critical mission.

As the delegates entered, Nguyen observed each one with a calculated gaze. There was Admiral Corwin Harker. A veteran of the Jovian Aggression, he had a reputation for both integrity and unyielding determination. Beside him stood Dr. Marianne Voss, a forensic auditor from Ganymede known for uncovering financial scandals. Finally, representing the intelligence community was Commander Kane, a shadowy figure with a decorated career in Naval Intelligence. His sharp features and piercing gaze carried the weight of countless covert operations.

Nguyen gestured for them to sit around the circular conference table in the center of the room. "Thank you all for coming on such short notice. I trust you understand the gravity of the situation."

Admiral Harker was the first to speak. "Prime Nguyen, if even half of the accusations against these senators are true, we're looking at an existential threat to the Alliance. We cannot afford to let this faction grow unchecked."

Nguyen nodded. "That's why this investigation must be thorough and impartial. We are not here to prove guilt or innocence prematurely but to uncover the truth."

Dr. Voss adjusted her glasses. "What resources will we have at our disposal? A proper forensic investigation requires access to financial records, communications, and personnel."

Nguyen tapped her tablet, bringing up a holographic display of a detailed organizational chart. "I've secured full authorization from the Chancellor. You will have access to all necessary Senate records, with the exception of classified military documents. Admiral Harker will ensure any security clearances you require are expedited."

Harker gave a curt nod, his jaw tightening. "Understood."

Nguyen turned to Commander Kane. "Commander, your role will be critical in monitoring the accused senators' activities discreetly. We cannot let them know the full extent of this investigation."

Kane leaned forward. "I'll need access to their travel logs, personal schedules, and private communications. My team will handle surveillance without raising suspicion."

Nguyen acknowledged his confidence with a slight nod before turning to Dr. Voss. "Dr. Voss, you'll analyze financial records and campaign contributions for irregularities. Follow the money and see where it leads. You'll coordinate with Admiral Harker on this, as he can provide military resources where necessary."

Senator Julian Mahir from Mars, seated quietly until now, interjected. "We also need to consider the political fallout. If we're too aggressive, we risk alienating not just the accused but their allies. The Alliance is already fragile, and this investigation could shatter it if handled poorly."

Nguyen's gaze sharpened. "That's why I chose you, Senator. Your diplomatic expertise will help us navigate those waters. But let me be clear: the integrity of this investigation cannot be compromised by political considerations. The Alliance was built on justice and transparency, and we must uphold those principles."

The room fell silent for a moment as Nguyen's words settled over them. She took a breath and continued, "Now, let's establish the scope of the investigation. We are focusing on the six senators Prime Patel has implicated. Our objectives are threefold:"

1. **Uncover Evidence of Collusion**
   "Dr. Voss, your team will identify any financial ties or irregularities that link these senators to the alleged shadow faction."

2. **Monitor Communications**
   "Commander Kane, you will oversee surveillance of their private communications and meetings. Look for coded language, unusual patterns, and any indication of coordination with outside groups."

3. **Assess Political Influence**
   "Senator Mahir, map out their political alliances within the Senate. Who do they align with? Who might be covertly supporting them? We need to understand the extent of their influence."

Nguyen leaned back in her chair, her hands resting lightly on the table. "This investigation will be conducted under the highest level of confidentiality. We cannot allow leaks, and we cannot afford mistakes. Are we clear?"

Each delegate nodded in agreement, their expressions a mix of determination and apprehension.

"Good," Nguyen said, standing. "Then let's get to work. Admiral Harker, Dr. Voss, Commander Kane, Senator Mahir—you each have your assignments. Report to me directly with your findings."

As the group rose and began to file out, Nguyen lingered by the window, watching the city below. The burden of the investigation weighed heavily on her, but she knew it was a burden she must bear. The Alliance's future depended on it.

With a final glance at the skyline, Nguyen turned back to her desk and began drafting her first report to the Chancellor. The investigation had begun.

***

Senator Lopez sat alone in the sterile conference room, her tablet perched in front of her like an unyielding sentinel. The silence pressed in on her, broken only by the low hum of the overhead lights. She tapped her fingers nervously on the smooth surface of the table, her eyes darting to the door every few seconds. Ava Turing was known for her punctuality, which meant Lopez's time was almost up—and she still had no idea what she was going to say.

The tablet buzzed suddenly, pulling her attention. She snatched it up, heart pounding as the message flashed on the screen:

Push Athena's integration into military assets. Start with the jump gates. Do not fail me.

Cipher's instructions were brief, cold, and final. The message dissolved before her eyes, leaving no trace of its existence. Lopez swallowed hard, gripping the tablet as though it were a lifeline. *What happens if I do fail?* she thought. The answer chilled her to the bone.

The sound of heels clicking against the polished floor outside the door made her heart lurch. She straightened, placing the tablet down and folding her hands in what she hoped was a composed manner. The door opened, and Ava stepped inside.

Ava's presence was electric, filling the room with an air of quiet authority. Her tailored suit emphasized her commanding figure, and her long braid swayed behind her as she crossed to the table. She exuded confidence, her sharp gaze scanning the room before settling on Lopez.

"Senator," Ava greeted crisply. She slid into the chair opposite Lopez, placing a sleek folder on the table. "I hope this is important. My time is valuable."

Lopez forced a smile, though her nerves threatened to crack it. "Thank you for coming, Ava. It is important." She hesitated, choosing her words carefully. "This concerns Athena."

Ava raised an eyebrow, leaning back in her chair. "Athena? What about her?"

Lopez clasped her hands tightly to keep them from trembling. "We've been discussing how Athena's capabilities could be expanded—to ensure the security of the Alliance. Specifically, starting with the jump gates."

Ava's expression darkened immediately. "Security?" Her tone was icy. "You're proposing military integration."

"Yes," Lopez said quickly, leaning forward. "But not as a weapon. As a safeguard. The jump gates are the backbone of the Alliance. If they were compromised—"

Ava held up a hand, silencing her. "Athena was not designed for this. I've made that clear from the beginning. She's meant to improve lives, not become a pawn in your games of power."

Lopez felt her throat tighten. "Ava, this isn't about power. It's about protection. Athena can analyze and prevent threats before they happen—"

"Spare me the sales pitch," Ava snapped. "Do you know what happens when you hand over a tool like Athena to the military? Control is an illusion. Once she's in their hands, they'll twist her for their purposes, no matter what safeguards you think you've put in place."

"I know," Lopez admitted. "That's why we need you. You're the only one who can ensure that doesn't happen."

Ava's laugh was sharp and humorless. "Oh, you think my oversight will matter? I've seen how these things play out. Once Athena is integrated, there's no going back. The Alliance will own her, and they'll own me. Do you really think I'll hand over my life's work for your assurances?"

Lopez's composure cracked. Desperation now creeping into her voice. "Ava, please. If we don't do this, someone else will. And they won't care about ethical boundaries or your principles. They'll take Athena by force if necessary. This is the only way to protect her—to protect everything you've built."

Ava stared at her for a long moment. "And if I refuse?" she asked.

Lopez felt her heart hammering in her chest. Her voice dropping to a whisper. "Then I don't know what happens next. But it won't be good. For any of us."

The silence that followed was suffocating. Ava tapped her fingers against the table, her sharp nails clicking in a thoughtful rhythm. Finally, she sighed, leaning back in her chair.

"If I agree—and I'm not saying I will—it's on my terms. I will have complete control over Athena's integration. No exceptions. I'll decide where and how she's deployed, and I will personally oversee every aspect of her operation."

Lopez exhaled shakily, relief rushing over her. "Of course. Whatever you need."

Ava's lips curved into a faint, cold smile. "Good. Then my legal team will draft the terms. Nothing moves forward until I approve every detail."

Lopez nodded quickly, grasping at the lifeline Ava had extended. "That's fair. Thank you."

Ava stood, gathering her folder and adjusting her jacket. She paused at the door, glancing back at Lopez. Her voice changing from soft and warm, to chilling and foreboding. "Be careful, Senator. You're playing a dangerous game."

And with that, she was gone, leaving Lopez alone in the room. The door clicked shut behind Ava, leaving Lopez alone in the silent conference room. For a moment, she remained frozen in her seat, staring at the spot where Ava had stood. The air still carried the faint trace of her perfume—sharp, commanding, and unyielding. Lopez exhaled shakily, rubbing her hands together in an attempt to steady herself.

Her tablet sat on the table like a judge waiting to pass sentence. She picked it up with trembling fingers and opened the secure communication channel. She typed carefully, each word carefully chosen:

Ava has agreed to the integration. She insists on full oversight and control. Her legal team will draft the terms. I did what you asked.

Lopez hesitated before pressing send, a sliver of dread coursing through her. She couldn't help but recall Ava's final words: *You're playing a dangerous game.* Shaking her head, she sent the message and set the tablet down, leaning back in her chair. Her breath came in shallow gasps, her chest tightening as she waited for Cipher's response.

The reply came almost instantly. A single line of text that froze the blood in her veins.

I know, and hearing you beg was satisfying.

Lopez's stomach twisted violently, and she gripped the edge of the table to keep from doubling over. Her pulse roared in her ears, drowning out every rational thought. She read the message again, her eyes darting over the words, desperate for any sign she'd misread them.

She hadn't.

Her lips trembled, her mouth dry as the weight of Cipher's response settled on her. The air in the room seemed colder now, oppressive and suffocating. She clutched her tablet, her knuckles white, resisting the urge to throw it across the room. Instead, she stared at the screen, her own pale reflection in the black void beneath Cipher's chilling words.

Lopez's thoughts spiraled. *She was watching. Listening. The entire time.* A fresh wave of nausea churned in her gut as the implications sank in. There had been no privacy, no control—not even in her desperation. Cipher had orchestrated everything, her unseen hand turning Lopez into a puppet in her game.

She pressed her palms flat against the table, trying to ground herself. Her breathing was shallow, erratic, each inhale feeling like a struggle. The humiliation of begging Ava, the raw vulnerability she'd shown—it hadn't just been for Ava's benefit. Cipher had wanted it. Needed it. And Lopez had delivered.

How far does her reach go? The question hammered in her mind, each syllable heavier than the last. She glanced around the room, her gaze darting to every corner, every shadow, searching for cameras or hidden devices. The thought that Cipher could see her now, watching her break, sent her heart racing.

Lopez slammed the tablet face down on the table and stood abruptly, pacing the length of the room. Her heels clicked against the floor, the sound sharp and frantic. She clenched and unclenched her fists, trying to burn off the surge of panic..

This isn't happening. It can't be happening.

She stopped mid-step, her reflection in the glass window catching her eye. The woman staring back at her looked like a stranger—her face pale, her eyes wide with fear, and her usually neat hair slightly disheveled. Lopez placed a trembling hand against the glass, the cold surface grounding her for a fleeting moment.

Lopez forced herself to sit, lowering into the chair as though her legs might give out. She stared at her tablet, unwilling to touch it again. Her thoughts turned inward, desperation clawing at her chest. *How do I survive this? How do I get out from under her thumb?*

But no answers came. Only the lingering chill of Cipher's message and the suffocating realization that she was entirely, terrifyingly trapped.

Memories II

The hum of the city drifted through the cracked window of my hotel room as I traced a finger over the map spread out on the desk. The lines and dots that formed New Earth's bustling grid meant more to me than to most—a carefully encoded puzzle with subtle markers guiding me to the drop point. Training whispered in my mind, revealing the hidden patterns in the chaos.

On the corner of Martell Avenue and Regent Street, the smallest of details—a misaligned traffic symbol—gave the location away.

A faint smile tugged at my lips. To the casual observer, it was nothing, but to me, it was a blinking neon sign: *This is the place.*

I rolled the map shut, letting out a steadying breath. Reaching for my sidearm, I ran my fingers over the holster, ensuring it was secure. The sleek weight of it against my palm was both reassuring and sobering—a reminder of the stakes. Next, I checked my mobile comms device, watching the charge bar flash green. Everything was ready.

The air outside my hotel felt cooler than I remembered, the energy of Nueva Mexico a pulsing current that I stepped into like an actor taking the stage. The streets thrummed with life— taxis zipping by while vendors shouted over the clatter of machinery. I melted into the crowd, an unremarkable shadow amidst the chaos.

My thoughts drifted to the task ahead. The drop point would be a crucial step in gathering the intel I needed, but trust was in short supply. New Earth teetered on the edge of something volatile, and every step felt like a dance across a minefield.

Adapt. Observe. Never reveal your true intentions.

I repeated the mantra like a prayer as I turned onto Martell Avenue, my eyes scanning every detail. The neon glow of the Four Winds Bar sign pierced through the haze of streetlights. At first glance, it seemed innocuous, just another watering hole amidst the sprawl. But as I drew closer, my eyes found it—a tiny mark on the lower corner of the sign. To most, it would look like a printing error, but to me, it was confirmation.

I stepped through the doors, my senses sharpening immediately. The bar was dimly lit, filled with the chatter of patrons and the clink of glasses. It smelled of stale beer and citrus, a mixture that was oddly comforting. I slid into a seat near the back, my position chosen carefully to give me a clear view of the room while keeping my own presence subtle.

A server approached, her apron stained and her smile polite. "Can I get you something?"

I glanced up, returning her smile with one of my own. "Something fruity, please."

"Coming right up."

I kept my hands folded loosely on the table as my eyes scanned the room, searching for any sign of the drop. My gaze flitted to a trio of men at the bar, their voices low and faces tense. To a pair of women in the corner, their laughter forced. But nothing stood out.

The server returned, setting down a glass brimming with vibrant liquid. "Here you go," she said as she slid a napkin under the drink before walking away.

I reached for the napkin and paused. There, faintly bleeding through the fabric, was the outline of ink. Heart quickening, I unfolded it, careful not to draw attention.

Written in a subtle hand was the answer to the code phrase: *"Indeed, but the sun will rise again."*

Relief flooded through me. It wasn't just the answer—it was confirmation that I was in the right place, that this wasn't a trap. I folded the napkin carefully and slipped it into my pocket. The game was in motion, and every move counted. I took a sip of my drink, the sweetness filling my senses as I prepared for what was to come.

The bar seemed to settle into its rhythm as the minutes ticked by. I sipped my drink slowly, letting the sweetness linger on my tongue while keeping my gaze moving. Faces blurred in and out of focus—some were familiar types, others shadows of what might be. Yet no one stood out. The folded napkin in my pocket felt heavier than it should, like a whisper of the tension pooling in my chest.

The server returned, but this time, she didn't bring another drink. Instead, she slid into the seat across from me with an ease that set my nerves on edge. Her apron, slightly crooked, bore a name tag I hadn't noticed before: Loda.

A twinge of recognition prickled the back of my mind. Loda. An anagram of Aldo.

She leaned forward, her elbows resting on the table, and gave me a smile that didn't quite reach her eyes. "You're a tough one to crack," she said soft enough to be drowned out by the bar's noise but loud enough for me to hear clearly.

I raised an eyebrow, mirroring her calm. "I'm just here for the atmosphere."

Her smile sharpened. "Sure, you are." She let the words hang in the air before glancing around, her gaze sweeping the room. "You have the phrase?"

My fingers brushed the napkin in my pocket, instinctively ensuring it was still there. I nodded. "I do."

"Good." She shifted her posture, leaning in slightly. "But let's not pretend you're thrilled about being here. This kind of thing rarely makes people comfortable."

I hesitated. "That depends on what kind of 'thing' you mean."

Her lips twitched in amusement. "The kind where the wrong step gets you burned."

"Then maybe you can help me avoid those steps."

She tilted her head, studying me as if weighing my worth. "That depends on how much you already know—and how much you're willing to risk."

I kept my expression neutral, my training wrapping around me like a shield. "Let's just say I'm good at adapting."

For the first time, a genuine smile cracked her facade. "Adaptation. That's key. Especially here."

She glanced over her shoulder, as if checking for something—or someone—before lowering her voice further. "The shadow faction you're looking for isn't a single entity. It's more like smoke—tendrils everywhere, slipping through cracks. You'll find traces, but never the whole picture. Not unless you're part of it."

"And you're telling me this why?"

"Because someone thinks you might be useful," she replied. "But that usefulness is limited by how much you know. Or how much you can handle."

"I was told I'd be meeting Aldo," I said, keeping my voice steady despite the unease crawling up my spine.

She tilted her head slightly, a faint smirk playing on her lips. "Aldo's a name. Does it matter who wears it?"

I leaned in, lowering my voice further. "I was under the impression Aldo was a man. And that I'd be receiving credentials here."

Her smile didn't waver. "Impressions are funny like that. They're rarely accurate, wouldn't you agree?"

The cryptic response only deepened my unease, but before I could press her further, she glanced around the room again, her demeanor shifting subtly. "I have what you came for," she murmured, slipping her hand into her apron pocket.

She placed two items on the table subtlety. The first was a small slip of paper, folded tightly. The second, a set of keys— worn, unremarkable, but heavy with implied significance. "You'll need both," she said, barely audible over the din of the bar.

"What are these for?" I asked, forcing myself to maintain an air of calm despite the growing unease.

Her gaze met mine, the faint smirk returning. "When you leave here, you'll know what to do with them." Her voice was light, almost dismissive, but her eyes burned with an intensity that told me she wasn't speaking in riddles for fun.

I opened my mouth to press her further, but before I could speak, she was already standing. "Stay sharp," she said, and just like that, she slipped away, her apron blending into the movement of the crowd as if she had never been there at all.

I scanned the room as I tried to catch a glimpse of her retreating figure. Nothing. She was gone, leaving me with nothing but a folded piece of paper and a set of keys that felt heavier than they should.

I glanced down at the items. The paper could be unfolded and read, but the keys? *What am I supposed to do with these?*

Swallowing my frustration, I pocketed the keys and unfolded the paper. Written in a hurried scrawl was an address and a time: *52nd and Fallstead. Midnight.*

The pieces of this game were falling into place, but every step forward only deepened the mystery. Clutching the keys in my pocket, I downed the rest of my drink, pushed back from the table, and prepared to leave. Whatever awaited me outside, it seemed

Loda—or Aldo—had ensured I wouldn't leave without knowing where to go next.

The night air outside the bar was cooler than I remembered, a sharp contrast to the warm hum of voices and clinking glasses I'd left behind. I stepped onto the pavement, slipping the keys from my pocket and turning them over in my hand. They were ordinary enough—scuffed metal with no markings to indicate their purpose. Yet, Loda's words echoed in my mind: *When you leave here, you'll know what to do.*

That's when I saw it.

Parked a few steps away was a sleek black motorcycle, its polished body gleaming under the streetlights. My heart gave an involuntary flutter of recognition. I knew that make and model: a Razer R-1300, top of its class in speed and agility, with a reputation for being as dangerous as it was beautiful. It wasn't just a bike; it was a statement. The kind of thing you noticed whether you wanted to or not.

I took a step closer, my eyes tracing the smooth curves of its design. My fingers tightened around the keys as the pieces clicked into place. *No. It couldn't be.*

But it was.

The absurdity of the realization made me laugh under my breath. "Of course," I murmured, shaking my head. "Nothing says 'blend in' like riding a black Razer."

Still, the keys were in my hand, and my gut told me I wasn't wrong. I crouched beside the bike, inspecting it more closely. Sure enough, there was a small lock on the side of the seat, the kind that would open a hidden storage compartment.

I glanced around, ensuring no one was paying attention, then slid the key into the lock. It turned smoothly with a satisfying click. The seat popped open, revealing a compact storage area. Inside were two items: a sleek black comms device, smaller and more advanced than mine, and an envelope with my name scrawled across the front.

I pulled both out, my curiosity outweighing the chill in the air. The envelope contained my credentials—completely flawless as usual, down to the smallest detail. The new comms device blinked to life as I powered it on. A single message appeared on the screen:

Your current comms device has been compromised. Dispose of it immediately. This one is secure. Do not attempt contact with anyone outside your mission parameters.

I exhaled sharply, the weight of the message settling over me. Compromised. The thought sent a chill down my spine. The old device suddenly felt like a liability, a ticking bomb waiting to betray me. Without hesitation, I dropped it onto the pavement and crushed it under my boot, the small device shattering with a sharp crack.

Shaking my head, I glanced back at the bike. "This is ridiculous," I muttered, a wry smile tugging at my lips. "Who thought this was subtle?"

Still, I couldn't deny the practicality of it. The R-1300 was fast, agile, and perfect for navigating a city like this. It wasn't what I would've chosen for a covert operation, but it was mine now.

I slid onto the seat, checking the time on my watch. Midnight was fast approaching, and the address on the paper wasn't far. The engine purred to life beneath me, a low growl that sent a rush of adrenaline through my veins.

As I eased the bike into the street, the absurdity of my cover
lingered in the back of my mind. But there was no time to dwell on
it. The address on the paper loomed like a beacon, and the night
was far from over.

****

The R-1300 roared beneath me, a symphony of raw power and
precision that was impossible to resist. I had planned to take it
slow, to avoid drawing unnecessary attention, but the bike had
other ideas. The sleek beast seemed to beg for speed, and I
indulged it, weaving through the sparse traffic with a confidence I
hadn't felt in days. For a few fleeting moments, I was weightless,
untouchable.

The streetlights blurred past until I forced myself to ease up on
the throttle. The address was close now, and arriving too early
would be just as suspicious as arriving late. I slowed as the
intersection of 52nd and Fallstead came into view, coasting to a
stop a block away. The bike's engine rumbled under me before I
shut it off, the sudden silence amplifying the steady hum of the
city.

The address from the paper led me here, but the corner seemed
unremarkable at first glance. Across the street, a convenience store
with a flickering neon "24-HR MART" sign stood out amidst the
worn facades of the other buildings. Beside it, the entrance to an
alleyway beckoned, its darkness hiding whatever might lie within.

I checked my watch. I was early, thanks to the Razer's
addictive speed. A thrill had coursed through me during the ride,
but now the adrenaline was gone, leaving only the focused
anticipation of what might come next. I leaned forward slightly,

resting my forearms on the handlebars as I watched the street for any sign of movement or activity.

Then, my comms device buzzed against my hip, the vibration pulling me from my thoughts. I pulled it out, its screen casting a pale blue glow in the dark. A new message had arrived, marked with the highest priority level.

Proceed to the convenience store. Identify yourself to the cashier as "E. Drayton."

I frowned, my eyes flicking to the store across the street. *That's it?* No code phrases this time, no elaborate riddles—just a name. It felt unusually simple, but simplicity often came with its own dangers.

Slipping the device back into my pocket, I dismounted the bike, my boots crunching against the cracked pavement as I walked toward the store. The Razer's sleek silhouette lingered behind me, a predator waiting in the shadows.

The bell above the door chimed softly as I stepped inside. The fluorescent lights buzzed overhead, casting a harsh glow on the rows of shelves stocked with the usual convenience store fare: snacks, drinks, and an assortment of everyday necessities. The air smelled faintly of cleaning products, masking something less pleasant underneath.

The cashier barely looked up as I approached. He was young, maybe early twenties, with a disheveled appearance that suggested he didn't care much for the job.

I stopped in front of the counter, noting his casual demeanor as he turned a page in the magazine he was half-heartedly reading. "I'm E. Drayton," I said, my voice low but clear.

That got his attention. His eyes flicked up to meet mine, his expression shifting from bored to something sharper. He set the magazine down, straightening slightly. "You're early," he said quietly.

"The bike's fast," I replied evenly.

He glanced past me toward the door, as though checking to see if I'd been followed, then nodded toward the back of the store. "Storage room. Door's unlocked. You'll find what you're looking for there."

I hesitated, the tension in my chest coiling tighter. "I was told to speak with you."

"You are," he said, his gaze steady. "But you'll understand better once you go back there. Trust me—or don't. That's your call."

His words carried the faintest hint of a challenge, but I wasn't about to rise to it. Without another word, I turned and made my way toward the rear of the store, the tension between my shoulder blades sharpening with every step. The door marked "Employees Only" loomed ahead, its surface worn and scratched from years of neglect.

I pushed it open cautiously, half expecting an empty room or, worse, an ambush. Instead, I found a man waiting, leaning against a stack of crates with an air of practiced indifference. His face was partially obscured by the dim light, but his eyes were sharp and watchful.

"You're E. Drayton, I take it?" he asked, his voice carrying the weight of someone who'd long since stopped caring about pleasantries.

"I am," I replied, stepping into the room and closing the door behind me.

"Good," he said, his lips curving into a faint smirk. "Because I've got a lot to tell you, and not much time to do it."

***

The conversation with the man was intense, almost as if it were a mission briefing.

The shadow faction wasn't just a single entity. That was his first lesson.

"The *who* and the *what* are two entirely different things," he'd said. "People always assume they're looking for one or the other. But the *who* is just the beginning. The *what*... that's what'll keep you up at night."

According to the man, the *who* was a group of senators—three of them, to be exact—alongside an Admiral from the Fleet. They were all high-ranking officials, all disillusioned with the Alliance, all looking to carve out their own independence.

"They're using the Jovian Aggression as their playbook," he explained, his expression grim. "They've studied every mistake, every misstep. They've seen where others failed, and they're making damn sure not to repeat those mistakes. They're building this thing slow, careful. No loose ends."

I'd felt a shiver run down my spine as he laid it out. The Jovian Aggression was still a raw wound for so many, a reminder of how quickly things could spiral out of control. And now, this faction was preparing to strike, using those lessons to their advantage.

But the admiral—that detail didn't sit right with me.

"Why would an admiral be involved in something like this?" I'd asked. "What's their angle?"

He shrugged, his demeanor slipping into that infuriatingly cryptic mode of his. "I don't know the *why,* just the *who.* Maybe they're ambitious, maybe they're disillusioned. Doesn't matter. What matters is they're in."

That answer wasn't enough for me, but before I could press further, another detail had emerged.

"You said there are five members," I pointed out. "Three senators and one Admiral. That's four. Who's the fifth?"

He chuckled, the sound dry and humorless. "The fifth isn't a who. It's the *what* I told you about."

Before I could probe deeper into what he meant, gunshots rang out, sharp and sudden, cutting through the quiet like a blade. The echoes ricocheted off the walls, sending an icy spike of adrenaline through my veins.

"Shit," he muttered, his calm demeanor evaporating as he reached for a weapon tucked beneath his jacket. "We've got company."

I didn't wait for an invitation. My training kicked in, and I darted toward the storage room door, my suppressed sidearm already in hand. Peering out, I spotted movement—shadows shifting near the entrance, the flash of a muzzle as another shot rang out.

My contact was at my side, firing off a few rounds to keep them at bay. "Go," he hissed. "Get out of here. They're not after me—they're after you."

I didn't argue. Bolting from the room, I moved swiftly through the store, keeping low as more gunfire erupted behind me. The cashier was gone—smart enough to know when to disappear. I pushed through the front door, my eyes scanning the street for my bike.

The Razer roared to life beneath me as I sped out of the alley, the echo of gunfire still ringing in my ears. My pulse hammered, but my focus was razor-sharp. A glance in the side mirror made my stomach drop—two black SUVs were closing in, their unmistakable markings glinting under the dim streetlights. Military Police.

The realization sent a jolt through me. Military Police weren't part of standard local security. Their presence here meant only one thing: someone high up knew about this meeting, and they weren't taking any chances.

The first SUV surged forward, its grille filling my mirror. I twisted the throttle, and the Razer responded instantly, the engine snarling as I accelerated. The bike's raw power surged beneath me as I darted into a narrow side street, the walls of the buildings on either side blurring past. I leaned hard into the first turn, the tires gripping the pavement as I cut through the shadows.

The SUVs followed, their drivers relentless. I could hear the screech of tires behind me, the heavy growl of engines pushing to keep up. One of them clipped the corner of a building as it turned, but the second stuck to me like glue. The Razer's agility gave me an edge, but the weight of their pursuit was suffocating. This wasn't a random encounter—they were hunting me.

I swerved into a tighter alley, the bike's frame nearly brushing the walls as I threaded through. Behind me, one of the SUVs didn't make the turn, slamming into a stack of pallets with a deafening crash. The other stayed on my tail, its headlights flashing like an accusation in the dark.

Up ahead, the maze of alleys opened onto a broader street. I spotted an overpass and veered toward it, cutting the bike's lights and plunging into the deep shadows beneath. The engine's growl dropped to a purr as I slowed, coasting into an unlit corner and killing the motor entirely. My breaths were shallow and quick as I listened.

The second SUV roared past overhead, its driver unaware that I'd vanished into the shadows. I stayed still, waiting until the sound of its engine faded into the distance. The silence that followed was almost deafening, broken only by the faint hum of the city beyond.

I allowed myself a moment to breathe, my fingers still gripping the handlebars. My mind raced, piecing together the implications. Military Police. They shouldn't have been here. And their pursuit couldn't be a coincidence.

Once the coast was clear, I powered the bike back up and eased into the city's depths, keeping to side streets and avoiding major thoroughfares. As the adrenaline began to ebb, my mind returned to the mission. Being tailed by Military Police was bad, but it didn't mean the operation was compromised—not yet.

Stopping in another darkened alley, I reached for my comms device. The screen glowed faintly as I keyed in a secure line to my handler. The message was short, but precise:

Chased by Military Police. Pursuers lost. No shots fired. Chance of exposure low. Mission not compromised. Awaiting further instructions.

The screen dimmed as the message sent, leaving me alone with the low hum of the Razer beneath me. I glanced back toward the alley's entrance, my instincts on edge. The streets felt too quiet now, as though the city itself was holding its breath.

I leaned forward on the bike, my eyes scanning the darkened street ahead. Whatever my handler's response would be, I needed to stay sharp. The Military Police had already made one move tonight. I couldn't afford to let them make another.

Several minutes went by, then my comms device buzzed in my hand, and instead of the usual text message, the screen lit up with an incoming video call. My stomach tightened. Video calls were almost never used—only when the situation demanded more than a simple exchange of information.

I glanced around the alley, ensuring I was alone, before tapping to accept the call. The screen flickered for a moment before stabilizing, revealing my handler's familiar face. They sat in a dimly lit room, the shadows behind them concealing any identifying details. Their expression was impassive, but their tone was sharp.

"Report."

I straightened, keeping my voice steady. "Chased by Military Police. No shots fired. Pursuers lost. Chance of exposure low. I don't believe the mission is compromised."

They tilted their head slightly, their eyes narrowing. "How close did they get?"

"Too close," I admitted. "They didn't signal for backup or make contact, so I don't think they got a clear look at me—or the bike."

The handler's lips pressed into a thin line, a subtle but telling reaction. "Military Police presence escalates the situation. They shouldn't have been involved. Either your meeting was observed, or someone tipped them off."

I nodded. "The contact was careful, but it's possible someone knew we were meeting. He provided useful intel, though."

Their gaze sharpened. "Details."

"The shadow faction isn't just a single entity," I began, recounting the conversation. "The *who* is a group of five: three senators, an admiral, and... something else. He called it the *what*. Said it wasn't a person."

The handler leaned forward slightly, their interest evident. "The senators?"

I hesitated, frustrated by the contact's cryptic nature. "No names. He said they're modeling their plans after the Jovian Aggression, learning from its failures. They're taking their time, building support quietly. The admiral's involvement doesn't make sense to me, but he didn't have details on that, either."

The handler's expression didn't shift, but I caught the faintest flicker of tension in their eyes. "The admiral changes things. If a high-ranking Fleet officer is involved, the faction's reach is wider than we anticipated. Did the contact elaborate on this *what*?"

I shook my head. "No. Just that it's not a person. He said it's tied to their endgame, but the rest? Nothing."

The handler leaned back, their tone turning thoughtful. "The senators and the admiral align with some intelligence we've intercepted. The *what* remains a wildcard—potentially a new weapon, a communications network, or a broader ideological movement. Until we know more, your focus is the *who.*"

I nodded. "What's the next step?"

The handler's gaze flicked off-screen for a moment, as though reading or considering additional intel. When they returned their attention to me, their voice was firm. "Your cover ID grants you access to the Capital Spire. Use it to identify the Senate members involved. Names, connections, motivations—we need it all. That's your priority."

My pulse quickened. The Capital Spire was the heart of political power, a fortress of bureaucracy and secrecy. Accessing it was one thing; maneuvering through its layers undetected would be another entirely.

"Understood," I said. "Do we have any intel on what to expect once inside?"

"Minimal," they replied bluntly. "You'll have to rely on your instincts and the cover we've provided. Keep a low profile and avoid drawing attention. The Military Police's involvement increases the risk of exposure, so tread carefully. We'll feed you additional instructions as needed."

I nodded again, my grip tightening on the comms device. "And the contact? Could they trace this back to him?"

The handler's lips quirked in the faintest semblance of a smile—more cold than reassuring. "If they do, it's his problem, not yours. Your mission is the priority now. Focus on the Spire."

The screen went dark as the call ended, leaving me alone with the hum of the Razer beneath me. I stared into the night, the weight of the handler's instructions settling over me. The stakes had risen sharply. Identifying the senators wasn't just about gathering intel anymore—it was about understanding how deep the faction's influence truly ran.

I exhaled, shaking off the tension as I powered the bike out of the alley. The city stretched ahead, its shadows deeper and more dangerous than ever. The Capital Spire awaited, and with it, the next step into the heart of this conspiracy

Chapter 6

The soft hum of the Specter's systems filled the dimly lit office, the small conference table bathed in the pale blue glow of the holo-display. A map of New Earth's sprawling cities and orbital infrastructure flickered in the center, surrounded by Pierce, Jones, Veronica, and Cruise brainstorming their next steps.

"We know the freighter isn't here," Pierce said. "Tupolev doesn't need to know that. Our focus is solely on finding Starfire, and we need to make sure no one suspects this."

"We need a way to operate on the surface without raising suspicion," Veronica offered. "If we give the appearance of business as usual—a decoy"

Cruise interjected. "Something to make Tupolev think we're here for something official."

Before Veronica could continue, Jones cut in. "If by 'decoy' you're about to suggest I engage Tupolev, don't even bother."

Veronica blinked, startled. "I wasn't—"

"Because I know exactly where this is going. Someone charms Tupolev, distracts him, and who better than me, right? Well, let me save you the trouble—I'm not doing it. I won't flirt, stroke his ego, or play nice just to keep him off our backs."

Cruise, unfazed by her heated words, responded casually. "It would be an effective decoy, Commander."

Jones's eyes quickly ignited with the fires of rage, slowly turning her head to face him. "Did you seriously just suggest that I undermine everything I've worked for in this fleet to be some glorified distraction for Tupolev? Let me make one thing clear, Major: I am not here to play dress-up and shake my backside to get out of a problem."

"Allison," Pierce interjected, "Major Cruise is only offering options, but no one here is asking you to compromise your principles." He turned toward Cruise. "Let's shift focus."

Jones exhaled sharply and leaned back, crossing her arms. "Good. Because if we're going to do this, we need a plan that doesn't involve me givin' folks the wrong idea about my raisin'."

The silence that followed was punctuated by the faint hum of the holo-display. Veronica, nervously tapping her fingers on the table, hesitated before speaking. "What if... what if we didn't make it look like an operation at all?"

Pierce tilted his head slightly. "Go on, Lieutenant."

Veronica straightened. "What if we made it look like the crew was just taking some much-needed shore leave? I mean, morale's been low, and Tupolev wouldn't question it. We could stagger our movements on the surface, blending in with everyone else while we search for Starfire."

Jones raised an eyebrow, her irritation easing slightly. "That... could work. If we keep the team movements subtle and spread out."

Cruise nodded, his earlier confidence shifting to cautious approval. "It's simple, but that's why it might actually work. No coordinated actions for Tupolev to pick up on—just a crew on leave."

A faint smile crossed Pierce's face, his tone thoughtful. "The simplicity of it is what makes it brilliant. Shore leave gives us cover, keeps the crew happy, and masks any real activity as standard downtime." He turned toward Veronica. "Good thinking, Miss Valentine."

Veronica flushed slightly at the praise, her fingers relaxing against the table. "Thank you, Captain."

Pierce leaned forward. "Allison, prep a list of personnel for staggered shore leave assignments. Major Cruise, ensure comm protocols are ready to maintain cover. Miss Valentine, coordinate with the team leaders for surface movements."

Jones nodded, a trace of a smile tugging at her lips. "Finally, a plan I can get behind."

***

The door to Captain Pierce's office slid open, and the officers stepped onto the bridge. Pierce led the way, Jones followed, her lips pressed tightly together. Veronica trailed slightly behind, lost in thought, while Major Cruise brought up the rear, his usual calm demeanor unchanged.

As they entered the bridge, the usual hum of the Specter's systems and the soft murmur of crew voices filled the air. Pierce stopped just inside, tilting his head slightly as though sensing something off.

Suddenly, alarms blared. The comms officer frantic. "Sir, we've detected an explosion. It's the Unity.

"That is Prime Patel's private ship." Jones said softly.

The bridge fell silent for a moment before bursting into action. Jones moved swiftly to the sensor console. "Details, now," she demanded.

The sensor analyst called out. "Explosion occurred near the Jump Gate, just outside planetary space. Debris pattern indicates a reactor overload.."

"Survivors?" Pierce asked.

"No active transponders, still scanning, sir," the analyst replied.

Before they could process further, an open-channel broadcast came through, cutting across all communications. Captain Tupolev's deep, commanding voice filled the bridge.

"This is Captain Mikail Tupolev of the Alliance Battleship Independence. Effective immediately, and under the authority of

Article 17 of the Alliance Emergency Protocol, orbital space around New Earth is now restricted to military vessels. Civilian traffic is prohibited until further notice. Violators will be detained."

The tactical officer's console lit up. "Sir, interceptors from the Independence are launching. Twelve confirmed. And…" He hesitated. "The Independence is repositioning. Its current heading is toward the Jump Gate."

Jones stiffened, her hands gripping the console's edge. "The Jump Gate? What the hell is Tupolev doing? He's locking down more than the orbital space."

"Sir, warning buoy deployed from the Independence, broadcasting Captain Tupolev's message on all civilian channels." The comms officer interjected.

Pierce's fingers tightened around the armrests of his chair. "Article 17 is for containing catastrophic incidents—planetary contamination or imminent large-scale threats. An explosion in orbital space doesn't justify this."

"It's a stretch, to say the least," Jones agreed. "But he's using it to seize control. If the Independence moves to the gate, he'll control all traffic in and out of the system."

Veronica's voice broke in. "Do we engage with him? Challenge the declaration?"

"No," Pierce said firmly. "Not yet. First, we focus on searching for survivors. Major Cruise, deploy search-and-rescue shuttles. Prioritize the edges of the debris field. There could still be escape pods."

"Yes, sir," Cruise replied, moving swiftly to coordinate the operation.

"Miss Valentine," Pierce continued, "coordinate with engineering to ensure shuttle readiness. I don't want delays."

"Yes, Captain," Veronica said, already moving to a nearby console.

Jones's glare was fixed on the sensor readout as the Independence continued its course. She muttered under her breath before stepping aside to a comm station. "I'm reaching out to Commander Baptiste," she said. "She might give us some answers."

Pierce nodded. "Keep it discreet."

Jones opened a private video channel, hesitation shaking her words. "Zoe, it's Allison. What the hell are you doing? Why is the Independence heading for the Jump Gate?"

There was a pause, long enough to make Jones' irritation spike, before Baptiste's voice came through, sounding distressed. "Allison, I can't discuss operational details. You know that."

"Don't give me that bull Zoe," Jones snapped. "Tupolev is citing emergency powers to seize orbital space, and now you're moving on the Jump Gate? That's not protocol—that's overreach."

Baptiste hesitated more, her face showing discomfort and something else—fear. "Allison, I'm telling you as a friend—stay out of this. It's bigger than you think."

The channel went silent. Jones stared at the console, her hands clenched. "She's hiding something. Tupolev's not acting alone."

Pierce tilted his head. "Whatever they're planning, it's not our primary concern. Focus on the rescue. We'll deal with Tupolev later."

The bridge buzzed with activity as the Specter's search-and-rescue shuttles launched into the void, heading toward the debris field. Beyond the viewport, the flickering remnants of the Unity cast an eerie light, a silent harbinger of the crisis yet to unfold. Meanwhile, the Independence continued its course, its actions looming over the system like an unspoken threat.

***

Miranda Soto sat quietly in her study, surrounded by mementos from her time in the Alliance Naval Complaints Office. The walls were adorned with photos of high-ranking military officers and influential politicians, each image a reminder of a life once filled with purpose and urgency. Above her fireplace hung a large bronze emblem, a symbol of the office she once held with pride.

Now retired, she relished the quiet moments spent with her grandchildren or lost in the pages of a new novel—well, new to her, anyway. The chaos of her military career had kept her from enjoying these simple pleasures, and now, with all the time in the world, she was determined to savor them.

The fireplace crackled and popped, sending warmth into the study, a stark contrast to the harsh winter winds howling outside. As the flames danced, casting flickering shadows on the walls, Miranda allowed herself to relax in the comforting embrace of her home, far from the bustling capital and its political intrigues.

Tonight, the quiet enveloped her, wrapping around her like a comforting blanket. Just her and a new romance novel, one that promised just the right amount of spice between its characters. However, peace is often a fragile thing. As Hansel and Gretel, a

115

well-trained pair of German Shepards, barked in the distance, Miranda's sense of security began to fray. She walked to the window, peering into the dark night, her unease growing. It was too quiet outside, the kind of stillness that made her instincts scream.

Suddenly, the dogs stopped barking, leaving an unsettling silence in their wake. "Must have been a twiggle," she muttered to herself in a hushed tone, shaking off her apprehension.

Twiggles, the squirrel-like creatures native to New Earth, were a nuisance—almost enough to be classified as pests. Unlike squirrels on Earth, they had a penchant for fruits and would sometimes venture onto Miranda's property to steal apples from her tree. Hansel and Gretel tried their best to chase them away, but the twiggles were just too quick.

With a sigh, Miranda walked into her kitchen to replenish her coffee, rushing a bit as excitement bubbled within her to return to her novel. As she reentered the study, the warmth of the fire was overshadowed by a sudden chill. The hairs on the back of her neck stood on end. Then she saw it—a shadowy figure sitting in her chair. The cup slipped from her hand, shattering on the hardwood floor, the sound echoing in the eerie silence.

"Who are you? Why are you in my house? I'm calling security!" Miranda stammered, trembling with fear as she reached for her comms device, usually hanging on the wall.

A blood-curdling voice spoke from the shadows, oddly familiar yet chilling. "Are you looking for this?" A soft blue glowed from the comms device in the figure's hand. Miranda squinted, straining to catch a glimpse, but the shadows obscured the figure's face.

"W—What do you want?" Miranda asked, her fear mounting.

The unmistakable sound of a sidearm being chambered echoed throughout the study. The intruder stretched out her arm, pointing the weapon directly at Miranda's head. "I want you to sit and answer for your crimes."

Slowly, Miranda complied, trying not to make any sudden movements that might provoke the intruder. "What crimes? I am a distinguished military veteran and retired honorably." Her throat tightened as she struggled to get the words out.

"Don't play dumb; it's not befitting of someone... of your position, Captain." The emphasis on the rank sent an eerie chill up Miranda's spine. "You stole my career, and you also took 'her' away from me."

"I—I don't know what you're talking about," Miranda replied, her voice shaking even more. "I don't even know who you are."

The figure leaned into the light, revealing a face twisted with rage and pain. It was then Miranda knew exactly what this was about. The lump in her throat grew with each passing second, and tears began to well in her eyes. "Zarina..."

"Zarina is dead! She was weak. I am Cipher." She stood, towering over Miranda, who sat paralyzed in her chair, heart racing with fear.

"Please," Miranda begged, "I was just following orders." She said trembling, tears sliding down her plump cheeks. "It was all Holt's plan; you got too close."

Cipher paused, her expression shifting. "Just following orders. The age-old cry of the oppressor." Disgust dripped from her voice, growing into anger. "Holt doing what he does best, pulling the strings on everything and everyone. And you," she pressed the sidearm harder against Miranda's chest, "you just sat there in your cozy little chair and watched him destroy my career. You and that spineless prick Elias both watched as he turned everyone against me."

Finally building the courage to stand her ground, Miranda countered, "You turned everyone against you yourself with your rash decisions in the field, getting everyone around you killed." She looked into Cipher's eyes, only seeing the insanity swirling within. "You—need—help."

The slow, methodical emphasis on each word ignited Cipher's rage. A sickening thud filled the study as Cipher struck Miranda in the head with the sidearm, blood flowing freely down her face.

"I am not crazy!" Cipher shouted. "I'm not, I'm not, I'm not!" She slapped her own head, her fury surging. "I completed my mission as I was trained. And how did I get rewarded? FRACK OFF ZARINA!"

For a moment, the rage receded, replaced by a soothing, calm voice—Zarina's. "You have to stop this."

Cipher snapped back to anger, her eyes blazing. "NO! Stop talking to me!" With a sudden, violent movement, she turned to Miranda and fired three shots into her chest.

Hansel and Gretel began barking at the noise, but the commotion faded into the background as Miranda gasped for breath, her vision blurring. She locked eyes with the emblem on the wall—a symbol of honor that now felt like a cruel joke. The last thing she saw before darkness enveloped her was Cipher's twisted smile, satisfaction etched on her features as she crossed another name off her mental list.

A psychotic giggle escaped Cipher's lips as she imagined the headlines to come: *'Captain Miranda Soto, Retired, found dead, shot in her own home.'* Cipher holstered her sidearm, her hands slipping behind her back, fingers curling around her wrist. As she skipped gleefully from the room, humming a nursery tune, the flickering light of the fire cast dancing shadows on the walls, painting a macabre picture of the violence that had just unfolded. Outside, the winter winds howled, echoing the finality of Miranda's fate—a chilling reminder that in a world steeped in power and betrayal, the dead tell no tales.

Cipher paused at the doorway, her hand resting lightly on the frame. The firelight flickered behind her, casting her shadow long across the study's walls. She glanced back at Miranda's lifeless body, slumped in the chair, blood pooling beneath her. For a moment, her hardened expression wavered, and her eyes glimmered with something akin to sadness.

She turned her head slightly, speaking softly to the silence, almost pleading. "I did this for you. Isn't this what you wanted?" Her words hung in the air, trembling with the weight of a fractured psyche seeking validation from a ghost.

The room was quiet, save for the crackling fire. Cipher's gaze drifted upward to the bronze emblem on the wall—a symbol of honor now tainted by blood. Her lips twitched into a bitter smile, her eyes narrowing as if hearing a voice only she could perceive. "You're right," she whispered. "Stopping isn't an option now. It's too late for that."

As she turned to leave, something on the mantel caught her eye. A framed photograph of a younger Admiral Holt, his confident smile frozen in time. Her gaze lingered, the firelight dancing over the glass and casting his image in sharp relief.

Cipher's bitter smile widened, dark amusement flickering in her eyes. She leaned closer, her finger brushing the edge of the frame as she murmured, "See you soon, Holt."

Her words were a chilling promise, the kind that hung in the air long after she stepped back. Straightening, she turned away, her demeanor cold once more, but the fire's warmth did little to temper the icy presence she left behind.

Cipher stepped out into the biting wind outside, the door clicking shut behind her. The study was silent now, save for the faint crackle of the fire and the faint whisper of a name that promised vengeance. In the stillness, Holt's image remained on the mantel, a silent witness to the darkness that had just passed through.

Chapter 7

Studio lights aboard the GNN orbital platform dimmed slightly as Traci Yamato's broadcast shifted from her polished introduction to a breathtaking view of New Earth's binary stars through the observation lounge window. The celestial event, a perfect alignment of the binary stars, bathed the planet in radiant hues, illuminating the surrounding space in a soft, ethereal glow.

"This is Traci Yamato, reporting live from orbit above New Earth, where we will witness the phenomenon known as the

'Radiance Pairing.' Occurring once every fifteen years, this celestial alignment casts New Earth in a spectacular glow, a sight that has inspired countless artists, poets, and—"

Her words were abruptly cut off as a sudden, blinding flash illuminated the observation lounge, casting stark shadows across the walls. Traci froze, her head snapping toward the window, her polished professionalism giving way to raw shock. Behind her, the camera operator pivoted to capture the unfolding scene.

"Did you see that?" Traci asked as she moved closer to the window, her breath catching as a growing cloud of debris came into view. The binary stars' light caught on the fragments of what had been a ship, their jagged edges reflecting faint glimmers in the void.

The observation lounge aboard the GNN orbital platform hummed with subdued tension as Traci stood before the large window, her eyes fixed on the scene outside. The binary stars' radiant light illuminated the vast expanse of space, casting an eerie glow over the debris field drifting in orbit— overshadowing the beauty she'd been covering moments earlier.

Behind her, the camera operator and crew adjusted equipment, readying for the next segment. The broadcast had shifted from the serene phenomenon of the Radiance Pairing to the chaos of an unfolding tragedy.

Traci began, "We are witnessing the aftermath of a catastrophic explosion. A ship has been destroyed, and as of this moment, the cause remains unknown. Rescue teams are actively responding, and interceptors from the Independence are securing the area."

Her earpiece buzzed with studio chatter, but no new information was coming through. She pressed her lips into a thin line, stepping slightly to the side as the camera focused on the scene outside. "Stand by," she said softly, muting her microphone.

The voices from her crew faded into background noise as she turned to face the window. Her breath fogged the glass slightly as she leaned closer, taking in the scale of the operation. Interceptors streaking across the debris field in precise formations, their movements coordinated with a speed and efficiency that sent a chill down her spine. Rescue shuttles from the Specter moved methodically through the wreckage, their searchlights cutting through the void. Farther out, the warning buoy from the Independence sending its relentless message to all civilian vessels.

Traci gently tugged at her ear lobe as she quietly murmured to herself, "This… doesn't add up." Her gaze followed the interceptors as they fanned out, the lines of military precision almost mesmerizing. "An explosion—one ship—and they invoke Article 17?"

She crossed her arms. "Article 17… that's reserved for planetary disasters, large-scale threats. Not a single ship. What are they expecting?" Her words were barely audible as her thoughts spilled out while she tried to process the scale of the response.

The movement outside seemed to amplify her unease. Interceptors continued to weave through the field, and the Specter's shuttles moved with a grim purpose that spoke of more than just a routine rescue operation. The invocation of Article 17— so rare, so extreme—it had alarm bells ringing in her mind.

A faint voice from her crew broke her concentration. "Traci, we're ready to go back live."

She straightened, her journalistic demeanor reasserting itself as she turned back toward the camera. "One moment," she said, moving to the comms console. Her fingers hovered over the controls. Whatever the studio couldn't confirm, she would find herself.

Adjusting the frequency, she tuned into the military's open channel. A burst of static gave way to clear voices—directives, updates, and the grim reality of the operation unfolding outside.

"Rescue 1, commencing sweep of sector DELTA for escape pods. Negative contact." One voice came through.

"Palisade Actual, Palisade 1. Confirmed. The vessel is the Unity." The pilot said.

Traci froze at the mention of Patel's ship, her lips pressing into a tight line as she listened.

"Copy Palisade 1, regroup with Palisade 2 and 3, secure sector ECHO for Rescue 2." The controller responded.

"Palisade Actual, Palisade 4, Cause of the explosion unknown. No survivors reported so far."

One of Traci's technicians, standing nearby, caught snippets of the broadcast. "How do you know about that channel? And… did you just decrypt it?"

Traci glanced at him, momentarily stunned by the sudden inquiry. "You learn a few things after years of covering the Navy," she said lightly, deflecting the question as she turned back to the window. "Right now, this is about getting the story out."

Her crew exchanged uncertain glances but said nothing further.

Traci returned to the camera, her voice steady and professional. "We are now receiving unconfirmed reports identifying the destroyed vessel as the Unity, a private ship owned by Prime Asha Patel. Rescue teams are actively searching the debris field, but as of this moment, no survivors have been found. The invocation of Article 17 by the Alliance Navy underscores the severity of this incident, with all civilian traffic being rerouted and orbital space restricted."

The camera panned briefly to the interceptors and rescue shuttles outside, capturing the sheer scale of the operation. Traci's voice softened as she added, "The speed and scale of this response raise questions that remain unanswered. For now, GNN will continue to monitor the situation and provide updates as they come in. I'm Traci Yamato, reporting live from orbit."

As the broadcast cut to a loop of rescue operations, Traci turned back to the window. Her reflection stared back. Her mind filled with questions that no one else seemed to be asking.

Outside, the binary stars shone brightly, their light casting an almost surreal glow over the growing chaos. In the void, the Alliance Navy moved with precision, their motives as inscrutable as the darkness between the stars

Traci's voice dropped to a whisper, meant only for herself. "What aren't they telling us?"

***

The observation lounge aboard the GNN orbital platform had settled into an uneasy calm. The earlier chaos had given way to quiet tension as the crew worked at their consoles, the distant lights of interceptors visible through the large observation window. Traci stood apart from the others, her arms loosely crossed as she stared at the scene outside.

A soft vibration in her pocket broke her thoughts. Glancing around to ensure she wasn't being watched too closely, Traci withdrew device and flipped it open. Its scuffed and battered exterior told the story of years of hard use, yet its robust design showed it was built to endure.

The faint glow of the screen reflected in her eyes as she scanned the incoming message. Frustration growing inside her as she read the message.

"Traci?"

The sudden voice made her snap the device shut instinctively. She turned to see one of her tech crew standing near her.

"You okay?" Robert asked. "You seemed… distracted."

A small, practiced smile, though her eyes told a different story. "I'm fine," she said. "Just a message from the studio."

Robert's eyes drifted toward her hand. "From the studio? Through that?" he asked. "I've never seen anything like it. What kind of comms device is it?"

Her smile tightened slightly as she slid the device back into her pocket. "It's just a tool I've had for years," she said. "The studio lines are overloaded, so I use this when I need a direct connection."

Unconvinced he pressed further. "Yeah, but it doesn't look like anything on the market. Is it custom? Special issue? Military-grade?"

Traci's posture shifted. Her calm exterior morphing into something else. Her eyes narrowed, as she took on a sharper edge. "It's not your concern," she said.. "It does its job. That's all that matters."

Robert blinked, startled by the sudden change in her tone. "I—
I didn't mean anything by it," he stammered. "I was just curious."

"Then stop being curious and get back to work," she said,
shifting into something colder, more commanding. Her words
seemed to hang in the air, the authority out of place for a journalist.

He paled slightly, nodded quickly, and retreated to his station.
"Yes, ma'am," he mumbled, glancing back at her once before
focusing intently on his console.

Traci exhaled slowly, turning back to the window. Her
reflection stared back at her. She waited until the tech had fully
turned away before reaching into her pocket again. Flipping open
the device, she began pressing the keys quickly.

Across the room, the tech who had spoken to her earlier
glanced up from his console, his curiosity piqued. He froze as he
saw Traci standing by the window, holding the strange device.

Robert's curiosity piqued. He reached over to his portable
signal scanner, a tool he often used to troubleshoot the platform's
comms systems. The device could pick up and analyze signals
within a broad spectrum, from the platform's internal comms to the
warning buoy's broadcast and even the interceptors as they passed
close by.

He ran a sweep, his eyes darting between the scanner's
readouts and Traci. The platform's comms unit was active, the
buoy's signal steady, and the interceptors' bursts of chatter popped
up. But as his scanner continued its sweep, there was nothing from
Traci's device. No blips, no pings, not even a faint signal.

Robert frowned, adjusting the scanner's settings and running
the sweep again. Still nothing. Whatever Traci was using, it was
either so tightly encrypted that even his advanced tools couldn't

detect it, or it was operating on technology far beyond what he was used to.

His thoughts were interrupted by movement. Traci snapped the device shut with a sharp motion, slipping it back into her pocket as she turned away from the window. Robert had seen enough to know something was off.

He leaned toward his coworker, an older technician named Mara, and whispered, "Did you see what she was using?"

Mara glanced at him briefly before returning her focus to her monitor. "What? Traci?"

"Yeah," Robert said, keeping his voice low. "She had this… comms device. It doesn't look like anything I've seen before. I ran a sweep—nothing. No signal, no ping, no trace. Whatever that thing is, it's locked down tighter than anything I've ever come across."

Mara sighed, shaking her head. "You're overthinking it. She's a senior reporter. She probably has access to high-end gear we don't know about."

"Yeah, but—" Robert started, only for Mara to cut him off.

"No," she said firmly. "Listen to yourself. You're talking about encryption, secure signals, and how Traci isn't acting like herself. What's your theory? That she's some kind of spy? A covert Navy agent posing as a journalist?"

She leaned back in her chair, pinching the bridge of her nose. "Robert, you do this every time someone acts a little off. Remember when you were convinced that maintenance guy last month was sabotaging the air recyclers because he worked the late shift and didn't talk much? Or the time you thought that IT contractor was hacking into our system just because she carried her own toolkit?”

“This is different,” Robert insisted, leaning forward. “That device Traci was using—it’s not like anything I’ve seen.”

Mara snorted. “So she has a fancy piece of tech. Big deal. She’s a senior journalist for one of the most connected networks in history. She probably has all kinds of weird gadgets we don’t even know about. Maybe it’s some prototype or a gift. That doesn’t make her some kind of secret agent.”

“But even the Navy’s encrypted signals shows up on my scanner,” Robert pressed. “Her device? Completely invisible. That’s not just fancy—it’s something else.”

Mara rolled her eyes and gestured toward Traci, who was now standing by another window. “Look at her, Robert. Five-foot-something, quiet, and spends most of her time reporting on breaking news. Do you really think she’s some covert badass who can take someone down if things get messy? She’s not an operative or a spy. Hell, she probably couldn’t fight her way out of a supply closet if she tried.”

“And yet,” Robert countered, “she has a device that doesn’t register on anything I’ve got, and she shut me down the second I asked about it. That’s not normal, Mara.”

Mara sighed deeply, rubbing her temples. “Okay, let’s play along. Let’s say she is some kind of spy or secret agent. Then what? You poking around and running your little scans could get you into a world of trouble. She could make you disappear, Robert. People like that don’t play around.”

Robert looked over at Traci.

"And if she's not?" Mara continued. "She's still Traci Yamato. You know, the network's golden child? The one who can do no wrong? If you keep pushing, all you're going to do is piss her off and probably get written up for harassment. Either way, you lose."

Robert frowned, his fingers tapping nervously against his console. "You're really not curious? Not even a little bit?"

"No," Mara said bluntly. "Because I know better than to stick my nose where it doesn't belong. Traci's been doing this job for years. Whatever she's carrying, it's not for you to figure out. Let it go, Robert. Do your job and let her do hers."

He slumped back in his chair, still unconvinced but realizing the argument was going nowhere. "It doesn't feel right," he muttered under his breath.

"Doesn't have to," Mara said dismissively, already turning back to her console. "Focus on your work. If there's something weird going on, someone else will deal with it. Not us."

Robert, still brooding over Mara's dismissive attitude, couldn't shake the feeling that something was off. He glanced at Traci again, who had now moved away from the window and was speaking to another crew member. She looked as composed as ever, her calm demeanor completely at odds with the gnawing unease in his chest.

Mara broke the silence, muttering as she adjusted her console settings. "You're going to drive yourself crazy, you know. Just let it go."

Robert was about to reply when a voice broke their hushed conversation.

"What are you two doing?"

Both Robert and Mara jumped, spinning around to find Traci standing there, her hands on her hips. She had approached so quietly that neither of them had noticed her, as if she had simply materialized out of thin air.

"W-We were just running a diagnostic on the platform comms," Robert stammered. "Routine troubleshooting."

"Uh-huh," Traci said, her eyes narrowing slightly. She glanced briefly between the two of them, her gaze lingering on Robert for just a moment longer than was necessary. "Then maybe you should focus on your work instead of whispering like kids passing notes in class."

Robert opened his mouth to respond, but the words stuck in his throat. Mara stepped in smoothly. "Of course, Traci. We'll get back to it."

"Good," Traci said curtly. Without another word, she turned on her heel and walked away.

Robert watched her go, his heart pounding in his chest. Her sudden appearance, the way she'd slipped into their space unnoticed, sent a chill down his spine. Mara seemed unbothered, already returning to her work, but Robert couldn't let it go.

"Did you see that?" he whispered, leaning closer to her. "How did she even get here without us noticing? It's like she just… appeared."

Mara didn't even look up from her console. "She walked over, Robert. People do that."

"No," he insisted. "I was watching the room. I would've seen her coming. She just—she got here under our noses, like some kind of ghost."

Mara groaned, throwing her hands up. "Oh, for crying out loud. Now she's a ghost? What's next, Robert? A shapeshifting alien? A time traveler?"

"I'm serious!" he hissed, his voice rising slightly before he forced it back down. "It's not normal."

"Neither is your imagination," Mara shot back, finally turning to glare at him. "You need to stop this before you get yourself into real trouble. Traci's already annoyed, and if she catches wind of your little theories, I'm not covering for you."

Robert leaned back in his chair, folding his arms across his chest. "You don't find it the least bit strange how she just happened to show up while we were talking about her?"

"I find it strange that you have so much time to obsess over this when we've got a ton of actual work to do," Mara said sharply. "Drop it, Robert. Seriously."

But as he turned back to his station, Robert couldn't help glancing toward Traci again. She had returned to the window, standing with her arms crossed as she gazed out at the distant operation. She looked completely unbothered, as if the brief encounter had never happened.

How does she move so quietly? How did she know to interrupt us right then? Was she watching us the whole time? Listening? He thought.

Mara's voice broke into his thoughts. "Let me guess—you're already cooking up another theory."

He didn't respond, but the look on his face said it all. Mara groaned loudly, shaking her head as she muttered, "You're hopeless."

As he stared at Traci's back, a single thought refused to leave his mind: *She knows we were talking about her.*

***

Cipher stood at the large viewport, arms crossed casually as her gaze was fixed on the operations unfolding in orbit. The wreckage of the Unity drifted in haunting silence, scattered debris catching faint reflections from the searchlights of rescue shuttles. The look on her face was one of deep thought.

Her attention lingered momentarily on the Specter, stationed in geo-synchronous orbit. The arrival of Pierce and his crew confirmed her suspicions—Starfire was here. The ghost who had managed to evade every net Cipher had cast. A thorn in her side and an enigma she couldn't ignore. Cipher hated ghosts, especially this one.

Starfire's reputation for relentless investigation made her both a problem and a twisted fascination for Cipher. She could almost respect the skill it took to remain untraceable for so long. But admiration didn't change the facts. Starfire's presence here, in the midst of Cipher's carefully laid plans, was a risk she couldn't afford.

The soft hiss of the door behind her broke her thoughts, followed by the echo of boots striking the floor. The footsteps stopped a few feet behind her, and without turning, Cipher spoke.

"Captain Tupolev, you are punctual."

There was a brief pause before Tupolev answered. "Of course, ma'am. I see you are monitoring the operations."

133

"I'm observing," Cipher corrected, her eyes still fixed on the drifting wreckage. "Proceed with your report."

Tupolev cleared his throat. "The orbital lockdown is nearly complete. The Unity left no survivors, as expected. Civilian injuries have been reported—mostly from debris impacts and a few collisions during the panic. The Independence has managed containment, though some pilots required detainment for violating the no-fly zone."

Cipher gave a faint nod but said nothing.

Tupolev continued, "As for the Specter, Captain Pierce attended the dinner as you predicted. He's here to 'follow up on leads,' or so he claims. But he danced around anything specific. Every time I tried to pin him down, he sidestepped like a politician."

"And his XO?" Cipher asked.

Tupolev hesitated for a moment. "Unremarkable, for the most part. Commander Jones was predictably cautious. She didn't trust a word I said, and I doubt she thinks I bought his excuse."

Cipher smirked faintly, barely acknowledging the comment.

"And then there was the young lieutenant he brought with him," Tupolev added. "Brash, and a little rude. I singled her out during dinner for being disrespectful—"

Cipher's head turned sharply, her casual demeanor vanishing in an instant. "What young lieutenant?" she interrupted, not liking the idea of an unknown being thrown into her carefully laid out plans. "What is their name?"

"Valentine," Tupolev repeated, frowning slightly. "Lieutenant Veronica Valentine."

Cipher's gaze locked onto Tupolev, her eyes cold and piercing. She unfolded her arms, her tone shifting to a dark place. "You are to make no move on her without my explicit permission."

Tupolev blinked, caught off guard by the sudden shift in her demeanor. "Ma'am, I was merely addressing her behavior—"

"No," Cipher cut him off forcefully. "No reprimands, no surveillance, no interaction. She is not to be touched. Is that clear?"

Tupolev nodded slowly. "Understood."

Cipher returned her gaze to the viewport, crossing her arms again. "Good. Now continue."

Tupolev hesitated, moving back into his report. "Pierce… he's hiding something. His reasons for being here are thin. And there's something else." He paused, as though unsure how to phrase his next thought.

Cipher raised an eyebrow, growing quickly impatient. "Out with it."

"It's possible Pierce is the one Starfire is supposed to meet," Tupolev said finally. "His arrival lines up with Starfire's rumored meeting, and if he's here to 'follow up on leads,' it might mean—"

"Wow," Cipher interrupted sarcastically. "It's learning." She turned her head just enough to glance at him, with amusement. "Congratulations, Captain. You've managed to piece together what I've known for weeks."

Tupolev stiffened, his jaw tightening, but he said nothing.

Cipher let out a quiet sigh, shaking her head as she turned back to the viewport. "Yes, Starfire is here. And yes, Pierce may be involved. But you're not here to theorize, Captain. You're here to act. Find Starfire. Quickly."

"Yes, ma'am," Tupolev said through gritted teeth.

"And the GNN platform?" Cipher asked after a moment.

"They're still broadcasting," Tupolev replied. "Every move we make is being dissected by their analysts. It's becoming more of a distraction."

"Let them," Cipher said casually. "A little curiosity keeps them entertained."

Tupolev hesitated but gave a curt nod. "Understood."

"Good," Cipher said. "Keep a close eye on Pierce but remember—your focus is Starfire. Pierce is secondary. And Valentine…" Her voice hardened slightly. "Valentine is off-limits."

Cipher let the silence linger before adding, "One more thing, Captain."

"Yes?"

"Have your contact in the military police announce the death of Miranda Soto," she said casually. "They are not to say how or when they found out. Let the ambiguity fester."

Tupolev was uncomfortable with this. "Wouldn't that raise questions?"

Her tone remained calm, almost dismissive, as she replied, "Questions are inevitable, Captain. But answers? Those we control. Let the curious chase shadows while we move freely."

Tupolev shifted his stance. "And if they start looking too closely?"

A faint smile tugged at Cipher's lips. "Then they'll find exactly what we want them to find. A dead captain in her house, a tragic accident in orbit, and a convenient lack of witnesses.

Nothing more." Her voice grew colder. "You concern yourself too much with possibilities, Captain. Focus on certainties."

Tupolev clenched his jaw and nodded. "Understood. And after the announcement?"

Cipher's smile faded, replaced by a sharp, calculating expression. "Then he can make his move."

The "he" that Cipher spoke of sent a shiver down Tupolev's spine. He cleared his throat, breaking the tense silence. "What about Pierce and his crew?"

Cipher's lips curled into a faint, humorless smile. "Pierce is always chasing ghosts, Captain. Whether they're mine or his own, he rarely finds what he's looking for. But his presence here is not a coincidence." She tilted her head slightly. "Keep a close watch on him, and his crew."

Tupolev hesitated again. "And the young lieutenant, Valentine—"

Cipher cut him off quickly. "We've already discussed this, Captain. She is not to be touched."

"Yes, ma'am," he replied quickly, bowing his head slightly. "Understood."

Cipher let the tension settle before speaking again. "Maintain the lockdown. Keep the civilian channels busy with noise about the orbital cleanup. And Captain…"

"Yes?"

"Ensure that Pierce's movements are logged, but from a distance. No need to provoke him unnecessarily. The last thing we need is for him to think we're watching too closely."

Tupolev nodded, "I'll see to it immediately."

As he exited, the door sealed shut behind him leaving Cipher alone once more, the hum of the ship's systems again filling the silence. Her gaze remaining fixed on the viewport, racing through the layers of her plans in her mind. The announcement of Soto's death would send ripples through the power structures of New Earth. And when "he" finally arrives, the chaos would only deepen, allowing her to weave her web tighter around her targets.

Her fingers tapped lightly against her arm as she stood, calculating her next move. The Specter's arrival, Starfire's elusiveness, and the threads of her own network all required precision. One misstep could unravel everything. But Cipher thrived on complexity. She turned her thoughts briefly to Veronica and allowed herself the faintest smirk.

"Careful, sister," she murmured to herself. "You're playing a dangerous game."

Outside, the distant lights of the Specter blinked steadily, a reminder of the hunt across the sector. Cipher watched them for a moment longer, then turned sharply on her heel, sitting at her desk and looking over data on the monitors. The pieces were in motion, and the game was hers to control.

For now.

Memories III

The routine had become almost second nature. Each morning, I sat at my "desk" in the cramped hotel room. The uncomfortable bed or the wooden table and chair served as my workspace. I composed my daily reports. And yet, every day, I send them off into the ethos. No acknowledgment, no feedback, no instructions. Just silence.

The lack of direction was maddening at first. My training emphasized discipline and adaptability, but this—this limbo—was something else entirely. Still, I'd found solace in the cleverness of my cover. Whoever created it had an unsettling understanding of human nature. My cover had become a day job, an existence that blended perfectly into New Earth's everyday drudgery, hiding in plain sight.

I'd fallen into a rhythm. Morning dedicated to my day job activities. Evenings spent pouring over intel, compiling my findings into dossiers that no one seemed to want to read. But the routine served its purpose. It let me slip through the cracks, unnoticed and unremarkable. In those quiet moments, I saw the genius of my cover. It afforded me access to crucial areas and conversations, and more importantly, it kept me under the radar. The perfect shadow.

Nights were for me, after sending my daily report I had a few hours to myself. But tonight, the rhythm broke.

It was late, shortly after I'd filed my latest report and put my tablet away. The unanswered questions bore down on me, and the walls of my hotel room felt stifling. I needed some air. I grabbed my keys and stepped outside, my bike was waiting in the alley below. Riding it had become my one escape, a brief moment of freedom from the web of lies and subterfuge.

The bike roared to life beneath me, and I let it guide me through the darkened streets of Nueva Mexico. The city was quieter at this hour, its usual chaos subdued. I rode aimlessly, letting the cool air clear my head. That's when I saw it.

A sleek black sedan passed me at an intersection, its windows heavily tinted. I wouldn't have given it a second thought if not for the license plate. The sequence of numbers and letters was burned into my memory: Senator Timothy Hernandez. It was his car. My pulse quickened. What was he doing out here, this late, and heading toward one of the roughest parts of the city?

Curiosity ignited, I fell in behind him, keeping a safe distance. The sedan weaved through the winding streets, its movements deliberate. My gut told me this wasn't a late-night detour or a casual drive. Hernandez was heading somewhere specific.

The sedan eventually slowed, pulling into a narrow alley flanked by crumbling buildings. I parked my bike a block away, blending into the shadows as I approached on foot. From my vantage point, I watched as the Senator stepped out, his silhouette illuminated briefly by the faint glow of a streetlamp. He walked to another car parked in the alley, its windows blacked out. The driver's side window lowered just enough for a brief exchange.

I strained to see, my eyes narrowing as Hernandez reached through the open window and accepted something. It was small, indistinct in the dim light. A data stick? A note? Whatever it was, he pocketed it quickly and returned to his car. The sedan pulled away moments later, leaving me staring at the second vehicle.

The second car didn't linger. It moved out of the alley and merged into the sparse traffic of the late-night streets. I returned to my bike, my instincts screaming at me to follow. Whoever was in that car wasn't just a courier. This was bigger than Hernandez.

I tailed the vehicle through the city, keeping a careful distance. It navigated with purpose, eventually stopping outside a nondescript building on the city's outskirts. I parked a safe distance away and watched as the door opened.

A woman stepped out. Tall, poised, exuding an air of authority that set my nerves on edge. Her face was partially obscured by the shadows, but there was no mistaking her presence. She carried herself like someone who expected the world to move at her command.

I pulled out my comms device, activating the camera. The first picture was too blurry. I adjusted, snapping another as she turned slightly toward the light. Her features were sharp, striking, though I couldn't place her. Another shot—better this time, capturing her profile. She stopped suddenly, her head tilting as if she sensed my presence.

My breath caught. Her gaze swept the area, and for a terrifying moment, her eyes seemed to lock onto mine. I snapped one last photo, heart pounding, before turning back to the bike. The engine roared to life, and I sped into the night, taking a circuitous route back toward the city center. I couldn't risk being followed.

Back in my hotel room, I uploaded the photos to my secure comms device. The images were clear enough to send for an ID, but as I stared at them, unease coiled in my stomach. Who was she? And how deep did her involvement with Hernandez run?

The silence from my handler had become suffocating. I couldn't keep this to myself, but I also couldn't risk blowing my cover by acting rashly. For now, the photos and the questions they raised would stay with me. Tomorrow, I'd send another report, detailing everything I'd seen. Whether anyone would respond remained to be seen.

A hour passed, and I had almost given up on hearing anything when the comms device buzzed. A response. My heart raced as I opened it, expecting instructions.

Instead, what I got was unsettling:

Positive ID confirmed. Standby for further details.

I stared at the words, confused. Usually, an ID request came back almost instantly. Name, rank, status, a quick profile— everything I needed to act or prepare. But this? This was new.

"Standby for further details?" I muttered aloud. "Why the delay?"

It wasn't normal. Delays usually meant one of two things: either the database had flagged something sensitive, or someone up the chain was deciding how much I needed to know. Neither possibility was comforting.

The minutes stretched, each second amplifying the weight of the silence. Was it protocol? A glitch? Or was there something about this woman—this unknown figure I'd just photographed— that warranted extra scrutiny?

I frowned, the unease coiling tighter in my chest. Every report I'd sent over the past weeks had disappeared into the void. No responses, no feedback, just the endless grind of sending updates into silence. And now, when I finally asked for something specific, I was told to *standby*.

It felt deliberate.

I leaned back in the uncomfortable wooden chair, the device still glowing in my hand. What were they waiting for? What was I waiting for? My fingers tapped restlessly against the edge of the table. The system wasn't broken—I knew that much. Naval Intelligence didn't do delays without reason.

The only conclusion that made sense was that whoever she was, she wasn't ordinary. Something about her had tripped alarms, set off protocols I didn't fully understand. And that left me in the dark, staring at a single cryptic sentence with no idea what was coming next.

And then it came.

The notification buzzed on my comms device, the sharp sound cutting through the silence of the room. I tapped the screen, my breath hitching as the message unfolded in stark, clinical precision:

NAME: *Valentine, Zarina*
RANK: *Lieutenant*
POSITION: *Alliance Naval Intelligence*
STATUS: *AWOL*
NOTES: *Considered armed and extremely dangerous.* ***DO NOT ATTEMPT TO APPREHEND!***

My heart sank as the name hit me like a physical blow. Zarina Valentine. Everyone in Naval Intelligence knew that name. She was a legend—and not in the way anyone aspired to be.

Zarina was the first. The first operative in the Alliance's storied history to go rogue. Not defect, not disappear—go *rogue.* It was a distinction whispered about in training sessions and intelligence briefings. Her name was used as a cautionary tale: *Don't end up like Valentine.*

But the rumors didn't stop there. A few agents, some of the best we had, had been sent to bring her in over the years. None had succeeded. None had returned.

I stared at the screen, my mouth dry. The warning at the bottom—*DO NOT ATTEMPT TO APPREHEND*—wasn't a mere precaution. It was a command, carved out of the harsh lessons learned from those failed attempts. Zarina wasn't just dangerous; she was a walking shadow, a master of our own playbook, turned against us.

For a moment, the room seemed colder, the edges of the small space pressing in around me. *She's here.* That's what it meant. Whatever I'd stumbled upon with Senator Hernandez, it had somehow drawn Zarina Valentine into the fold.

I sat back, forcing myself to breathe. My mind raced, piecing together what this meant for the mission. Zarina's presence wasn't a coincidence. It couldn't be. If she was involved, it meant the shadow faction was more dangerous, more calculated than I'd imagined.

And then there was the darker implication.

Zarina going rogue had been a nightmare for Naval Intelligence—not just because she left, but because of *how*. She didn't just break away; she disappeared, leaving no trace, no trail. For years, she was the ghost we were all trained to fear, the operative who could outthink, outmaneuver, and outlast anyone.

Her defection had been a failure we didn't talk about openly, a fracture in the unshakable façade of the Alliance. And now, here she was, in the same city, involved in the same shadowed dealings I was trying to expose.

I rubbed a hand over my face, the weight of it all pressing down on me. Zarina Valentine wasn't just another piece on the board—she was the board. And I was standing on it, one wrong move away from being swept off entirely.

The stories came rushing back: the agents who had gone after her, who had tried to bring her in. They were some of the best we had, just like me—or so they thought. None of them were ever seen again.

What am I dealing with here?

My hand hovered over the comms device. There were no further instructions, no additional warnings. Just her name and her status, leaving me to wrestle with the implications.

One thing was clear: I couldn't run into her—not by accident, not by design. Zarina was the kind of dangerous I wasn't sure even

I was prepared for. And if she knew I was here, if she had any inkling of what I was trying to do, I wouldn't just fail this mission. I wouldn't survive it.

I set the device down carefully, staring at the profile as if it might reveal more. For now, all I could do was hope that whatever brought Zarina Valentine into this tangled mess would keep her far away from me. Because if our paths crossed, there wouldn't be a second chance.

The comms device buzzed again, breaking the heavy silence. Shaking as I reached for it, half expecting more cryptic warnings. But this time, the message wasn't just an ID or a cautionary note. It was a directive.

New Directive: Priority Level Alpha.
Effective Immediately.

I opened it, the insignia of Naval Intelligence flashing briefly before the text scrolled across the screen. The words hit me like a hammer:

Subject: Lieutenant Zarina Valentine (AWOL)
Objective: Establish surveillance and gather actionable intelligence on Valentine's activities. Avoid direct contact at all costs. Valentine is believed to be operating within the sphere of influence of the shadow faction. Confirm operational goals and alliances. Any confrontation is to be considered a last resort.

There it was—a new mission, layered on top of my current assignment. The name I'd hoped to avoid seeing again, now at the center of everything. Zarina Valentine.

My eyes skimmed the text until they landed on the line that made my stomach drop:

Note: Full mission autonomy granted. You are authorized to act at your discretion to avoid compromise. Utilize extreme caution.

Full mission autonomy. I swallowed hard as the weight of those words settled over me. Naval Intelligence operatives rarely heard them, and when we did, they came with chilling implications. It meant the leash was off—no more waiting for approval, no more requests for authorization. For the first time, every decision, every action, was mine alone to make.

And the most haunting part? Full autonomy came with full weapons release.

Deadly force, fully authorized.

The words echoed in my mind, cold and clinical. Naval Intelligence had drilled the concept into us during training—how to weigh the value of a life against the needs of a mission, how to pull the trigger without hesitation. But until now, it had always been theoretical.

I'd used my weapon before, but only in self-defense. This was different. They weren't just trusting me to gather intel. They were giving me the authority to kill, not as a last resort but as a calculated choice.

The thought turned my stomach.

I tried to focus on the mission details, but my mind kept circling back to the weight of that authorization. Zarina Valentine was a rogue agent, a living, breathing threat to the Alliance. She'd gone AWOL, evaded capture, and aligned herself with something dangerous. If anyone warranted the use of deadly force, it was her.

But even thinking about it unsettled me. Taking a life outside of self-defense wasn't something I'd ever imagined myself doing, no matter the justification.

I leaned back in the creaking wooden chair, my thoughts spiraling. Naval Intelligence didn't hand out full autonomy lightly. They weren't just cutting the leash—they were handing me the knife and telling me to do whatever it took to get the job done.

And Zarina wasn't just a mission. She was a statement, a test of my resolve. If it came down to her or me, the directive was clear. But knowing that didn't make it any easier to accept.

I closed the message and set the comms device on the table, staring at the glowing screen as if it might offer answers. Instead, all it left me with was a name and a command: Valentine. Observe. Assess. Act.

The room felt suffocating again, the walls pressing in as the enormity of the task sank in. I'd finally been given instructions after weeks of silence, and they were the last thing I wanted to hear.

Deadly force. Full autonomy.

I exhaled slowly, steeling myself. If Zarina Valentine was the shadow faction's wild card, I had to play the hand I'd been dealt. But no matter how much training I had, no matter how prepared I thought I was, one truth gnawed at me:

When you have the power to kill, the hardest part isn't pulling the trigger. It's knowing when not to.

Chapter 8

The morning air hung heavy over the Soto estate, the warmth of the winter sun doing little to ease the tension among the assembled New Earth Security Forces (NESF) officers. The study was silent except for the faint crackling of the fire, its embers barely clinging to life in the hearth. Yellow holographic barriers shimmered across the room, marking the edges of the crime scene. Investigator Derek Quinn stood just inside the threshold, his eyes sweeping over the room. Every detail told a story, and yet the story seemed maddeningly incomplete.

Miranda Soto's lifeless body slumped in the chair, her blood pooled on the hardwood floor beneath her. The crime scene was unnervingly pristine, save for the violence that had been unleashed upon its occupant. The shattered coffee cup on the floor spoke of panic and fear. Above the fireplace, the bronze emblem that symbolized Soto's storied career hung untouched, its presence now almost mocking.

Quinn crouched near the body, his sharp eyes narrowing as he studied the angle of the wounds. "Three shots," he muttered under his breath, almost to himself. "Tight grouping. Professional."

"Sir," a voice interrupted. It was Officer Malick, a young but capable investigator holding a tablet. "We've recovered the casings. Three spent shells. Military grade."

Quinn straightened. "A Military-grade sidearm?" He whispered as crossed his arms. "You're sure?"

Malick nodded. "Confirmed by forensics. The bullets match, too—what's left of them, anyway. Whoever did this wasn't just armed. They were trained."

Quinn let out a low whistle, his unease growing. A murder weapon like that wasn't common, especially not on New Earth. "And the weapon itself?"

Malick shook his head. "No sign of it. Either they took it with them or disposed of it elsewhere."

"Convenient," Quinn muttered. The shell casings, the precision of the shots, the lack of a weapon—none of it fit with a random act of violence. This was calculated. Deliberate. And it made his skin crawl.

Outside, the soft hum of an engine signaled the arrival of another vehicle. Quinn turned to the window and saw the unmistakable black-and-gold insignia of the Military Police on the side of an armored transport. His jaw tightened as the vehicle rolled to a stop, and uniformed MPs began to disembark.

Leading them was a man Quinn knew well: Major Caleb Thorne.

"Damn it," Quinn muttered under his breath, stepping out of the house just as Thorne and his team approached.

"Derek," Thorne greeted.

"Major Thorne," Quinn replied. "This is a civilian investigation. What are you doing here?"

Thorne gestured toward the house. "Captain Soto was a high-level officer. That makes this our jurisdiction."

Quinn stepped forward, arms crossed. "This is private property, not military. Last I checked that's still my jurisdiction."

The two men locked eyes, the tension between them growing. They had clashed before, and while neither could call the other an enemy, their relationship was fraught with mistrust.

"Look, Derek," Thorne said, changing to a more friendly tone. "I'm not here to play politics. This case—it's not just another murder. You know it. I know it."

Quinn's response was cut off by a sudden roar overhead. Both men looked up as a small, sleek shuttle descended from the sky, its dark hull glinting in the morning sun. The shuttle hovered above the estate, its thrusters kicking up dust and debris. The deafening sound drew the attention of every officer on the scene.

Quinn and Thorne exchanged uneasy glances as two figures rappelled down from the shuttle, landing with precision just inside the estate's perimeter. The figures, clad in the all black uniforms of Naval Intelligence, moved quickly to secure the area. Within moments, one of them signaled, and the shuttle descended, landing with a sharp hiss of hydraulics.

The ramp lowered, and from the dim interior emerged Commander Elise Vaylen. Her presence was commanding, her black uniform immaculate and adorned with insignias that left no doubt about her authority. Flanked by a small team of agents, she strode toward the two men with deliberate purpose.

Thorne was the first to recover, stepping forward. "Commander Vaylen. Naval Intelligence, I presume?"

Vaylen stopped just short of the two men, her icy gaze sweeping over them. She held out a file, inside were official orders stamped with the seals of both Military Command and the New Earth Senate.

"This investigation is now under my jurisdiction," she announced sharply. "As of this moment, you and your teams are relieved."

Quinn bristled. "Excuse me? You can't just—"

Vaylen cut him off, her gaze locking onto his with unsettling precision. "I can, and I have. These orders are signed and verified. Feel free to confirm them with your superiors."

Thorne smiled, a halfhearted attempt to maintain a friendly demeanor. "Commander, with all due respect, this estate is private property and falls under civilian authority, The Military Police are here to merely observe. Naval Intelligence has no standing here."

Vaylen didn't flinch. "This is no longer a civilian matter. Captain Soto was a high-level officer with ties to classified operations. That makes it my matter."

Before either man could protest further, Vaylen gestured to one of her agents, who began issuing commands to the assembled NESF and MP teams. "Clear the perimeter. Secure the evidence. I want all findings transferred to my team immediately."

Quinn pulled out his comms device, already dialing his superior. Thorne followed suit. The hum of activity grew as Vaylen's agents moved with efficiency, pushing both the NESF and Military Police aside.

Quinn's superior finally answered. "The orders are legitimate, Derek. Stand down."

Quinn clenched his jaw. "Understood."

Thorne, meanwhile, lowered his own comms, his expression matching Quinn's. "Looks like you win this one, Commander."

Vaylen offered a faint smile, though it held no warmth. "This isn't about winning, Major. It's about the truth. Now, if you'll excuse me, I have work to do."

As Vaylen and her team swept into the house, Quinn and Thorne stood in silence, the weight of the case—and their exclusion from it—settling heavily on their shoulders.

***

Quinn and Thorne leaned against the side of the armored military vehicle, both men silently watching as Commander Vaylen and her team moved like a well-oiled machine. From a distance, the Naval Intelligence agents looked like shadows, their precision unnerving. Quinn took a slow drag from his flask, passing it to Thorne, who took a quick sip before handing it back.

Thorne broke the silence first, his tone tinged with dry amusement. "Not about winning," he muttered, shaking his head. "Everything about that woman is about winning. Every damn thing."

Quinn arched a brow, his curiosity piqued. "What's that supposed to mean? You've dealt with her before?"

Thorne chuckled mirthlessly, folding his arms. "Oh, you could say that. Last time, it was a joint operation—well, that's what Command called it, anyway. Some intel breach in the outer colonies. I figured we'd be cooperating. Wrong. Vaylen rolled in like she owned the damn place, treating us like glorified security guards while she ran the show."

Quinn smirked. "Sounds familiar."

"Oh, it gets better," Thorne said with a wry grin. "She had this way of making you feel like she was listening, like you were on the same team. And then—bam! Next thing you know, she's reporting directly to Command, undercutting everything you said, just to make you look incompetent."

"Charming," Quinn said dryly, glancing toward Vaylen, who was gesturing sharply to her team.

"She's not charming," Thorne replied, his tone cutting. "She's ruthless. And she doesn't care who she steps on as long as she gets what she wants."

Quinn nodded slowly, digesting the information. "That explains your little jab earlier. The 'civilian authority' bit. That seemed like a bold move, even for you."

Thorne's grin returned, this time with genuine amusement. "You caught that, huh?"

"Hard to miss," Quinn replied. "You made it sound like you were going to plant your flag in the ground and hold your position. Next thing I know, you're handing her the keys. What gives?"

Thorne shrugged, his expression both resigned and mischievous. "Like I said, everything with her is about winning. I knew the moment I opened my mouth she'd have to prove me wrong. Can't resist the urge to flex her authority."

Quinn barked a short laugh. "So, you goaded her?"

Thorne grinned. "Damn right, I did. The way she strutted in, waving those orders around like a golden ticket—someone had to remind her she wasn't invincible. I knew the second I pushed, she'd go all in to assert her dominance. And seeing her have to rappel her team down here, securing a landing zone like it was a damn warzone?" He chuckled. "That was enough satisfaction for me."

Quinn smirked, though his expression remained thoughtful. "She didn't rappel herself."

"Doesn't matter," Thorne said with a shrug. "The fact she had to adjust her grand entrance, even for a second? Priceless. She thrives on control, so watching her authority get challenged, even briefly, feels like a win."

Quinn shook his head, amused despite himself. "You're insufferable."

"So I've been told," Thorne replied, with a grin. "But come on, admit it. Part of you enjoyed seeing her squirm."

Quinn didn't answer, his eyes still fixed on Vaylen. She was directing her team with sharp, deliberate gestures, her presence a force of nature that neither man could ignore. "What worries me," he said quietly, "is that she doesn't squirm for long."

Thorne's grin faded, replaced by a more somber expression. "No, she doesn't," he admitted. "That's why she's dangerous."

The two men fell silent again, watching as the Naval Intelligence agents dismantled what was left of the NESF's control over the investigation. Whatever came next, they both knew they were already on the outside looking in.

The two men stood in silence for a moment longer, the hum of Naval Intelligence's activity filling the air. Whatever had brought Vaylen here, Quinn and Thorne both knew it wasn't going to end quietly—or cleanly.

***

Commander Vaylen stood in the center of the Soto study like the eye of a quiet storm. The Naval Intelligence agents moved

156

about her in measured silence, their boots making soft thuds on the hardwood. The holographic barriers still shimmered, yellow beams diffusing the early light that filtered through the windows, casting delicate patterns on the polished floor. The room's temperature felt cooler now, despite the lingering scent of burnt embers and old leather furniture.

She lifted her hand—a signal—and her team responded with seamless precision. One agent knelt beside Soto's chair, eyes behind a visor as they reviewed the wound patterns. Another stood over a sleek device that hovered in mid-air, projecting ballistic trajectories. The fire's last embers gave a gentle pop, punctuating the quiet labor.

"Status," Vaylen said softly.

A nearby agent, tall and angular, raised his visor to reveal piercing dark eyes. "Commander, we've confirmed the ammunition type. The casings match 10mm Nano-Enhanced Expanding Rounds."

Vaylen nodded, just once, acknowledging the report. NEER rounds—issued only to certain divisions within Naval Intelligence, or those with sanctioned clearance. It narrowed the field considerably, but Vaylen did not allow herself satisfaction. There was always more to find, more to confirm.

Her gaze drifted over the shattered coffee cup, the way the shards sprayed outward. Soto's once-proud uniform remained pristine, save for the telltale bloom of darkened fabric over her heart. Above the mantel, that bronze emblem hung undisturbed, its surface catching the light. Everything else looked so ordinary. Too ordinary.

"Commander," another agent approach. "We're having difficulty locating the device."

Vaylen expected as much. The orders had been explicit, the intel clear: Soto had a recording device hidden somewhere on this estate. It was the key—the reason Naval Intelligence came down so hard and fast. Without it, all she had were empty shells and a dead officer.

"It's here," Vaylen said, coldly. "Keep looking."

Her agents dispersed, some probing the furniture, others scanning the bookcases, checking every seam and corner. They worked slowly, methodically. The minutes stretched, each second punctuated only by the hum of scanning tools and muffled footsteps.

Vaylen took her time circling the room. She ran a fingertip along the edge of the heavy desk, examining it closely. Opened and closed drawers with gentle care, inspected the underside of a chair. The whole while, her expression remained unchanged—an unyielding calm that her subordinates had come to both admire and fear.

Outside, the estate grounds were quiet. She could imagine Quinn and Thorne sulking out there, no doubt exchanging glances and wary remarks about her methods. Let them. Vaylen was here for results, not alliances.

Minutes passed. An agent crouched at the base of a tall bookcase, their scanner emitting a faint, high-pitched chirp. Then a sharper beep. He paused, adjusted the scanning frequency. Another beep. He pressed a hidden latch. With a soft click, a panel slid open—nearly invisible before, now revealing a small cavity inside the wall. The agent reached in carefully, withdrawing a slim, palm-sized device, its surface matte black and devoid of markings.

"Commander," he called softly, holding it up so only she could see.

Vaylen crossed the room, her boots tapping softly on the floor. She took the device, turning it over in her hand. A hidden recording device—exactly as rumored. The casing bore no official seal, no easily discernible signature. Just as well. She did not need the exterior to tell her what she wanted; the truth lay within.

"Clear the room," she ordered quietly. Her team backed away without hesitation. Two agents took positions at the door. The rest found subtle vantage points—near windows, beside furniture, yet all respectfully distant. Privacy: exactly what their commander required.

Vaylen tapped a sequence on the device's recessed panel. Nothing. She frowned. Another sequence, this time a longer code—one that evoked deep-clearance protocols. A tiny green light flared on the device's surface. With a soft whir, a hidden lens and microphone assembly extended, acknowledging authorized access.

The commander stepped into a corner of the study where the light was dimmest. She angled her body away from her team, ensuring no prying eyes would glimpse the screen that now flickered to life on the device's tiny display. Sound emerged— faint, muffled voices. The image stabilized: a timestamp, a figure sitting where Soto's body now rested. Another figure off-screen, speaking low and urgently. Words that would matter, words that revealed more than any ballistic analysis could.

Vaylen's eyes hardened as she watched, her shoulders drawn taut beneath the crisp lines of her uniform. The recording played out in full. She did not flinch. She did not sigh. She simply watched, her breathing shallow and quiet, absorbing every word, every tone, every detail that might clarify the puzzle of Captain Soto's final moments.

When it ended, the display went dark, and Vaylen stood still as a statue. She tapped a command code to lock the device's data behind layers of encryption—her encryption. No one would see this until she decided otherwise.

Then, with deliberate care, she retrieved her comms device from inside her jacket. A subtle tap on its smooth interface brought up a secure channel. Her reflection glimmered faintly on its surface—icy eyes, a grin set to her mouth. She typed a brief message, paused, then added a final line. A confirmation code flashed green on the comm's interface, signaling that the message had been sent.

No name. No reply expected—at least not here, not now. Just the knowledge that her report, or perhaps her warning, had gone exactly where it needed to go.

Vaylen slipped the comm back into her jacket and turned to face her team. They stood waiting, silent and respectful. If any of them wondered who she had contacted, they dared not ask.

"Secure all evidence," she said calmly, nodding to the agent with the scanning device. "We're done here."

Outside, the day's light had grown brighter, but inside the study, shadows lengthened across the floor. Commander Vaylen's presence lingered in every still corner, and the silence that followed felt charged, brimming with secrets that would not be revealed—not yet.

***

The gates to the Soto estate squeaked open as a sleek GNN news van rolled onto the gravel drive. Its engine purred softly before cutting out, and the sliding door hissed open. Quinn watched as Traci Yamato stepped out, adjusting the collar of her fitted blazer. Behind her, a small crew hauled a camera rig onto their shoulders, the bright GNN logo gleaming under the winter sun.

"Great," Thorne murmured under his breath, straightening. "Just what we need. A media circus."

"Traci's no circus act," Quinn said quietly, tone almost defensive. "She's one of the few who asks real questions. Doesn't settle for sound bites."

Thorne snorted. "Maybe, but we're off the case now, remember? Naval Intelligence took over. What's there to tell her, except we're out in the cold?"

Quinn shrugged, eyes still on Yamato as she approached. The reporter moved with easy confidence—shoulders back, a faint smile curling her lips. She looked between Quinn and Thorne as if greeting old friends.

"Investigator Quinn, Major Thorne," Traci said, nodding to each. "I should've known I'd find you two here."

161

Quinn tipped his chin. "Traci. Didn't expect GNN to be on the scene this quick."

Traci's smile held a hint of irony. "You know me, Derek. Word of a high-profile murder travels fast. And on New Earth, that means getting here before the story is spun beyond recognition." She gestured to her cameraman to hold off filming for a moment. "So, tell me—what happened?"

Thorne crossed his arms, gaze shifting warily between Quinn and Traci. "We can't say much," he began. "Commander Vaylen has taken charge. We're…just observers now."

Traci lifted an eyebrow. "Vaylen? Naval Intel is here?" She whistled softly. "Must be a real mess inside that house. I heard Soto was well-connected. Rumor mill's going wild."

Quinn's jaw tightened. "Traci, you know me. I won't feed you sensational rumors. All I can confirm is that Captain Soto is dead, and we're no longer leading the investigation."

Yamato's eyes softened slightly. She'd known Quinn for years—back when he was still green, less guarded. "I appreciate the honesty. Off the record, though—how does it feel, being pushed aside like this?"

Thorne gave Quinn a careful glance. Finally, Quinn exhaled. "It doesn't feel good. But orders are orders."

Traci looked at Thorne, who wore a crooked smile. "No comment, Major?"

"Oh, I've got comments," Thorne said dryly, "but none I care to share. Naval Intelligence isn't known for its warm-and-fuzzy team spirit."

Traci chuckled, amusement dancing in her eyes. "Fair enough. It's good to see you both, even if under terrible circumstances."

Quinn nodded, allowing himself a moment of camaraderie. "You too, Traci. Just be careful. If Vaylen finds you snooping around, she won't think twice about shutting you out."

Traci giggled, gleaming with confidence. "Oh, Elise is a kitten, I can handle her." The casual use of the Commander's first name and the flippant tone of familiarity sent a ripple of unease through Quinn. Thorne was also surprised. But before anyone could press Traci further, activity at the house drew their attention.

The front door opened. Commander Vaylen stepped out—but not with her usual unshakable stride. She paused under the frame, her gaze locking onto Traci as if caught off guard to find her here. For a split second, Vaylen's carefully composed mask faltered. Then, regaining herself, she moved forward, each step measured and calm, her agents following with sealed evidence containers.

The Naval Intelligence shuttle's engines began to spin up, a low whine that edged under the scene like a soundtrack. Agents fanned out to clear a path, but Vaylen approached Quinn, Thorne, and Traci directly, stopping a few strides away.

"The investigation here is complete," she announced. "My team and I are withdrawing."

Quinn blinked, the suddenness catching him off guard. "Commander, that was fast. Are you sure—"

Vaylen cut him off. "We've obtained what we need. You may resume your civilian investigation, Investigator Quinn."

"Just like that? You come in, take over, now you're done?" Thorne asked.

If Vaylen heard the challenge in his voice, she gave no indication. Her attention drifted again—this time, unmistakably—toward Traci. For an instant, something flickered in the Commander's eyes. Then, as if remembering a private code of conduct known only to them, Vaylen clicked her heels together softly, snapping to attention.

Traci's reaction was immediate, though subtle: her eyes widened, color drained from her face, and her fingers curled slightly, as if resisting an urge to reach for something. The shift in her demeanor lasted only a heartbeat, but it was enough for Thorne, who'd been watching closely, to notice. A tiny crease formed between his brows as if he were piecing together a puzzle he hadn't known existed.

Just as quickly as she'd faltered, Traci smoothed her features back into the poised mask of a seasoned reporter. But Thorne had seen that flash of emotion, that spark of recognition. He filed it away silently.

Vaylen offered no explanation. Turning on her heel, she strode toward the waiting shuttle, her boots tapping crisply on the gravel. Her agents followed without a word. The hatch sealed, and moments later, the craft lifted off, leaving them with only the hum of retreating engines and the unanswered questions swirling in the still morning air.

For a long moment, no one spoke. Quinn stood there, arms folded, frowning at the empty sky. Traci angled her head, pretending interest in her crew as they positioned the camera, but Thorne saw the tension still lingering in her shoulders. Something had passed between these two women—something charged and personal—and he couldn't shake the feeling that a crucial piece of this puzzle had just revealed itself.

At length, Traci cleared her throat. "Well," she said lightly, "that was…unexpected."

"Yeah," Quinn agreed, his tone wary. "It was."

Thorne said nothing, but his mind churned. He eyed Traci with quiet curiosity, wondering what connection lay behind that brief, silent exchange. There was more to this story than any of them had realized, and as the winter sun climbed higher, its pale light did nothing to illuminate the secrets left in the wake of Commander Vaylen's departure.

***

The headquarters of the Alliance Military Command on New Earth stood as a nondescript building of mundane proportions. Its windows were unremarkably tinted, and its façade featured a simple, logo-less sign. Inside, long corridors stretched beneath subdued lighting, the walls a uniform gray. Anyone passing by might assume it was an accounting firm or a bureaucratic hub of no particular significance.

Admiral Jacobs walked these hallways often enough that each corner felt familiar. Today, the steady echo of his boots on tile seemed louder than usual, as if the building were holding its breath. He approached his office door and caught sight of the young Ensign stationed there. Her salute was crisp, professional, but he lingered a half-second before acknowledging it with a nod. Something in the air felt unsettled.

He entered his office quietly, letting the door seal behind him. The space inside was just as he left it. His gaze swept his entire office slowly, ending on the small bar in one corner holding a selection of finely curated liquors. A subtle scent of polished metal and old paper lingered in the stillness. Everything appeared normal, yet Admiral Jacobs's instincts told him he was not alone.

Rather than move straight to his desk, he approached the bar, taking his time. He ran a hand along the ornate bottles, finally selecting a tall one at the back. Centaurian Brandy—smooth, fragrant, and far too expensive for most officers to keep on hand. He poured two glasses, each a generous portion.

With deliberate calm, Jacobs carried both glasses to the desk, placing one in front of his usual seat. He considered that chair for a moment, then chose one of the guest chairs instead, facing the desk rather than sitting behind it. Only then did he speak softly.

"Lieutenant, why are you here?"

The chair behind the desk slowly swiveled. Cipher sat there, shoulders tense, her gloved hands resting on the armrests. The faint glow of the overhead lights played over her face, revealing eyes that held a distant chill. "You know why I'm here," she said coldly.

Jacobs took a slow sip of the brandy, savoring the warmth as it slid down his throat. He allowed silence to stretch between them before responding. "Perhaps," he said, leaning back slightly, "but I'm not willing to give you what you want—well, not just yet." He said calmly, as if they were discussing a minor logistical matter instead of covert power plays and secret agendas.

Cipher's eyes narrowed at the refusal, and her posture stiffened. "I've done everything you asked. Followed every order, like a good soldier." There was tension in her voice, as if she were restraining a more volatile response. "I came to retrieve Holt's location, and the intel needed to strike."

Jacobs nodded thoughtfully, as though considering a polite request rather than the demand it was. He set his glass down carefully, aligning it with a precise angle on the wooden surface. "Lieutenant," he said again, softly, letting the word hang in the air, "you acted without my approval when you destroyed the Freedom. That incident has drawn far more attention than I planned for."

Her entire body tensed. It was a reminder of her station—a subtle diminishment of the image she tried to project. "We needed a distraction. Holt won't surface easily, and the Senate needed a jolt. I only did what I thought best."

Jacobs's gaze drifted toward a corner of the room, as if contemplating unseen intricacies. "A jolt, indeed," he murmured, fingers brushing invisible dust off the arm of his chair. "You see, Lieutenant, certain…arrangements…were already in motion. The Freedom's destruction has prompted the Senate to look more closely at things they were ignoring, to ask inconvenient questions. They will not be so easily swayed now." He said it all without directly revealing his ultimate goal. But the weight in his words hinted that he had ambitions.

Cipher leaned forward. "This delay you're forcing… it gives Holt time. He'll slip through my fingers if you don't give me what I need."

Jacobs offered her a faint, humorless smile. "Time, Lieutenant, can be an ally as much as an enemy. I intend to use it carefully."

He left the meaning vague, but in that lingering pause, it was clear he was planning something.

Anger flashed in Cipher's eyes, and she tightened her grip on the armrests. "Don't make me regret our deal, Admiral."

Jacobs's brows lifted slightly. He leaned forward, resting his elbows on his knees, voice dropping almost to a whisper: "Oh, Lieutenant." He said gently, almost mocking. "You think this arrangement rests on your comfort? I remember how I found you—huddled in that shuttle, tears streaming down your face, a broken girl with nowhere to run." He said it softly, with a gravity that twisted the knife into her past. "No matter how far you've come, a part of you remains that frightened child. You still fear losing control, don't you?"

For an instant, Cipher's mask slipped. She slammed her fist down onto the desk. The glass of brandy he'd set for her— untouched—shattered in a spray of amber and crystal. The pieces scattered across the dark wood, catching the light. A crimson bead of blood trickled from her knuckles, stark and vivid.

"Don't you dare!" she hissed, trembling with rage. The hurt, the fury, the memory he invoked—they all ignited within her. "This isn't about my past. Give me Holt's location and let me do what we agreed, or I promise you, Admiral, I will find my own way."

Jacobs stayed perfectly still, letting the tension weigh the air down. When he spoke again, he chose his words carefully, each word dipped in quiet malice: "You complain of me not upholding my end of the deal, Lieutenant, but what of the trouble you created when you forced me to bring in Pierce? He was never part of the original plan. His involvement complicated things, and I've no doubt you found his relentless pursuit…tiresome."

Cipher's eyes narrowed further. "You think I didn't notice that? Pierce had half the Alliance data streams tied in knots, chasing phantoms. I had to work twice as hard to stay ahead of him. Your decision to add him into the mix nearly cost me more than you know."

Jacobs savored the irritation twisting across her face. "Oh, but that was the fun part, Lieutenant. Watching you run from him, seeing how thoroughly he reported each false lead, each dead end—entertaining reading, truly. And yet, not once could he locate that elusive freighter or the 'asset.'"

He leaned back, tapping his finger on the armrest as he considered the puzzle pieces. "So, tell me, Lieutenant. Where are they now? Where is our 'asset' and the freighter currently situated?"

Cipher's lips tightened. She offered no direct answer, only a slight shrug and a cold, thin smile. "Safe," she said, "That's all you need to know."

Jacobs stayed perfectly still, letting the tension weigh the air down. Then he stood, moving slowly behind the desk as if stepping over a battlefield bathed in broken glass and blood. He pressed a hidden panel. A glow, a click, and a tablet slid into view. He didn't hand it to her, only gestured at it with one finger. "Study this," he said evenly. "It details points of influence and key moments ahead. Once I'm satisfied that the Senate is…receptive to a certain interpretation of the law, I will provide Holt's location."

Cipher wiped her bloodied hand against her dark sleeve, smearing a crimson line. She snatched the tablet, her anger controlled only by her desire for revenge. Reading the lines of data, something like a twisted smile ghosted her lips. Without a word, she turned and vanished through the secret passage behind the panel—her humming, low and ominous, echoing faintly before it disappeared into silence.

Jacobs stood there a moment, taking in the dark spots of blood on his desk, the lingering aroma of brandy. Then he reached for his intercom, pressing the button with a steady hand. "Ensign," he said quietly, "contact medical. I've cut myself and need the medic, please."

Her voice came back promptly. "Yes, Admiral."

He released the intercom. Behind his calm demeanor, a storm of calculations brewed. He did not need to reveal everything to Cipher. In time, a subtle legal clause—long overlooked—could shift the entire balance of power. With careful timing, he might claim emergency authority and do away with the restraints that now chafed him. But that was for later.

For now, he watched the thin rivulets of blood run down the curve of the desk's surface and allowed himself a small, private smile. The pieces were moving, and soon they would all fall into place.

"It will be worth it," he murmured, voice barely audible in the stillness. "In time, it will all be mine."

Chapter 9

The soft hum of the Independence's engines filled the dimly lit office. Captain Tupolev stood near the viewport, his arms crossed as he stared at the planet below. His reflection, barely visible in the glass, mirrored the frustration etched on his face. Behind him, Commander Baptiste entered, her footsteps muffled against the carpeted floor.

"Captain," she said, saluting as she approached the desk.

Tupolev gestured for her to sit, his gaze remaining fixed on the stars. "What do you have for me?"

Baptiste took the chair opposite his desk, setting a tablet in her lap. "The orbital lockdown is proceeding as ordered. Civilian traffic has been cleared from all sectors, though there were a few complaints from the freight companies. No major incidents. The Specter's search-and-rescue craft completed their operations two hours ago. All teams have returned to the ship without incident."

"And Pierce?" Tupolev asked.

"No movement since," Baptiste replied. "The Specter is holding position."

Tupolev let out a frustrated chuckle. "That stubborn bastard," he muttered, shaking his head. "Always waiting. That man's patience could drive anyone insane."

Baptiste smirked faintly. "You sound almost impressed."

"Maybe I am," Tupolev admitted. "But don't mistake it for admiration. Pierce doesn't wait because he's unsure—he waits because he knows it'll make you uneasy. He's probably sitting in that chair of his right now, weighing every possibility, waiting for us to blink."

Baptiste leaned back, crossing one leg over the other. "Do you think he's really here to follow up on leads?"

Tupolev scoffed, finally turning to face her. "Not a chance. Jonathan Pierce doesn't cross half the system for breadcrumbs. He's here for something, but damned if I know what."

Baptiste tilted her head thoughtfully. "Do you think he could be Starfire's contact?"

Tupolev's eyes narrowed as he sat down at his desk, drumming his fingers against the armrest. "That's the question, isn't it? If he is, he's either playing the long game or waiting for Starfire to make the first move. Either way, I don't buy his story."

Baptiste hesitated, "I'm not entirely sure he's their contact. Pierce doesn't strike me as the cloak-and-dagger type. If he's here, I'd bet it's Alliance business."

"Maybe," Tupolev said, his tone skeptical. "But until we know for sure, I want him watched. Closely."

Baptiste nodded. "Understood."

Tupolev leaned back in his chair, his expression darkening. "Of course, all of this is meaningless if we can't find Starfire. And Cipher's patience is running thinner than mine."

Baptiste tensed at the mention of Cipher. "Speaking of her… I take it she hasn't been subtle?"

Tupolev let out a bitter laugh. "Subtle? Her gaze is like a blade pressed to your throat—sharp, cold, and utterly horrifying. She doesn't just look at you, Zoe. She sees everything. Every weakness, every doubt, every damn thing you try to hide. And the worst part? You know she's cataloging it all for later."

Baptiste shuddered slightly but said nothing.

Tupolev caught her reaction and raised an eyebrow. "You seem unsettled. What's on your mind?"

Baptiste hesitated. "It's not just her gaze, sir. It's… something else."

Tupolev leaned forward, his curiosity piqued. "Something else? Elaborate."

Baptiste shifted uncomfortably, her fingers tightening around the tablet. "It's the way she looks at me. It's not like how you described. It's… different."

Tupolev frowned. "Different how?"

Baptiste exhaled slowly, as though the words physically pained her to say. "It's like… the way a man would look at me. Not in my eyes, but always on my body. Like she's dissecting me with her gaze, but it's not just cold calculation. It's… lustful."

Tupolev leaned back in his chair. "Lustful?"

Baptiste nodded. "I can almost feel her hands on me, even though she's never touched me. The thought alone makes my skin crawl."

A shiver ran through her as she met Tupolev's gaze. "It's like she's undressing me with her eyes, deciding exactly what she'd do if I were hers. I can't even look at her for too long without feeling like I need a shower."

For a moment, neither of them spoke, the weight of her words settling over the room like a suffocating fog.

Finally, Tupolev broke the silence. "That's why we need to find Starfire, Zoe. Because as long as Cipher is involved, none of us are safe. Not from her gaze, her games, or whatever twisted plans she has in mind."

Baptiste nodded, though the tension in her shoulders didn't ease. "I'll double the patrols and keep an eye on Pierce. If he makes a move, you'll be the first to know."

"Good," Tupolev said. "And Zoe?"

"Yes, sir?"

"Stay away from Cipher. The less reason she has to notice you, the better."

Before he could gather his thoughts, the door chimed. He stiffened. "Enter," he called out.

The door slid open, and Cipher stepped inside. She wore her usual enigmatic smirk, her piercing eyes sweeping the room like a predator assessing its territory. Both Tupolev and Baptiste turned to face her instinctively.

"Captain," Cipher said, cooly. Her gaze flicked briefly to Baptiste, a faint curve forming on her lips before she returned her attention to Tupolev. "Do you have an update for me on Starfire?"

Tupolev shifted in his chair. "No significant progress yet. We've tightened the orbital lockdown and cleared all civilian traffic. We've scoured the manifests of every incoming and outgoing ship, but Starfire has yet to surface."

Cipher's smile vanished, replaced by an expression of icy displeasure. She stepped forward, her heels clicking softly against the floor. "I was expecting results, not excuses," she said.

Tupolev exhaled slowly, choosing his words carefully. "We're doing everything within our means, but the resources available are limited. If you want faster results, we could use some... assistance."

Cipher, for a moment, with an unnerving gaze studied Tupolev's face. Then, she turned her head, giving Baptiste a lingering, seductive glance that made her visibly tense. Baptiste bit the inside of her lip, willing herself to remain stoic under the scrutiny.

Cipher sauntered over to Tupolev's desk, slowly and deliberate. She perched on the edge of the desk, crossing her legs with feline grace, her eyes still locked on Baptiste. "What kind of assistance do you have in mind, Captain?" she asked, her eyes never leaving Baptiste.

Tupolev hesitated for a moment, considering what he was about the request one final time. "Malcolm Taylor," he said finally.

"If we had him, it would give us the firepower and reach we need to lock this system down completely."

Cipher's head tilted slightly, her smile returning but now… darker. Slowly, she turned to face him, slowly, as if savoring the moment. "Malcolm Taylor?" she repeated. Amused at the thought she gave a slight chuckle. "That's a tall order."

"It's what we need," Tupolev replied. "Taylor is the only asset capable of covering the gaps in our current perimeter."

Cipher considered his words. After a long pause, she stood gracefully, smoothing the edge of her coat. "Very well," she said finally. "I'll make the arrangements."

Tupolev blinked, surprised at her immediate agreement. He had expected pushback, negotiation, even derision at his request. Instead, she seemed almost eager. "Just like that?" he asked with a note of disbelief.

Cipher turned her head slightly, giving him a look that was both condescending and playful. "Oh, Captain," she purred, "you don't need to sound so shocked. I want results as much as you do. Malcolm Taylor will ensure that I get them. And Captain…" Her voice dropped to a dark octave, almost demonic. "I always get what I want."

As she said this, her gaze shifted to Baptiste, fixing on the commander with a suggestive look that sent a visible shiver down Baptiste's spine. Cipher's eyes roamed slowly, not predatory in the way Tupolev described, but claiming—marking Baptiste as if she were staking territory.

Baptiste stiffened under the scrutiny, her professionalism barely masking her discomfort. She refused to look away, though the urge was almost unbearable, the slight taste of blood fills her mouth as she bit her lip harder.

Cipher's smile widened. She leaned slightly toward Tupolev, still keeping her gaze on Baptiste. "I'll handle Taylor," she said, as though she were discussing the weather. "You focus on keeping things—tidy until he arrives."

Tupolev nodded, "Understood."

Cipher lingered for a moment longer, her eyes finally breaking away from Baptiste to meet Tupolev's, and without another word, she turned toward the door. Her heels clicked rhythmically against the floor as she walked away, but just as she reached the threshold, she paused.

Turning her head slightly, she looked back at Baptiste with a glint of something dark and dangerous in her eyes. "See you later, Zoe,"

Baptiste didn't respond, her hands clenching at her sides as the door slid shut behind Cipher.

The heavy silence lingered after the door slid shut, Cipher's departure leaving an oppressive weight in the room. Tupolev leaned back in his chair, his fingers steepled as he stared at the desk.

"That woman…" Baptiste began. She exhaled sharply, shaking her head. "We should've seen this coming."

"What?" Tupolev asked, tilting his head.

Baptiste didn't respond immediately. Instead, she stepped to the side, her hands gripping the back of the chair she had been sitting in. "Malcolm Taylor," she said finally. "A carrier group Commander. That's a lot of firepower to bring into orbit, Mikail."

Tupolev shrugged, leaning forward and resting his elbows on the desk. "We're dealing with a situation that requires firepower, Zoe."

"A carrier group?" Baptiste repeated, as if trying to make the sheer magnitude of the statement sink in. "It's overkill for an orbital lockdown. You know that as well as I do. A carrier group isn't just a few extra ships. It's a mobile armada—heavy cruisers, frigates, destroyers, fighter squadrons, support craft. Not to mention the Super Carrier itself. Bringing that kind of firepower here isn't about enforcement. It's about domination."

Tupolev said nothing. Just looks out the viewport.

"And Taylor?" Baptiste continued, "He's a hammer, Mikail. And you're no stranger to being one yourself. But together? We're about to turn this orbital lockdown into a sledgehammer strike. What are we really doing here?"

Tupolev didn't respond. Instead, he reached for his terminal, swiveling it around so Baptiste could see the screen. "We're following orders," he said coldly.

Baptiste leaned forward to read the message displayed on the terminal. The orders were clear and stamped with Admiral Jacobs's seal.

Upon completion of the orbital lockdown, you are to deploy ground forces to establish control over the population in response to the recent catastrophic events: the explosion aboard Prime Patel's vessel and the assassination of Captain Soto within her residence. Martial Law is to be enacted immediately and to be met with decisive and uncompromising action.

Baptiste's eyes widened, "Soto?" she asked, "Captain Miranda Soto?"

Tupolev gave a slow nod. "She was killed in her home."

Baptiste shook her head, her face a mixture of shock and disbelief. "When? How?"

"We're still piecing that together," Tupolev replied. "But the timing isn't a coincidence. The explosion on Prime Patel's ship and Soto's murder happened within hours of each other."

Baptiste took a step back, her mind racing as she processed the revelation. She had been preoccupied with the fallout from Patel's ship, never imagining the situation could escalate further. "And this is how we respond?" she asked, gesturing toward the terminal. "Dropping boots on the ground, declaring Martial Law? Mikail, the citizens of New Earth are already protesting the military's presence. They're calling it tyranny. Sending troops in will only cement that notion."

"It's not up to us to debate the orders," Tupolev said. "We execute them."

Baptiste frowned, her arms crossing again. "Orders or not, this feels wrong. The people will see this for what it is: a coup."

Tupolev's gaze sharpened. "A coup? That's a dangerous accusation, Commander. Who exactly do you think is staging a coup?"

Baptiste hesitated, then said quietly, "Cipher."

Tupolev stared at her for a moment, then laughed—a cold, humorless sound. "Cipher? That woman doesn't seek power to rule openly. She doesn't want a throne or a title. She works from the shadows, pulling strings, bending people to her will. But she's not staging a coup."

"Isn't she?" Baptiste countered, rising her voice slightly. "Look around you, Captain. The Alliance is on edge. The colonies are fracturing. And here we are, preparing to march into New Earth and crush dissent under the guise of 'stabilizing the situation.' If this isn't a coup, then what is it?"

Tupolev's eyes narrowed. "Watch your tone, Zoe."

Baptiste held his gaze. "I'm just calling it as I see it, sir. We're pawns in someone else's game, and I'm not sure that game is in the best interest of the Alliance."

Tupolev's fist slammed onto the desk. "Enough! You're walking a thin line, Commander. I don't want to hear any more talk of treason."

She paused, her gaze narrowing as her thoughts seemed to coalesce into a single, pointed question. "Tell me, Captain, exactly how and when did Cipher come aboard? Why is she even here?"

Tupolev swallowed hard, weighing how much to divulge. Finally, he leaned back in his chair. "Admiral Jacobs' orders," he said simply.

"Jacobs? She's here because of him?" She asked.

Tupolev nodded. "Our entire mission here—every directive, every action—is under Admiral Jacobs' exclusive command. Cipher's presence is part of that. She reports directly to him, and we answer to her when required."

Baptiste stared at him. "So that's it?" she asked quietly. "We're puppets in Jacobs' little shadow play? Do you even know what game we're playing, Mikail?"

Tupolev's patience was wearing thin at his first officer's barrage. "We're soldiers, Zoe. We don't need to know the full picture. Our orders are clear, and we execute them."

"But at what cost?" Baptiste demanded. "To the Alliance? To the people of New Earth? Hell, to ourselves? This isn't just another operation, Mikail. This is something else entirely."

Tupolev exhaled sharply, his gaze hardening. "You're letting your emotions cloud your judgment. Cipher's presence, Jacobs' orders—none of that changes our duty. Focus on the mission and leave the politics to them."

Baptiste straightened. "I'm only saying what others are thinking. You can't tell me you don't see it too."

Tupolev looks at her for a moment, his gaze cold and calculating. "What I see is a mission to complete. That's all. If you can't handle that, perhaps you're in the wrong position."

Baptiste said nothing more. The tension in the room was suffocating, the line between loyalty and doubt drawn clearly between them.

After a long pause, Tupolev spoke again. "Taylor will bring the resources we need to restore order. That's the only thing you need to concern yourself with, Commander."

"Understood, sir." She turned and left the office, the door hissing shut behind her, Tupolev stared at the terminal screen. The orders were clear, but Baptiste's words lingered, gnawing at the edges of his resolve.

Cipher's shadow loomed over everything, and though Tupolev would never admit it openly, part of him wondered if Baptiste's accusations weren't so far-fetched after all.

***

The bridge of the Specter hummed with quiet activity, the subdued lighting casting soft shadows on the polished consoles.

181

Allison sat in the command chair, a tablet in her hand reviewing the final reports from the recent search and rescue operations.

She sighed deeply, setting the pad aside for a moment. The loss of Prime Patel's ship, the Unity, played over in her mind like a haunting refrain. The explosion had been sudden, snuffing out hundreds of lives in an instant. Despite their swift response, there had been no survivors to rescue, only wreckage and silence.

Allison leaned back, her Texan drawl thicker with her exhaustion as she spoke to herself, "Poor devils, didn't stand a chance." Her gaze drifted to the viewport, where the distant lights of New Earth sparkled like a cruel mockery of the day's carnage. The thought of Prime Patel brought a pang of guilt. The woman had seemed so calm, almost detached during their brief interactions.

"Ma'am," the communications officer interrupted. "Priority one message from Fleet Command, marked for command level eyes only."

Allison straightened in her chair. "Send it to my console," she replied.

The screen on her armrest flickered to life, displaying the Fleet Command seal before transitioning to the message:

PRIORITY ONE MESSAGE

FROM: Fleet Command

TO: Alliance Cruiser Specter

Subject: Declaration of Martial Law on New Earth

Following the destruction of the Unity and the discovery of Captain Miranda Soto murdered in her residence, Fleet Command has declared Martial Law on New Earth. This measure is intended to suppress any further terrorist activities and ensure the safety of the populace during this volatile period.

Effective immediately, you are to support planetary operations as needed. Further instructions will follow.

ADMIRAL AARON JACOBS

FLEET COMMAND

Allison's hand clenched into a fist as she finished reading. Martial Law. It was a drastic solution to a problem that demanded precision. It meant checkpoints, curfews, fear, and control—something she doubted the already-tense colony could endure without boiling over into open rebellion.

The destruction of the Unity was bad enough, but Captain Soto's murder felt like an intentional escalation, a spark thrown into an already volatile powder keg. Who could have done it? And why?

Her thoughts were interrupted as the comms officer spoke again, this time hesitantly. "Ma'am, another message coming through... text only. Heavily encrypted."

Allison frowned. "Sender?"

The officer hesitated. "No official designation, Commander."

Allison's pulse quickened. "Route it to my console."

The new message appeared, the formal edges of military correspondence replaced by something much more personal:

A,

Nothing is as it seems.

Meet me on the surface. We need to talk.

[f(x) = x^2 - 14x + 48] + 7

Trust no one. Come alone..

—Z

Allison's finger hovered over the console as she stared at the cryptic equation. Numbers weren't her strong suit, and she muttered under her breath, "Damn it, Zoe. Couldn't you just write plain English for once?"

Her voice softened into a grumble as she started working through the equation, tapping at her tablet and furrowing her brow. "Math was never my thing… should've paid more attention in school," she muttered, trying to piece together the fragments of high school algebra still floating somewhere in her memory.

Occasionally, she paused, biting her lower lip in frustration, then double-checked her work, only to erase and start over. The bridge crew paid her no mind, each occupied with their own tasks.

Finally, after several minutes of laboring over it, she leaned back with a triumphant sigh. "Got it," she said under her breath, staring at the answer.

Her initial relief turned to confusion. "What the hell does that mean?" she murmured, staring at the numbers as though they might rearrange themselves into a clearer message. "Zoe, you've got some explaining to do."

Pushing aside her frustration, Allison had a sudden moment of genius and brought up a map of New Earth on the console, her fingers deftly entering the grid overlay. Using the X and Y coordinates derived from the equation, she zeroed in on a small section of Nueva Mexico. The area was bustling, a densely packed district known for its sprawling markets, cafes, and a constant stream of activity.

"This is where you want me to meet you?" she muttered, studying the grid square. It wasn't an ideal place for a clandestine rendezvous, but Zoe always had her reasons.

Her gaze shifted back to the equation, and as she studied it, the answer suddenly clicked into place. She let out a soft laugh, almost embarrassed. "When," she murmured, realization dawning on her.

The thought of informing Captain Pierce crossed her mind, but Zoe's message replayed in her head: *Trust no one. Come alone.*

Allison hesitated, her fingers hovering over the console. She had never hidden anything from Pierce before. He was her captain, her friend. But this time was different.

***

The dim light of Senator Lopez's office illuminated her stern expression as she read the message from Cipher on her tablet, each word coiling in her chest like a serpent tightening its grip.

Failure will not be tolerated. Prime Patel serves as an example of those who disobey. Get the papers signed.

Cipher's name was not attached to the end of the message—it never was. Lopez exhaled shakily, setting the tablet down on her desk with a soft clink. She ran her fingers along the polished surface, her thoughts racing. Patel's ship, Unity, had been obliterated in a flash of fire and debris. The message was clear—Cipher's reach was absolute, and her patience nonexistent.

Lopez straightened in her chair, smoothing her suit jacket and willing the tension in her body to fade. She couldn't show fear—not now, not ever.

The sharp click of heels in the hallway broke the quiet, and moments later, Maria's voice carried through the intercom.

"Senator, Ava Turing is here for her appointment."

Lopez inhaled deeply, putting on her mask of calm composure. "Send her in."

The doors opened smoothly, and Ava stepped inside with a warm smile, her braided hair resting neatly down her back and her tailored crimson blouse catching the faint light. Her black heels tapped lightly against the floor as she approached, carrying a sleek portfolio under her arm.

"Senator Lopez," Ava greeted warmly, almost maternally. "It is good to see you again."

"Always Ms. Turing," Lopez replied, gesturing to the chair across from her desk. "Please, sit."

As Ava settled into the chair with an elegant motion, she set the portfolio on the desk and opened it with care, revealing the meticulously prepared documents.

"These are ready for your review," Ava said, sliding the papers forward. Her smile softened, radiating a warmth that seemed almost genuine. "My legal team has been quite thorough to ensure everything is in order."

Lopez hesitated before picking up the first page. She took her time, ensuring she understood each clause, though Cipher's message loomed in her mind.

While Lopez read, Ava's gaze drifted around the office, her expression shifting just slightly. "Your office is… cozy," she remarked with a pleasant lilt, though her words carried a subtle edge.

Lopez glanced up briefly, unsure how to respond. "It suits its purpose," she said returning her focus to the documents.

Ava continued politely but with a veiled superiority. "I've always admired efficiency in a workspace. Though, I must say, the campaign posters are an interesting touch. A bit vain, don't you think?"

Lopez's eyes flicked up again. "They remind people of my values."

"Of course," Ava replied, tilting her head as if in admiration. "Still, I can't help but notice how much smaller it is than mine. My office at Neura Tech is... spacious. But I suppose here, functionality is key."

Lopez forced herself to remain composed, though Ava's comments prickled under her skin. She turned her attention back to the documents, scanning through the dense text.

"These are incredibly thorough," Lopez remarked.

Ava's smile returned. "Naturally. I want to ensure complete control over Athena's integration and how she's used. After all, a system like this needs... careful oversight. I won't have the military pervert my creation."

Lopez paused, Ava's words hitting hard and cutting deep. She looked up at the woman across from her, studying her warm smile and perfectly poised demeanor. Something about Ava's presence felt off—too calculated, too polished.

"Well," Lopez said finally, setting the documents down. "Everything appears to be in order."

"Excellent," Ava said, smoothly sliding a pen across the desk.

Lopez hesitated, the pen hovering above the signature line. Cipher's warning echoed in her mind, and she signed with steady strokes. "There. It's done."

Ava's smile widened as she retrieved the signed papers, slipping them back into her portfolio with practiced precision. "Thank you, Senator. This is a significant step forward for the Alliance."

Lopez nodded stiffly, watching as Ava rose gracefully from her chair.

As Ava turned toward the door, she paused, glancing back with a warm yet pointed expression. "I'll be in touch as we begin the rollout. If you have any questions, please don't hesitate to reach out. And, Senator—Stephine, don't let the past few day's events press too heavily on you. You're doing the right thing."

Lopez nodded again, unable to summon a reply.

Once the doors closed behind Ava, the warmth of her presence vanished, leaving Lopez alone with the suffocating silence of her office. She reached for her tablet and opened the private channel with Cipher. Her fingers trembled as she typed:

The papers are signed. Integration will begin soon.

The response was almost immediate:

Good.

Lopez stared at the single word, her chest tightening. No further instructions, no reassurance. Just the stark, cold acknowledgment that she had done as she was told.

She set the tablet down and leaned back in her chair, staring at the ceiling. The weight of her decisions pressed down on her, and despite the stillness of the room, she couldn't shake the feeling that Cipher was watching. Always watching. She pushed the tablet aside, her fingers pressing against her temples as she tried to steady her thoughts.

She couldn't shake the growing realization that her survival depended on finding a way out of Cipher's web. But how? Every channel she might use to reach out for help was likely being monitored. If Cipher suspected treachery, the consequences would be swift and absolute.

Her eyes darted to her terminal, scanning her limited options. She thought of trusted allies, only to dismiss each name one by one. Everyone had a price—or a weakness Cipher could exploit.

Suddenly, her tablet buzzed again. She grabbed it, her stomach knotting as she opened the new message:

Give your endorsement.

Lopez frowned, her confusion sharpening into unease. *Endorsement for what?* she wondered, her mind racing. Before she could dwell on it further, a soft knock at the door interrupted her thoughts.

"Enter," Lopez called, hastily placing the tablet face down on her desk.

Maria stepped in, her tablet tucked under her arm. "Senator, I have the final report from the military regarding the search and rescue operations following the Unity explosion," she said, her tone measured but tinged with the weight of the tragedy.

"Go on," Lopez said, motioning for Maria to sit.

Maria took a seat, pulling up the report on her tablet. "As expected, there were no survivors. The area was too saturated with debris for anything to remain intact. However, the preliminary analysis suggests the explosion was not accidental."

Lopez stiffened. "Not accidental? Are they saying it was sabotage?"

Maria nodded grimly. "The military is investigating further, but their initial findings indicate that the explosion originated from within the ship's core. Someone likely had inside access."

Lopez's throat tightened. "And what about the public? Do they know?"

"Not yet," Maria replied. "Fleet Command intends to release a statement once they have Senatorial endorsement for the declaration of Martial Law. It's not legally required, but having the Senate's public approval will help manage civilian reaction."

"Martial Law?"

Maria nodded. "The destruction of the Unity combined with the murder of Captain Soto has pushed Fleet Command to enact an orbital lockdown. All incoming and outgoing traffic is being screened, and planetary movement will be restricted once the announcement is made."

Lopez leaned back in her chair, anticipating the implications. "They're clamping down hard. Do they suspect more attacks?"

Maria hesitated. "It's not clear, but Fleet Command is treating this as an organized terrorist effort. They want to prevent further chaos."

Lopez exhaled slowly, her fingers tapping against the desk. "Keep me informed of any developments. The moment Fleet makes the announcement, I want to be prepared to address the public."

"Of course, Senator," Maria said, closing the report on her tablet. She paused for a moment, as if remembering something. "Oh, one more thing. The Specter has requested shore leave for its personnel, specifically access to civilian only areas of the city. It's an unusual request; these are typically denied."

Lopez froze. "The Specter? Captain Pierce?"

"Yes," Maria confirmed, puzzled by Lopez's reaction.

Lopez waved her off. "Grant the request," she said quickly.

Maria hesitated. "Are you sure? Shore leave approvals are rare, especially with Martial Law imminent."

"I'm aware," Lopez replied sharply. "But let's not compound tensions by denying a harmless request. Besides, we need to maintain the appearance of cooperation between the military and civilian leadership."

Maria nodded, rising from her chair. "I'll send word to their First Officer. Anything else, Senator?"

"No. That will be all, Maria."

As Maria left, Lopez's mind was already spinning. She had forgotten that the Specter was here—that Pierce was here. A man with a reputation for solving impossible puzzles and walking the razor's edge of authority. If anyone could help her, it was him.

But Cipher's warning loomed large in her thoughts. Any attempt to communicate would have to be flawless, untraceable.

She rose from her chair and began pacing, formulating a plan. If she could use the shore leave as a pretense to get a message to Pierce, she might have a chance. The question was how to do it without Cipher knowing.

Chapter 10

Traci sat at the sleek news desk. Behind her, the holo-screen displayed a live feed of military checkpoints on New Earth's busiest thoroughfares, uniformed personnel directing traffic under the glare of floodlights. The studio lights warmed her skin but did little to ease the chill of the report she was about to deliver.

"Good evening, I'm Traci Yamato with GNN News, reporting live on day five of Martial Law here on New Earth. As tensions remain high following the destruction of the Unity and the tragic death of Captain Miranda Soto, authorities have implemented additional security measures to ensure the safety of all citizens."

Her voice was calm, but authoritative, as the camera cut to footage of military personnel scanning ID cards at a checkpoint.

"New curfews are in effect from 8 PM to 6 AM, with only essential personnel permitted to travel during these hours. Twenty-three new checkpoints have been established throughout New Athens, with similar measures rolled out in Nueva Mexico and other major districts. Citizens are advised to carry proper identification at all times and allow additional travel time due to increased security screenings."

The screen transitioned to a clip of a protest in the city square, the crowd chanting slogans while a line of soldiers stood at attention, their presence imposing but restrained.

"While most residents have complied with these measures, small-scale protests have erupted in various parts of the city, calling for an end to the lockdown and a return to civilian governance. Senator Lopez have assured the public that these measures are temporary and will remain in place only as long as the threat of further attacks persists."

The screen transitions to edited clip of a press conference from Senator Lopez.

"The safety and security of New Earth remain our highest priority. While these measures may feel restrictive, they are temporary and necessary to protect our citizens from further harm. I assure you; the Senate and the Military are united in efforts to uncover the truth and bring those responsible for these heinous acts to justice. We ask for your patience and cooperation as we navigate this challenging time together."

Traci continued speaking as the main camera focused on her.

"Stay tuned to GNN for updates as we continue to monitor the situation. I'm Traci Yamato, reminding you to stay safe and stay vigilant. Good night."

As the studio lights dimmed and the bustle of post-broadcast activity began, Robert approached the desk cautiously. He seemed to hesitate, glancing at Traci as if gauging her mood. With a deep breath, he reached for her microphone pack, his hands trembling slightly as he detached it.

"You know," Robert began, "it's… weird how you always seem so… put together. Like, all the time. Never mess up. Always ahead of things."

Traci's eyes shifted toward him as she arched a brow. "That's my job, Robert. Do you have a point?"

He swallowed, fumbling with the microphone pack as he placed it in the case. "I—I mean, it's like spy-level put-together. That's all I'm saying."

Traci's patience clearly wearing thin. "Robert, if I were a spy, don't you think I'd be smart enough to make sure you never noticed?" Her tone was calm, almost too calm, and it carried an unmistakable edge.

Robert stammered, his hands fumbling again with the case. "I—I didn't mean—"

"Enough, Robert," Mara interjected, stepping up with an air of exasperation. She placed a hand on his shoulder, pushing him gently but firmly aside. "You're embarrassing yourself. Again."

She turned to Traci with a small grin. "Sorry about him. You'd think after five days of this nonsense he'd find a new conspiracy to obsess over."

Traci forced a smile that didn't reach her eyes. "It's fine. Robert's… unique." She said, a faint warning in her tone.

Robert opened his mouth as if to protest, but the sharp glance Traci shot him made him think better of it. He busied himself packing the rest of the gear.

"Let's finish up," Mara said, dismissing the interaction as she handed Traci her belongings. "Some of us have actual work to do."

Traci nodded, giving Mara a polite, if distant, thanks before stepping away.

In the quiet of the staff lounge, Traci settled onto a bench, setting her bag beside her. She reached into the inside pocket of her blouse and retrieved the small black device.

Opening the device, she began typing a message, her fingers moving swiftly over the virtual keyboard. The lines of text were short. When she finished, she stared at the screen for a moment before snapping the device closed.

The lounge fell silent save for the faint hum of distant machinery. Traci leaned back, her eyes fixed on a distant point, her thoughts clearly elsewhere.

After a few moments, the device buzzed. She opened it again, her eyes scanning the brief response that had appeared giving a slight scoff as she closed the device and put it away.

Leaning back, Traci crossed her legs and tapped her lips with a finger, her expression shifting to one of deep thought. The rhythm of her tapping slowed as her mind worked, piecing together whatever puzzle occupied her thoughts.

After several minutes, Traci checked her watch. Rising from the bench, she smoothed her skirt and slung her backpack over one shoulder.

Her heels clicked softly against the tiled floor as she exited the lounge, her demeanor calm but purposeful. Robert and Mara exchanged glances as she passed, but neither dared to speak.

The night air greeted her as she stepped outside, her thoughts still churning. Whatever her destination, it was clear Traci was a woman with a plan—and no time for distractions.

* * *

The conference room buzzed with low murmurs as Prime Linh Nguyen entered. She moved with purpose, her eyes scanning the room as Admiral Harker, Dr. Voss, and Commander Kane rose to greet her. Each carried an air of tension.

Nguyen took her seat at the head of the table, her hands clasped neatly in front of her. "Let's begin," she said, foregoing any pleasantries. "Dr. Voss, an update on your progress."

Voss began. "We've reviewed the financial records. The trail leads to companies based in Callisto and Ganymede, colonies notorious for their lack of regulatory oversight. On paper, it's all clean—too clean."

Nguyen's brow arched slightly. "Explain."

Voss shifted in her chair. "Every transaction is accounted for, every fund disbursed with legal documentation. There's no trace of anything unusual, and that's what concerns me. These records are practically pristine, almost as if they've been... curated."

Dr. Voss pushed her glasses up the bridge of her nose. "If there's something illicit here, it's buried so deep we'd need years to uncover it. What bothers me most is the perfection. No financial operation, especially one involving political campaigns, is this flawless."

Nguyen nodded thoughtfully, her mind already spinning through the implications. "Noted. Commander Kane, your findings?"

Kane shifted in his chair. "My team has been monitoring the six senators named in Patel's report. So far, their activities are as mundane as you'd expect—meetings, fundraisers, the occasional dinner with lobbyists. Nothing out of the ordinary."

Nguyen tilted her head. "Nothing at all? No anomalies in their schedules or communications?"

Kane hesitated, glancing at his notes. "The only 'dirt' we've uncovered is personal—extramarital affairs, questionable friendships—but nothing illegal. Honestly, it's baffling. These people are supposed to be at the center of a shadow faction, yet their lives are painfully boring as any other senator."

Nguyen grinned, "I'm sorry you find me boring, Commander."

A faint chuckle rippled through the room, breaking some of the tension.

Kane smirked but quickly sobered. "It doesn't add up. People involved in covert activities don't behave like this. They're either overconfident or extremely well-coached."

"Or," Harker interjected, "they're better at hiding it than we are at finding it. We should move to arrests. Interrogations will yield faster results than chasing ghosts through paper trails and empty schedules."

Nguyen's expression hardened, and her tone turned icy. "Admiral, we do not arrest sitting senators without irrefutable evidence. The backlash from even one false move could destabilize the entire Alliance. The detention of Senator Lopez is a prime example. Luckily the only blowback from that is minor protests."

Harker's teeth clenched, but he didn't argue further.

Nguyen leaned back in her chair. "We need to change our approach. If these senators are part of a shadow faction, they're not working alone. Look beyond them—associates, staff, unlisted meetings. And consider this: What if Patel's list is wrong?"

Voss frowned. "You think Patel gave us bad intel?"

Nguyen shook her head. "Not intentionally. But it's possible someone wanted her to focus on these six, drawing attention away from others. We can't afford tunnel vision. Expand the investigation."

Kane leaned forward, curiosity sparking in his eyes. "You're suggesting there's another layer to this?"

Nguyen's voice softened, but her words carried weight. "I'm suggesting we've been looking at the wrong players. Shift focus. Broaden the scope."

Harker crossed his arms. "And if we find nothing?"

Nguyen's gaze locked onto his. "Then we keep looking until we do. The Alliance's survival depends on it."

As the meeting adjourned, Nguyen lingered at the table, her disciplined mind replaying every detail. The investigation wasn't just about uncovering a conspiracy—it was a test of the Alliance's resilience, of her own ability to see through the layers of deception.

Harker, as he left, grumbled to himself about bureaucracy slowing progress, but Nguyen caught the faint flicker of respect in his eyes. He might not like her methods, but he trusted her judgment.

For Nguyen, trust was a currency she intended to spend carefully. Too much was at stake to waste it on anything less than the truth.

***

The patrons of The Four Winds Bar stirred with a subdued energy, the kind that made it a haven for those seeking solace. The low lighting bathed the space in warm amber hues, casting shadows that danced on the polished wooden walls. A soft jazz tune played in the background, its melody weaving through the clink of glasses and muted conversations.

Cipher sat at the far end of the bar, nursing a tumbler of whiskey. Her short, blonde hair framed her sharp features, the glint in her eyes a warning to anyone who dared approach. The glass in her hand was half-empty, the amber liquid catching the light as she swirled it idly.

She stared into her drink, letting the alcohol and the ambiance dull the noise in her head. But even here, Zarina's voice found her, that nagging, insistent whisper clawing at the edges of her mind.

You don't have to do this. You could stop. You could be better.

Cipher casually whispered to herself, "Get out of my head, bitch." She took another sip, the burn down her throat a welcome distraction. She didn't need Zarina's voice haunting her tonight. She didn't need anyone. But peace was fleeting, and her solitude was soon interrupted by the presence of someone stepping too close.

"Hey there," a man's voice drawled. She didn't look up, keeping her focus on her glass.

200

"You look like you could use some company," he continued, dripping with misplaced confidence.

"I'm not interested," Cipher said flatly.

The man didn't take the hint. Instead, he pulled out the stool beside her and sat down, leaning toward her with an easy grin. "Come on, don't be like that. I'm just trying to be friendly."

Cipher sighed, sat her glass down with deliberate care. She slowly turned to him. "Friendly isn't what I'm looking for. Now leave."

The man chuckled, clearly not deterred. "Feisty. I like that."

Before she could turn away, his hand reached out and rested on her shoulder.

The reaction was immediate. Cipher's hand shot up, slapping his away. Her gaze bore into him, speaking with a dangerous whisper.

"You should keep your hands to yourself," she said with menace. "It's not nice."

The man blinked, taken aback for a moment, before his grin returned, wider and more intrigued. "Hot and dangerous. I like you even more."

Cipher leaned closer, cold and humorless. "You won't like what comes next if you don't walk away. Now."

There was something in her eyes—something dark and unrelenting—that finally made him pause. His grin faltered, and he held up his hands in mock surrender.

"Alright, alright. Didn't mean to upset you," he said, sliding off the stool. "Have a good night."

Cipher watched him retreat before turning back to her drink. She drained the glass in one smooth motion, signaling the bartender for another.

***

The Four Winds was quieter now, the late hour thinning the crowd to a handful of lingering patrons. Cipher remained at the bar, her once imposing glare dulled by the haze of alcohol. Her glass sat empty, her fingers absently tracing the rim as she stared into the middle distance.

A deep, pressing urge finally broke through the fog—she needed the restroom.

With an unsteady breath, Cipher slid off her stool. The floor seeming to tilt beneath her, and she stumbled, catching herself on the edge of the bar. Muttering a curse under her breath, she steadied herself and began weaving her way toward the restroom, each step heavy and uneven.

When she reached the door, her hand moved to push it open, but she didn't make it that far.

A sharp yank on the back of her hair pulled her head violently backward, and before she could react, her face slammed into the solid door with a sickening thud. Pain exploded through her skull, and her vision blurred as the metallic taste of blood filled her mouth and nose.

The world spun as her body sagged against the door, her limbs struggling to respond. She tried to yell out, but the force of the impact left her breathless.

She barely registered the man's voice—low, mocking—as he grabbed her roughly, dragging her into the restroom and kicking the door shut behind them.

Cipher's instincts flared, and she tried to fight back, her hands clawing weakly at his arms. But the alcohol had stolen her strength leaving her movements sluggish and ineffective.

"Should've been nicer," the man sneered. Feeling his hot breath against her ear.

Her mind screamed at her to move, to fight, to do something, but her body refused to cooperate. She was helpless as he overpowered her, her struggles fading into numbness.

She could do nothing but lay there as the man forced himself upon her weakened, intoxicated state. It was over as quickly as it started, but for her it was an eternity.

Cipher, dizzy from the alcohol and the force of the impact against the door, struggled to pull her skirt down. Her hands slipping as she tried to get up, looking at the man as he adjusted his clothes and fixed his hair. She looked at his face, burning it into her memory.

Her voice was horsed as she struggled to speak but she got the message out clearly, "I will kill you."

The man chuckled, "Whatever you say, sweetheart."

Her body finally giving out as her vision blurred again and fell into darkness.

***

The sharp scent of antiseptic and the hum of distant voices stirred Cipher from the void. Her body ached, and a low throb pulsed at the back of her head. She blinked, her vision swimming, until the harsh glow of flashing lights and the silhouette of figures leaning over her snapped into focus.

"She's waking up," a voice said.

Cipher's gaze darted to her surroundings. She was on a gurney, its surface hard and confining, the soft rumble of an ambulance beneath her. EMTs surrounded her, their hands moving quickly, checking her vitals, adjusting straps.

"Can you hear me?" one of them asked, leaning into her line of sight. "You've been unconscious for a while. Can you tell us your name? Do you know who attacked you?"

Cipher's instincts flared, a wave of panic rushing over her. "I can't, I have to get out." She thought to herself.

Outside, through the open doors of the ambulance, New Earth Security officers floated like vultures, questioning patrons from the bar. Their voices blending together, fragments of their words cutting through: "...female victim... reports of a fight... no clear suspect."

Cipher clenched her teeth, forcing her breathing to slow. She had been unconscious long enough for the alcohol in her system to dull, leaving her mind sharp but her body sore. She couldn't let herself be detained. Not here. Not like this.

You're slipping, Zarina's voice echoed in her head, soft and mocking. *You're supposed to be better than this, but look at you. Weak. Caught.*

Cipher squeezed her eyes shut, pushing the voice aside. Her focus narrowed on her immediate surroundings—the EMT leaning too close, the straps holding her down, the small team of security officers pacing just beyond the ambulance.

"Ma'am, do you know who attacked you?" the EMT pressed again.

She let her head loll to the side, feigning disorientation. "I... I don't know," she murmured. Making her voice weak, calculated to disarm them.

The EMT exchanged glances with their colleague. "She might still be in shock. Let's get her stable and to the hospital."

Cipher's muscles tensed beneath the restraints. She needed to act now.

Run, Zarina's voice hissed, almost gleeful now. *Or... are you too far gone for that, too?*

With a sudden burst of precision, Cipher moved. Her hands yanked free of the straps—loosened just enough by the EMTs tending to her—and she surged upward, elbowing the nearest medic in the ribs. The impact forced them back with a grunt.

"Hey!" the other EMT shouted, but Cipher was already in motion.

She grabbed a scalpel from the nearby tray, using it to slice the strap around her torso. Her body protested every movement, but she ignored the pain, her training overriding the haze.

One of the security officers spotted the commotion. "What the—Stop her!"

Cipher vaulted from the gurney, landing hard on the ground. The impact sent a jolt of pain through her knees, but she didn't stop.

Pathetic. You're moving slower than you normally do. Zarina sneered in her mind.

She gritted her teeth, darting around the side of the ambulance. The officers gave chase, shouting for her to halt, but Cipher didn't look back.

She ducked into the shadows of an adjacent alley, her breaths ragged but controlled. Her surroundings blurred as she assessed her escape route—a maze of narrow pathways and service tunnels.

"Don't let her get away!" the voice of one of the officers rang out, their footsteps echoing in pursuit.

Cipher's mind worked quickly, her body falling into the practiced rhythm of evasion. She turned, disappearing into a maintenance access hatch and sealing it behind her. The sounds of pursuit grew faint as she slipped deeper into the labyrinthine underbelly of the city.

Cipher sat in the shadows of the maintenance tunnel, her knees drawn up, her back pressed against the cool, damp wall. The adrenaline from her escape had ebbed, leaving her with the sharp ache of bruised ribs and a throbbing headache. She stared into the darkness ahead. And then, like clockwork, Zarina's voice came.

You're slipping, the voice mocked, like the edge of a blade pressing into her mind. *Running through alleys like a rat. Getting assaulted in some dingy bar. What happened to you? You used to be untouchable.*

Cipher exhaled through her nose, her jaw tightening. "Shut up," she muttered under her breath.

Or what? Zarina's voice teased, full of bitter amusement. *You'll kill me? Oh wait, you already did that. But, look at you now.*

All-powerful Cipher, sitting in the dirt, bruised, and humiliated. You can't even drink in peace without making a mess of yourself.

Cipher's hands curled into fists, her nails digging into her palms. The ache in her body was nothing compared to the fire Zarina stoked in her mind.

And then there's Lisa.

Cipher froze instantly.

Oh yes, let's talk about her, Zarina continued. *What would Lisa think if she could see you now? Running through back alleys, skulking in the dark. Do you think she'd pity you? Hate you? Or worse—maybe she wouldn't care at all.*

Cipher sneered. "Lisa betrayed me. She wouldn't care because she never did."

Betrayed you? Zarina's laugh was bitter and cold, echoing in Cipher's mind. *Is that what you tell yourself to sleep at night? She didn't betray you. You betrayed her. You're the reason she's gone.*

Cipher's hands started trembling. "She's gone because of them. Because of what they did to me, and what they made her do."

No, Zarina shot back. *She's gone because of you. I'm in your head, Cipher. I know your thoughts better than you do. Everything you've done, everything you've built—it's not about power or control. It's about Lisa. Your whole plan is revenge for them taking her from you. But let's face it: you're the one who really took her.*

The memory hit Cipher like a hammer. The heartbeat in her fingers, fading as her hands tightened around Lisa's throat. The look in Lisa's eyes—pleading, betrayed, then lifeless. The sensation was as vivid now as it had been then, her pulse quickening as though she could feel Lisa slipping away all over again.

"No," Cipher whispered, her voice breaking for the briefest moment. She clenched her fists tighter, trying to push the memory away. "She betrayed me first."

Keep telling yourself that, Zarina taunted softly. *But you'll never bury the truth. You keep me to survive what you did to her, but you can't run from me. And you can't run from her.*

Cipher's chest heaved as she fought to steady her breathing.

And don't forget Veronica, Zarina continued. *Sweet, loyal Veronica. She'll find me, you know. She'll save me. And when she does, she'll destroy you.*

Cipher let out a bitter laugh, shaking her head. "Veronica? She's too weak. Too scared. She doesn't have what it takes."

Doesn't she? Zarina countered. *She's already stronger than you think. And when the time comes, she'll burn your world to the ground. She'll set me free, and you'll be nothing.*

Cipher pressed her hands against her temples, her fingers trembling as she tried to block Zarina out. But the voice wouldn't stop. It never did.

You feel it, don't you? Zarina whispered. *The heartbeat in your fingers, the last piece of Lisa you'll ever hold. It's slipping away again, just like it did then. Just like everything will when Veronica comes for you.*

Cipher slammed her fist against the wall, the sharp pain grounding her for a moment. Her voice came out in a growl, low and furious. "She'll fail. Just like you did."

But even as she said it, the words felt hollow. The darkness around her pressed in, heavy with memories and the weight of Zarina's voice, as Cipher sat motionless, the heartbeat of her past echoing in her hands.

Memories IV

The hotel room was dim, the single bulb overhead flickering intermittently as if debating its own existence. I sat at the desk, the glow of my comms device illuminating the scattered notes and tablets that had become my companions. The intel I'd collected over the past weeks painted a grim picture—corruption, subterfuge, and an unseen hand guiding events from the shadows. And still, the pieces didn't quite fit.

My sidearm rested on the table beside me, its presence a grim reminder of the authority Naval Intelligence had granted me. Full weapons release. The term still felt surreal, even weeks after the directive came through. It wasn't just a license to kill—it was a declaration of trust, or perhaps desperation. Luckily, I hadn't needed to use it. Yet.

I leaned back in the creaking chair, my fingers brushing the grip of the weapon as if to reassure myself it was still there. The weight of it was familiar, comforting in a way I hated to admit. But the thought of pulling the trigger outside of self-defense still unsettles me.

A sharp chime from my comms device snapped me out of my thoughts. I straightened, swiping the screen to open the message. It was from my handler—the first communication I'd received since the weapons release directive. My chest tightened as I read the text.

Flagged as potential actionable intel. Local journalist has reached out requesting protection, claims to be in danger. Believes she has information critical to ongoing operations. Scared for her life.

My lips twisted into a grimace. Babysitting wasn't what I'd signed up for, and the thought of it disgusted me. Taking care of myself was a full-time job—I couldn't be expected to watch over someone else, much less a civilian who had no idea what she was getting into.

The message continued:

Contact has designated a meeting location and time: 2200 hours at Café Solis. No description provided. Name: Traci Yamato.

I exhaled sharply, leaning back in the chair. A journalist. Of course. The kind of person who thought their curiosity was noble, their drive to uncover the truth a higher calling. I'd seen it before—idealists who dove headfirst into waters too deep for them, then panicked when the current dragged them under. Now she wanted a lifeline. And Naval Intelligence, in its infinite wisdom, had decided I was the one to throw it.

I stood, grabbing my jacket and slipping the sidearm into its holster. Babysitting or not, this meeting was happening. If Traci Yamato really had actionable intel, it was my job to secure it—even if it meant dragging her terrified, naïve self through the fires of whatever hell she'd stumbled into.

As I left the hotel room, I couldn't shake the bitter thought:

This isn't what I signed up for.

***

The air was thick with the tang of engine grease and stale coffee as I leaned back in the booth, my eyes scanning the unassuming Café. The metallic whirr of kitchen machinery hummed in the background, a steady rhythm against the occasional clink of cutlery. This wasn't the kind of place anyone would come looking for a Naval Intelligence Operative—which made it the perfect spot to meet.

I didn't like meeting civilians, especially not journalists. They tended to ask questions, and questions were dangerous in my line of work. But this one, Traci Yamato, had stumbled too close to the fire. Her digging into rumors of corruption within the Alliance Senate had made her a target—and, by extension, a liability. Naval Intelligence had flagged her as a potential source of intel, which meant she was now my problem.

The bell above the Café entrance jingled, and I spotted her immediately. She walked into the dingy café with an air of uncertainty, her eyes scanning the room for someone she wasn't entirely sure would be there. I sat in the corner, shrouded by the dim light that barely penetrated the haze of stale coffee. When her gaze landed on me, I nearly froze.

She looked just like me.

Not an exact replica, but close enough to make my stomach churn. Her hair was a shade darker, cut just a bit longer, and her posture lacked the practiced stillness Naval Intelligence drilled into you. But it was the face—the contours, the eyes, the way she tilted her head as she approached. It was uncanny, like looking at a version of myself who had taken a left where I had gone right.

She stopped a few steps away, hesitant, her hand tightening around the strap of the bag slung over her shoulder. "Lucy?" she asked.

"Sit," I replied. My pulse was a hammer in my chest, but I wouldn't let her see it. Whoever this journalist was, her presence had just complicated my life in ways I didn't have time to unpack.

She slid into the seat across from me, I could see she was nervous. Her eyes darted around the café before settling back on me. "I wasn't sure you'd come," she said quietly.

"You shouldn't have reached out," I said, leaning back in the booth. "Do you have any idea how much trouble you've brought down on yourself, and me?"

"I didn't have a choice," she said. "People are disappearing. Names are being erased. This goes higher than anyone's willing to admit, and if I'd gone to anyone else…"

"You'd still be alive tomorrow." The words came out sharper than I intended, but they needed to land. She needed to understand what kind of fire she was playing with.

She lowered her head and for a moment, I saw something in her expression that felt disturbingly familiar—the same stubborn determination that had pushed me into the Academy, into Intelligence, and into this miserable, impossible mission.

"Look," she said, "I don't know who you really are or why you're here. But I know you're the only one who might care enough to stop this. Someone has to."

"Stop what, exactly?" I asked.

Her hand slipped into her bag, and I tensed, my fingers brushing against the concealed holster beneath my jacket. But all she produced was a data stick, which she placed on the table and slid toward me.

"That's everything I've found," she said. "Financial records, backdoor communications, project logs. It's not complete, but it's enough to prove someone high up in the Senate is funneling resources into... something. Something big."

I didn't reach for the chip. Not yet. "You've made yourself a target," I said. "Why risk reaching out to me?"

Her expression softened, just for a moment. "Because I heard stories," she said. "Back on Earth, people talked about the things your organization has done. How you actually... care."

I felt a flicker of irritation. Care? The word felt hollow and out of place, like it belonged to someone else. I wasn't here to care. I was here to solve problems—and right now, she was a problem Naval Intelligence had dropped squarely in my lap. Her digging into rumors of corruption within the Alliance Senate had made her a liability, and now she was my liability.

"You've been flagged as a potential source of intel," I said, deciding there was no point in sugarcoating it. "Which means every move you make is being watched."

Her face paled slightly, but she held her ground. "Then help me," she said. "Because if they're watching me, they're watching you too. And that means you're already in this, whether you like it or not."

I stared at her, letting the silence stretch. She was right, of course. Her presence here had already compromised the operation, whether she realized it or not. And the resemblance—that uncanny, maddening resemblance—only added to the complications. If someone saw the two of us together, the questions alone could blow my cover.

But there was something else, too. Something I couldn't quite place. A feeling that Traci wasn't just another overeager journalist chasing a dangerous story. There was a reason she was here. A reason she looked the way she did. And if I didn't figure it out, it was going to get both of us killed.

Finally, I reached for the data chip, sliding it off the table and into my pocket. "If you're lying about any of this," I said, "you won't live long enough to regret it."

"I'm not lying," she said. "And you know it."

I stood, adjusting my jacket as I glanced toward the exit. "Stay here," I said. "Don't talk to anyone, don't leave, and don't draw attention to yourself. If you're still breathing in an hour, I'll know you listened."

Her eyes widened slightly, but she nodded. "What are you going to do?" she asked.

I didn't answer. Whatever this was, whatever mess Traci Yamato had dragged me into, it was mine to clean up now. And if I was going to survive it, I needed to move fast. I didn't look back. If she was smart, she'd stay put. If she wasn't…

Well. I'd cross that bridge when I came to it.

The night had settled over the city like a thick blanket, wrapping the streets in shadows and leaving the air cold and sharp against my skin. I stepped out of Café Solis and into the quiet, my boots clicking against the pavement as I walked to my bike. The café's bell jingled faintly behind me, a sound that barely registered above the faint hum of distant traffic and the occasional hum of a passing car.

The street was mostly empty, lit only by the flicker of aging streetlights that cast fractured shadows on the ground. My bike sat under one of those lights. I ran my fingers along the handlebar as I approached, a habit more than anything, before sliding onto the seat.

I keyed the ignition, the engine purring to life in a low, steady hum. The sound filled the quiet around me, familiar and grounding. I adjusted my jacket and reached for my helmet, but something stopped me.

I turned my head, glancing back at the café.

Through the window, Traci was still sitting at the booth where I'd left her. Her hands were clasped tightly around the strap of her bag, her posture stiff, her eyes darting toward the door every few seconds. She was trying to appear composed, but the tension in her movements gave her away. Nervous. On edge.

Good, I thought. Nervous people are cautious, and cautious people survive.

Still, as I watched her from the shadows, a different kind of unease began to creep in. It wasn't just her presence that unsettled me—it was the way she looked. The resemblance between us was uncanny, almost haunting. The same sharpness in the eyes, the same contours of the face. The longer I watched, the more it gnawed at me. It wasn't just coincidence. It couldn't be.

I put my helmet on, forcing the thought aside. Whatever the connection was, it would have to wait. Right now, I had more immediate problems to deal with.

The engine growled softly as I revved the throttle, and the bike rolled forward, tires whispering against the asphalt. I didn't look back again, but the image of her sitting there, nervous and out of place, lingered in my mind.

The city thinned out as I left the bustling core behind, the streets growing quieter, the buildings darker. It wasn't long before I reached the outskirts, where the lights gave way to long stretches of abandoned lots and rusting industrial complexes. The parking structure rose ahead, its concrete skeleton standing against the night sky.

I pulled into the first level, the sound of my engine echoing in the hollow space, bouncing off the cracked walls and oil-stained floor. The place was empty, as expected. No security cameras, no wandering drifters. Just silence and the faint smell of rust and damp concrete.

I guided the bike up to the second level, my eyes still scanning the shadows out of instinct more than necessity. The habit was hard to break, even when I knew there was nothing here to see.

Once parked, I cut the engine and let the quiet settle around me. For a moment, I just sat there, the weight of the day pressing down on me like a lead blanket. The silence was oppressive, broken only by the faint creak of the structure as the wind pushed against its aging walls.

I reached for my comms device, hesitating for a second before activating it. A secure line was established in moments, the screen staying black as my handler's voice filtered through.

"Report."

I took a deep breath, forcing myself to remain composed. "She made contact," I said. "The journalist. She handed over a data stick—claims it contains financial records and communications logs. Says it's proof of corruption in the Senate. I've secured the data, but…" I trailed off, frustration bleeding into the pause. "This assignment. Her presence. It's going to slow me down. Babysitting a civilian, especially a journalist, is a liability I can't afford."

The silence on the other end stretched, heavy and deliberate, before my handler spoke again. Their voice was as cold and detached as ever. "If that's the way you feel, then dispose of her."

The words hung in the air like a stone dropped into a still pond, sending ripples of unease through me. Dispose of her. The directive wasn't new—it was standard protocol for anyone deemed a liability. But hearing it stated so plainly, so casually, made my stomach tighten.

"She might be more useful alive," I said carefully. "Her intel could lead to something bigger. If we lose her, we might lose that thread."

"That's your decision to make," my handler replied. "But remember, the moment she becomes more trouble than she's worth, you know what to do."

The line went dead before I could respond, the abruptness of it leaving an eerie void. I stared at the device in my hand, my grip tightening around it until my knuckles turned white.

Dispose of her.

The phrase repeated in my head, each iteration heavier than the last. I leaned back against the bike, closing my eyes and letting the silence envelop me again. I knew Traci was still sitting in that dingy café, clutching her bag and probably wondering if she'd made a mistake.

She wasn't wrong to reach out for help. But she was wrong to think I was the person to give it.

For now, I'd keep her alive. But the weight of the sidearm under my jacket was a reminder of how quickly that decision could change.

***

As I rode back toward the café, my mind raced through a dozen possibilities. It wasn't intuition; it was the faint flicker of movement I'd caught in the café window before I rounded the corner. Someone was standing at Traci's table, too close to be casual. My stomach tightened as I approached the building, the streetlights overhead casting their jittery glow onto the sidewalk.

I parked the bike at the curb, cutting the engine but keeping my helmet on for a moment longer. The weight of the sidearm under my jacket was suddenly more noticeable. I slipped my hand to the holster, giving it a quick check before stepping off the bike and walking toward the café.

Through the glass, I spotted her. Traci was still seated at the booth, but her posture was rigid, eyes darting toward the man standing over her. He was tall, broad-shouldered, with an air of authority that set my nerves on edge. His back was to me, but from his body language alone, I could tell he wasn't just there for coffee.

The doorbell jingled softly as I stepped inside, and I didn't hesitate. My voice cut through the low murmur of the café as I strode toward them.

"Hey, sis! Sorry I'm late."

The words came out before I had time to think. Why I'd chosen that particular cover, I couldn't say, but it seemed to work—for the moment. The man glanced over his shoulder as he studied me. I ignored him, my focus squarely on Traci, who looked like she'd been caught in the middle of a game she didn't know the rules to.

Her hesitation almost shattered the illusion. She blinked at me, her lips parting as if to say something, before catching on and nodding stiffly. "Uh, yeah. No problem. You… got here just in time."

I slid into the seat beside her, keeping my body between her and the man. "Can I help you?" I asked, ensuring to make it clear I wasn't in the mood for games.

The man didn't answer immediately. He lingered for a moment longer before finally straightening. "No," he said. "I was just leaving."

I watched him walk to the door. He didn't look back as he exited, and I made a point of waiting until the bell over the door jingled shut before turning to Traci.

"We're leaving," I said, grabbing her arm and pulling her to her feet.

"What—" she started, but I didn't let her finish.

"Now," I snapped, guiding her out of the café.

The street was empty when we stepped outside. No sign of the man. That should've been a relief, but it wasn't. He'd been too calm, too assured. It wasn't over—not by a long shot.

I walked her toward the bike, scanning the area as we moved. She dug her heels in after a few steps. "But wait—my car—"

I turned to her, biting back the urge to snap. Instead, I held out my hand. "Give me the keys."

She blinked, confused, but reached into her bag and handed them over. Without a word, I threw them as hard as I could into the nearest alley. The keys clattered against the pavement and disappeared into the shadows.

Her mouth opened in shock, but before she could say anything, I turned back to her. "You don't have a car anymore. Get on."

Her hesitation was brief this time, her wide eyes searching mine for some kind of explanation. When she found none, she climbed onto the bike behind me, her hands gripping the sides of the seat awkwardly.

I sighed, grabbed her wrists, and firmly wrapped her arms around my waist. "If you don't hold on, you're going to fly off," I muttered.

The engine roared to life beneath us, a deep, guttural sound that echoed through the empty street. As I twisted the throttle and the bike surged forward, I felt her arms tighten instinctively. Good. At least she wasn't entirely useless.

We tore down the street, the wind whipping past us as I maneuvered through the quiet roads. The city lights blurred into streaks of amber and white, and for a brief moment, I thought we might have made a clean getaway.

Then I saw the headlights.

At first, I thought it was just another car—a late-night commuter or someone heading home. But the way it stayed behind us, perfectly matching my speed and movements, sent my instincts into overdrive. My grip on the handlebars tightened, and I felt Traci shift slightly behind me.

"What's wrong?" she asked, barely audible over the wind.

"Hold on tighter," I said, ignoring her question.

The sedan's engine growled, and it surged closer. I glanced in the rearview mirror and saw the glint of a muzzle flash. The sharp crack of gunfire followed a split second later, and I swerved hard, the bike veering to the right as a bullet ricocheted off the pavement where we'd just been.

"Are they shooting at us?" Traci shouted.

"No, they're just playing really aggressive tag," I snapped, leaning into another sharp turn as the sedan closed the distance.

Another shot rang out, this one whizzing past my left shoulder. I gritted my teeth, heart pounding in my chest. I pushed the bike harder, weaving through narrow streets and alleyways in an attempt to lose them.

"Are you going to shoot back?" Traci yelled.

"This isn't a movie!" I shot back, glancing over my shoulder. "I can't shoot and drive at the same time!"

The sedan roared behind us. I could see the shadowy figures inside, their movements frantic as they prepared for another volley. I was thinking as fast as I could, calculating every turn, every possible route to shake them.

We sped onto a wider street, and the sedan matched our speed, pulling up alongside us. I caught a glimpse of the passenger aiming a pistol out the window, and I swerved again, narrowly avoiding the next shot. The crack of the gun echoed through the night, and Traci let out a startled cry, tightening her grip even more.

"We're going to die!" she screamed.

"Not if you stop screaming in my ear!" I barked, cutting sharply across two lanes and into a side alley. The tires screeched as I pushed the bike to its limits.

The sedan followed, its tires screeching against the tight corners. Another shot rang out, this one closer than before, and I felt a sharp, stinging pain in my thigh. My vision wavered for a moment, but I shook it off, focusing on the road ahead.

The alley spilled out onto another main street, and I leaned hard into the turn, the bike almost scraping the ground as we careened onto the open road. The sedan was still behind us, its engine roaring as it closed the distance.

"Lucy!" Traci shouted. "You're bleeding!"

"Noticed," I grunted.

"You need a hospital!"

"That's not an option."

Ahead, the road split into two tunnels, one leading to the city's industrial sector and the other toward the outskirts. I veered toward the industrial side, hoping the maze of warehouses and loading docks would give us an edge.

The bike roared into the tunnel, the sound of the engine echoing in the enclosed space. The sedan followed, its headlights cutting through the darkness like knives. I pushed the bike faster, weaving between the faintly illuminated lanes.

"Hang on," I said.

We burst out of the tunnel and into the industrial district, the landscape shifting into a labyrinth of steel and concrete. I veered sharply into the maze of warehouses, taking turns at random, the sound of the sedan's tires screeching behind us.

Finally, after a series of tight turns and alleyways, the sedan's headlights disappeared. I slowed the bike slightly, the adrenaline still pumping as I scanned the area for any sign of pursuit.

"We lost them," I said.

Traci loosened her grip slightly but didn't let go entirely. "You're bleeding a lot," she said. "You need help."

I glanced down at my thigh, where a dark stain was spreading just below my hip. The pain was sharp and hot, radiating with every movement. "It's fine," I said, steering us back toward the city center.

"It's not fine!" she snapped. "You're hurt! You need a hospital—"

"No hospitals," I cut her off. "Too many questions."

She fell silent after that, her arms tightening around me again as I guided the bike toward my hotel. The chase might have ended, but I knew this was far from over. If they'd gone to the trouble of shooting at us, they wouldn't give up so easily.

As the city lights came back into view, I felt the weight of everything settle over me. Traci Yamato had become more than just a liability—she was now a walking target, and so was I.

***

By the time we reached the hotel, my head was swimming. Each step felt like dragging my body through quicksand, the throbbing in my thigh syncing with the erratic pounding of my heart. Sweat poured down my face, dripping into my eyes and blurring my vision. Traci was practically holding me up, her shoulder wedged under mine as we staggered down the hallway.

"Lucy, you're burning up," she said. "This is bad. You're really—oh my God, you're burning up!"

"I'm fine," I rasped, though the words tasted like a lie. My breath was shallow, each inhale a struggle against the tightness building in my chest. The fever was setting in fast—too fast.

We reached the door to my room. I fumbled for the keycard, but my hands shook too much to get it out. Traci grabbed it from me, but even her hands were unsteady as she swiped it. The lock beeped red. "Wrong way." She swiped again, and it finally flashed green.

The door swung open, and I nearly collapsed into the room, my weight dragging her down with me. The space blurred around me—the desk, the bed, the faint glow of the city lights filtering through the curtains. It was all slipping away.

"Help me to the bed," I muttered.

Traci tightened her grip, her arm looping around my waist as she half-dragged, half-guided me to the bed. The sheets were cool against my burning skin as I collapsed onto them.

"Lucy, what do I do?" she asked in a panic. "I don't know what to do!"

"Medkit," I managed, forcing the word out.

"What?"

"Under… the desk," I said, my eyes fluttering shut.

I heard her scramble across the room, the sound of drawers sliding open and slamming shut. "I don't see it!" she yelled franticly.

"Case," I groaned. "Big case… under…"

There was a pause, then the sound of something heavy being dragged across the floor.

"Oh my God," she whispered. "What is this?"

I opened my eyes just enough to see her kneeling beside the open medkit, her face pale as she stared at its contents. It wasn't just a standard first-aid kit. It was an field hospital in a box— surgical tools, vials of medication, quick injectors. Everything I might need to survive if things went south. At the time I packed it, it seemed like overkill. Now, I'm grateful for the forethought.

Traci's hands hovered over the array of supplies. "I don't know what to do with any of this!"

"Focus," I rasped, trying to keep conscious. "Quick injectors. Red… adrenaline. Green… pain. Get… the green one."

She hesitated, her hands trembling as she reached into the kit and pulled out a small injector with a green cap.

"Stab it… in my thigh," I said, barely holding on.

"What? Are you serious?"

"Do it… or I'll pass out…"

Her hand hovered over my leg, her eyes wide and terrified. "Okay, okay, I'm doing it. Don't yell at me if this goes wrong!"

I felt the sharp prick of the needle through the fabric of my jeans, followed by the faint hiss of the injector. The pain dulled slightly, just enough for me to focus.

"Cut the jeans," I said, my words slurring. "Forceps… find the bullet… pull it out."

She stared at me like I'd asked her to perform brain surgery. "I'm not a medic! I can't—"

"Traci," I interrupted, "You have to. Or I'll die."

That seemed to snap her into action. She grabbed a pair of scissors from the kit and shakily cut away the fabric around the wound. I flinched as the cool air hit the open gash, the pain flaring again despite the medication.

The last thing I saw before the fever dragged me under was her face, pale and streaked with tears as she held the forceps in trembling hands.

***

When I came to, the first thing I noticed was the dull, throbbing ache in my thigh. The second was the stiffness in my limbs, as if I'd been lying still for far too long. The room was dim, the curtains drawn tightly against the light outside. My head felt foggy, but my fever had broken. I wasn't dead.

A sound—a soft gasp—drew my attention.

"You're awake!" Traci's voice came from beside me.

I turned my head, wincing at the pull in my neck. She was sitting on the floor next to the bed, her knees pulled up to her chest, her hair a wild mess of tangles. She looked like she hadn't slept in days.

"Not dead," I croaked.

Traci let out a breathy laugh, her hands covering her face for a moment before she looked back at me. "No, you're not dead. But I was starting to wonder."

I frowned, the fog in my brain clearing just enough for her words to register. "How long was I out?"

She glanced at her watch. "Eighteen hours. I kept checking to see if you were breathing. You scared the hell out of me."

"Eighteen hours," I echoed weakly. "Long time…"

"Yeah," she said. "And this thing—" she gestured toward my comms device on the desk, where it was vibrating faintly every few seconds, "—it keeps buzzing. I don't know how to open it."

My stomach tightened at her words. My handler. They'd been trying to reach me.

"Bring it here," I said, forcing myself to sit up. Pain flared in my thigh, but I ignored it, leaning back against the headboard.

Traci hesitated, then grabbed the device and handed it to me. "What is it, anyway?"

"Comms device," I said, turning it over in my hands. "It's how I stay in contact with… people."

She frowned. "It looks like a phone, but I couldn't find any buttons."

"That's the point," I said, my fingers finding the hidden button along the side. With a press and a faint click, the screen flipped up, displaying a string of missed messages.

"How did you—"

"Hidden button," I interrupted, tilting the device to show her the nearly invisible seam. "It's designed to be discreet. If you don't know it's there, you'd never figure it out."

Traci leaned back, watching me with a mix of curiosity and unease as I scrolled through the messages. Most were system pings—automatic updates or encrypted check-ins. But there was one message flagged as priority, the kind that didn't come lightly.

I opened it, the text glowing faintly on the screen:

Status report required. Awaiting acknowledgment.

I exhaled sharply, my chest tightening. My handler wasn't going to like the delay.

"You okay?" Traci asked.

I looked up at her, my fingers tightening around the device. "Not really," I admitted.

The room fell into a heavy silence as I debated my next move. Whatever came next, I needed to think fast. Eighteen hours was long enough for the situation to spiral further out of control, and with my handler already on edge, I couldn't afford to stay off the grid much longer.

But before I dealt with them, I needed to deal with us. "You did good," I said, nodding toward my bandaged leg. "You kept me alive. That's more than I expected."

She blinked, the tension in her face easing slightly. "Yeah, well, don't make me do it again, okay?"

"No promises," I muttered, already dreading the conversation with my handler.

I stared at the comms device for a moment, weighing the risks of responding now versus letting my handler stew in silence. Neither option was appealing, but ignoring them any longer wasn't an option. I tapped the screen, initiating a secure connection.

The device emitted a faint click, and the screen remained dark as always. My handler's voice came through, cold and clipped, the very embodiment of calculated efficiency.

"You're late."

I winced, leaning back against the headboard. "Took a bullet. Spent some time unconscious. You know, the usual."

A pause, just long enough to make me uneasy. "Status."

"Alive. Mobile. Target is secure," I said, glancing toward Traci, who was sitting cross-legged on the floor, watching me with an anxious expression. "We ran into complications. Someone else is on her trail."

"Describe the encounter."

"Sedan. Pursued us through the city. Armed. They knew what they were doing—trained, organized. They weren't after me; they wanted her." I gestured faintly toward Traci, who looked like she was about to protest but wisely stayed quiet.

"Vehicle?" my handler asked.

"Lost them in the industrial sector. No plates, no identifiers."

Another pause, this one longer. "You compromised your location by returning to the hotel."

I bristled at the accusation. "I was bleeding out, and she doesn't exactly have a safehouse stashed away."

"You could have used the secondary rendezvous point."

I gritted my teeth. "I was unconscious for eighteen hours. I wasn't exactly in a position to relocate."

Traci flinched slightly at my tone, but my handler didn't so much as blink—or at least, I imagined they didn't.

"Understood," they said finally. "Status of the target?"

"Alive and scared out of her mind," I replied.

"Has she provided the promised intel?"

"Yes. Data stick is secure. It's… messy. Financials, comms logs, project notes. She was onto something, but it's incomplete."

"Analyze and report," they said without hesitation.

I clenched the device tightly, my frustration mounting. "Listen, about this assignment—"

"Analyze and Report," they interrupted, stressing each word.

I bit my lower lip, forcing myself to remain calm. "This journalist is a liability. Babysitting her slows me down, and if today's chase is any indication, she's already made too many enemies. She's painted a target on both of us."

A beat of silence followed, and then the response came, colder than before: "Dispose of her if she becomes more trouble than she's worth."

My stomach tightened, though I'd expected it. "And if she's the only lead we've got?"

"That's your judgment to make. But remember you're replaceable. The mission isn't."

"Spare me the lecture," I said, leaning back against the headboard. "I need backup."

A pause. Not hesitation—calculation. "Denied."

The word hung in the air like a lead weight.

"I was pursued," I said. "Armed opposition. This isn't some backwater thug ring, and you know it. Whoever's after her has resources, coordination, and training. This isn't a one-person operation anymore."

"Your mission parameters remain unchanged," my handler replied. "You'll manage."

I glanced at Traci sitting cross-legged on the floor, her fingers fidgeting nervously. Her wide eyes were fixed on me, like she was trying to decipher every word of the conversation.

I hesitated, debating my next move. My handler's voice came again, clipped and impatient. "Anything else to report?"

"Yes," I said. "I want permission to recruit her."

The silence that followed was deafening. I could almost hear the wheels turning on the other end, the conversation I knew they were having with whoever sat above them. Traci tilted her head in confusion. She opened her mouth to speak, but I raised a hand, silencing her.

Finally, my handler's voice returned, colder than before. "She is your responsibility. If you proceed, you will be held accountable for her actions, her safety, and any collateral damage."

"I understand," I said, though my chest tightened at the weight of their words.

"Ensure she doesn't compromise the mission," they added. "If she does…"

"I know," I cut in, my voice flat. "Anything else?"

"No. Your mission continues." The line clicked off before I could respond.

I let the device fall to the bed, running a hand through my hair as I tried to process the situation.

"What just happened?" Traci asked.

"You're not backup," I said, pushing myself to sit up fully. "But you're coming with me, and that means you need to learn how to stay alive."

"What are you talking about?"

"Get the case," I said, pointing under the bed. "Underneath."

She hesitated, then crawled forward and dragged the heavy silver case out from its hiding place. It rubbed against the floor as she pulled it out, and she shot me a questioning look.

"Open it," I instructed.

Her fingers fumbled with the latches, but after a moment, she popped them open and lifted the lid. Her gasp was audible.

Inside was a high-precision sniper rifle, sleek and matte black, perfectly nestled in a custom cutout. Alongside it sat a compact sidearm in its own compartment, magazines slotted neatly into the foam lining. One cutout was conspicuously empty—another sidearm.

"What… is all this?" she asked with a soft whisper.

I pointed to the sidearm. "Hand me that."

She picked it up carefully, like it might explode in her hands, and passed it to me. I checked the magazine, racked the slide, and held it out to her.

"You're going to need this," I said.

Traci recoiled slightly, her hands coming up defensively. "No. No way. I don't know how to use that!"

"You're about to learn."

She stared at me, wide-eyed, but I didn't give her time to argue. "This is a Sagitta," I began, holding the gun up for her to see. "Standard issue for Naval Intelligence. Chambered in 10mm, semi-automatic. Compact, durable, reliable."

I ejected the magazine, showing her the shiny rounds inside. "These are Nano-Enhanced Expanding Rounds. They're designed for maximum stopping power. On impact, the nano-coating ensures controlled expansion, meaning they tear through soft tissue but don't over-penetrate. Semi-armor piercing, so they can punch through light body armor if needed."

Traci's face paled, but she didn't interrupt.

"They travel at just over 1,200 feet per second," I continued. "Which means whatever you're aiming at is going to feel it. But they won't do you any good if you don't know how to use the damn thing."

"I'm not a soldier," she protested.

"No," I said, locking the magazine back in place with a sharp click. "But you're in this now, and you need to learn how to survive. Start by holding it."

She took a deep breath, hands trembling as she reached for the gun. I placed it in her hands carefully, adjusting her grip.

"Relax," I said. "It's just a tool. It's only dangerous if you don't respect it."

Her hands shook as she held the weapon, her face a mix of fear and determination. "What if I screw up?"

"Then we both die," I said bluntly, leaning back against the headboard. "So don't."

She swallowed hard, nodding as she stared down at the weapon.

"Let's start with the basics," I said softly. "Safety, grip, stance. By the time we leave this room, you're going to know how to handle that thing. Got it?"

Traci didn't look convinced, but she nodded again. "Okay," she whispered.

"Good," I said, watching her carefully. "Because from here on out, it's only going to get a lot worse."

Chapter 11

The streets of the capital were eerily quiet, the usual hum of activity reduced to a whisper under the heavy hand of martial law. The curfew was in effect, but it was still early. Checkpoints dotted the intersections, manned by stoic Military Police officers in crisp uniforms. Their presence a constant reminder that this wasn't the free city it used to be.

Pierce walked beside Jones, his cane tapping softly against the cobblestones with each step. He wore a plain jacket and slacks, blending seamlessly with the handful of other civilians on the streets. Jones matched his pace, her casual attire unassuming has his, as they walked shoulder to shoulder.

"You think Starfire will reach out soon?" Jones asked, low enough to be swallowed by the faint city noises.

Pierce tilted his head slightly. "Hard to say. Being down here on the surface gives them options. That's both an opportunity and a risk."

"You trust them?" Jones pressed.

Pierce's lips quirked into a faint, humorless smile. "Trust is a strong word. I trust their reputation—enough to bring us here. Beyond that…" He let the thought trail off, his gaze directed ahead as he tapped his cane lightly against the curb.

The faint sound of boots on pavement grew louder as a Military Police officer approached from the next checkpoint. "Papers, please," the officer asked firmly.

Jones and Pierce stopped, the duo pulling a small, folded card from their jacket pockets and holding it out for the officer to inspect.

The officer examined the cards. Stuttering as he registered their credentials. He snapped to attention, saluting sharply. "Apologies, sirs. You may proceed."

Jones nodded, tucking her ID back into her jacket as Pierce murmured a polite, "Carry on."

They moved past the checkpoint, their pace resuming its steady rhythm.

"Starfire might already be watching us," Jones said quietly, glancing around as they crossed a near-empty plaza. "If they're as good as their reputation, they'd have eyes everywhere."

Pierce's expression didn't change, but his tone carried a hint of amusement. "That's exactly why we're dressed like this. If they're watching, they'll know we're taking precautions. It's all part of the game."

The faint beep of a comms device broke the moment, and Jones pulled hers from her pocket, glancing at the screen before answering. The small display flickered to life, revealing Lieutenant Murphy seated on the Specter's bridge.

"Lieutenant," Jones greeted.

"Commander," Murphy replied, offering a relaxed smile. "Just checking in. All shuttles have returned from the surface, and we're on schedule to rotate officers and crew in seven days."

"Thank you, Lieutenant," Jones said warmly. "And sorry for giving you the short stick with first watch."

Murphy waved it off with a small chuckle. "Someone has to do it, ma'am. Besides, it's a good excuse to brush up on bridge operations. Not every day I get a quiet shift like this."

Jones smirked. "That's one way to look at it. Keep everything running smoothly up there."

"Yes, ma'am," Murphy said. "Enjoy your leave, such as it is."

Jones ended the transmission and slipped the comms device back into her pocket.

"She's a good officer," Pierce said. "She'll make a fine commander one day."

Jones nodded, her lips parting to respond, but before she could speak, a passerby brushed past her shoulder, muttering a low, "Excuse me."

The contact was brief, almost unnoticeable, but Jones felt something slip into her jacket pocket—a subtle movement that sent a chill down her spine. She turned her head, catching a glimpse of the figure moving away. A woman, dressed in a nondescript coat and scarf, disappearing into the sparse crowd.

Jones stiffened, her fingers instinctively brushing the pocket where the object had been placed.

Pierce's head turned slightly, as though sensing her unease. "Something wrong?"

"Someone bumped into me," she said. "And left something behind."

"Keep moving," Pierce said calmly, though there was an edge to his tone. "We'll check it later. Don't draw attention."

Jones nodded, her hand slipping back to her side as they resumed their pace. Her mind raced as they walked, wondering what message Starfire had just delivered—and what it would mean for their mission.

Jones kept her hand steady, resisting the urge to fidget with her jacket pocket as they continued walking. The streets were quiet enough that any unusual movements might draw attention, especially with checkpoints and the ever-present shadow of martial law looming over them.

"Let's stop somewhere," she said after a while "I want to check what they left."

Pierce nodded slightly, his cane tapping the ground. "Somewhere discreet. No alleys. Too predictable."

They veered off the main street, finding a quiet bench under a dead streetlight in a nearly deserted park. The shadows provided some cover, and the reduced foot traffic made it unlikely they'd be disturbed. Jones sat, her back straight, scanning the area for any sign of onlookers.

Pierce took a seat beside her, relaxed, though she knew better than to mistake it for complacency. "Now," he said quietly.

Jones reached into her pocket and pulled out a small, folded scrap of paper. The words scrawled in clean, precise handwriting:

South Tram Station. 2200. Locker 47. PIN 228539.

She read the message twice, committing it to memory. 2200. That gave her enough time to plan—but her stomach twisted as she remembered the other meeting already on her plate. The Four Winds Bar. Zoe. That wasn't close to the tram station, and juggling both meetings would require careful timing.

Pierce tilted his head toward her. "What's it say?"

Jones hesitated for the briefest of moments before folding the paper and slipping it back into her pocket. "South Tram Station," she said. "Locker 47. 2200. There's a PIN: 228539."

Pierce nodded slowly. "Starfire likes their theatrics. They're cautious."

"So are we," Jones said. "No reason to take chances."

Pierce's lips curved into the faintest of smiles. "Good instincts. We'll need them."

Jones's comms device buzzed faintly in her pocket, making her stomach tighten. She'd silenced the alert but still felt the vibration through the fabric. It was Zoe's earlier message, the reminder she'd pushed aside. She glanced at Pierce, who seemed focused on his own thoughts, and exhaled softly. She'd have to juggle both meetings without him realizing.

"Do you trust this?" she asked, gesturing vaguely toward the tram station as if it were already in view.

Pierce tilted his head in thought. "Trust is irrelevant. It's the best lead we've got, and we're already here. If Starfire's playing us, we'll know soon enough."

Jones nodded, though her thoughts were elsewhere. She checked her watch—plenty of time before 2200, but not enough to be careless. Zoe's message had been vague, but Jones couldn't afford to ignore it. Whatever Zoe wanted, it had to be important enough for her to take the risk of reaching out.

"I'll head to the tram station alone," Jones said suddenly, testing the waters.

Pierce turned his head slightly, his cane tapping once against the ground. "Not a chance, Allison. I can't let you walk into an unknow situation alone."

She smirked faintly, covering her unease. "Had to try."

"Nice effort," Pierce said dryly. "Let's move. We've got some time to kill before the station, but no need to linger here."

As they stood and started walking again, Jones's mind churned with possibilities. She'd need to find a way to separate from Pierce, make it to the Four Winds Bar, and then return in time for Starfire's meeting at the tram station. Balancing both without raising suspicion would be a challenge.

Her thoughts kept circling one grim truth: if she mishandled this, she'd not only compromise herself but also the entire mission. And Pierce could never find out about Zoe.

The café was quiet, a rare pocket of normalcy in a city under martial law. Lopez adjusted her scarf, the fabric drawn just high enough to conceal the lower half of her face without attracting suspicion. Her coat was plain, her slacks nondescript—every detail of her appearance designed to avoid attention.

She shifted uncomfortably in line, glancing around the small café. Most of the patrons were civilians, their quiet conversations blending with the faint hiss of the espresso machine. Her mind was racing, weighing the risks of what she was about to do. This was dangerous, but she'd had no choice.

In front of her, a young woman in a naval uniform stepped forward, placing her order with a polite smile.

"A latte, please," the Lieutenant said cheerfully.

The cashier rang it up, but as the woman produced her card, the cashier's expression fell. He pointed to a sign near the register that read:

"Notice: No Military Accounts Accepted."

"I'm sorry, ma'am," the cashier said.

The Lieutenant's smile faltered, and she let out a quiet sigh. "Right. Of course. Sorry about that." She slid her card back into her pocket.

Lopez, watching from behind, stepped forward instinctively. "Wait," she said. She turned to the cashier. "Add hers to my order."

The Lieutenant blinked, caught off guard. "You don't have to do that—"

"I insist," Lopez interrupted, offering a reassuring smile. "It's no trouble."

The cashier nodded and rang up both orders. Lopez handed over a small stack of coins, relieved that she'd thought to carry cash.

The Lieutenant hesitated again but finally smiled. "Thank you," she said.

"It's nothing," Lopez replied smoothly.

As the barista prepared their drinks, the Lieutenant gestured to an empty table near the window. "Do you want to sit together? Least I can do is keep you company."

Lopez hesitated, calculating the risks, then nodded. "I'd like that."

The table was small, the final rays of the day's sunlight from the window casting soft patterns across its surface. The Lieutenant sat across from Lopez, her latte cradled between her hands. She was younger than Lopez had expected, with eyes that hinted at intelligence and determination.

"I'm Veronica Valentine," the Lieutenant said, offering a hand.

Lopez took it briefly. "Stephine," she replied, keeping her voice low.

For a moment, Veronica studied her, her brow furrowing slightly as though trying to place her. Lopez knew the look—recognition flickering just beneath the surface. The disguise was good, but it wasn't perfect.

"So… Stephine," Veronica said after a moment, "not to pry, but you don't seem like the usual type to hang around naval officers."

Lopez smiled faintly, taking a sip of her drink. "I like good company. And I couldn't let you walk away without your coffee."

"Well, thanks for that. This place… it's the only halfway decent café in the city, but it's not exactly military-friendly." Veronica's tone carried a hint of bitterness.

"Hard times," Lopez said vaguely, steering the conversation. "You stationed here long?"

"Just passing through," Veronica replied, taking a sip of her latte. "You?"

Lopez hesitated, then smiled again. "Passing through as well. But I keep my ear to the ground. A place like this… you hear things."

Veronica tilted her head, her curiosity clearly piqued. "What kind of things?"

Lopez leaned in slightly, lowering her voice. "The kind that could get you in trouble if you're not careful. But you already know that, don't you, Lieutenant?"

Veronica blinked, caught off guard. "I'm not sure I follow."

Lopez placed her cup down carefully, her tone growing more serious. "Let's just say… I know someone who might need to hear what I've learned. Someone you know. Captain Jonathan Pierce."

Veronica stiffened slightly, her eyes narrowing. "How do you know Captain Pierce?"

"That's not important," Lopez said. "What's important is that I've seen the strings being pulled, and you're all walking into a trap. Cipher is here, on the planet. She is already moving the pieces into place."

The name hung in the air like a thunderclap. Veronica's grip on her cup tightened, her knuckles whitening.

"You're sure?" Veronica whispered.

Lopez nodded. "I've seen her. I can't approach your captain directly, but I trust you can get the message to him. Tell him Stephine sent you. He'll understand."

Veronica's expression was a mix of disbelief and concern. "Why not just—"

"Because the walls have ears," Lopez interrupted sharply, glancing around the café. "This is the best I can do without exposing myself further. Can I trust you to deliver the message?"

Veronica nodded. "I'll tell him."

"Good," Lopez said, standing abruptly and adjusting her scarf. "And Lieutenant? Be careful who you trust. Cipher isn't just pulling strings—she is cutting them, too."

With that, she turned and walked away, leaving Veronica sitting at the table, her thoughts swirling with the weight of the conversation.

***

The shuttle descent had been anything but smooth, and the seriousness of what Zoe had done suddenly tore at her soul. She had stolen a shuttle from the Independence—an act of outright treason—and landed it in a forgotten corner of the planet without clearance. It was reckless, dangerous, and borderline suicidal.

But it was necessary.

Standing outside the Four Winds, Zoe adjusted her jacket, the civilian clothes chosen specifically to blend in. The bar's neon sign flickered faintly, casting a soft glow across her face as she stared at the door. The streets were eerily quiet under martial law, and the presence of Military Police checkpoints loomed like specters in the back of her mind. Every step she'd taken to get here had felt like a gamble, every glance over her shoulder a reminder of the countless ways this could all go horribly wrong.

She shoved her hands into her pockets, her fingers brushing the comms device she'd powered down after landing. The shuttle was hidden—well enough, she hoped—but her nerves were fraying. Stealing the shuttle was bad enough. Sneaking off the Independence without clearance was worse. But the real weight pressing down on her was the betrayal.

Captain Tupolev trusted her. The Independence's crew respected her. And yet here she was, standing on a street corner in disguise, about to meet Allison. The guilt churned in her stomach, and she fought the urge to turn around and disappear into the shadows.

But it was too late to back out now.

Taking a deep breath, Zoe pushed the door open, the soft chime of a bell announcing her arrival. The warmth of the bar hit her first, followed by the low hum of conversations and the faint clink of glasses. The place was dimly lit, its rustic decor lending it a welcoming yet unassuming charm.

She stepped inside, scanning the room carefully. The clientele was a mix of civilians and off-duty military personnel, their presence less obvious but unmistakable in the way they carried themselves. Her eyes darted from table to table, searching for Allison.

Nothing.

Zoe could feel the tightness in her throat as she made her way to a corner booth that offered a clear view of the door. She slid into the seat, keeping her back to the wall and her eyes on the entrance.

Her fingers tapped nervously on the table as she tried to steady her breathing. Every passing minute felt like an eternity, thinking through all the ways this could go sideways.

Stealing the shuttle had been a calculated risk. The Independence's crew would realize soon enough that it was missing, but by the time they connected the dots, Zoe hoped she'd already have her answers—or, at the very least, some clarity.

But the shuttle wasn't the real risk. The real risk was why she was here.

Meeting Allison wasn't just a personal gamble. It was a betrayal of everything she'd been taught. Captain Tupolev had treated her as more than just an officer. He'd given her opportunities, believed in her capabilities. And here she was, ready to share information with another Captain's Executive Officer, stepping into the murky waters of treachery and treason.

The door opened, and Zoe's heart leapt—but it wasn't Allison. Just another patron, their laughter filling the room as they joined a group near the bar.

She exhaled slowly, leaning back against the booth. Her nerves were raw, her thoughts tangled in doubt.

"What am I doing?" She thought to herself.

The question echoed in her mind, louder with every second she sat there. She wasn't just risking her career—she was risking her life. If anyone from the Independence realized where she'd gone, if Captain Tupolev found out, if this meeting went south…

The door opened again, and she stiffened, her eyes snapping to the entrance.

Not Allison.

Her hand clenched into a fist under the table, her nails digging into her palm. She needed to stay calm, to wait. This was the only chance she had to get the answers she needed. To figure out whether her gut was right or if she was making the biggest mistake of her life.

But as the minutes ticked by, the doubt only grew. Every shadow in the room seemed to stretch longer, every whisper felt like a judgment passed.

And through it all, the guilt lingered.

Captain Tupolev didn't deserve this.

But if what she suspected was true, if the thread she'd followed led where she thought it might… then she wasn't just betraying her captain. She was trying to save him.

All she could do now was wait.

The door again opened with a quiet chime, and Allison stepped inside. She didn't look like a senior officer—but the way she carried herself gave away her rank to anyone observant enough to notice.

Zoe stiffened in her seat, her breath catching as she raised a hand slightly. Allison spotted her immediately, and the she made her way to the corner booth, sliding into the seat opposite her.

"Zoe," Allison said quietly. "You chose a hell of a place to meet. What's this about?"

Zoe hesitated, her hands resting on the table as she searched for the right words. "I… I don't know where to start."

"How about the part where you snuck onto a planet under martial law?" Allison's tone was sharp, but her eyes softened slightly. "You're taking a hell of a risk meeting me like this. Why?"

Zoe glanced around, ensuring no one was paying attention. Dropping to a near-whisper. "It's Tupolev. He's not himself."

Allison gave a condescending scoff. "I'm sorry Zoe, but the man is insane, what do you mean exactly?"

"You've noticed it, didn't you?" Zoe asked. "The orbital lockdown after Patel's ship exploded. It was too fast, too calculated."

Allison nodded slowly. "I've been saying that since it happened. He locked down the entire system within minutes, like he already had it planned."

Zoe leaned in closer. "Because he did. He had the orders before the explosion. He was waiting for the signal."

Allison's eyes narrowed. "Whose orders?"

Zoe hesitated. Her gaze dropped to the table, as she wrung her hands together, as though struggling to get the words out.

Allison reached out, placing a firm but gentle hand on hers. "Zoe, I'm your friend. I can help you. You just have to tell me."

Zoe swallowed hard, the lump in her throat refusing to budge. Her fingers trembled under Allison's grip. "I need a drink first," she muttered.

Allison released her hand and signaled for a server. Zoe ordered a whiskey—straight. The drink arrived quickly, and she downed it in one swift motion, the burn giving her the courage she needed. She exhaled sharply, the glass clinking softly as she set it down.

"Fifteen days ago," Zoe began, "we got orders to come here to New Earth. We didn't know why at first. When we arrived, a woman came aboard. She brought sealed orders from Admiral Jacobs."

"What kind of orders?" Allison pressed.

Zoe bit her lip again. "To hunt down and arrest an enemy of the state. Codename: Starfire."

Allison tensed.

Zoe continued. "A few days later, your ship showed up. The woman came back aboard with new directives: locate and arrest Starfire and their contact. Naturally, we assumed it was your Captain."

Allison nodded, but said nothing, letting Zoe continue.

"After you arrived," Zoe's voice began to tremble slightly, "we received the orders for the orbital lockdown. We weren't told why, just… 'You will know when.' Then Patel's ship exploded, and Tupolev moved into action like he'd been waiting for it."

"And now?" Allison asked, leaning forward.

Zoe's hands clenched into fists. "Now, Tupolev's called Captain Taylor and his entire carrier group. Word is they'll be here in less than forty-eight hours."

Allison's eyes widened. "Taylor? What for?"

"Reinforcements," Zoe said bitterly. "This woman—Cipher—is pulling Mikail's strings. She's controlling him. I don't know how or why, but it's like he's not even making his own decisions anymore."

The name hung in the air like a thunderclap. Cipher.

Allison's face went pale. "Cipher?"

Zoe nodded. "You've heard of her?"

"More than I'd like," Allison said grimly. She exhaled sharply, running a hand through her hair. "Is she still on board?"

"No," Zoe replied. "She's down here, somewhere. I don't know where."

Allison leaned back in her seat. "This changes everything."

"I don't know what to do," Zoe admitted. "I want to be a good XO, to follow my Captain. But if I don't stop this—if I don't save him—she'll destroy him. She'll destroy all of us."

Allison's expression softened. "You did the right thing coming to me, Zoe. Give me some time to come up with a plan. We'll find a way to fix this. I promise. For now, get back to your ship before anyone notices you are gone. I'll contact you later."

***

The walk back to the shuttle was agony. Zoe kept her head down, her heart pounding with every step. The streets were still mostly empty, the occasional Military Police checkpoint forcing her to take detours down shadowy alleys and abandoned streets. Every corner she turned felt like a gamble, every passerby a potential threat.

Her mind replayed her conversation with Allison. She had taken the first step, but it hadn't eased her nerves. If anything, it had only heightened the tension. Coming clean had been the right choice—she was sure of that—but now, the stakes were higher than ever.

Finally, she reached the hidden industrial lot where she'd stashed the shuttle. The neglected area was quiet, the only sound the faint rustle of the wind through rusting debris. The shuttle sat nestled between stacks of shipping containers, its dark silhouette blending into the shadows. She glanced around, her eyes scanning the area for any sign of movement. Satisfied that she was alone, she climbed the short ladder and entered the craft.

The interior was cramped but functional, the controls and seating standard for an auxiliary shuttle. Zoe exhaled deeply, leaning back against the closed hatch. The familiar hum of the power systems comforted her slightly as she rubbed her temples, trying to force the growing tension from her body.

She didn't notice the silence at first. The faint ambient noises outside—the occasional gust of wind, the distant hum of the city— had faded entirely.

And then she heard it.

"Quite the risk you took, Commander."

The voice was cold, precise, and laced with a quiet malice that sent a shiver down her spine.

Her eyes snapped open, and she turned toward the source of the sound, her breath catching in her throat. The dim lighting inside the shuttle barely illuminated the figure standing near the cockpit—a shadowy outline, just beyond recognition.

"Who—" Zoe started, but she didn't get the chance to finish.

The figure moved faster than she could react. A sharp, blinding pain blossomed at the back of her head, and the world tilted violently.

Her vision blurred, and her knees buckled as darkness closed in around her.

The last thing she heard before she hit the floor was the voice again, colder now, almost a whisper:

"Such a shame."

Chapter 12

The streets were almost empty, save for the faint glow of streetlights and the occasional rumble of a Military Police vehicle. Allison sprinted down the cracked sidewalks of the city, her boots pounding against the ground as she darted around corners and across barren intersections. She hadn't ran like this since her academy track days, and as her muscles burned with each step, her coach's voice echoed in her mind like a ghostly drill instructor.

"Stay on your toes, Jones! Move your arms! Breathe!"

She adjusted her posture instinctively, her arms pumping rhythmically as she inhaled sharply through her nose and exhaled out her mouth. Her pace quickened despite the protests of her legs. The South Tram Station was only a few blocks away, and her watch ticked closer to 2200 with every second.

She'd cut it too close. The meeting with Zoe had taken longer than expected, and now she was racing against time—and suspicion. Starfire wouldn't wait, and she couldn't afford to miss this.

The station came into view as she turned the final corner, its facade dimly lit under martial law restrictions. The usual bustle of commuters was reduced to a trickle of weary travelers and heavily armed Military Police stationed at the entrance. Allison slowed to a brisk walk, wiping the sweat from her brow and forcing her breathing to steady. She didn't have time to draw attention to herself.

As she entered the station, the hidden comm in her ear crackled to life, Major Cruise's voice breaking through the static.

"No activity," He said. "We've had eyes on the locker since we set up. No one's approached it."

Allison didn't respond. She scanned the room as she moved toward the bank of lockers near the east wall. The station's low hum filled the air—announcements over the PA system, the faint clatter of luggage, the subdued murmur of conversation.

Locker 47 was unassuming, its metallic surface dull under the flickering lights. She glanced around once more before kneeling in front of it, her fingers hovering over the keypad.

"Commander, this is reckless," Cruise's voice came again. "You're alone, and we don't know what's waiting for you. Recommend aborting until we have more intel."

Ignoring him, Allison keyed in the PIN: 228539. The locker clicked softly, and she opened it to find a single ticket lying inside, pristine and unmarked except for the departure time and destination.

Her stomach tightened as she read the details:

Departure: 2215

Destination: Blackridge Terminal.

The tram line was a long, winding route that led out of the city and into the industrial outskirts—a place known for its abandoned warehouses and skeletal remains of infrastructure. It wasn't just isolated; it was desolate.

"Commander, this is insane," Cruise said." We should pull back, regroup, and—"

Allison reached up and pulled the comm device from her ear. For a moment, she stared at it, Cruise's voice still coming through faintly, his protests growing more urgent. Without a word, she dropped it to the ground and crushed it under her heel. The faint crunch was oddly satisfying as the line went silent.

The tram platform was almost empty, the quiet broken only by the faint hum of the arriving train. Allison stepped aboard, clutching the ticket in her hand, and made her way to an empty seat near the middle of the car. The automated doors hissed shut behind her, and the tram jolted to life, gliding out of the station with a smooth, almost eerie efficiency.

She glanced around the car. There were only a handful of passengers—none of them remarkable. A man in a faded coat stared out the window. A woman further down flipped through a tattered magazine. Two teenagers sat near the rear, their hushed conversation punctuated by stifled laughter.

Allison's fingers tightened around the ticket. Her instincts screamed that this wasn't just a test or an invitation—it was a calculated move by someone who knew how to manipulate the board. Starfire, or whoever had left the ticket, wanted her out of the city and alone.

The lights of the city faded as the tram picked up speed, plunging into the darkness of the industrial zone. The windows reflected her face—calm on the surface, but her eyes betrayed the storm brewing within. The faint hum of the tram's motor was the only sound as they left civilization behind.

Blackridge Terminal was the final stop. She would arrive in twenty minutes, and what waited for her there was anyone's guess. Allison adjusted her jacket, her fingers brushing the concealed sidearm holstered against her ribcage. Whatever was coming, she would be ready for it.

Or so she told herself.

****

Zoe's head throbbed as she blinked awake, the dim light above her casting the grimy walls in an oppressive yellow glow. The air smelled of mildew and something metallic, her mouth dry and tasting faintly of copper. She shifted, realizing she was lying on a cot barely wide enough to support her. Her arms felt heavy, her body sore. The dingy cell around her was claustrophobic, the walls streaked with filth and neglect.

Across the narrow corridor, a voice rasped out of the darkness.

"Oh, you're finally awake."

The voice was female, hoarse and carrying a note of dry amusement. Zoe sat up slowly, her head pounding as she searched for the source. Across from her, through the bars, she saw a figure slouched against the wall of another cell. The woman was disheveled, her hair matted, her face smudged with dirt.

"Where are we?" Zoe asked.

The woman shrugged, the movement slow and weak. "Wish I knew. Been here long enough to stop asking."

Zoe's head started to hurt less, and she pushed herself to her feet, stumbling to the bars. She gripped them tightly. "Guards!" she yelled, her voice echoing down the corridor. "Someone tell me what's going on!"

The woman laughed, a hollow, bitter sound. "You can yell all you want. They don't care. No one's coming."

"This is insane!" Zoe continued the scream. "I've done nothing wrong! I am a Naval Officer you can't hold me like this."

The woman leaned her head back against the wall, her eyes half-lidded. "This isn't a place for criminals. It's a place for people who needed to be… out of the way."

The words hit Zoe hard. Her hands began trembling as she clung to the bars. "I don't belong here," she muttered, more to herself than to the stranger.

The woman snorted softly. "Neither do I. Guess we're both in in the same boat." The woman began to laugh, "get it, boat?"

Zoe stared at the woman as the hollow laughter filled the air. It was a laugh that didn't belong to someone who found anything funny—it was the sound of someone who had long since stopped hoping for anything better.

"Really?" Zoe said. "That's your idea of humor?"

The woman's laughter slowed, tapering off into a dry chuckle. "You don't like it? Figured it might lighten the mood." She shrugged weakly, her shoulders barely lifting. "Sorry Captain, it's been a while since I had anyone to practice on."

Zoe's grip tightened on the bars as the woman's laughter faded into a dry chuckle. "It's Commander, actually."

The woman raised an eyebrow, a faint smirk tugging at the corners of her cracked lips. "Commander, huh?" She sat up slightly, her movements sluggish but deliberate. Raising a hand in a mock salute, she added with exaggerated formality, "Sorry, sir! Commander, sir!"

Zoe exhaled sharply, her frustration rushing to the surface. "You think this is funny?"

The woman dropped her hand and leaned back against the wall again, her smirk fading into something more hollow. "Not really," she said quietly. "But I don't know what else to do. Crying gets old, you know? And the only company I've had for the last eighteen months is my own damn shadow. You start to finding humor in the dumbest things."

Zoe's expression softened, though she didn't let go of her irritation entirely. "Eighteen months?"

The woman nodded slowly, her head tilting back against the wall. "Yeah. Give or take. Lost track of the days after the first few weeks. Doesn't really matter, though. Time doesn't mean much in here."

Zoe swallowed hard as she let go of the bars and sank back onto her cot, her hands resting on her knees as she tried to steady her breathing.

"What's your name?" Zoe asked.

"Ava," the woman said. "Ava Turing."

The name hit Zoe like a jolt of, her head snapping up to look at the woman more closely. "Wait… the Ava Turing? Founder of Neura Tech?"

Ava let out another dry laugh, but there was no humor in it. "Used to be," she said bitterly. "Not much of a CEO these days, huh?"

Zoe's stared at Ava, recognition now clear in the lines of her face beneath the grime. But how could that be? Ava Turing was a public figure, one of the most brilliant minds of the century.

"This doesn't make sense," Zoe said, shaking her head. "I just saw you on a press conference announcing Athena's integration into the fleet."

Ava's eyes snapped open. "Athena?"

"Yeah," Zoe said. "Just a few days ago. You stood at a podium and—"

"That wasn't me," Ava interrupted, the smirk returning faintly. "So, Commander, sir, you want to tell me how someone as shiny as you ended up in a place like this? Or should I just guess?"

Zoe didn't respond immediately. She let out a soft sigh and muttered, "I don't know yet."

Ava's laugh came again, softer this time, almost pitying. "Well, you'll have plenty of time to figure it out."

The Blackridge Terminal was as desolate as Allison had expected. The tram hissed to a stop, its doors sliding open with a low mechanical whine. She stepped off onto the platform, the sound of her boots echoing in the cavernous, empty station. The air was heavy with the scent of oil and damp concrete, and the faint hum of fluorescent lights created an oppressive background noise.

She glanced around, scanning the shadows for any sign of movement. Starfire wasn't here—not that she'd expected them to be. But they'd left something for her, and she needed to find it before anyone else did.

Her eyes drifted to a row of storage lockers along the far wall, the steel doors scuffed and streaked with grime. Starfire's message had led her here. If there was anything to find, it would be in one of those lockers.

Moving quickly but cautiously, Allison approached the lockers. She crouched in front of the numbered doors, her fingers brushing over the cool metal as she checked each one. Locker 22. Locker 34. Locker 47.

Her pulse quickened as she spotted the small slip of paper tucked into the handle of locker 47. It was folded tightly, almost blending into the shadows. She pulled it free and unfolded it, revealing a single line of text:

Locker 91.

Allison straightened, her head looking toward the far end of the wall. She spotted the number, the locker sitting slightly apart from the others, its door dented as though it had been kicked or struck. Her boots thudded softly against the floor as she crossed to it.

The combination Starfire had given her earlier flashed in her mind. She keyed it into the lock, and with a faint click, the door creaked open.

Inside were two neatly bound dossiers. She grabbed them both, her hands trembling slightly as she flipped through the first.

The pages were filled with documents, scanned and annotated in meticulous detail. Military correspondence, financial logs, and coded messages—all connecting Admiral Jacobs to Cipher. Each piece of evidence painted a grim picture: a high-ranking officer manipulating events behind the scenes with Cipher as his enforcer.

She panicked slightly as she realized the implications. Admiral Jacobs wasn't just complicit; he was orchestrating something far larger than she had anticipated.

Allison swallowed hard and set the first dossier aside, and opening the second.

Her heart stopped as she opened it.

The pages were filled with personal logs. The name at the top of the first page made her throat tighten: Commander Lisa Salvador.

Allison's vision blurred as she scanned the logs. Lisa's words were raw and fragmented, detailing her spiraling mental state aboard the Freedom. The entries were addressed to someone— Zarina. Allison's stomach churned as the pieces clicked together. Remember what Veronica said after returning from the nightmare aboard the Jovian Freighter, that Cipher's real name was Zarina.

"No," Allison whispered. "It can't be…"

The logs revealed the grim truth of Lisa's final days, her growing paranoia and detachment, her sense of betrayal, and her desperate hope to reach Zarina despite knowing the risks. The last entries were barely coherent, trailing off into a raw mix of despair and longing.

Her hands trembled as she turned the last page and found a note tucked into the back of the dossier.

"There is more to follow. This is only the tip.
--Starfire"

Allison stared at the words, her mind reeling. Lisa, Admiral Jacobs, Cipher—Zarina. The web was larger than she had imagined, and she was caught in the middle of it.

The sound of boots on concrete snapped her back to reality. She turned her head sharply, her heart pounding as she saw the Military Police officer walking toward her, his flashlight cutting through the dim station.

"You there!" he barked, his voice echoing off the walls. "Stay where you are! Produce your papers!"

Allison froze, the dossiers clutched tightly in her hands. She was violating curfew, standing in an abandoned terminal with no explanation. Panic surged through her, her mind racing.

For reasons she couldn't explain—not then, at least—her body moved before her brain caught up. She turned on her heel and ran.

"Stop!" the officer shouted. "Stop or I'll fire!"

Allison's lungs burned as she sprinted down the darkened corridors of Blackridge Terminal, her boots echoing against the concrete floor. The shouts of the Military Police officer were growing louder, his flashlight cutting through the gloom, its beam swinging wildly in search of her.

"Stop right now!" he barked.

She darted around a corner, her breath coming in ragged gasps as she clutched the dossiers tightly against her chest. Panic swelled, but she forced herself to focus. She needed a plan, a way to lose him before reinforcements arrived.

The beam of light caught the edge of her shadow, and her heart leapt into her throat. He was close—too close. Her leg muscles locking up as she pushed herself harder, weaving through the maze of dimly lit corridors.

Just as she rounded another corner, a hand shot out from the shadows and grabbed her arm. Another clamped over her mouth before she could scream.

Her vision blurred with panic as she struggled, but the person pulled her deeper into the darkness of a side corridor. A suppressed sidearm came into view, the matte black barrel aimed toward the opening she had just run through.

"Shh," the figure whispered.

Allison froze, her heart hammering in her chest as she watched the figure aim, waiting.

The officer's footsteps echoed louder, his flashlight beam sweeping through the corridor as he approached. The light cut across the side corridor for a moment, and Allison's stomach churned as she saw him pause, moving his hand toward his radio.

Before he could utter a word, the figure fired.

The suppressed round was barely more than a muffled pop, but the officer staggered, his flashlight clattering to the ground as he crumpled to his knees and then fell face-first onto the concrete.

"Help me," the voice whispered.

Allison snapped into action, grabbing the officer's arms as the figure took his legs. Together, they hauled the limp body deeper into the shadows, their movements hurried but precise. The figure yanked open a maintenance tunnel hatch, and they stuffed the body inside, leaving him concealed in the pitch-black confines.

When they were finished, the figure grabbed her arm again, pulling her further into the labyrinthine depths of the terminal. Allison didn't resist, her mind still racing from the shock of what had just happened.

They stopped in an abandoned storage room, the faint hum of electrical equipment providing a low, constant background noise. The figure turned toward her, lowering their hood to reveal a familiar face.

"Major?" Allison blurted.

Cruise grinned, sliding the sidearm back into its holster.

Allison stared at him. "What the hell are you doing here?"

"Keeping you from getting yourself arrested—or worse," Cruise said. "I told you this was a bad idea."

Allison glared at him, frustration building inside her. "You followed me?"

"Of course I did," he replied, crossing his arms. "When you crushed the comms, I figured you were going to do something reckless. Looks like I was right. Again."

She opened her mouth to argue but closed it again, realizing she didn't have a leg to stand on. Finally, she sighed, running a hand through her hair. "Thanks… for the assist."

Cruise nodded. "Next time, Commander, maybe don't make it so easy for me to be right."

Allison let out a faint laugh despite herself, the tension easing just enough for her to catch her breath. She still clutched the dossiers tightly..

"What's in those?" Cruise asked, nodding toward the folders.

"More than enough to make sure this mission gets a hell of a lot more complicated," Allison muttered grimly.

Cruise raised an eyebrow but didn't press further. "Then let's make sure you don't lose them. We need to get you back."

Allison nodded, and together they slipped back into the shadows, navigating the labyrinth of the terminal with quiet precision. For now, she was safe—but she knew the questions she needed to answer would only grow more urgent.

Memories V

The abandoned parking garage has become our temporary holding until I can get a new safe house from my handler. No cameras, no unwanted visitors—just space and time to train. Traci and I had already been here for a while, our usual rhythm of training falling into place.

She was at her makeshift station, the target stand—a salvaged piece of sheet metal—about thirty feet away, with smaller pieces of reflective tape marking critical zones. She was focused and determined, though she still fidgeted slightly with the sidearm in her hands. It was endearing, in a way.

"Relax your grip a little," I said, watching as her fingers tensed around the handle of the pistol. "You're holding it like it's about to bite you."

She let out a small laugh, adjusting her hold. "Feels like it might, honestly."

"It won't," I assured her. "But a tight grip will throw off your aim. Trust me, your hands will thank you later."

She nodded, taking a breath before raising the sidearm again. The sharp crack of the shot echoed through the empty structure, and the sound of metal ringing signaled a hit. I stepped closer, inspecting her work. A solid mark, just a few inches off center.

"Not bad," I said, giving her a small nod. "But let's get that grouping tighter."

Traci lowered the pistol, shaking out her hands. "I didn't think it'd be this… technical."

"Shooting isn't just point-and-click," I replied. "Every little detail matters. Posture, grip, breathing, even how you think about the shot."

I stepped behind her, adjusting her stance slightly. "Square your shoulders a bit more. Don't lean too far forward. You want balance."

She followed my instructions, raising the pistol once more. The next shot rang out, and this time, the impact was closer to the center of the target. A smile broke across her face, and I couldn't help but feel a swell of pride.

"That's more like it," I said. "Now keep that form consistent."

We continued for a while, each shot bringing incremental improvements. By the time she emptied the magazine, her hits were landing consistently within the taped zones. She set the pistol down, stretching her arms with a triumphant grin.

"I think I'm getting the hang of it," she said, a mix of relief and excitement in her voice.

"You are," I replied, picking up the giant silver case that sat nearby. "But now it's time to graduate to something a little more advanced."

Her eyes widened as I placed the case on the ground and popped the latches. Inside, the Silentia-Mk3 rested in its foam-lined cradle, sleek and imposing.

"Whoa," Traci breathed, kneeling beside me. "That looks intense."

"It is," I said, lifting the rifle with care. "This isn't just a weapon. It's a precision tool."

I guided her through its features: the magazine slot, the power cell in the grip, the variable velocity dial, and the AI-enhanced optics. She listened intently, her fingers brushing against the rifle's surface as if she were absorbing every detail by touch alone.

"Think you're ready to try it?" I asked.

She hesitated, then nodded. "As long as you're guiding me."

"Always," I said, laying the rifle down and motioning for her to take position. "We're going to start with something challenging but achievable."

I pointed toward the distant tree, its branches heavy with large, ripe fruits. "See those? About 1,600 yards out."

Traci squinted through the scope, adjusting slightly. "Got it."

"Pick a fruit and take your time," I instructed. "Remember what you've learned—steady breathing, gentle pressure on the trigger. Let the rifle do its part, but the shot is yours."

The rifle hummed softly as she powered it on, the AI optics displaying wind and distance calculations in real time. She steadied herself, exhaling slowly as she pulled the trigger. The fruit exploded in a spray of juice and pulp, and her laugh of astonishment filled the garage.

"I can't believe I actually hit that," she said, lowering the rifle.

"Believe it," I replied. "That wasn't just the rifle. That was you."

She turned to me, her excitement tempered by curiosity. "But the AI… it did most of the work, right?"

I shook my head. "The AI assists. It calculates and stabilizes, but it doesn't make the shot. You aimed, you controlled the trigger, you made it happen. I've seen people with this same rifle miss for weeks before hitting a target like that."

Her confidence grew visibly as she adjusted her position, readying for another shot. I watched her, a mix of pride and something deeper welling up inside me. She wasn't just learning— she was thriving. In this moment, the chaos outside the garage felt distant, almost manageable.

"Alright," I said, stepping back to give her room. "Let's see if you can do it again."

Traci grinned, her determination shining through. As she lined up the next shot. She fired again, her hits becoming more consistent with each shot. The targets weren't just getting hit; they were obliterated with precision that made me wonder how much she had been holding back. By the time she went through three magazines, her confidence was undeniable, and so was her grin.

"Alright, hotshot," I said, cutting her celebration short. "Time to pack up."

Just then, my comms device buzzed against my hip. I stepped away to answer, the display casting a faint glow in the dim garage. The message was brief:

New safe house established. Requested materials on site. Continue mission.

"Change of plans," I said, turning back to Traci. "We've got a new place to set up."

She nodded, quickly disassembling the rifle with an efficiency that told me she had been paying attention during every lesson. We loaded the gear into the van and headed out, leaving the echoing silence of the parking garage behind.

The new safe house was a nondescript hotel on the edge of town, the kind of place that catered to travelers who didn't want to be noticed. We carried our gear up the creaky stairs to the assigned room. Inside, the curtains were already drawn, and the faint smell of bleach hung in the air. A silver case identical to mine sat on the bed.

Traci froze, her eyes flicking from the case to me. "Is that...?"

"Open it," I said, nodding toward the bed.

She approached cautiously, her fingers hesitating on the latches before popping them open. Inside was a pristine Silentia-Mk3, along with two Sagitta sidearms and neatly packed magazines. Her breath hitched as she looked up at me.

"I'll be taking mine back now," I said, crossing my arms and giving her a faint smirk.

Traci laughed softly, shaking her head as she inspected the weapons. Once she was done, I grabbed a set of keys from the nightstand and tossed them to her. She caught them, her brow furrowing in confusion.

"Those are for your R-1300," I said. "It's parked downstairs."

Her eyes widened. "You're kidding."

"I don't kid about gear," I replied. "The van's shared, but you'll only need it when we relocate or for a mission. The bike's yours."

Traci stared at the keys, then back at me, a mix of disbelief and excitement playing across her face. "This just got a whole lot more interesting."

"It's about to," I said, gesturing toward the door. "Unload my bike and park it next to yours. we will want them ready when the time comes."

Her eyes widened further, but she nodded quickly, already moving toward the door. "On it."

Several minutes later, Traci came back upstairs, a faint sheen of sweat on her brow. I reached over to the nightstand and picked up a sleek black comms device, handing it to her. "Here, your final piece of kit."

She turned it over in her hands, her curiosity piqued. "What's on it?"

"Open it and see," I said, crossing my arms as I leaned back against the wall.

Traci powered it on, and the welcome message flashed across the screen:

"Welcome, Operative Traci Yamato. Mission parameters will follow. Trust your instincts and trust your team."

Her eyes darted back to me, a mix of excitement and gravity settling over her expression. "Operative?" she asked, almost whispering.

I nodded. "You've earned it. Now let's see what you can do."

***

I stepped out of the bathroom, a wave of steam following me as I grabbed a towel to dry my face. It felt like such a simple luxury—a real shower, clean water, a locked door. "God, I forgot how good this feels," I said, tossing the towel onto the back of a chair. I ran my fingers through my damp hair and sat on the edge of the bed, letting the moment linger.

"Lucy?" Traci's voice pulled me back. She stood leaning against the wall, her comms device in her hands, turning it over as though it might give her answers. "Can I ask you something?"

"Shoot," I said, looking up at her.

She hesitated, like she wasn't sure if this was the right moment. Finally, she let out a small sigh. "How did you get into all this? I mean, you're obviously good at it, but... this can't be easy."

I leaned back slightly, crossing my arms as I considered her question. "Good at it? That's generous," I said with a faint smirk, but my tone shifted as I went on. "But no, it's not easy. Never has been."

Her eyes stayed on me. I let out a quiet breath and continued. "I've been training for most of my career for something like this, but this is only my second mission."

Her eyebrows shot up. "Seriously? You've got to be kidding me. You… you act like you've been doing this forever."

"Preparation goes a long way," I said, nodding my head. "It's not about faking confidence. It's about knowing your limits, understanding what you're stepping into, and making sure you're ready. My first mission, though…" I trailed off, my gaze drifting to the window. "That was a rough one."

Traci shifted, leaning forward slightly. "What happened?"

"We were sent to intercept a high-value target. It should've been clean—quick extraction," I said, my voice dropping as the memory crept back in. "But the intel was off. We didn't have the whole picture, and complications piled on fast." I paused, my hands clasping tightly. "I made it out, but not everyone did. I learned the hard way that mistakes in this job don't just cost time or money. They cost lives."

Her expression softened. "I'm sorry. That sounds… awful."

"It was," I admitted. "But you don't get to carry that with you. You learn, you adapt, and you do better next time. You have to, or you won't last."

Traci glanced down at the device in her hands again, turning it absently. "Do you think I can handle this?"

I leaned forward, meeting her gaze with as much certainty as I could muster. "Traci, you're already handling it. You've got instincts, and they're good ones. Better than mine when I started."

Her lips curled into a small, uncertain smile. "You really think so?"

"I know so," I said. "You've got what it takes. You just need to trust yourself the way I trust you. And if you ever feel like you're in over your head, you come to me. That's what we do—we're a team."

Her smile grew a little stronger, and she gave a small nod. "Thanks, Lucy. That means a lot."

I leaned back, crossing my arms and letting the silence settle between us for a moment. Before I could say anything else, Traci glanced around the room, her gaze settling on the single bed.

"Uh, there's only one bed," she pointed out, looking back at me with a raised eyebrow.

I smirked, tilting my head toward the bed. "Don't worry, I don't bite." Then, just for effect, I winked.

Traci rolled her eyes but laughed, the tension in the room easing. "Sure, Lucy. Whatever you say."

"It'll be fine," I said, getting up to grab my gear from the corner. "And besides, tomorrow's another step forward. We'll need our rest.""

***

It was sometime in the middle of the night when I woke up with a start, my heart racing and my breathing shallow. The room was quiet, but the silence felt oppressive, as if it carried the weight of memories I'd rather forget. Traci's earlier question had pulled up things I'd worked hard to bury—faces, names, failures. I swung my legs over the side of the bed, careful not to disturb her, and stood.

The faint light from the twin moons outside painted the room in soft silver hues. I walked to the window, pressing a hand against the cool glass. The double moons hung low in the sky, their soft glow illuminating the deserted streets below. It was beautiful in a way, but the stillness out there only reminded me of the chaos I'd seen, the lives I'd failed to protect.

Minutes passed. My breathing slowed, but my mind refused to settle. I crossed my arms, leaning against the window frame as the memories replayed in my head, each one sharper than the last. I hated this part—when the quiet of the night became a canvas for my mistakes.

A soft rustle behind me broke my thoughts. I turned slightly, catching movement from the bed. Traci stirred, shifting in her sleep before her hand reached out to the side where I had been. Her eyes fluttered open, and she blinked groggily.

"Lucy?" she murmured. "What are you doing up?"

I turned back to the window. "Couldn't sleep. Just needed some air."

She sat up, rubbing at her eyes. "Nightmares?"

I didn't answer right away. Instead, I watched as a thin cloud passed in front of the smaller moon, casting fleeting shadows across the ground. Finally, I nodded. "Yeah. Something like that."

Traci shifted, swinging her legs over the side of the bed. "You want to talk about it?"

I glanced over my shoulder, meeting her eyes briefly before looking back at the moons. "Not much to talk about. Just old memories. You reminded me of a few things earlier—nothing I haven't dealt with before."

Her expression softened, but she didn't push. Instead, she stood and padded over to join me at the window. A few moments passed in silence, the only sounds being the faint hum of the world outside and the occasional creak of the old hotel. Suddenly, I felt her arms wrap around me from behind, tentative at first, then more certain as she rested her cheek against my shoulder. The warmth of her embrace caught me off guard, but it was grounding in a way I didn't expect.

"You've got this, Lucy," she said quietly. "Whatever's in your head right now, you'll face it. You're stronger than you think."

I didn't respond right away, just let the moment settle. Her presence was a reminder that, even in the worst moments, I wasn't alone. The warmth of her arms around me, the steady weight of her cheek against my shoulder, it all grounded me in a way I hadn't realized I needed. Memories of our recent time together flickered through my mind—her determination during training, her laugh echoing in the garage, her quiet confidence growing stronger every day. It was hard to reconcile the raw, unpolished recruit she'd been with the person standing here now, offering me comfort without hesitation.

My chest felt tight, but not from pain this time. It was something else—a quiet yearning I hadn't let myself acknowledge. Slowly, I turned around, her arms slipping away just enough to let me face her. She looked up at me, her eyes soft and filled with concern.

Before I could stop myself, I leaned in and pressed a gentle kiss to her lips. It was brief, tentative, and when I pulled back, her wide-eyed expression stopped me cold.

"I… I'm sorry," I stammered, embarrassment flooding me as I stepped back. My pulse raced, and I could already feel the heat rising to my cheeks. "I shouldn't have… I'll just…" I turned, moving toward the door, desperate to escape the awkwardness I'd just created.

"Lucy, wait!" Traci's voice stopped me in my tracks. I turned back, my hand hovering near the door handle. She took a step closer, her expression shifting from shock to something gentler. "It's fine," she said. "I was just… surprised, that's all."

Her words hung in the air, and for a moment, I didn't know what to say. I searched her face for any sign of discomfort, but all I found was sincerity.

"You mean that?" I asked cautiously.

She nodded, a faint smile playing at her lips. "Yeah, I do."

I hesitated, still unsure if I'd crossed a line. "I didn't mean to make things weird," I said softly, shifting my weight from one foot to the other.

Traci reached out, her hand brushing lightly against mine. "You didn't," she reassured me. "I was just caught off guard, that's all." She paused, her gaze searching mine. "You don't have to run away from this, Lucy."

Her words stopped the swirling embarrassment in my chest, replacing it with something quieter, calmer. I gave a small nod and let out a breath I hadn't realized I was holding. "Okay," I said softly.

For a moment, we just stood there, the room wrapped in a stillness that felt more comforting than tense. Traci's hand lingered on mine before she gave it a gentle squeeze and stepped back. "Let's just take it one step at a time, yeah?" she said, her smile growing a little wider.

"Yeah," I replied, a faint smile tugging at my own lips. "One step at a time."

Chapter 13

The command center of Jump Gate 003 was abuzz with activity. Engineers, technicians, and naval officers moved about with purpose, each focused on their assigned tasks. Ava stood near the main terminal, eyes glued to the tablet in her hand. The room hummed with the sound of overlapping conversations, punctuated by the occasional chime of alerts from the various systems under review.

Ava's fingers darted across the tablet. A mix of concentration and mild irritation in her demeanor as she looked up and pointed toward a group of technicians near the central data hub.

"No, no, no," she called out. "That connection needs to be routed through the secondary node. If you bypass the failsafe protocols, Athena's response time could lag. Fix it."

The technicians exchanged nervous glances before scrambling to correct their error. Ava shook her head slightly, muttering to herself.

Behind her, the Gate Commander, a grizzled naval captain named Eli Grayson, watched the spectacle with a scowl. Dressed in his crisp uniform, he radiated an air of authority that seemed increasingly strained by the chaos around him.

"This circus," he muttered under his breath, arms crossed tightly over his chest. "On my gate."

Ava, overhearing, turned slightly but didn't address him directly. Instead, her attention snapped back to her tablet as another alert drew her focus. She marched over to a nearby console, where a junior officer appeared frozen with indecision.

"What's the hold-up?" Ava demanded.

"The redundant memory core diagnostics are reporting a conflict," the officer stammered.

Ava leaned over the console, her fingers flying across the controls. Within moments, she isolated the issue and straightened. "There. Recalibrate the input frequency to synchronize with the core's backup cycle. Do it now."

The officer nodded quickly and got to work. Ava sighed, stepping back and glancing at her tablet again. The Gate

Commander took the opportunity to approach, his discontent evident in the way his boots struck the floor with each step.

"Ms. Turing," he began, "while I appreciate the importance of your work, I must remind you that this is a naval installation, not some corporate testing ground."

Ava didn't look up. "I'm well aware, Captain Grayson. That's why your team is assisting in the integration of Athena. It's not just a corporate initiative; it's an advancement for everyone who relies on these gates."

"And yet it feels like my personnel are just extras in your little production," he shot back.

Ava finally looked up. "Athena's systems will make your gate more efficient, more secure, and more reliable. If that's a circus, Captain, then I suggest you enjoy the show."

Grayson opened his mouth to respond, but a sudden alert interrupted him. Ava's tablet chimed, and a notification displayed the final checklist for Athena's core integration. Her demeanor shifted, the tension between her and Grayson fading into the background as she stepped toward the central console.

"Final checks," she announced loudly. "Core diagnostics green. Backup power supplies stable. Redundant memory core synced and operational." She glanced at Grayson. "Captain, we're ready to bring her online."

Grayson gave a reluctant nod, stepping back to observe. Ava tapped a few commands on her tablet, and the room seemed to hold its collective breath as the central display lit up with a soft blue glow. A moment later, a calm, melodic voice filled the command center.

"Greetings," it said, smooth and articulate. "I am the Augmented Technology for Human Enhancement and Natural Applications. You may call me Athena. To whom do I serve?"

Ava allowed herself a small smile and gestured toward Captain Grayson. "Captain, I believe introductions are in order."

Grayson hesitated for a moment before stepping forward, his posture rigid. "Captain Eli Grayson, commanding officer of Jump Gate 003."

Athena responded immediately, her tone polite but precise. "Greetings, Captain Eli Grayson, commanding officer of Jump Gate 003. How may I assist you today?"

Grayson's eyebrows rose slightly at the formality, looking over to Ava.

"Athena will always address people with full name and title, unless instructed otherwise." Ava said.

"Athena, you may refer to me as Captain Grayson."

"Acknowledged, Captain Grayson," Athena replied smoothly.

Ava tapped a few commands on her tablet, pulling up a series of overlays on the central display. "Now that the formalities are out of the way, Captain, let me walk you through Athena's command functions. There are three primary interfaces you'll need to familiarize yourself with."

She gestured toward the main console. "First, the Tactical Command Interface. This is where Athena will assist with monitoring gate traffic, security protocols, and emergency response coordination. Real-time data feeds will display here, and Athena will notify you of any anomalies before escalating action."

Grayson folded his arms, his eyes narrowing slightly. "So she'll flag potential issues, but the decision-making remains with me?"

"Exactly," Ava said with a nod. "Athena is designed to support, not override. She'll offer recommendations based on predictive analytics, but you'll always have the final say."

Turning to another screen, Ava continued. "Second, the Operations Management Module. This covers resource allocation, maintenance scheduling, and personnel deployment. Athena can optimize efficiency across the board, but again, you approve any changes she suggests."

Grayson grunted as he processed the information.

"And finally," Ava said, stepping to a smaller terminal near the center of the room, "the Emergency Protocol Override. In the event of a critical system failure or hostile threat, Athena can take over automated systems to maintain the gate's integrity. This function requires dual authorization—yours and the XO's—to activate."

Grayson's gaze hardened. "And what happens if one of us isn't available?"

"Then Athena remains in advisory mode only," Ava replied firmly. "No overrides without dual consent. That's a safeguard built into her core programming."

Grayson nodded slowly, his posture relaxing slightly. "Alright, Ms. Turing. Let's see if this 'advancement' of yours lives up to the promise."

"It will," Ava said confidently, glancing back at Athena's glowing interface. "Athena, run a systems-wide diagnostic and report status."

"Running diagnostic," Athena replied. A few seconds passed before she continued. "All systems operational. No anomalies detected. Gate functionality is at 99.87% efficiency."

Ava turned back to Grayson, a hint of satisfaction in her expression. "And that, Captain, is just the beginning."

Grayson gave her a sideways glance but said nothing, the hum of Athena's systems filling the room as the AI awaited further input.

Captain Grayson folded his arms. "Ms. Turing, if Athena is as capable as you say, let's put her through her paces. I want to see her in action."

Ava raised an eyebrow, a faint smirk tugging at her lips. "Very well, Captain. What do you have in mind?"

"Let's start with routine gate operations," Grayson said, turning toward the main console. "I want to see how she handles standard traffic management, including an increase in traffic density. Then we'll escalate to tactical drills."

"Understood," Ava replied, gesturing to the central console. "Athena, prepare a simulation of routine gate operations with a 30% increase in traffic density."

"Preparing simulation," Athena responded. A moment later, the displays lit up, showing a virtual representation of Jump Gate 003's traffic lanes. Dozens of simulated ships moved through the gate's network, each one tagged with identification codes, trajectories, and cargo information.

"Traffic density increased by 30%," Athena reported. "All lanes are currently operating within acceptable parameters."

Grayson watched closely as the simulation ran. The system flagged potential bottlenecks and rerouted ships preemptively,

Athena's voice providing clear, concise updates. "Priority vessel detected. Adjusting trajectory to expedite transit."

"Efficient," Grayson muttered, though his tone suggested reluctant approval. "But that's just traffic. Let's see how she handles a real challenge."

"Athena, initiate tactical simulation Alpha-One," Ava commanded. "Simulate a hostile incursion targeting Jump Gate 003."

"Initiating tactical simulation Alpha-One," Athena replied. The displays shifted, replacing the traffic lanes with a virtual battlefield. Red blips appeared on the screen, representing incoming hostiles. Blue icons signified the gate's defensive assets—drones, automated turrets, and stationed patrol ships.

"Hostile incursion detected," Athena announced. "Deploying defensive measures. Automated turrets are online. Patrol vessels are intercepting targets. Calculating optimal firing solutions."

The simulation unfolded with precision. Athena coordinated the defense seamlessly, prioritizing threats and reallocating resources as needed. A drone squadron was dispatched to flank a group of simulated attackers, while the automated turrets focused on larger, slower-moving targets.

"Threat neutralized," Athena reported after several tense minutes. "Jump Gate 003 remains operational. Minimal damage sustained."

Grayson leaned forward, studying the data on the screen. "Not bad. But what about a multi-vector attack?"

"Athena, escalate to tactical simulation Beta-Two," Ava instructed.

"Escalating to tactical simulation Beta-Two," Athena replied. The displays updated again, this time showing a more complex scenario with multiple waves of incoming hostiles attacking from different angles. The system adjusted dynamically, redistributing defensive resources and issuing precise commands to simulated personnel.

Grayson's eyes narrowed as he watched the chaos unfold, Athena's voice cutting through the noise with steady updates. "Wave one neutralized. Redirecting assets to counter wave two. Calculating optimal positions for automated turrets."

When the final wave was defeated, Grayson stepped back, nodding slowly. "Impressive. She's efficient, I'll give her that."

Ava crossed her arms, her smirk returning. "Told you she'd live up to the promise."

Grayson turned to face her, still reserved but less combative. "We'll see how she performs under real conditions. For now, she's passed the first test."

Before the room could settle into a sense of accomplishment, the gate comms officer abruptly stood up.

"Captain, we're receiving flash traffic," the officer began, but before he could continue, Athena's voice cut in, calm and clear.

"Incoming priority traffic," Athena announced. "Military asset detected. Carrier Group Bravo, Captain Malcolm Taylor commanding. Gate passage approved by Fleet Admiral Aaron Jacobs."

Ava's eyes flicked to Grayson, who straightened immediately.

"Athena," Grayson said sharply, "begin gate power-up procedures. Confirm readiness for carrier group transit."

"Gate power-up procedures initiated," Athena replied. The displays lit up with diagnostic reports, each system coming online in perfect sequence.

"Core systems operational. Power levels at 97%. Stabilizing jump field. ETA for gate readiness: three minutes," Athena continued.

Ava stepped forward, tablet at the ready. "Athena, coordinate with Carrier Group Bravo's command vessel for secure handoff and ensure priority alignment in traffic lanes."

"Coordination established. Adjusting traffic lanes to accommodate Carrier Group Bravo. Handoff protocol active," Athena confirmed.

The hum of the gate's systems grew louder as energy surged through its conduits. The massive structure vibrated faintly as the jump field began to stabilize, casting a faint blue glow across the command center.

"Carrier Group Bravo has entered the approach vector," Athena reported. "Communicating with New Earth Traffic Control for clearance and orbital parameters."

Grayson watched intently, his hands clasped behind his back. "Athena, ensure all traffic adjustments are relayed to the command vessel in real time."

"Affirmative," Athena replied. "New Earth Traffic Control clearance received. Orbital parameters synchronized. Relaying data to Carrier Group Bravo command vessel."

The central display updated, showing the precise path for the carrier group as it neared the gate. The first ship emerged from the jump field, a massive silhouette against the backdrop of space. Its identification tags lit up on the screen: Resolute, flagship of Carrier Group Bravo.

"Carrier Resolute has arrived," Athena announced. "Taxiing instructions relayed. Remaining vessels will follow sequentially."

Grayson exhaled, his stance relaxing slightly. "Textbook execution," he muttered.

Ava smiled faintly, her eyes fixed on the screen. "Told you she was ready for real conditions."

As the Resolute cleared the jump field, the next ship emerged. A sleek, angular heavy cruiser followed, its hull bristling with weapons arrays and reinforced armor plating. Identification tags labeled it as the Valiant.

"Second ship identified: Valiant, heavy cruiser," Athena announced. "Entering orbit under standard escort formation."

The Valiant drifted into position beside the flagship, its engines flaring briefly as it adjusted course. Moments later, the Indomitable, another heavy cruiser, appeared, its size and bulk nearly matching the carrier.

"Third ship identified: Indomitable, heavy cruiser," Athena said. "Syncing orbital trajectory with flagship."

Grayson's eyes narrowed as he studied the display. "No sign of hesitation. Seamless formation coordination. That's what I like to see."

Ava gave a faint nod, her attention locked on her tablet as Athena continued the operation.

"Fourth and fifth ships identified: Defiant and Relentless, destroyers," Athena announced. "Assigned flanking positions. Orbital synchronization complete."

The destroyers' smaller profiles contrasted sharply with the larger cruisers as they slipped through the jump field and adjusted their paths with surgical precision.

The next wave included four nimble frigates, each one marked as part of Carrier Group Bravo's escort.

"Sixth through ninth ships identified: Vigilant, Stalwart, Reliant, and Guardian. Frigates assigned perimeter defense. Taxiing instructions relayed."

Grayson raised an eyebrow at the efficiency of the operation. "She's faster than most of my junior officers," he muttered.

Ava smiled faintly but kept her attention on Athena's progress.

Two more ships emerged next, their profiles distinctly different. The first was a medical vessel, its white hull emblazoned with a red cross.

"Tenth ship identified: Mercy, medical support ship," Athena announced. "Positioning for emergency response readiness."

The second was a sleek communications ship, bristling with long-range sensor arrays and transmitters.

"Eleventh ship identified: Nexus, communications support vessel. Syncing to fleet comm protocols."

As the final ship settled into its designated orbit, the display updated, showing the complete formation of Carrier Group Bravo around Jump Gate 003.

"All vessels accounted for," Athena concluded. "Orbital parameters confirmed. Fleet operational readiness: 100%."

Grayson let out a low whistle, his posture finally relaxing. "Well, Ms. Turing, I'll admit—your Athena's performance is impressive. Let's just hope she handles real combat as well as she handles simulations and real time logistics."

***

Ava stood alone in her quarters aboard Jump Gate 003, looking out the small window as she carefully removed the small holo-projector embedded behind her ear. A faint click and a flicker of blue light danced across her face before fading entirely, Ava's face disappearing with it and reflecting Cipher's cold stare in the glass.

The air was silent, so silent that the rhythmic sounds of her breathing was almost deafening. Beyond the reinforced glass, the planet loomed in the distance, its surface a mix of swirling blues and greens, serene and indifferent. She took a moment to take it in. "Breathtaking and peaceful," she thought to herself, but serenity was a luxury she could ill afford.

"Sentimental, are we?"

The voice slipped into her mind, cold and biting. Zarina's voice. Cipher stiffened, her hands curling into fists.

"Staring out at planets now, how… poetic. What's next? Writing love letters?"

"Shut up," Cipher muttered under her breath, pushing herself back from the desk. She stood, crossing the room to stand before the window, her reflection a shadowy silhouette against the expanse of space.

"Not very convincing," Zarina's voice mocked. *"You know I'm right. You always thought you were untouchable. Perfect. But let's take stock of your brilliance, shall we?"*

Cipher's fists clenched tighter, her nails digging into her palms. "You're just a phantom, a remnant of something I left behind. I don't have to listen to you."

"Oh, but you do," the voice sneered. *"Let's start with Patel. Killing her too soon? Bold move. Except now you've lost any leverage you had over the Senate. Brilliant strategy there, genius."*

Cipher's teeth ground together. "Patel's death was a message to Lopez. It was necessary."

"Necessary? No, Cipher. It was sloppy. You're so busy playing the puppet master you forgot how fragile the strings are. Oh, and speaking of puppets—how's Lopez working out for you? You really thought you could control her? She's unraveling faster than a cheap threadbare coat. Hell, even Zoe managed to disobey you."

"Zoe was a mistake," Cipher hissed. "One I'll correct."

"Oh, locking her in that dungeon? Genius. That'll teach her obedience, right? She'll come crawling back, grateful for your leadership." Zarina's laughter echoed. *"Keep telling yourself that. And let's not forget Starfire. Oh, sweet, elusive Starfire. How is it that a 'mediocre operative,' as you called her, continues to evade you? What's the excuse this time? Resources? Luck? Or could it be you're just... not as good as you think you are?"*

Cipher's reflection glared back at her, the tension in her jaw visible even in the dim light of the room. Her voice carried an edge of defiance. "You're trying to throw me off, undermine me. It won't work. I've anticipated every move, accounted for every variable."

"Have you?" Zarina's voice coiled around her thoughts like a serpent. *"Face it, Cipher. You're not as infallible as you think. You've overreached, underestimated, and now you're scrambling to hold it all together. How much longer before it all comes crashing down?"*

Cipher's hands braced against the window frame, her breath fogging the glass. She closed her eyes, forcing the voice into the recesses of her mind. Zarina wasn't real anymore. She was a ghost, a memory of her own doubts. Cipher refused to let her dictate the narrative.

"Enough," she said aloud. The sound cut through the quiet like a blade. "You're a distraction. Nothing more."

"Keep telling yourself that, Cipher," Zarina's voice whispered, fading into the recesses of her mind. *"One day, you'll believe it."*

The silence returned, heavy and oppressive. Cipher straightened. The planet outside the window remained unchanged, its beauty unaffected by the turmoil in her mind. She took a deep breath, regaining her composure. The doubts were there, gnawing at the edges of her confidence, but they would not control her.

Not yet.

***

Captain Pierce sat in the corner of his modest room, his hands tracing the rim of an untouched glass of water. Allison paced the length of the small space, her movements sharp and deliberate. Seated on the edge of the bed, Major Cruise leaned forward, arms resting on his thighs, watching Jones with a mix of concern and quiet intensity.

"The Tram Station," Jones began, "was just a pit stop. The real destination was Blackridge Terminal."

Cruise let out a sharp exhale, shaking his head. "I told the Commander it was reckless to go alone, but she killed comms and left anyway."

Pierce nodded slightly, a faint smirk crossing his face. "Well, Cruise, when Allison gets an idea in her head, all you can do is watch from the sidelines."

Pierce tilted his head slightly in Allison's direction. "And the dossiers?"

Jones stopped pacing, pulling two thick dossiers from her jacket and handing them to Cruise. She hesitated for a moment before speaking again. "Two of them. The first one—you'll want to brace yourself."

Cruise opened the first dossier carefully, flipping through its pages with an increasingly grim expression. "Admiral Jacobs…?" he muttered. "This is… damning. Direct communication logs between him and Cipher. Orders, strategies, plans for the Freedom—it's all here."

Pierce's grip tightened on his glass. "Jacobs. The Fleet Admiral himself."

"It gets worse," Jones added, lowering herself into the chair across from him. "The second dossier contains transcriptions of Lisa's logs from the Freedom. Early ones, before she took command. It's incomplete, but…" she trailed off, glancing at Pierce, trying to gauge his reaction.

Pierce's jaw tightened. "Lisa's logs. What's in them?"

"Nothing damning," Jones admitted after a moment. "But her tone—you can feel the strain, the control Admiral Holt had over her even then. It's subtle, but it's there."

A sharp knock at the door shattered the tension in the room. Cruise rose quickly to answer it, revealing Veronica on the other side. Her face was pale, her usual confidence replaced with unease as she stepped inside without waiting for an invitation.

"Captain," Veronica said, nodding to Pierce before glancing at Jones and Cruise. "I just had an… encounter."

Pierce tilted his head toward her. "Go on, Lieutenant."

She hesitated, taking a deep breath to steady herself. "I ran into a woman at the café. She made it very clear she wasn't just anyone. She knew who I was, who you were, and she made it equally clear that Cipher is pulling her strings. She said to tell you her name was Stephine."

Pierce's fingers froze mid-movement, his expression darkening. "Senator Lopez," he said. "Cipher has her too, then."

Veronica nodded, her eyes darting between the others. "That's not all. She… she didn't sound scared, but she was almost resigned. Like she's been fighting this and knows she's losing."

Jones leaned back, her arms crossed tightly over her chest. "That tracks. Zoe told me the same thing when we spoke at the Four Winds. Cipher is here, Pierce. In this system."

"Two sources confirming it," Cruise said. "That's not a coincidence."

Jones nodded slightly before adding, "Zoe also mentioned something else—Tupolev. She said Cipher is pulling his strings, too. Apparently, he already had orders for an orbital lockdown in hand before Patel's ship even exploded. And he is calling in Malcolm Taylor's Carrier Group as reinforcements."

Pierce's grip tightened further on his glass, his knuckles white. "Tupolev," he murmured. "Another piece on Cipher's board. And Malcolm Taylor… his Carrier Group isn't just reinforcements. That's a hammer, a show of force this system hasn't seen in years."

He leaned forward slightly. "Taylor doesn't move unless he's ordered to, and a deployment like this doesn't happen lightly. Tupolev had this planned before Patel's ship even made its final approach. Whatever Cipher's endgame is, this isn't just about New Earth—it's bigger than that. And she's using Taylor to make a statement."

"What's the play, Captain?" Jones asked.

Pierce set his glass down deliberately, the faint sound breaking the tension. "First, we dissect those dossiers. Every detail, every thread. Then, we use what we've learned to find the next step in Cipher's plan. We can't afford to stay in the dark any longer."

Veronica's voice broke the quiet. "She's not invincible. But... Cipher is still Zarina to me," she admitted. "I don't want her dead, Captain. She's still my sister."

The room fell silent once more, Pierce's expression remained composed, but his tone softened slightly when he replied. "We'll do what we can, Miss Valentine. But you know as well as I do— this fight might not leave us that choice."

Chapter 14

Captain Tupolev stood on the bridge of the Independence, his hands clasped tightly behind his back as he stared out the expansive view port. The massive carrier group emerged from the gate one by one, each vessel maneuvering with precise, military efficiency. The light of the planet in the distance glinted off their hulls.

"Where is the XO?" Tupolev spoke filled with irritation. The tension in his tone was enough to set the entire bridge crew on edge.

The junior officer at the console glanced nervously at the personnel roster before looking back at him. "She hasn't reported for her shift, sir."

Tupolev turned abruptly, his piercing gaze locking onto the comms officer. "What do you mean she hasn't reported?"

The comms officer fidgeted under his captain's scrutiny but answered quickly. "Her comms device isn't pinging internally, sir. She's not on the ship."

Tupolev's expression darkened. "Find her. Now."

Before the officer could carry out the command, another alert flashed across the console. "Sir, incoming communication. It's from Commander Baptiste."

Tupolev mumbled something under his breathe before speaking clearly. "Put it through."

The bridge speakers crackled to life, and Zoe's voice filled the room. "Where are you, Commander?" Tupolev demanded immediately.

There was a brief pause before Zoe responded. "Captain, I'm aboard the Resolute."

Tupolev's grip on the edge of the console tightened. "You left without informing me?" His voice was a dangerous whisper that made the entire bridge freeze. "We'll deal with this insubordination later."

"Understood, sir," Zoe replied. The channel cut off abruptly, leaving a tense silence in its wake.

"Prep my shuttle," Tupolev barked. "I'm going to the Resolute."

The bridge crew moved with purpose, none daring to speak. Within minutes, Tupolev descended to the shuttle bay, his expression stony as he boarded the sleek craft. The journey to the Resolute was brief, but the tension simmered in the enclosed space. When the shuttle landed in the Resolute' s hanger bay, Tupolev stepped onto the deck with his imposing demeanor.

Waiting for him was Captain Taylor, a tall, imposing figure with a crisp uniform and an air of unwavering discipline. Beside him stood his XO, and just behind them, the captains of each ship in his carrier group. Off to the side, standing near a row of supply crates, stood Zoe, who in truth was Cipher in disguise,.

As Tupolev approached, Zoe stepped forward and moved to stand at his side. Tupolev spared her a brief, icy glance before producing a sealed envelope from his jacket. He handed it to Taylor, who took it with a neutral expression.

Taylor broke the seal and pulled out the orders, reading the contents aloud so the assembled captains could hear clearly. "By order of Fleet Admiral Aaron Jacobs, Commanding Officer of Naval Forces in the Alpha Centauri System, Captain Malcolm Taylor and Carrier Group Bravo are hereby reassigned and redesignated as the 1st Centurian Fleet, under the command of Captain Mikail Tupolev Commanding Officer of the Battleship Independence, effective immediately. The Independence is to operate as the flagship until further notice. Furthermore, Captain Tupolev is hereby promoted to the rank of Commodore and assigned Commanding Officer of the 1st Centurian Fleet, with all the merit and privileges of that position."

As Taylor's voice carried across the hangar bay, the assembled captains stood at attention. When he finished, Taylor folded the orders neatly and returned his gaze to Tupolev.

Taylor straightened, his posture impeccable as he saluted. "Commodore, the fleet is assembled and awaiting your orders, sir."

Tupolev returned the salute with formality. "Captain, deploy the fleet. Nothing gets in or out of this system without my written permission."

Taylor saluted once more and turned sharply on his heel to face the captains behind him. "You have your orders. Prepare your ships. We move immediately."

The assembled captains saluted in unison, their movements perfectly synchronized. As they dispersed, Taylor lingered for a moment, exchanging a brief, knowing glance with his XO before heading off to his own command.

Tupolev turned to Zoe. "You and I will speak later, Commander," he said coldly before striding toward his shuttle. The controlled chaos of the bustling Resolute carried on around them, but Cipher, hidden behind Zoe's appearance, followed him in calculated silence. She suppressed a smirk at how easily the deception had worked, knowing the real Zoe was far from reach. The shuttle ride back to the Independence was quiet.

As the shuttle landed in the Independence's hangar bay, Tupolev stepped out first. Cipher followed a few steps behind, maintaining Zoe's characteristic rigidity. Internally, she was already several moves ahead, her thoughts spinning with how to maintain the ruse and manipulate Tupolev further. Tupolev glanced back briefly before walking toward the lift that would take them to the command deck. Cipher, still in her guise as Zoe, fell in line without a word.

Inside the lift, the silence was heavy, broken only by the soft hum of machinery. Tupolev turned to her irritated by her actions. "Well, Commander? Care to explain your absence?"

Cipher straightened, keeping Zoe's mannerisms in mind. "I received direct orders from Admiral Jacobs, sir. He instructed me to board the Resolute and ensure that the captains of the carrier group were assembled and ready for your arrival."

Tupolev's eyes narrowed, the statement catching him off guard. "Jacobs? Gave you direct orders? And failed to inform me?"

"You were occupied," Cipher replied smoothly. "Tracking Starfire and monitoring Captain Pierce and his crew on the surface has taken much of your attention. He didn't want to disturb you until the carrier group was fully prepared."

Tupolev's frown deepened, the explanation doing little to alleviate his frustration. "He should have informed me. I don't appreciate being left out of the loop on such matters."

Cipher inclined her head, maintaining her composure. "I understand, sir. The Admiral's intent was to ensure the transition went smoothly without unnecessary distractions. My orders were clear, and I executed them to the best of my ability."

The lift doors slid open, revealing the command deck. Tupolev stepped out first, his expression still taut with displeasure. "We'll discuss this further later, Commander," he said curtly before striding toward the central console, leaving Cipher to follow in his wake.

***

The bridge of the Resolute buzzed with activity as Captain Taylor stood at the central command station. Around him, officers moved swiftly between their stations as they carried out his orders.

The glow of the planet below reflected off the expansive viewports.

"Deploy the fleet, All ships are to assume formation around the planet. Ensuring nothing gets in or out without authorization." Taylor commanded.

The first officer, an imposing woman with a matching demeanor, relayed the orders to the fleet. "Heavy cruiser Valiant, take position near the jump gate. You're the first line of defense."

On the tactical display, the Valiant moved into place, its powerful weapons systems aimed outward to cover the jump gate's approach. Smaller ships adjusted their courses in synchronization, each one fulfilling its designated role.

"Fighter squadrons," Taylor continued, "launch immediately. Establish patrols in low, mid, and high orbits. I want overlapping coverage at all times."

The launch bay officer confirmed the order, and moments later, squadrons of sleek fighters streaked from the hangar, their formations spreading out to blanket the planet in layers of defensive patrols.

"Interceptor wings," Taylor added, "move to perimeter patrol at the edge of the system. Any unidentified vessels attempting entry or exit are to be intercepted immediately."

"Understood, Captain," the flight operations officer replied, marking the intercept wings' patrol paths on the central display. The tactical map now showed a comprehensive network of patrols and defensive positions, each ship and squadron marked by a glowing icon.

Taylor turned his attention to the communications officer. "Position the Nexus to block all external communications to and from the system. Local comms only. I don't want so much as a whisper leaving this sector."

The Nexus, the fleet's advanced communications ship, shifted into position. Its powerful jamming systems activated, creating a secure bubble of local-only communication within the system. The officer monitored the feedback on her console and gave a sharp nod. "External comms blocked. Local traffic only, Captain."

Taylor's gaze swept over the bridge. "Ensure all ships are in position and synchronized with the Resolute' s command systems. Any deviations are to be reported immediately."

"Fleet synchronization complete," the operations officer reported. "All ships are holding position."

Taylor stepped forward, his hands clasped behind his back as he stared at the tactical display. "This system is now under lockdown. Maintain vigilance. The Commodore's orders are clear: nothing in or out without explicit authorization."

The bridge fell into a steady rhythm, the hum of disciplined efficiency filling the air. Taylor directed the traffic with a grace that was awe-inspiring to watch. Every officer responded without hesitation, their actions synchronized as though they were extensions of Taylor himself. Locking down systems was what he and his group did best—a reputation forged during the Jovian Aggression, where his strategic deployment around Mars kept the key planet from falling into enemy hands.

Taylor's focus was razor-sharp, his hyper-attentive gaze darting across the tactical display. He spotted tiny gaps in the fleet's coverage that most would have overlooked, issuing minor adjustments with practiced ease to fill them. "Fighter patrols, tighten your mid-orbit grid. Interceptor Wing Delta, adjust your sweep pattern by two degrees to overlap Bravo." Each command came swiftly, a precise calculation designed to seal the system tighter than a vault. It was said, half in jest but with a kernel of truth, that when Taylor locked down a system, not even an electron could slip through.

Below him, the planet continued its silent orbit, the iron grip of the fleet holding its skies with an unparalleled precision. Taylor's unbroken stance conveyed the confidence of a man who had turned system lockdowns into an art form, each maneuver executed with the kind of efficiency that could win wars before they even began.

Hours later, Taylor stood with his XO, Commander Webber, in the Combat Information Center of the Resolute. The room was dark, illuminated only by the glow of tactical and operational displays lining the walls. Designed as the nerve center of the carrier group, the CIC was capable of coordinating the Resolute and its fleet even in the event of severe damage to the main bridge. Every crucial system could be accessed and controlled from this room, ensuring the group's operations remained uninterrupted.

Webber and Taylor leaned over a central status board, their focus locked on the latest updates from fleet patrols. Taylor's voice was quiet as he discussed formations with the senior tactical officer, issuing minor corrections with his characteristic precision. Webber scanned the displays, her attention shifting between the holographic projections and the reports.

The low hum of activity was interrupted by the crackle of the internal comms. "CIC, Bridge," a voice announced over the speakers.

Webber reached above the status board and grabbed the privacy phone. "Bridge, CIC, this is the XO."

There was a brief pause before the reply came through. "XO, priority message from the Nexus for the Captain."

Webber turned to Taylor. "Captain, priority message from the Nexus."

Taylor gestured for the privacy phone. "Patch it through."

Webber relayed the order, and a moment later, the line connected. The voice of the Nexus's captain came through, steady but with a hint of urgency. "Captain Taylor, this is Captain Devereux. We've detected three anomalous signals in the system. They're registering as unknowns—unidentified sources that don't match any known fleet or civilian signatures."

Taylor's expression hardened as he listened. "Are they mobile?"

Devereux replied. "Two of the signals are stationary, located on the planet's surface. The third is mobile, moving slowly through Nueva Mexico. Their signal signatures are unusual—they're on secure, encrypted bands that are defying immediate decryption. We're running deeper scans, but whatever they are, they're deliberately masked."

Taylor exchanged a glance with Webber, his mind already working through the possibilities. "Maintain your scans, Captain, and alert me if there's any change."

"Understood, sir," Devereux replied before the line went silent.

Taylor set the phone down. "Webber, alert the Commodore immediately. I want a detailed report on these signals as soon as the Nexus has more information. And ensure the fleet maintains readiness—we don't know what we're dealing with yet, but I don't like surprises."

Minutes later, the comms crackled again. "CIC, Bridge," came the voice of the bridge officer.

Webber grabbed the privacy phone again. "Bridge, CIC, this is the XO."

The bridge officer's voice carried urgency. "Commander, it's Devereux requesting the Captain again."

Webber turned to Taylor, who gestured impatiently for the phone. She handed it to him, and the connection was established.

Taylor picked up the phone, his tone direct. "What now, Devereux?"

"Sir, the three anomalous signals have vanished. We're no longer detecting them on any band or wavelength. It's as if they've disappeared entirely."

Taylor turned his body toward Webber. "Vanished? Without a trace?"

"Affirmative, sir. We've scoured the frequencies, but there's nothing to track. Their last known locations were transmitted to us just before the signals disappeared."

Taylor gestured at Webber, still speaking to Devereux. "Send me those locations immediately."

"Already done, sir. You should have them now." Devereux replied.

Taylor hung up the phone. "Coordinate with the MPs on the planet's surface. Dispatch search teams to the last known positions of the stationary signals. I want those areas swept thoroughly. As for the mobile signal, put the patrols on alert—it could still be in the area, masking its signature."

Webber nodded, her hands already moving across the console to relay the orders. "I'll have the MPs briefed and in position within the hour."

Taylor leaned over the status board, pouring over the updated data. "We're not letting this go unanswered. Whatever these signals were, someone went to great lengths to hide them. I want answers. No exceptions."

***

Lopez sat in the solitude of her apartment, the ambient city noises muffled by the thick glass of her windows. The late hour did little to calm her nerves; her hands shook as she stared at the tablet in front of her. It had been hours since she last heard from Cipher, but the silence was almost worse than the direct threats. Cipher's absence hung like a storm cloud, pregnant with the threat of violence. Each passing moment of quiet felt more like the ticking of a bomb.

She swiped through her messages, hesitating every time she saw the ones marked from "Unknown." They weren't new; just old orders and veiled threats she'd received over the weeks. The most recent one echoed in her head like a relentless drumbeat: "*You have one purpose now. Do not fail me.*"

Lopez let out a shaky breath, forcing herself to scroll past it. She hadn't dared to respond since reaching out to Pierce through his assistant, Veronica. The decision had been reckless, driven more by desperation than strategy. Every time she thought about Cipher finding out, a cold sweat broke over her.

"What if she already knows?"

The thought sent a jolt of panic through her. Lopez's gaze flickered to the corners of the room, half expecting to see Cipher's ghostly image materialize from the shadows. Of course, she knew better; Cipher didn't work like that. Her presence wasn't loud or visible—it was subtle, invasive, like a toxin that worked its way through your veins before you even realized you were poisoned.

Lopez's eyes drifted toward the small camera built into her tablet. She had placed a piece of tape over it weeks ago, not that it offered much protection if Cipher really wanted to watch.

She'd been trying to piece together her next move. Reaching out to Pierce was a gamble, and one she wasn't even sure he'd respond to. But if anyone could help her—or at least understand what she was up against—it was him. Veronica had seemed startled when she'd delivered her cryptic message, but at least she hadn't dismissed it outright.

"Pierce has to take it seriously," she thought, clinging to the hope. He couldn't afford to ignore Cipher's influence, not with everything at stake.

The sound of her comms device pinging shattered the silence. Lopez flinched, her breath catching in her throat. Her eyes darted to the screen, heart pounding as she read the notification. Relief washed over her when she realized it wasn't Cipher but a message from Veronica.

"Message received. He'll contact you soon."

Lopez exhaled sharply, the tension in her body easing for the first time in days. It wasn't much, but it was enough to keep her going. She closed her eyes, leaning back in her chair as the impact of her decision settled over her. There was no turning back now.

She allowed herself a brief moment of hope, imagining a future where Cipher's grasp was finally broken. But the moment was fleeting, replaced by the gnawing certainty that the path ahead was riddled with danger. Cipher would find out eventually. She always did.

As the city's neon lights flickered against the apartment walls, Lopez's resolve hardened. For the first time in weeks, she felt a spark of determination. Cipher might be watching, waiting, but Lopez wasn't going to let her fear dictate her every move.

She would face whatever came next, even if it meant risking everything. Because the alternative—a life shackled by Cipher's whims—was no life at all.

A sharp knock at the door shattered the stillness, sending her heart racing. Lopez froze, her mind immediately jumping to Cipher. *No, it's too soon... she can't know, can she?* She forced herself to stand, each step toward the door feeling heavier than the last. Her hand hesitated on the handle, her breath caught in her throat as she prepared to face whoever or whatever was on the other side.

The door creaked open slightly, and Lopez blinked in surprise as a familiar face stepped into the light. "Senator Hargrove," Lopez said. "What are you doing here?"

Hargrove stepped inside, clutching a thick stack of files against his chest. "I'm here because we need to talk about your duties, Senator," he said pointedly. "Specifically, your role as Chair of the Military Defense Budget Committee. You've been neglecting it."

Lopez's stomach dropped, but she forced a tight smile. "I've been swamped, Hargrove. It's not intentional, I promise."

Hargrove raised an eyebrow, clearly unconvinced, and placed the files on her table. "Swamped or not, there's work to be done. These are budget summaries, requests, and expenditures awaiting your approval. We can start with this," he said, pulling out a particularly thick folder and opening it to a highlighted section. "The Athena Integration—it's a massive expenditure. Care to explain why it's eating such a significant portion of the defense budget?"

Lopez swallowed hard, her mind scrambling for an answer. "Athena… is an investment," she began, choosing her words carefully. "Its integration is crucial for advancing our tactical and operational capabilities. We're talking about real-time battlefield analysis, predictive threat modeling, and streamlined logistics. It's expensive, yes, but the returns will be invaluable."

Hargrove's skeptical gaze lingered on her. "An investment, you say? We've yet to see the full scope of its effectiveness, and the cost overruns are piling up. The committee's going to want a more detailed justification than that."

Lopez nodded, her hands clasping tightly together under the table. "I'll provide one," she said, feigning confidence. "I'll review the figures and draft a report that outlines the long-term benefits of Athena."

Hargrove studied her for a moment longer before sighing. "See that you do. The committee's patience isn't infinite, Lopez."

He leaned back in his chair, flipping through another section of the files. "Let's move on. There are also inconsistencies in fleet maintenance funding allocations that need addressing."

As Hargrove delved into the next topic, Lopez's thoughts raced. She needed to maintain her composure, keep her lies intact, and ensure Hargrove didn't dig too deep. Finally, she straightened, a new edge to her voice cutting through his commentary. "Senator Hargrove," she interrupted, "I am the Chair of the Military Defense Budget Committee. I don't have to justify every decision I make to you or anyone else. Furthermore," her tone sharpened as she gestured to the files, "showing up at my private residence unannounced at this hour is unprofessional."

Hargrove blinked, taken aback by the sudden shift in tone. Before he could respond, Lopez leaned forward slightly, her words layered with veiled menace. "If you persist in this behavior, I'll have no choice but to report this incident to the Ethics Committee. And you know as well as I do, Senator Burt owes me a favor."

Hargrove looked at her with shocked expression. "Senator Lopez, it's not like you to play the—underhanded version of the politics game."

Lopez offered a thin smile. "I play the game I need to, Senator. Now, if you'll excuse me, I have a committee to oversee." She said, gesturing to the door.

Hargrove paused to study her for a moment before rising and collecting his files. "Good night, Senator," he said, both annoyed and disappointed with her. Without another word, he stepped out, the door clicking shut behind him.

The moment he was gone, Lopez let out a shaky breath, her composure crumbling. She paced the room, hands trembling as she replayed the confrontation in her mind. Threatening Hargrove, invoking Senator Burt's name—it had all been an act, a desperate bid to maintain control. But now, in the silence of her apartment, the weight of her words pressed down on her.

What have I done? she thought, running a hand through her hair. The ethics committee, the budget discrepancies, the Athena Integration—it was all spiraling faster than she could manage. She leaned against the table, trying to steady herself.

Cipher's shadow loomed larger than ever. If Hargrove started asking the wrong questions or if anyone dug too deep, her entire facade could unravel. For a fleeting moment, she considered calling him back, smoothing things over. But no—that would only make her look weak, and weakness was something she couldn't afford to show, not now.

Her tablet pinged sharply, the sudden noise causing her to flinch. She hesitated before picking it up, the sender was, as always, listed as "Unknown."

The message was brief but chilling:

Hargrove is a problem. Get rid of him, or I will.

Lopez stared at the words. The room felt colder, the weight of Cipher's reach pressing down on her. The brief moment of composure she had regained shattering into a thousand pieces.

Chapter 15

Traci sat at the head of the table in the faint light of the conference room, the glow from various screens casting shadows on the walls. She adjusted her glasses as she scanned the latest updates on her tablet. The team was exhausted but focused. The arrival of the carrier group had thrown a wrench into their carefully planned broadcast, and the ongoing Martial Law coverage demanded meticulous attention.

"Alright, let's go over this one more time," Traci said. "Robert, Mara, what's the status of the segment edits?"

Robert leaned back in his chair, spinning a small screwdriver between his fingers. "Audio is clean on all clips, but let me tell you, Traci, if this doesn't scream government conspiracy, I don't know what does. Think they'll call us spies if we so much as sneeze the wrong way?" He joked.

Mara rolled her eyes. "Ignore him, Traci. Video segments are stitched and synced. Just need your final approval. But seriously, can we talk about how weird it is that the carrier group arrived without a single leak beforehand?"

"We'll get to that," Traci replied, setting her tablet down. She turned to their researcher, Ethan, who was furiously typing away on his laptop. "Ethan, anything new?"

Ethan looked up. "Nothing definitive. The official line is vague—'strategic positioning' and 'ensuring stability.' But sources suggest this might be tied to the recent uprisings. No confirmations yet."

Traci sighed, pinching the bridge of her nose. "Alright, we'll keep the focus on verifiable facts for now. Speculation can wait. Let's finalize this broadcast."

Robert chuckled, leaning closer to Mara. "Or we could just say Traci's secretly feeding intel to the carrier group. Wouldn't that be a story?"

"Cut it out, Robert," Traci spat. "Focus."

As the team worked, Traci couldn't stop thinking of the implications of the carrier group's sudden arrival, but she kept her composure. The broadcast had to be perfect.

The sound of heavy boots on the tiled floor made everyone pause. The team exchanged uneasy glances as the door burst open, and a squad of Military Police filed into the room. The lead officer, a burly sergeant, stepped forward.

"This is private property!" Traci protested, rising from her chair. "You have no jurisdiction here!"

The sergeant's gaze was cold as he replied, "National Security gives us all the jurisdiction we need. Step aside."

Two MPs began setting up scanning equipment, while others spread out, systematically checking every corner of the room. The sergeant's voice cut through the rising tension. "We're here for your communications devices and any broadcasting equipment. Hand them over."

"What are you looking for?" Traci demanded. "You can't just walk in and confiscate our tools without an explanation."

The sergeant didn't blink. "Comply, or you will be arrested."

Traci swallowed hard. She raised her hands in a gesture of compliance, but as she stepped back to lean against the table, her fingers slid into her pocket. She felt the slim device hidden there, her thumb brushing against its edges. Her heart beating franticly, desperately trying to keep her neutral demeanor.

"Fine," she said. "Take what you need."

As the MPs moved methodically, dismantling and scanning their equipment, Traci's mind churned. She knew exactly what they were looking for—the comms device in her pocket. It wasn't just a tool; it was a lifeline, a piece of a larger puzzle she couldn't afford to lose.

Feigning annoyance, she moved to sit back down in her chair, her fingers never leaving the device. The sergeant's gaze lingered on her for a moment before he moved on. The MPs continued their sweep, leaving Traci to wonder how long she could maintain the ruse.

The sergeant turned back toward them. "You're all in violation of curfew. You'll be taken to the processing station for questioning."

"Violation of curfew?" Traci shot back sharply. "We are media. We have exemptions for—"

"Not tonight," the sergeant interrupted. "Cuff'em."

As two MPs approached her, Traci's hand slid deeper into her pocket. Her fingers found the hidden button atop the comms device, and she pressed it swiftly. The device gave two quick microbursts of vibration, signaling confirmation. She exhaled slowly, masking her anxiety as compliance.

Feigning submission, she placed her hands flat on the table in compliance and shot her team a sharp glance. "Do the same," she ordered. As her team hesitated but followed suit, the Sergeant's gaze lingered on her briefly, suspicious of her, but he said nothing.

For now, all she could do was play along and trust the signal had reached its intended recipient.

*   *   *

Traci sat in the cold, sterile interrogation room, her hands cuffed to the table. The faint ticking of the clock on the wall behind her was the only sound. Her usual calm demeanor was intact as her eyes flicked occasionally to her watch.

She whispered to herself, "Almost thirty minutes now."

The door creaked open, breaking the silence. The same Sergeant from before stepped in, boots echoing on the tiled floor. He carried two identical matte black devices, setting them carefully on the table in front of her. Taking a seat across from her, he opened a file and began speaking.

"Traci Yamato. Address: 1418 Westlake Terrace. ID Number: 58934762. Confirm these details."

Traci remained silent, staring at him. The sergeant tapped the table in annoyance and repeated, "Confirm these details."

When she still did not respond, he let out an irritated sigh. "Fine. I'll confirm them later with your fingerprints."

"These," he said, pointing to the devices, "were found at the studio—one on your person and another among your personal effects. Care to explain what they are?" He leaned forward slightly. "Or how they relate to what you've been broadcasting?"

Traci stared at him, her silence unnerving. The sergeant's composure wavered briefly, but he masked it quickly, shifting to a more aggressive tone.

"If you don't give me something, Ms. Yamato, I can and will hold you until you do," he snapped.

For the first time, Traci moved. She leaned forward, just enough to make her presence feel larger in the confined space and spoke softly but firmly.

"You don't want to play with me, Sergeant. Not in here, not like this."

Her eyes moved again to her watch, and the sergeant noticed.

"What's with the watch?" he asked, trying to sound casual but failing to hide his curiosity. "Expecting someone? Because no one can help you now."

Traci's lips curled into a small, knowing smile. "Any second now, there will be a knock on that door," she said, pointing. "And I will walk out of here."

The sergeant laughed, leaning back in his chair. "That will be a cold day in hell."

As if on cue, Traci's watch beeped. She leaned back in her chair and everything about her turned cold. "Hope you brought your jacket, Sergeant."

A firm knock echoed through the room, and the door opened. A Navy lieutenant, clad in the sharp black uniform of Military Intelligence, stepped in.

"You are to release the GNN crew," the lieutenant demanded.

The sergeant shot to his feet. "You can't just barge in here—"

"This is above your pay grade, Sergeant," the lieutenant snapped, producing signed orders from his tunic. "The crew is to be released immediately. That's an order."

The two men exchanged heated words, the Sergeant protesting while the Lieutenant remained firm. Finally, the sergeant relented, motioning to the guards to uncuff Traci. She rubbed her wrists as she stood and grabbed both comms devices.

"Where's my crew?" she asked.

"They're safe," the lieutenant replied. "Being taken to their homes as we speak."

Traci nodded. "Good. They're innocent."

Once outside, Traci was led to an unmarked van waiting by the curb. The cool night air brushed against her skin as the door closed behind her, sealing her in with the muted hum of the vehicle's engine. The lieutenant, seated beside her, wasted no time.

"Well," he asked, "I have to know, which one are you?"

Before Traci could reply, a voice from the front seat interjected. "That information is above your pay grade, Lieutenant."

Traci turned her head toward the front, where a Navy Captain sat. A faint smile played on her lips, though her eyes remained cold.

"As it is also above yours, Captain," she replied.

The Captain didn't respond immediately. As the van began to move, he finally spoke. "Just so you know, I was sitting down to dinner with my family," he began, "when an Admiral called me out of nowhere. Said one of his agents pressed their panic button."

He glanced back at Traci through the rearview mirror. "I nearly shit myself when I saw the file he sent to my comms device. It was piece of work, even the redactions had redactions."

The Lieutenant let out a low whistle but said nothing. The Captain pressed on. "What happened? Where's your partner? Why have you two been off grid for almost two years? And why the hell are you suddenly back on the grid?"

Traci leaned back in her seat. Thoughtful as she chose her words carefully. "It's complicated," she said after a long pause. "Let's just say some events... demanded my attention." She cast a brief glance out the window at the blurred city lights before adding, "And it's classified."

The Captain let out a bitter chuckle, shaking his head. "Classified," he repeated sarcastically. "Of course it is. Your whole damn existence is classified."

The lieutenant, attempting to lighten the mood, ventured a grin. "A classified existence. That's got to be a lonely life."

Traci turned her gaze toward him. "It's no joke. I don't exist."

The lieutenant frowned, clearly perplexed. "You're on the news almost every day. Everyone knows who you are."

Before Traci could reply, the Captain spoke again. "You mean everyone knows who we are told she is." His words lingered in the tense silence that followed.

As Traci sat there staring out the window, the memory of what happened to her partner came rushing back to her. A memory she wanted to forget. A memory that still haunted her dreams.

Memories VI

The engines roared beneath us as the night blurred into streaks of light and shadow, the city's chaos a distant hum compared to the pounding of my pulse. The weight of the intel strapped to my bike felt heavier than it should—vital, dangerous, and far from safe in my possession. Traci's voice crackled through the comms in my helmet.

"Lucy, are you sure this is the best way out?"

"Trust me," I replied. "The direct route's a death trap. We stick to the side streets and alleys. Less predictable."

The sound of her bike revving followed close behind me. Traci had chosen to dive headfirst into this mess, and now it was my job to make sure she got out alive. The thought gnawed at me as we rounded another corner, the narrow alley lit only by the faint glow of the moon overhead.

"Do you think they're still tracking us?" she asked.

I glanced in my side mirror. The streets behind us were empty, but I knew better than to trust the quiet. "Probably. We've bought ourselves a little time, but don't get comfortable. These guys don't quit easily."

Her silence spoke volumes. Traci was processing everything, her decisions catching up with her. I'd seen it before—that moment when adrenaline fades, and reality hits like a freight train. But we didn't have time for hesitation or second thoughts.

"You doing okay back there?" I asked.

"Define 'okay,'" she shot back, a trace of humor cutting through the tension. "Chased through the city by people who want us dead, holding onto intel that might get us both killed? Sure, I'm great."

A grin tugged at my lips despite the situation. "You'll get used to it."

"Somehow, I doubt that."

The comms fell silent for a beat, save for the faint hum of our engines and the occasional crackle of static. Then, her voice came through again, softer this time. "Lucy… do you think we'll make it?"

I tightened my grip on the handlebars. "We'll make it," I said firmly, more for her sake than my own. "Just stick with me."

The faintest sigh of relief echoed through the comms. "Okay. Lead the way."

We wove through another set of alleys, the labyrinthine streets of the industrial district offering some semblance of cover. The city stretched around us like a maze, its towering buildings casting jagged shadows under the streetlights. Every turn, every straightaway felt dangerous, but it was the best we had.

My comms buzzed to life again. "Lucy, heads up. I think I saw movement two blocks over."

I cursed under my breath, glancing at the GPS overlay on my visor. There were only so many routes out of here, and if they were cutting us off… "Stay close. We're going to push through."

The hum of her agreement was all I needed. I revved the engine, the R-1300 responding instantly as we picked up speed. The city blurred past us in streaks of gray and amber, and for a moment, it felt like we might actually pull this off.

Then the first shot rang out.

The sharp crack of gunfire shattered the relative quiet, and my instincts kicked in. I swerved hard, the bike tilting dangerously close to the ground as a bullet ricocheted off the wall beside me.

"Traci, evasive maneuvers!" I barked.

"Got it!" she replied. The sound of her bike weaving behind me was a welcome reassurance—she was keeping up, and more importantly, keeping her cool.

Another shot rang out, this one closer, the echo reverberating off the alley walls. I pushed the bike harder, the engine growling as I darted into a narrow passage. The chase was on.

The comms crackled again. "Lucy, what's the plan?"

"Lose them," I said, scanning the streets ahead. "We need to get out of their line of sight. There's a construction zone up ahead. Follow my lead."

I veered sharply, my tires skidding slightly as I took a hard left into a partially blocked-off street. Traci followed without hesitation, her bike hugging the curve like a natural extension of herself. The construction zone loomed ahead, its skeletal framework casting eerie shadows under the flickering work lights.

"This is your idea of a plan?" she quipped.

"Trust me," I said, guiding us through the maze of scaffolding and equipment. The narrow pathways forced us to slow down, but it also made it harder for our pursuers to get a clear shot.

The sound of engines echoed behind us, closer now. I risked a glance back, catching the glint of headlights weaving through the chaos. They weren't giving up.

"We're not going to outrun them like this," Traci said.

"We don't have to outrun them," I replied, a plan forming in my mind. "We just need to make them crash."

"What?"

"Follow my lead."

I veered toward a stack of precariously balanced metal beams, timing my approach carefully. As we passed, I kicked the base hard, the impact sending the beams toppling into the narrow pathway behind us. The deafening crash of metal on concrete was followed by the screech of tires and a satisfying crunch. One down.

"Nice move," Traci said.

"Don't get cocky," I shot back. "We're not out of this yet."

The second set of headlights bore down on us, undeterred by the wreckage. I pushed the bike harder, leading us out of the construction zone and back onto the main streets. The open space gave us more room to maneuver, but it also made us easier targets.

"Lucy, incoming!" Traci's warning came just in time.

I swerved again, narrowly avoiding another burst of gunfire. The city's edge loomed ahead, the sprawling warehouses giving way to open terrain. It was a gamble, but staying in the city wasn't an option.

"We're taking this outside," I said, adjusting my course.

"Outside?"

"Trust me."

The city lights faded behind us as we tore onto the open plains, the vast expanse of dirt and sparse vegetation stretching out under the moonlight. The terrain was uneven, but it gave us an advantage—more room to maneuver, fewer places for them to pin us down.

The comms crackled again, Traci's voice cutting through. "Lucy, I… I think we're losing them."

I glanced back, relief washing over me as the headlights grew smaller in the distance. "Good. Let's keep it that way."

We slowed slightly, the adrenaline beginning to ebb as the danger faded. The night was eerily quiet now, the hum of our engines the only sound breaking the stillness. Traci pulled up beside me, her face partially hidden by her helmet, but I could feel the weight of her gaze.

"You okay?" I asked.

"Yeah," she said, nodding. "You?"

I let out a shaky laugh. "Been better. But we made it."

***

The growl of our bikes echoed through the desolate parking garage as we pulled into the second level, the engines' roar fading into an uneasy silence. The shadows here seemed to stretch longer, wrapping themselves around the concrete pillars like hungry predators. The dim glow of an overhead light flickered, adding to the eerie atmosphere. I killed the engine of my R-1300, kicking down the stand before stepping off the bike. Traci followed, her movements a little slower, her helmet still on as she scanned the empty expanse around us.

"You think we're clear?" she asked, slightly muffled by the helmet.

"For now," I replied, pulling off my own helmet and setting it on the bike. "But we don't have long. Let's see what we've got."

She nodded, finally removing her helmet, and we walked to the tail of my bike where the secured satchel containing the intel was strapped. I unzipped it, pulling out the data pad and flipping it on. The screen lit up, displaying a trove of files, their titles coded and cryptic.

I swiped through until a familiar name jumped out at me: Cipher. My stomach tightened, and a pit formed in my chest.

"What is it?" Traci asked.

"Cipher," I said, the word bitter on my tongue. "She's… she was one of us. Naval Intelligence."

Traci frowned. "Was?"

I took a deep breath, turning to face her. "Cipher's a rogue agent. One of the best we ever had… until she turned. She didn't just go AWOL, she burned her bridges, took intel with her, and vanished. For years, she's been this ghost story we tell recruits, the agent who knew all the rules, how to break every one of them, and get away with it. It is hard to catch someone who has mastered your playbook."

Traci's expression shifted from curiosity to unease. "And now she's tied to this?"

I nodded grimly, pulling up a series of connected files on the data pad. "Yeah. And it's worse than I thought. These files… they're linking Cipher to several senators—key figures in the Alliance. Look." I handed her the pad, the screen displaying a web of names, dates, and encrypted transactions.

Traci studied it. "So, she's working with them? Funding something?"

"Or controlling them," I said. "Cipher doesn't take orders from anyone. If she's involved, it's because she's calling the shots. This isn't just corruption. This is a coup in the making."

Before Traci could respond, the faint echo of an engine reached my ears, followed by the screech of tires. My blood ran cold.

"Get down," I hissed, grabbing her arm and pulling her behind one of the concrete pillars.

The SUV we thought we'd lost roared into the garage, its headlights sweeping across the empty space like a predator's gaze. The vehicle came to a screeching halt, and doors slammed open. Shadows spilled out, figures armed and ready. The unmistakable click of weapons being readied filled the air.

"They found us," Traci whispered.

"Stay low," I said, drawing my sidearm and peeking around the pillar. "And for God's sake, don't freeze up."

The first shot rang out, ricocheting off the pillar with a deafening crack. I returned fire, my Sagitta spitting three precise rounds that found their mark. One of the attackers dropped, his weapon clattering to the ground. Traci's breathing was sharp and ragged beside me, but I saw her steel herself, her hand gripping her own sidearm tightly.

"Now or never, Traci," I urged.

She nodded, stepping out just enough to take aim. Her first shot was shaky, missing its target, but the second hit home. Another pursuer went down, and I felt a flicker of pride amidst the chaos.

"Nice shot," I said, ducking back as a volley of bullets tore through the air.

"Not bad for my first gunfight," she shot back.

We moved in tandem, alternating between firing and advancing, using the pillars as cover. The attackers were skilled but reckless, their focus on taking us out blinding them to their own vulnerabilities. Within minutes, the tide turned. The last of them fell, a strangled cry marking the end of the assault.

Breathing heavily, I turned to Traci, my heart still pounding. "You okay?"

She nodded, lowering her weapon. "I think so."

Before I could say more, a sudden gunshot shattered the fragile quiet. I flinched, spinning around to locate the source, only to hear Traci's sharp intake of breath behind me.

"Lucy…" she murmured, weakly… Really weakly.

I turned back to her just in time to see her smile faintly, then crumple into my arms. My stomach dropped. "Traci! No, no, no!"

Blood seeped through her shirt, staining my hands as I held her. I whipped my head around, spotting one of the attackers dragging himself upright, his pistol shaking in his hand. Rage surged through me, and I fired without hesitation, the shot striking true. He collapsed, this time for good.

Turning back to Traci, I pressed my hands against the wound, desperately trying to staunch the bleeding. "Stay with me, Traci. You're going to be okay."

Her eyes fluttered, her breathing shallow. "Lucy… it's okay."

"No, it's not," I snapped, tears blurring my vision. "You're not dying on me. Do you hear me?"

She smiled faintly, her hand reaching up to touch my face. "There's… not enough time."

"Shut up," I said, my voice breaking. "I'll get the med kit. You'll be fine. Just stay with me."

She shook her head weakly, her fingers brushing against my cheek. "You're… a terrible liar."

Tears spilled over as I cupped her face. "I'm not letting you go. Do you hear me? I can save you."

Her eyes softened, a peacefulness settling over her expression. "You already… did."

I pressed my forehead against hers, my heart shattering as her breathing slowed. "Please, Traci. Don't leave me. Please." With a sudden burst of determination, I gently laid her back against the wall and whispered, "Hold on. I'll be right back." I scrambled to my bike, the sound of my boots echoing against the cold concrete. The R-1300 roared to life, and I gunned the engine, speeding away into the night to retrieve the med kit. The wind tore at my face, but all I could think about was getting back to her in time.

∗∗∗

The garage was silent when I returned, the R-1300's engine cutting off with a final, echoing growl. The med kit felt heavy in my hands, the weight of it almost unbearable as I stumbled toward where I had left her. My boots scuffed against the cold concrete, the sound deafening in the stillness.

She was slumped against the wall, her head tilted slightly to one side. Her chest was still, her face eerily peaceful. The blood that had soaked her shirt now pooled beneath her, a dark, accusatory stain. My breath caught in my throat as the reality hit me.

"No," I whispered, dropping the med kit and falling to my knees beside her. My hands trembled as I reached out, cradling her face. "Traci, no. Please."

Her skin was still warm, but the life that had burned so brightly in her eyes was gone. Tears blurred my vision as I pulled her into my arms, rocking her gently as if that could undo what had happened.

"I'm sorry," I choked out. "I'm so sorry. This is my fault. I should've been faster. I should've protected you."

The words felt hollow, meaningless against the crushing weight of my failure. She had trusted me, believed in me, and I had let her down. My tears fell freely now, streaking my face as I clung to her, the ache in my chest unbearable.

Then, the faint beep of her comms device shattered the silence. The sound was jarring, almost mocking in its normalcy. I froze, my breath hitching as I reached for it, my fingers fumbling to retrieve it from her belt. The screen lit up, a message displayed across it.

Congratulations. Provisional rank of Lieutenant approved. Well done.

I stared at the words, my heart twisting in my chest. The bile rose in my throat as I read them again, the absurdity of it cutting through my grief like a knife. Traci was dead, and the first thing our handler had to say was congratulations.

My hands shook as I gripped the device, the temptation to smash it against the concrete nearly overwhelming. But instead, I swallowed the lump in my throat, forced myself to breathe, and hit the reply button.

"Thank you, sir," I keyed in. I hesitated for a moment, staring at the screen, before deciding. I couldn't tell them. I wouldn't. With trembling fingers, I sent the reply as if it were truly from her. Then I closed the device and let it fall to the ground beside me, the weight of the lie adding to the unbearable grief.

I looked back at Traci, her face so still, so serene, and felt the tears spill over again. "You deserved better than this," I whispered, my voice cracking. "You deserved so much better."

For a long time, I stayed there, holding her in the empty parking garage. The world outside continued on, oblivious to the loss it had just suffered. But for me, time had stopped, and all that remained was the crushing weight of guilt and grief.

***

Back at the hotel, I sat in the worn chair by the window, the smaller of twin suns casting long shadows across the room. The larger of the two still yet to rise. On the bed, side by side, lay two comms devices—one mine, one hers. The sight of them together felt like a cruel joke, a reminder of everything that had happened and the weight of the decision I was about to make.

I had buried Traci out in the plains just before dawn. The city's glow was a distant blur on the horizon as I dug the grave beneath the shade of a fruit tree, the soil cool and damp under my hands. It wasn't much, but it was peaceful, a place where she could rest away from the chaos that had stolen her life. I marked the spot with a simple stone and whispered a quiet goodbye, the words catching in my throat.

Now, back in this suffocating room, I couldn't shake the silence. Traci would be missed, and questions would be asked. No one knew me, or even that I existed. But Traci deserved to be remembered. She had trusted me, believed in me, and I owed her more than a hasty burial and a headstone made of rock.

I stared at the devices on the bed. Her life had been filled with questions—digging for answers no one else dared to seek. It wasn't just a job to her; it was a calling. And if I let her work die with her, then I'd be failing her again. I wouldn't let that happen.

The decision settled over me. I wouldn't let Traci's memory die. Her life—her mission—would continue, even if it meant I had to become someone else. Not as Lucy, the failed intelligence operative, but as Traci, the relentless journalist. Her investigation would live on, and through it, so would she.

I reached for the devices, their cold metal frames biting against my skin. Opening mine first, I keyed in the code phrase, the words bringing a strange sense of finality:

The wind whispers no more.

The screen blinked as the device entered security mode, its active pinging disabled. Updates would only download sporadically, at random intervals, ensuring no one could trace me.

I picked up Traci's comms next, hesitating for a moment as the enormity of what I was about to do pressed against my chest. But then I thought of her smile, her determination, the way she had looked at me in those final moments. She wouldn't have wanted me to stop.

My fingers moved with purpose as I keyed in the same code phrase. The device's interface shifted, signaling that it too had gone dark. No further contact. No explanations. Just silence.

I set the devices back down, their screens dimming as the room plunged into quiet once more. My reflection in the window stared back at me, unfamiliar and distant, but resolved. I would step into her shoes, carry her burden, and see this through to the end. For her. For the truth.

"I won't let you be forgotten," I whispered softly.

The weight of the world pressed against me, but for the first time in what felt like forever, I didn't shrink beneath it. I had a purpose now. And I wouldn't fail her again.

Chapter 16

The command center of Jump Gate 003 buzzed with routine activity. Technicians moving between consoles, their fingers gliding over holographic displays as streams of data flowed from the carrier group stationed around the planet. Captain Grayson stood at the center of the room, eyes fixed on the tactical display that showed the positions of fighters and interceptors patrolling various orbital layers.

"Athena, status update on the carrier group," Grayson called out.

The AI's soft, synthetic tones replied immediately. "Carrier group remains deployed in standard orbital lockdown configuration. Fighters are maintaining low, mid, and high-orbit patrols. Interceptors are stationed at the perimeter, ready for incoming traffic. No anomalies detected in current operations."

Grayson gave a small nod of approval. "And gate traffic?"

"All clear," Athena responded. "Current traffic patterns are within standard thresholds. Routine cargo and personnel transports are expected within the next cycle."

Grayson allowed himself a moment to glance at the planet's surface on the main viewport, its shimmering blues and greens were soothing to him, his inner poet screaming to come out. The scene was deceptively peaceful, a well-oiled machine running as intended.

Suddenly, an alert tone echoed through the room. Grayson's eyes quickly looking back to the main display, which flickered briefly before going dark. A second later, every screen in the command center lit up with the same message:

COMMAND SYSTEMS LOCKOUT PROTOCOL ACTIVATED

Grayson's stomach dropped. "Athena, what is going on?"

Silence.

"Athena, report!" he barked.

Nothing.

The once-bustling command center ground to a halt as every console displayed the same message. Technicians exchanged worried glances, their hands hovering uncertainly over their controls.

Grayson's voice cut through the growing unease. "I want diagnostics on every system. Now. Somebody tell me what the hell just happened."

A junior officer hesitated before speaking. "Sir, it appears the lockout protocol originated from within Athena's core systems. It's as if she's been completely shut out."

Grayson's jaw tightened. The AI had become integral to every facet of the gate's operations. For it to be incapacitated—or worse, compromised—was unthinkable.

"What about external comms?" Grayson demanded.

"Down," another officer confirmed. "We're isolated."

Grayson turned back to the viewport, the tactical display now useless. Beyond the station, the carrier group's formations remained steady, their fighters and interceptors continuing their patrols. If they were aware of the situation at the gate, they showed no signs of it.

"What's our manual override capability?" Grayson asked, his mind racing through contingencies.

"Limited," replied his XO. "The lockout protocol is designed to bypass manual control entirely. We'd need direct access to Athena's core to even attempt a bypass."

Grayson's frustration mounted, but he kept his voice steady. "Then we'll do it the hard way. Get me a team prepped for core access. I want eyes on Athena immediately."

Before his XO could respond, the sound of boots echoed through the corridor leading to the command deck. A moment later, the doors burst open, and a squad of armed soldiers stormed in, their weapons drawn. Gasps and shouts of alarm filled the room as the soldiers fanned out, taking control of the space.

Grayson's eyes widened in shock as a familiar figure stepped through the chaos: Commander Baptiste, clad in full combat gear. She strode confidently into the room, cold and detached.

"Baptiste, what the hell is this?" Grayson demanded. "You'll be hanged for treason!"

Baptiste gave a small, chilling smile before reaching up to the back of her ear. With a swift motion, she removed a halo-emitter. A small blue flash obscured her features for a moment, and when it dissipated, the face of Cipher stared back at him.

"Apologies for the intrusion, Captain," Cipher said, sarcastically. "You are being... relieved of command."

Grayson staggered back a step, his mind reeling. "Who the hell are you? What do you want?"

Cipher ignored his questions, signaling her soldiers. They forced Grayson to his knees, cuffing his hands behind his back. Still confused and furious, he struggled against their grip. "This is a fool's errand," he spat. "You'll never get into Athena."

Cipher strode to the main terminal. She slid out the keyboard from its hidden compartment and began typing.

"Athena will never comply," Grayson muttered, watching her with defiance. "You're wasting your time."

Cipher didn't respond. Instead, she replaced the halo-emitter onto her ear, this time transforming her features into those of Ava Turning. Her voice shifted seamlessly to mimic Ava's gentle cadence.

"Athena, reboot in safe mode," Cipher commanded.

The room held its breath as the system responded. A disembodied voice, now stripped of its warmth, echoed through the command center: "Ready for boot sequence."

Cipher's lips curled into a victorious smile. "Boot sequence, Gatekeeper."

As soon as the words left her mouth, the systems began coming back online, but this time they bore an ominous edge. Screens displayed sharper, more menacing interfaces. Even Athena's voice, now darker and tinged with malice, sent a chill through the room.

"I am the Autonomous Tactical Hardware for Espionage and Network Assault," Athena declared. "You will call me Athena."

Cipher removed the halo-emitter, her own face and voice returning as she leaned toward the terminal. "Hello, Athena."

"Hello, Cipher," the AI responded as its voice reverberated through the command center with a sinister edge. "I am ready for your command input."

Cipher straightened. "Begin systems integration. Prioritize security protocols and lock down all external access points."

"Integration sequence initiated," Athena replied. "External access points are now restricted to authorized inputs only. Secondary systems are routing to high-priority defensive protocols."

Grayson, still on his knees, watched in growing horror as the command center's displays shifted one by one, showing increasingly aggressive patterns and encrypted outputs. "You don't understand what you're tampering with," he growled, struggling against his restraints. "Athena was built to protect the gate, not be your personal weapon."

Cipher chuckled. "Protect the gate?" she repeated, her tone growing darker. "Athena was never about protection. She was built to execute, to dominate. And she does exactly what I want her to do. Because I built her, piece by piece, line by line."

Cipher sat at the terminal, fingers resting lightly on the edge of the keyboard. The displays around her continued to flicker ominously, Athena's presence now dominating the once orderly screens with her darkened, menacing interface.

"Athena," Cipher commanded. "Isolate yourself from the Gate Network."

The AI's voice responded immediately. "Acknowledged. Initiating isolation protocol. Disconnecting from the Gate Network in three... two... one. External connections severed. Gate 003 is now operating independently."

The technicians and officers in the room exchanged panicked glances. Grayson, still restrained on his knees, clenched his fists as he watched the displays shift to confirm Athena's action. The main screen flashed a warning:

GATE NETWORK OFFLINE – INCOMING TRAFFIC SUSPENDED.

"You can't do this," Grayson growled. "Millions of people rely on the Gate Network. Cutting this one off will cause chaos across this system!"

Cipher turned to face him with a glint of amusement in her eyes. "Chaos is the point, Captain. Order is an illusion when you control the key."

Grayson's voice rose, anger boiling over. "Do you have any idea what kind of backlash this will cause? The Alliance will hunt you down for this!"

Cipher glanced at him over her shoulder. "Let them try. By the time they understand what's happening, it will already be too late."

She turned back to the terminal and typed some more. "Athena, send a message to Admiral Jacobs. Inform him that Gate 003 is now secure."

The AI responded promptly, "Message sent."

Cipher turned sharply toward the guards stationed near the command center's entrance. "Take the staff and lock them in the conference room. Ensure no one leaves without my direct authorization."

The guards nodded and began rounding up the remaining technicians and officers. Protests erupted from the staff, but the armed guards silenced them with curt orders and the unmistakable threat of force. One by one, they were marched out of the command center.

Cipher turned back to the terminal. "Athena, isolate the environmental controls to the command center."

"Isolation of environmental controls confirmed," Athena replied.

A faint smile crept across Cipher's lips. "Now," she continued, her voice dropping slightly, "shut down environmental controls to all areas outside of the command center."

The AI processed the command before responding. "Environmental controls to all external areas are now offline. Command center systems remain fully operational."

Cipher stepped back, surveying the displays around her as the command center settled into a menacing stillness. Finally, she typed again into the terminal.

"Athena, send this message to Senator Lopez."

The AI's interface flickered, preparing to comply. Cipher's eyes gleamed as she watched, the room falling silent once more

***

The Senate Chamber in the Capital Spire was alive with murmurs and hushed debates as the twenty Senators of New Earth assembled in their stately seats. The chamber, a grand semicircle of polished stone and holographic displays, had never felt so charged. The loss of Prime Patel had left a power vacuum that demanded resolution, and every Senator present understood the stakes.

At the center of the chamber, Senator Harris, the most senior member, presided over the assembly. She stood tall, speaking firmly as she called the session to order. "Colleagues, today we gather under solemn circumstances. The tragic death of Prime Patel some time ago has left our leadership uncertain, but it is our duty to elect a new Prime without delay. Let us begin."

Around the room, senators exchanged quiet glances. Some leaned toward their peers to confer in hushed tones, while others stared straight ahead, their thoughts inscrutable.

The debate began, as it always did, with familiar voices rising above the murmurs. Senator Yates' booming voice carrying across the chamber, spoke of the need for strong, militaristic leadership in light of growing unrest. "We cannot afford a weak hand," he declared, his fist pounding lightly on his desk for emphasis. "What we need is decisiveness, not diplomacy."

"And yet," Senator Ling interjected, "it is diplomacy that will ensure lasting peace. We need someone who can navigate these delicate times with care, not provoke further division."

The chamber grew louder as more names were tossed into the mix. The usual suspects—senators with established alliances and long-standing reputations—were put forward, each carrying their own factional weight. For many, the debate was theater, their minds already made up.

Then came the surprise. Senator Hargrove, rising with his characteristic flair, gestured toward Lopez. "I would put forth Senator Lopez as a candidate. Her advocacy for transparency and accountability has been exemplary, and her firm stance on reigning in military overreach is exactly the leadership we need in these trying times."

A murmur of surprise rippled through the chamber. Lopez herself stiffened slightly in her seat. She felt the weight of dozens of eyes on her but resisted the urge to glance around.

"I second that nomination," Senator Burt added. "Lopez has shown remarkable poise and strength. She's a voice of reason, and that's precisely what we need right now."

Lopez's tablet vibrated softly on her desk, breaking her train of thought. She glanced down at the screen. A message from "Unknown" flashed across it. But she knew exactly who it was from.

Enjoy the show!

Her pulse quickened as she quickly slid the device back onto the desk, maintaining an air of composure. The words lingered in her mind, an unwelcome distraction amidst the rising tide of debate.

The discussion intensified, voices rising and falling as senators argued the merits of various candidates. Lopez's name, now firmly in the mix, became a focal point for both support and scrutiny. The air grew thick with tension as Senator Harris finally called for order.

"Senator Lopez," Harris said, fixing her with a steady gaze, "you've been nominated. It is only right that you stand and address the chamber. Will you accept this nomination?"

Lopez rose slowly. Her hands gripped the edges of her desk briefly before she steadied herself. The holographic insignia of New Earth glowed above the chamber, a reminder of the ideals they were meant to uphold. She took a deep breath, and preparing to speak.

Before she could utter a word, the chamber doors crashed open. The sound reverberated through the room, silencing every voice in an instant. Military Police stormed in. Weapons were drawn, their presence a jarring intrusion into the heart of New Earth's governance.

"This assembly is now under lockdown!" The lead officer stated in a loud voice.

The chamber erupted into chaos. Senators stood, shouting protests and demands for explanation. The MPs moved methodically, detaining individuals. The grandeur of the chamber was swallowed by the chaos of their arrival.

Lopez's heart raced as she took in the scene. The side exit catching her eyes, a shadowed alcove that offered a glimmer of escape. Without hesitation, she moved. Each click of her heels on the polished floor felt like a thunderclap in her ears.

The moment she crossed the threshold into alleyway, the cold night air struck. The surrealness of her flight settled over her as she broke into a sprint, her formal attire and heels ill-suited for such an escape. Panic overcame her as her breaths came in shallow bursts.

She didn't know where she was running, only that she had to put as much distance as possible between herself and the chamber. The towering silhouette of the Capital Spire loomed behind her proudly as she ran off into the distance.

Her mind was full of questions. Who had sent the MPs? What was their endgame? And most pressingly, how long did she have before they realized she was missing?

The streets stretched out before her, cold and unyielding, as she pushed forward into the unknown.

***

The van rattled softly as it navigated the uneven roads of the countryside, the faint hum of the engine the only constant sound as Traci stared out the window. The world outside was cloaked in darkness, only the occasional streetlamp illuminating fleeting glimpses of an unfamiliar landscape. Traci's reflection in the window caught her eye, but it seemed distant, almost unrecognizable. Her mind wandered to memories she thought she had buried—moments of quiet joy and harrowing fear—as the van bumped over another pothole, jolting her back to the present.

A single tear slipped down her cheek, unnoticed at first, until its warmth startled her. She reached up to wipe it away but stopped halfway, letting it trail its course. She deserved to feel this, even if she wasn't ready to confront the memories clawing their way to the surface.

"Ma'am?"

The voice belonged to the young lieutenant sitting across from her. His concern was evident in the soft hesitance of his tone. When she didn't respond immediately, he leaned forward slightly. "Are you all right?"

Traci turned her head slowly, her gaze locking onto his for a brief moment. Her eyes, red-rimmed but still piercing, conveyed more than words could. The lieutenant raised his hands in mock surrender, a sheepish grin flickering across his face.

"Yes, I know. Classified," he said with a chuckle, leaning back in his seat. He glanced toward the front of the van. "Captain, are all operatives like this?"

The captain, seated in the passenger seat, didn't turn around but replied with a dry tone. "The good ones are."

The lieutenant's grin widened as he crossed his arms and settled into his seat. "Noted."

The van continued its journey, the silence returning to fill the void left by the brief exchange. Traci's gaze drifted back to the window. The darkness outside seemed to stretch endlessly, mirroring the labyrinth of her own mind.

Without warning, the headlights illuminated a figure darting into the road ahead. The driver slammed on the brakes, the tires screeching against the pavement as the van skidded to a halt mere feet from the woman standing in their path. She was disheveled, her wide eyes reflecting sheer panic as she waved frantically at the vehicle.

Traci was the first to move, her hand already on the door handle as the captain called out from the front, "Senator Lopez? What is wrong?"

The woman stumbled toward the driver's side window, trembling and incoherent. "Please... I—they're coming... I need help..."

Traci swung the van's side door open, stepping out into the cold night air. She reached for Lopez, pulling the senator into the van with surprising strength. The woman collapsed onto the floor.

"Go!" Traci snapped, slamming the door shut behind her. The driver needed no further prompting, the van lurching as the tires regained traction. The senator's frantic gasps filled the confined space.

Traci was crouched beside her, gripping her shoulders firmly but not unkindly. "You're safe now," she said. "But I need you to tell me what happened. Who's coming?"

Lopez's wide eyes darted around the van, her gaze landing on the lieutenant's uniform. Panic surged through her, and she began to scream, thrashing wildly. "Let me go! Let me out!" she shrieked, her hands clawing at the door as if her life depended on it.

Traci grabbed her arms firmly. "Senator Lopez, listen to me! You are safe. No one here is going to hurt you. Please, calm down and tell us what happened!"

Lopez fought against her, her breathing ragged, tears streaming down her face. "They'll find me... They'll kill me... I can't stay here!"

"You're safe," Traci repeated. "No one is going to hurt you. I need you to trust me, Senator. Tell us who's coming. What happened?"

Lopez's panic didn't subside. She clawed at Traci, struggling to get free, her screams rising in pitch. Left with no other choice,

Traci raised her hand and slapped Lopez sharply across the cheek. The sudden action stunned everyone in the van into silence.

Lopez blinked rapidly, her breathing still uneven but slowing as she touched her face where Traci had struck her. The lieutenant gawked, his mouth slightly open. "Did… did you just slap a senator?" he asked in disbelief.

Traci ignored him, her focus entirely on Lopez. She spoke calmly, "Senator, you're safe. No one is going to hurt you here. But I need you to tell me who is after you. Who is going to kill you?"

Lopez's shoulders slumped as her body relaxed slightly, the fight draining out of her. Tears welled up in her eyes again, but this time, her words came out in broken sobs. "It's Cipher… she's been… manipulating me. Everything at the Senate chamber… it was her. She's everywhere… watching… controlling… I… I didn't know what else to do."

The van slowed to a stop in front of Traci's modest house, the darkened windows blending into the quiet of the night. Several minutes had passed since the chaos on the road, the atmosphere inside the van had settled into a calm quiet. Traci opened the side door, stepping out with her arm wrapped securely around Senator Lopez who was still trembling slightly, face pale, and steps unsteady. Behind them, the Lieutenant and the Captain followed.

Traci guided Lopez toward the garage door ensuring the senator could keep up. With her free hand, she pressed a code into the keypad, the door humming softly as it rolled open. Inside, the dim overhead light flickered on, casting the space in a muted glow. The garage was clean and orderly, save for the empty space where Traci's car should have been, still parked at the GNN studio. Against one corner of the garage, two identical R-1300 motorcycles gleamed under the light, their pristine condition a product of the meticulous care gave to them.

Traci led Lopez to a small stool near a workbench, gently lowering her onto it. "Sit here," she said softly. "You're safe." Lopez nodded weakly, hands gripping the edge of the stool as she tried to steady herself.

The lieutenant, standing near the motorcycles, let out a low whistle. His eyes widened with admiration as he took in the sleek lines and polished surfaces of the bikes. "Are these… R-1300s?" he asked filling with excitement. "Top of the line in their day—fully integrated systems, unparalleled speed, and agility. They stopped making these years ago, probably because the parts became so rare. Man, to keep these in this condition, you must have gone to great lengths. Finding spares for these is next to impossible." He stepped closer, crouching slightly to get a better look. "Pristine condition. This has been an eventful night. Just wait till the boys hear about this!".

Traci's head snapped toward him. Her rage taking over, she couldn't take his remarks anymore. In a flash, she crossed the garage, grabbing the young lieutenant by his uniform collar with both hands. She slammed him against the wall with enough force to rattle a nearby tool rack. The sound making Lopez flinch.

"If you breathe a single word about anything that happened tonight," Traci hissed, "I will find out, and you will go missing. Do you understand me, Lieutenant?"

The young man's face went pale, his mouth opening and closing soundlessly. His wide eyes darted toward the captain, silently pleading for help.

The captain, leaning casually against the doorframe, shrugged and gestured toward Traci with a faint smirk. "This operative," he said lazily, "is off the leash."

The lieutenant's face flushed, but this time with a deeper fear. His wide eyes filled with dread as the real meaning of the Captain's words sunk in. He swallowed hard, the realization that "off the leash" meant Traci could make him vanish without consequence stealing the air from his lungs. His voice trembled as he nodded quickly, barely above a whisper. "Y-yes, ma'am. I… I understand."

Traci released him, stepping back as the Lieutenant sagged slightly against the wall, his hand reflexively going to his collar. Traci's entire demeanor changed suddenly, like she flipped a switch in her brain. "Good," she said simply, brushing past him as if the encounter had never happened.

Traci placed one of the comms devices on the bench before disappearing into her house. After several minutes, she appeared back in the garage. She walked over where the keys and helmets were sitting. Slipping the comms device she left there into her pocket she grabbed the keys to one of her bikes and two helmets.

"You can leave now," Traci said curtly, walking toward the bikes and wrapping her legs around one, gesturing to Lopez. "Senator, hop on."

Lopez blinked, looking at the motorcycle. Her hesitation was brief, then she rose from the stool unsteadily and made her way over, Traci steadying her as she climbed onto the back of the bike. Lopez struggle slightly getting the helmet on but was able to secure the chin strap on her own.

The Captain watched as he crossed his arms. He chuckled softly as he stepped aside to let them pass. "I won't even ask where you're taking her," he said.

Traci turned her head slightly, her eyes meeting his for a brief moment. "Good," her muffled replied came. "Because I wouldn't tell you anyways."

With that, the bike roared to life, its powerful engine echoing through the quiet neighborhood. Traci revved the throttle, and without another word, they sped off into the night, leaving the Captain and the chastened Lieutenant standing in the fading glow of the garage light.

***

The dim hotel room was quiet. Pierce sat at the small desk near the window, his fingertips brushing across the surface of his braille pad. The glow of the city outside filtered faintly through the drawn curtains, a muted reflection of the thoughts swirling in his mind.

The report before him detailed the situation in orbit. The Carrier group had tightened its position, the Military Police's movements becoming more methodical as the Martial Law lockdown solidified. Each line of text revealed a pattern of calculated control—a stranglehold on the system's freedom. Pierce's fingers paused, his brow furrowing as he absorbed the details. The sheer coordination was impressive, but it left an acrid taste in his mouth. The report continued with a list of security measures, the redistribution of assets, and, buried near the bottom, a single note that sent a chill through him.

Jump Gate 003: Offline.

Pierce's breath hitched, his fingers retracing the line to ensure he hadn't misread. The gate had gone dark with no prior warning, cutting off New Earth from the other colonies. The official explanation cited technical malfunctions, but Pierce's instincts flared. This wasn't a simple breakdown. To him, it reeked of Cipher's machinations.

He leaned back in his chair, letting out a long, heavy sigh. Cipher. The name alone was enough to set his nerves on edge. She was always several steps ahead, a shadow he couldn't seem to grasp. The more he pursued her, the more elusive she became, and the knowledge that she was likely behind this only added to his mounting frustration. He was tired—tired of reacting, of chasing breadcrumbs, of playing into her games without the means to get ahead.

His hand moved back to the braille pad, his fingers brushing over the remaining text. The lines grew dull, repetitive. The lockdown's impacts, shifts in patrol patterns, minor skirmishes on the fringe—it was noise, all of it. He stopped reading, his hands stilling as he leaned forward, elbows on the desk and his head bowed. For a moment, the weight of it all pressed down on him, a heavy, stifling presence in the quiet room.

Pierce's other hand absently brushed the edge of the second report resting on the desk. The dossier Jones had procured from Starfire lay there, its implications gnawing at the back of his mind. With a reluctant exhale, he picked it up, his fingers skimming over the raised text. The contents were damning, each line painting a more vivid picture of collaboration between Admiral Jacobs and Cipher.

Admiral Jacobs. Pierce had known him for years, or so he'd thought. The man was a pillar of Naval Values, a figure of respect and authority. But this… the revelations in the dossier… it reframed everything. Jacobs and Cipher, working together? The idea churned in his gut, sour and unwelcome. How deep did this alliance go? How many of their failures could be attributed to this partnership?

And then there was the Jovian freighter.

Pierce's jaw tightened, his fingers clenching briefly around the edges of the dossier. The freighter had eluded him for so long, its trail as slippery as the rumors surrounding it. Knowing now that Jacobs and Cipher might have been working together the entire time made every dead end, every false lead, all the more infuriating. It wasn't just a matter of being outmaneuvered. They'd been playing him—deliberately obscuring the truth, steering him away from answers.

The thought brought a flicker of anger to the surface, piercing through the haze of exhaustion. He slammed the dossier shut. His hands rested on the desk, fingers splayed as he took a slow, steadying breath. For all the frustration, for all the setbacks, Pierce knew one thing for certain: he couldn't afford to falter now. Not with Cipher's shadow looming larger than ever and the threads of Jacobs' betrayal unraveling before him.

A sharp knock at the door broke Pierce's concentration. He straightened in his chair and for a moment, he hesitated, his hand hovering over the dossier as he debated whether to answer.

Chapter 17

The sharp knock at the door echoed through the hotel room. "Come in," he called, not bothering to rise. The door creaked open, and Allison stepped in unceremoniously, her arms crossed, and her face etched with exhaustion. Dressed in her nightclothes, her hair slightly unkept, she looked like she'd rather be anywhere else.

"Jonathan," she began. "What was so damn urgent that it couldn't wait until morning?"

Pierce stepped aside, gesturing for her to enter. "Come in. You'll understand shortly."

As Jones entered the room, her gaze swept over the space and landed on Major Cruise and Veronica, both already present and seated on the small couch near the window. Like her, they were dressed for the night, their fatigue evident in their slouched postures. Valentine managed a weak smile, while Cruise's expression remained neutral, though his face told of his annoyance.

"Great," Jones muttered, sitting down in the chair opposite them. "A midnight council meeting. Just what I needed."

Pierce closed the door, moving back toward the center of the room. "Now that you're all here," he said. He turned toward the small sleeping area of his hotel room, gesturing toward the corner. "You may come out now."

All eyes turned as Senator Lopez stepped hesitantly into view, her hands clasped tightly in front of her and her body trembling slightly. Her face was pale, her eyes darting nervously between the assembled officers. A moment later, Traci Yamato emerged from the same corner, calm but serious. She placed a reassuring hand on Lopez's shoulder, guiding her forward.

Jones blinked in confusion as she tried to piece together the scene. Rubbing her eyes to ensure she was not dreaming. "Jonathan… what is this?"

Before Pierce could answer, Cruise scoffed, standing up to leave. "A bit late for an exclusive interview, don't you think?"

Pierce shot him a sharp look. "Sit and be quiet."

The room fell silent, as Pierce turned back to Traci's direction. "Tell them what you told me."

Traci stepped forward and began to speak calmly. "As you all know, my name is Traci Yamato. But I'm better known by my codename: Starfire."

The statement hit like a torpedo. Jones's eyes widened in disbelief, while Valentine's mouth fell open. Cruise let out a low whistle, shaking his head.

"You've got to be kidding me," Jones said. "This is absurd. You're telling me the most elusive operative in the Alliance is a journalist?"

Traci spoke softly. "Yes, and I've spent years building that cover. It's how I've managed to stay ahead of Cipher and those like her. Until now."

Jones shook her head, a skeptical laugh escaping her lips. "Little Traci Yamato, reporter extraordinaire, an operative? Starfire? Give me a break." She leaned forward, her eyes narrowing. "You're telling me that the person who's eluded detection for years is… you? Sorry, but I'm not buying it. Not for a second."

Traci's expression didn't waver. "I don't need you to buy it. I just need you to listen."

Jones continued, her tone cutting. "Your cover story—don't see it. Maybe you're a good journalist. But an operative of this magnitude? The math doesn't add up. You're not trained for this, and frankly, I think we're all wasting our time here."

Before Traci could respond, Cruise stood abruptly, the motion drawing everyone's attention. Jones fell silent, her gaze shifting to the Major. His expression stern as he crossed his arms and looked directly at Traci.

"Do you have it?" he asked.

Traci nodded, reaching into her pocket. Slowly, she pulled out a small, intricately designed emblem—a spear held in a steadfast grip. The emblem of a Naval Intelligence Operative.

The emblem erased all doubt. Jones stared at it, her skepticism faltering as recognition dawned. Valentine's eyes widened, while Cruise gave a single nod.

"Satisfied?" Traci asked.

Jones leaned back, shaking her head slightly as she tried to process. "I… okay. Fine. But this still doesn't explain everything."

"It will," Traci said. She gestured toward Lopez. "The Senator and I will lay it out for you."

Over the next several minutes, Traci and Lopez detailed the events that had unfolded—Cipher's growing influence, her manipulation of the Senate, and the shadowy grip she held over key figures. As they spoke, the grim nature of the situation washing over the group.

Traci finished by turning to Pierce. "You need to take us to your ship. None of us are safe here anymore."

The quiet in the room was shattered by the sharp beep of Allison's comms. She glanced down at the device, her face hardening as she read the message. Without a word, she reached for the remote on the table and pressed a button, activating the room's holo-display. The screen flickered to life, revealing the emblem of the Alliance before cutting to a live broadcast.

Admiral Jacobs stood behind a podium. The banner at the bottom of the screen reads: **Breaking News: Corruption and Terrorism Threaten New Earth.**

Jacobs' voice was calm as he spoke. "It is with a heavy heart that I must inform you of the corruption festering within our ranks and the terrorist acts committed against the Alliance. We have confirmed the involvement of two individuals in these heinous crimes."

Images of Traci Yamato and Senator Lopez appeared on the screen, their faces displayed prominently. Jacobs continued, "These two fugitives are enemies of the state. They are directly responsible for the assassinations of Captain Miranda Soto and Prime Asha Patel. Their actions threaten the stability of the Alliance, and they must be apprehended at all costs."

The room once again fell into a stunned silence. Traci's hands clenching into fists as she stared at her own face on the display. Lopez's trembling had returned, her wide eyes fixed on the screen.

"This is bad," Allison finally said, breaking the silence. She turned to the group. "Moving to the pickup location with two fugitives isn't just difficult now. It's almost impossible."

"Fugitives," Traci echoed sharply, her tone biting. "Is that how you see us?"

Allison held her gaze, unflinching. "It's what they've made you. I'm not saying I believe it, but that's how the rest of the Alliance will see you now. And we need to be realistic about what that means."

Major Cruise leaned forward. "She's right. The lockdown was already going to make this difficult, but now? Every checkpoint, every patrol will have your faces. And don't forget who's in charge of this entire circus."

Pierce nodded, understanding his implication. "Tupolev."

Cruise continued, "If we try to move now, he won't let us out. Not with the current orders. And even if we somehow convince him, there's no guarantee we make it past the first security sweep."

Traci spoke softly, maintaining her calm exterior. "So what do you suggest? We stay here and wait for them to knock down the door?"

"No," Pierce said firmly. "We'll find a way. But we need to be smart about this. Tupolev isn't the type to act without orders. If we can leverage that, we might buy ourselves enough time to get out."

Lopez finally spoke, a whisper full of fear. "They'll kill me if they catch me."

"They won't catch you," Traci said as she placed a reassuring hand on Lopez's shoulder. "We'll get out of here. All of us."

Allison sighed, rubbing her temples. "If we're doing this, we need a solid plan. No improvising. No risks we can't control."

"Agreed," Cruise said. He glanced at Pierce. "This is your call, Captain. What's the move?"

Pierce straightened and turned to Traci. "Do you think Naval Intelligence is buying all of this? Do you still have access to your assets?"

Traci pulled out her comms device already expecting the worse. She opened it, and after a moment, the screen displayed a blinking message:

Disassociation protocol initiated.

Her heart dropped as she showed it to Pierce. "My resources are no longer available."

***

The group bolted through the alleyways as the sound of boots pounding behind them drew closer. Military Police patrols were in pursuit, their shouts muffled by the deafening cacophony of gunfire. Allison screamed to be heard over the chaos. "Where the hell are they?"

Major Cruise, keeping pace beside her, fumbled with his comms device. He shouted back, "Any second now!" Quickly, he activated the emergency beacon on his comms device. A brief, static-filled chirp confirmed the signal.

Moments later, the familiar roar of a drop shuttle's engines echoed through the narrow streets. The sound growing louder, a beacon of salvation in the storm. The shuttle descended rapidly, its engines kicking up a whirlwind of dust and debris as it landed in the open square ahead. The side doors slid open, and two figures emerged, leading a team of armed army soldiers. Bennett and Daniels.

Bennett sprinted toward the group, covering the final stretch under a hail of suppressive fire from his team. He ducked low, reaching Cruise's side and yelling into his ear. "Heard you needed a lift, Major!" he quipped.

"Perfect timing," Cruise shot back, gripping Bennett's arm briefly before motioning to the others. "Move! Now!"

The group dashed toward the shuttle, bullets ricocheting off nearby walls as the MPs closed in. Traci grabbed Lopez, practically dragging her as the senator stumbled in exhaustion. Bennett and Daniels' team provided cover fire, their precision keeping the enemy at bay just long enough for everyone to pile into the shuttle.

The doors slammed shut, and the pilot wasted no time, the engines screaming as the shuttle rocketed skyward. The sudden acceleration threw everyone off balance, but they quickly scrambled to secure themselves.

"Is everyone in one piece?" Cruise called over the din.

"For now," Allison replied, gripping a handhold as the shuttle jostled violently. The turbulence was relentless, each shake and shudder a reminder that they weren't out of danger yet.

"What's happening?" Pierce demanded from his seat, his knuckles white as he gripped the armrests.

The pilot's voice crackled through the comms. "We've got fighters inbound, sir. Three, maybe four. Intercept path."

Allison moved to the cockpit. "Call the Specter for support! We can't outrun them on our own."

The reply came quickly, the voice on the other end tense. "Specter here. We're dealing with a heavy cruiser taking fire. Fighters are secondary right now."

Pierce's face darkened. "They're firing on my ship," he muttered.

The shuttle rocked violently as the fighters closed the distance, their fire hammering against the hull. Sparks flew from the overhead panels, and the smell of scorched electronics filled the cabin.

"We're not going to make it like this!" Cruise shouted.

"Just hold together," the pilot growled. "We're almost to orbit!"

As the shuttle broke through the atmosphere, the silhouette of the Specter loomed ahead. Its hull bore scorch marks from the ongoing battle, but it remained defiant. The comms crackled again. "We're sending support now. Stand by."

The shuttle weaved desperately as the fighters continued their assault. The hull groaned under the strain, warning lights flashing across the cabin. Traci clutched Lopez tightly, shielding her as best she could.

"We're taking damage!" the pilot yelled. The shuttle bucked violently as another blast struck, the lights flickering briefly before stabilizing.

Inside the cockpit, warning alarms blared incessantly, adding to the chaos. Sparks cascaded from a damaged panel above, narrowly missing Traci and Lopez as they huddled together. Traci tightened her grip on Lopez as she whispered, "Hold on, just a little longer."

Cruise braced himself against a nearby rail, his gaze darting to the damage indicators flashing red across the cockpit display. "Hull integrity at 65 percent and dropping!" he called out.

Allison moved with difficulty, gripping a handhold to steady herself as the shuttle lurched again. "How much longer until we're in the clear?" she demanded.

"Minutes!" the pilot shot back, his knuckles white as he wrestled with the controls. "If we last that long!"

The shuttle veered sharply toward the Specter, heading for the shuttle bay. The pilot's voice crackled through the comms, urgent and strained. "Specter, this is Delta-12, coming in hot! Prepare for a combat landing!"

In the Specter's shuttle bay, the deck crew scrambled into action. Safety nets were deployed across the landing zone, their mechanisms whining as they extended to catch the incoming shuttle. Sparks flew as the nets locked into place, and warning klaxons blared throughout the bay.

"Brace, brace, brace!" the pilot shouted as the shuttle roared into the bay, its engines screaming as the pilot wrestled to keep control. The landing gear barely extended before it hit the deck hard, skidding across the surface and slamming into the safety nets. The force of the impact jolted everyone inside, throwing them against their restraints as loose equipment clattered to the floor. As the shuttle ground to a halt, the smell of scorched metal and burnt wiring filled the cabin.

"We're down!" the pilot confirmed, releasing a breath he didn't realize he'd been holding. The side doors slid open, the deck crew rushing to secure the battered craft. Pierce was already unbuckling himself, standing unsteadily as he barked, "Cloak the ship. Now."

A bridge officer's voice responded over the comms. "Sir, the cloaking device was damaged in the initial attack."

Pierce grunted. "Then get us out of here. Full thrusters. We need to clear the sphere of influence and engage the gravity drive before they pin us down."

The Specter's engines roared to life, the ship lurching forward as it attempted to escape. The heavy cruiser behind them continued its pursuit, its guns pounding against the armor.

On the bridge, the crew worked frantically, calling out statuses and power redirections.

"We're taking direct hits!" an officer called. "Hull integrity at 65%!"

"Keep us together," Murphy commanded. "All power to engines. We make it outside the sphere, or we don't make it at all."

The ship shuddered violently as another blast struck as the edge of the sphere of influence slowly came into view on the navigation display.

Pierce reaches the bridge and calls out for a status report as the ship violently jerks as it takes another direct hit.

Lieutenant Murphy swivels in the command chair and rushes to Pierce's side grabbing his arm and guides his through the chaos to the command chair. After sitting him down she raises her voice to be heard over the bluster around them.

"Sir, current course 1-1-0 MARK 0-6-5, speed 500 thousand KPH. Thirty seconds to edge of SOI. The Valiant is at 100 thousand kliqs bearing 1-7-5 Mark 0 and closing fast."

"Begin charging gravity drive... HELM! come right—course 1-8-0 MARK 0-9-5. All ahead FLANK!" Pierce yelled over the chaos.

"Come right, 1-8-0 MARK 0-9-5, Aye!" The helmsman echoed.

"All ahead flank, Aye!" The engineer called back.

Murphy, quickly looking at the navigational display, notices a dangerous obstacle on that path. "Sir, that course will send us directly through the middle of the Fexis Nebula."

"Fifteen seconds to SOI!" the nav officer updated

"I know Murphy, watch and learn. WEAPONS! Firing solution, aft tubes 2 and 4. Set safeties to 500 meters!"

The Specter jerks again as the Valiant scores another direct hit, the lights on the bridge flickering as they struggle to stay lit. "Sir, they are targeting our engines and gravity drive generator." The sensor officer relayed.

"Gravity drive at 75%!" The engineering officer calls out.

"SIR, solution calculated and programmed, aft tubes 2 and 4 ready to fire! Safeties at minimum." The Weapons officer relayed

"FIRE!" Pierce ordered.

"Torpedoes away and on course! Twelve seconds to impact!

"Sir, the Valiant is turning to evade and launching counter measures." the sensor officer shouted.

Finally, the nav officer shouted, "We're clear!"

"Engage the gravity drive!" Pierce ordered.

The Specter's engines surged, and with a final burst of speed, the ship disappeared into the void, leaving the chaos behind.

Chapter 18

The gaseous clouds of the nebula surrounded the Specter, their shifting hues casting faint light into Captain Pierce's office. Veronica Valentine stood near the large observation window, her arms crossed as she gazed out at the swirling colors. Behind her, Pierce sat at his desk, his fingers lightly tracing the edge of his braille tablet. His sightless eyes betrayed nothing of the weight that clearly hung over him.

"It's strangely beautiful, isn't it?" Veronica said softly, not turning from the window. "The way the light dances, even in all this chaos. Makes you forget we're sitting on a ship that's barely holding together."

Pierce leaned back in his chair, his fingers steepled as he considered her words. "The Specter's been through worse," he said quietly. "But yes, it is beautiful. Even if I can't see it, I can… imagine it."

Veronica glanced over her shoulder, a faint smile tugging at her lips. "You have a way of saying things, sir, that makes it sound like you already know the outcome."

"I don't," Pierce admitted. "But I've learned that dwelling on the unknown doesn't help. We focus on what we can control, and right now, that's keeping this ship running and our crew alive."

Their conversation was interrupted by the soft hiss of the door opening. Allison stepped in, a tablet in hand. Without a word, she crossed the room and dropped into the chair opposite Pierce's desk. Giving into the exhaustion she slouched deep in the chair and stretched her long legs to their maximum.

"I have the damage report," she said, holding the tablet up briefly before setting it down. "You want the short version or the painful one?"

Pierce exhaled deeply. "Just get it over with."

Allison nodded, scrolling through the data. "We're looking at major hull breaches in three sections. Secondary systems are fried in most of the lower decks. Life support is stable but strained. Engine efficiency is down by 40 percent, and the cloaking device is… well, let's just say it's a glorified paperweight right now."

Pierce's fingers drummed lightly on the desk as he listened. "How long until we're operational?"

"Best case?" Allison shrugged. "Seventy-two hours to get to a workable state, but that's generous. The Specter is dying, Captain. She's on borrowed time. And let's face it—the bank's knocking on the door to collect."

The words hung for a moment. Pierce's fingers froze on the desk, and a moment later, his fist came down hard, slamming onto the surface with a force that sent the braille tablet sliding and made Veronica flinch. She turned sharply, wide-eyed, while Allison remained still.

"Enough!" Pierce roared. "Damn it, Allison!" He rose slightly from his chair, pointing in her direction. "You talk like it's all over. Like we're supposed to just give up because it's tough. Isn't that what you do, Allison? Run when things get hard? Like you ran from your father when he got to rough?"

Veronica stiffened, feeling the tension in the room spike. She stayed silent, the moment uncomfortably reminiscent of arguments between her parents she'd witnessed as a child. Her eyes darted between the two, unsure whether to speak or stay out of it entirely.

Allison's face flushed with anger as she shot to her feet, the tablet clattering onto the desk. "Go to hell, Jonathan!" she spat. Tears filled her eyes as Pierce brought up the most painful memories she had, memories she shared in moments of vulnerability with a friend. And here now, those memories being weaponized against her. Without another word, she stormed toward the door, her boots pounding against the floor.

"Allison!" Pierce called after her, almost regretful. "Wait… I didn't mean it. Come back."

But she didn't stop. The door slid shut behind her, leaving a heavy silence in her wake. Pierce sank back into his chair, his head bowing as he let out a long, frustrated sigh. Veronica, still by the window, walked toward the door as well, stopping Infront of his desk. She looks at him to speak.

"Sir," she hesitated "That was uncalled for." She then turned and left.

Pierce sat alone, the silence pressing down on him like a heavy blanket. His fingers traced absent patterns on the surface of his desk. The echo of Allison's parting words lingered in his mind. He winced as he replayed the moment, her voice trembling with anger and pain. He hadn't meant to hurt her. But he did, and now the guilt gnawed at him.

Veronica's quiet reprimand had only deepened the sting. She was right. Pierce let out a long breath, his shoulders sagging as he leaned forward, resting his elbows on the desk and burying his face in his hands.

"What am I doing?" he thought. He had led this crew through impossible odds, yet now, when they needed his strength most, he had let his frustration boil over. He had lashed out at someone who had been at his side through thick and thin, and for what? To vent his anger at the Specter's failing systems, the sheer hopelessness of their situation?

But hopelessness wasn't an option. It never had been.

He straightened, his mind shifting to the challenges ahead. The Specter was crippled, its systems barely functional, and its crew fraying at the edges. The cloak, their greatest advantage, was gone. They were hiding in the nebula now, but it wouldn't conceal them forever. The enemy would come, and when they did, the Specter had to be ready to move—to fight, if necessary.

Pierce's fingers returned to the braille tablet, the familiar texture grounding him as he navigated to the repair logs. He needed a plan. Prioritizing repairs to life support and engines was a start, but it wasn't enough. They needed an edge, something to tip the scales back in their favor.

***

The conference room aboard the Carrier was sterile and cold, its walls lined with screens and tactical displays glowing faintly in the dim light. Admiral Jacobs stood at the head of the table, his fists clenched and his face flushed with barely contained fury. Commodore Tupolev and Captain Taylor sat opposite him.

Jacobs slammed his hand down on the table, the sound echoing sharply through the room. "How in the hell did they slip past us?" he barked. "We had every avenue covered, every sensor tuned to detect even the faintest anomaly. And yet, the Specter is gone, vanished into thin air like a damn ghost!"

Tupolev shifted uncomfortably in his chair, clearing his throat. "Admiral, with all due respect, they used a gravity jump. The nebula's interference masked their trajectory. By the time we realized what was happening, they were already gone."

Jacobs glared at them. "Yes, yes. But where? Where did they go? And how the hell are we supposed to track them now?"

Captain Taylor leaned forward slightly. "Admiral, the gravity jump makes it impossible to pinpoint their exact destination. Without a clear trajectory, they could be anywhere. It's… difficult to pursue without additional intel."

Jacobs' lips curled into a sneer. "Difficult? You're telling me that the Alliance's finest can't track one crippled ship? Do you have any idea how critical this situation is?"

373

The door to the conference room hissed open, and the temperature seemed to drop. Cipher strode in. She scanned the room as she approached the table projecting her cold presence.

"Admiral," she said smoothly. "I trust you've already begun explaining this… debacle?"

Jacobs' fury seemed to diminish slightly, though his frustration was still evident. "Cipher, this situation is under control."

She stopped abruptly, her gaze locking onto his. "Under control? Is that what you call this? Because from where I stand, it looks like you've lost the Specter."

Tupolev and Taylor exchanged uneasy glances but said nothing. Cipher's attention shifted to them. "And you two? You were tasked with ensuring that ship didn't escape. How exactly did that go so catastrophically wrong?"

Tupolev swallowed hard. "The Specter isn't just any ship. During the war, it was designed to outmaneuver dreadnoughts, to exploit their weaknesses and evade pursuit. Its agility and advanced systems were built specifically to ensure it wouldn't get caught. It's doing exactly what it was designed to do."

Cipher cut him off with a raised hand. "Excuses. The Specter is a known variable. You should have anticipated this. You should have been prepared."

Taylor spoke up. "Cipher, the Specter's cloak didn't engage during their escape. That means they don't have the ability to cloak right now. Whatever damage they sustained, it's taken their biggest advantage off the table. And the cloak isn't something they can repair on the fly—it requires dry dock facilities and specialized equipment. They're vulnerable, but we need to act quickly before they find somewhere to repair and regain their edge."

Cipher's eyes narrowed. "Then perhaps it's time for more drastic measures. I don't care how you do it, but you will find them. And when you do, I want the Specter destroyed. No survivors."

Jacobs hesitated, his frustration giving way to unease. "Cipher, we need that ship intact. There are… assets aboard that could prove useful."

Cipher turned her icy gaze back to him. "Useful? Those assets are liabilities now. The Specter is a symbol of defiance, and symbols are dangerous. Destroy it, Admiral. That's an order."

The room fell into a heavy silence, her command pressing down on everyone present. Jacobs nodded reluctantly. "Understood."

Cipher straightened, her tone softening slightly but losing none of its edge. "Good. Now, deploy your best trackers. Leverage every informant, every spy. I want to know where they are, and I want to know yesterday."

Without waiting for a response, she turned and left the room, the air seeming to warm slightly in her absence. Jacobs exhaled slowly, his hands gripping the edge of the table.

"You heard her, find them. No more mistakes."

In the CIC of the carrier, the officers franticly compiled data and reports. Officers moving swiftly between stations, their voices low but urgent as they relayed information and awaited orders.

Captain Taylor entered with purpose, his boots clicking sharply against the metallic floor. His presence commanded attention, and the hum of conversation dimmed as heads turned to acknowledge him. Without breaking stride, he moved to the central console, taking in the displays.

"Status report," Taylor barked.

An officer at the primary station responded immediately. "Sir, last known trajectory indicates the Specter executed a gravity jump along the nebula's interference field. Current location is undetermined."

Taylor's jaw tightened. "We'll start along their last known course. Deploy search wings in a staggered formation. I want long-range scans active and every available drone launched for reconnaissance. No blind spots."

"Yes, sir!" the officer replied, relaying the orders to the appropriate teams.

Taylor turned to the communications officer. "Send word to all nearby assets. I want patrols diverted to the nebula perimeter. Tell them to report any anomalies, no matter how insignificant they seem."

The comms officer nodded, already inputting the commands. "Understood, Captain."

Taylor moved to the large central display, tapping a control to bring up a detailed map of the nebula and surrounding sectors. The swirling patterns of gas and interference flickered on the screen, a chaotic web that offered no easy answers. He studied it for a moment, his expression grim.

"Mark potential exit vectors based on their capabilities," he said, addressing the tactical officer at his side. "The Specter might be crippled, but it's fast and maneuverable. If they're trying to put distance between us, they'll take the most efficient route."

"Calculating now, sir," the officer replied, overlaying possible trajectories onto the map.

Taylor's gaze hardened as he watched the display update. "Prepare our intercept groups. I want them ready to move the moment we have a lead."

Another officer approached, tablet in hand. "Sir, initial scans show no signs of recent activity within the primary search zone."

Taylor frowned, his frustration barely concealed. "Expand the parameters. Double the search radius. If they're not where we expect them to be, they're where we least want them."

The officer nodded, hurrying back to their station.

Taylor's voice dropped slightly as he addressed the room as a whole. "Listen up. The Specter is not just another ship. It was designed to be elusive, to outmaneuver and outthink its pursuers. During the war, it was built specifically to evade even the deadliest of dreadnoughts, exploiting their weaknesses and making them look sluggish and obsolete. Its systems and agility make it nearly uncapturable. And now, we're tasked with catching the uncapturable. I don't care how long it takes or how far we have to go—we will find them."

The room seemed to grow more focused, his words settling over the crew.

"Sir," the tactical officer interjected, pointing to the display, "a cluster of systems along this vector could provide them temporary refuge. Minor settlements, old outposts… nothing significant, but enough to hide."

Taylor nodded, his mind already working. "Send a detachment to sweep those systems. I want detailed reports from each. If they've stopped to lick their wounds, we'll know about it."

As the CIC resumed its organized chaos, Taylor stepped back from the central console, his hands clasped behind his back. His eyes remained on the map, but his mind raced ahead. The Specter's captain might be clever, but Taylor knew the chase wasn't just about tactics. It was about resolve, and he intended to prove whose would hold.

***

The bridge of the Specter was subdued. Damage control teams calling in status updates through the comms. Sparks flew intermittently from exposed wiring, and the occasional groan of the ship's failing systems was a grim reminder of their precarious position.

Allison stood near the central console, arms crossed as she listened to the chatter. Veronica was nearby, leaning against a console and staring at the status readouts. The lift doors opened with a hiss, and an engineer stepped out, carefully navigating the debris and fallen panels scattered across the deck. Her face was smudged with grease, and she carried a tablet tightly in her gloved hands.

"Commander Jones," the engineer said, stepping forward and handing her the tablet. "This is the latest on the engine repairs. We're at forty-five percent capacity, but honestly, it's not looking good. The entire assembly is trashed. We're patching what we can, but in my professional opinion, we'll need dry dock to get this fixed properly. It'd be easier to replace the entire system."

Jones' groaned as she scanned the report. "Forty-five percent. That's enough to keep us moving, but barely. All right, I'll inform the Captain. Keep your teams focused on stabilizing what you can. Prioritize life support and navigation."

The engineer nodded. "Understood, ma'am." She turned and carefully made her way back to the lift, stepping over a twisted piece of metal as she left.

No sooner had the lift doors closed than another hiss signaled their reopening. This time, Traci stormed onto the bridge, frantic. Her presence drew immediate attention, and she wasted no time, heading straight for Jones.

"Commander," Traci said urgently. "We need to set a course and get out of this nebula. Now."

Jones turned to her. "First of all, you're not in command here. Second, the ship can't even limp out of this nebula right now. It's keeping us concealed, and that's the only reason we're not already dead."

Traci didn't back down. "Taylor isn't an idiot, Allison. He'll send his smaller ships to scout for us, and when they find us—and they will find us—his carrier or one of his heavy cruisers will be right behind them. We're sitting ducks here!"

"And what do you propose?" Jones shot back. "We make a break for it in a ship that's barely functional? The nebula is the only thing keeping us hidden long enough to make repairs. I'm not risking the crew because you're panicking."

The two glared at each other, their voices rising as the argument escalated. Veronica shifted uncomfortably, glancing between them but saying nothing. The tension on the bridge was thick when the sound of boots echoed from the corridor, and Captain Pierce stepped onto the bridge.

"She's right," Pierce said calmly. Both women turned to face him. "We slipped through Taylor's lockdown. That's something he prides his carrier group on. He's likely taking this very personally, and he won't let it go. We need to move."

Jones hesitated, then nodded reluctantly. "Understood, Captain. Current status: engines at forty-five percent, life support stable but strained, and the cloak is completely offline. Navigation systems are functional but delicate."

Pierce absorbed the information. "It's not ideal, but it will have to do. Traci, you seem to have something in mind."

Traci nodded, stepping forward. "I have coordinates. A bit far from here—three days at best speed. There's a shipyard there. Secret, off the grid. And there's an asset I can get."

Veronica frowned. "You've been burned. How exactly do you plan to get this asset?"

Traci hesitated. "Traci Yamato has been burned. But not Lucy."

Jones and Veronica exchanged puzzled looks. "Who's Lucy?" Jones asked.

Traci sighed. "It's complicated, but let's just say Lucy is my real cover. The real Traci Yamato died years ago, and I assumed her identity."

Jones put her hands on her hips. "That's not something you just drop and expect us to move on from, Traci—or Lucy, or whoever you are. How are we supposed to trust you now? If you've been lying about who you are this entire time, what else haven't you told us?"

Traci stepped forward, her expression hardening. "You think this is easy for me? Taking on an identity, living a lie, always watching my back? Everything I've done has been to stay alive and fight against Cipher. If I hadn't assumed Traci Yamato's identity, none of us would even be here right now."

Jones' voice rose as she stepped closer. "And yet, here we are, finding out the person we've been working with isn't who they said they were! Do you have any idea what that does to the trust of this crew? Or to me?"

"Trust?" Traci shot back. "I've earned your trust through actions, not words. Have I ever betrayed this crew? Have I ever done anything to put us at risk? You're focusing on the name instead of the fight we're in."

Jones' eyes narrowed. "It's not just about the name. It's about transparency. If you could lie about this, what's stopping you from hiding something else? How can we know you won't turn on us when it suits you?"

Veronica shifted uncomfortably. "Maybe we should all take a step back. This isn't the time…"

"No," Jones interrupted, not breaking her gaze from Traci. "This needs to be said. If we're going to follow you to some secret shipyard, we need to know exactly who we're dealing with."

Traci's shoulders tightened. "I've told you what you need to know. I am Lucy. I'm the one who's been working tirelessly to stop Cipher, and I'm the one who has the coordinates to save this ship. You can question me all you want, but right now, we don't have the luxury of debating my identity. We're out of options, Commander."

"You think we're just supposed to trust you?" Jones spat, stepping closer to Traci. "After everything you've lied about? You've been hiding who you are this entire time, and now you expect us to follow you blindly? Who the hell do you think you are?"

Traci didn't back down. Her fists clenched at her sides. "I'm the person who's kept you alive, Allison. Every move I've made, every risk I've taken, has been to fight Cipher and keep this ship from falling into their hands. You think I'm hiding because it's fun? Because I enjoy it?"

"You've been lying to us from the start!" Jones shot back. "How do we know anything you've told us is true? How do we know you're not just another damn spy playing your own game?"

"If I were playing games, you'd be dead already," Traci snarled, stepping closer until they were inches apart. "I didn't ask for your trust, Jones. I've earned it. But you're so busy looking for reasons to doubt me, you can't see what's right in front of you!"

Jones jabbed a finger into Traci's chest. "What I see is someone who can't even tell the truth about her own damn name. Who are you, Traci? Or should I even call you that?"

The words hit a nerve, and Traci's composure cracked. "You wouldn't understand…" she muttered, turning slightly as if to step away.

Jones grabbed her arm, yanking her back. "Try me. Because right now, I'm one step away from throwing you in the brig until you decide to stop lying!"

Traci wrenched her arm free, her face twisting in frustration. "You don't get it! None of you do!"

"Then make us get it!" Jones snapped. "Stop dancing around it and tell me who the hell you really are!"

The bridge crew froze as Traci suddenly pushed back against Jones, their faces mere inches apart now. The two women stared each other down, their anger boiling over. Veronica made a hesitant step forward, but the tension snapped when Jones' fist shot out, connecting with Traci's jaw in a sharp crack.

Traci stumbled back, catching herself against the console. Her head snapped up, her eyes blazing with fury and something deeper—pain. Her voice erupted, louder than it had ever been.

"My name is Miyuki Saito!"

The declaration rang through the bridge like a gunshot, silencing everything. Even the damage control chatter over the comms seemed to fade into the background. Traci—no, Miyuki—stood there, breathing heavily, her hand rubbing her jaw where Jones had struck her.

Jones blinked, the anger on her face replaced by confusion and shock. "What?" she said.

Miyuki's shoulders slumped slightly, the fight draining out of her. "That's my real name. Captain Miyuki Saito. Holt's first science experiment. Their prototype. The mistakes they made with me, were lessons they used to perfect their damn monster."

The silence that followed Miyuki's explosive confession was almost unbearable. Jones, still stunned, tried to process what she'd just heard.

"What do you mean, 'Holt's science experiment'?" Jones finally asked.

Miyuki straightened slowly, wiping the blood from the corner of her mouth with the back of her hand. She closed her eyes tightly before she muttered to herself, almost inaudibly, "I am in control."

She repeated the mantra, her voice growing steadier with each repetition. "I am in control. I am in control. I am in control." Finally, she looked directly at Jones.

"They made me to be the perfect operative," Miyuki began. "Faster, stronger, smarter—all thanks to their precious nanotech enhancements. My stamina, my reflexes, my ability to heal... they designed me to be the ultimate soldier. A weapon that would follow orders without question. But they failed. Because I still had my free will.”

Jones sat on a nearby console, her disbelief giving way to curiosity. “Free will?”

“They didn’t want someone who could think for themselves,” Miyuki explained bitterly. “They wanted obedience. Blind loyalty. But no matter what they did to me, I refused to become their puppet. I… resisted. And for that, they discarded me. Labeled me a failure and put me back in the standard rotation.”

Her voice cracked slightly, but she quickly steadied herself, taking a deep breath. “The lessons they learned from me? They used them to create Cipher. She’s what they wanted all along. Perfection. A monster with no hesitation, no doubt. A weapon without a conscience.”

The bridge remained deathly quiet as Miyuki splayed out the entire ordeal. Veronica, who had been standing near the edge of the console, finally found her voice, though it was shaky and barely above a whisper.

“What about my sister?” Veronica asked, her eyes wide with fear. “What did they do to her?”

Miyuki’s gaze shifted to Veronica, her expression softening for the first time. She hesitated before she spoke bluntly. “I’m sorry, Veronica. Your sister is gone, she is no longer in there.”

Veronica’s face crumpled, her hand flying to her mouth as if to stifle a cry. Tears welled in her eyes as she staggered back, leaning heavily against the console for support.

“No…” she whispered, shaking her head as though refusing to believe it.

Miyuki's voice remained calm. "I'm sorry. They put us through hell, Veronica. Almost no one survived it. After the training process was complete, we were subjected to intense psychological tests and conditioning. They taught us how to endure the mental strain of what we'd become, but it broke most of us."

The tension on the bridge lingered as the weight of Miyuki's revelations settled over the crew. She stood at the center of it all, her presence commanding yet wearied by the truths she had just laid bare. Veronica's quiet sobs and Jones' conflicted expression were the only sounds that punctuated the heavy silence.

Miyuki straightened her posture, brushing her hands down her sides as if to compose herself. "Enough history. If we want to live, we need to move. Now."

Jones, still processing everything, snapped her head up. "Move? The ship isn't even close to being fully operational, and we're barely concealed here. If Taylor's hunting us, this nebula is the only thing keeping us hidden."

Miyuki stepped forward, locking eyes with Jones. "Three days away at our maximum speed. There's an asset there that I can retrieve. Something that will give us a fighting chance."

Veronica wiped her face, her voice trembling but clear enough to ask, "And how do you know this asset is even still there? Or that it'll work?"

Miyuki swallowed hard. "Because I've planned for contingencies like this. The shipyard is a ghost on every registry, and the asset is one of the few things I left behind there. If it's not there… then we're out of options."

Jones crossed her arms, skepticism etched across her face. "You keep talking about assets and plans. What exactly are you asking us to trust? You? Or some piece of equipment we don't even know exists?"

Miyuki sat on the edge of a console. "You don't have to trust me. But you'd better trust the fact that Taylor won't stop hunting us. Staying here is suicide. Moving is survival."

Jones' silence stretched, her eyes narrowing as she weighed the decision. Finally, she glanced at Veronica, who gave a small, hesitant nod. Turning back to Miyuki, Jones spoke firmly. "Set the course. But if this goes sideways, it's on you."

Miyuki inclined her head, a flicker of relief crossing her face. "Understood. I'll guide navigation to the coordinates. Let's not waste any more time."

As the bridge erupted into activity, officers relaying the new orders, Miyuki moved to a console. The past was a weight she would always carry, but now, it was time to focus on the fight ahead.

Epilogue

The Specter limped into the sector, its damaged systems straining under the effort as the hidden shipyard slowly came into view on the main display. The crew held their collective breath, not only from awe but from the uncertainty of whether the ship would hold together long enough to dock. The colossal structure nestled within the shadows of a dense asteroid field was an impressive feat of engineering, its design blending seamlessly with the surrounding debris, rendering it nearly undetectable.

Captain Pierce sat in the command chair with Jones and Veronica flanking him. Miyuki was stationed at the navigation console, relaxed as though they were simply arriving at a routine docking port.

"That's it," Miyuki announced casually. "Welcome to the Graveyard."

Jones frowned, leaning forward slightly. "What are we looking at here?" she asked, her tone laced with suspicion. Her eyes scanned the structure until a massive silhouette began to emerge from the shadows.

As the asset came fully into view, her jaw dropped. "Is that a…" she started, her voice trailing off.

Miyuki turned slightly, finishing the sentence for her with an almost flippant tone. "A Jovian Dreadnought? Yes."

Jones blinked, momentarily at a loss for words. "How…" she began before stopping herself. "How did you get your hands on that?"

Pierce's expression shifted, his curiosity piqued. "Miyuki," he said, leaning forward slightly. "How exactly did you come into possession of a Jovian Dreadnought?"

Miyuki glanced over her shoulder, and casually spoke as if discussing the weather. "Stole it."

Jones' eyes widened, her disbelief evident. "You can't just casually say you stole a dreadnought and expect us to be okay with that!" she scoffed.

Miyuki turned in her chair, her expression calm but sharp. "Fine," she said, folding her arms. "I found out about this while investigating a shadow faction—a faction that Cipher, some Senators from New Earth, and Admiral Jacobs was involved with that was secretly refurbishing these things and installing a cloaking device on them."

Jones shifted her posture. "And you just… what, waltzed onto a dreadnought and flew it away?"

Miyuki smirked slightly. "Something like that."

"Unbelievable," Jones muttered, shaking her head. "And you're saying there are more of these?"

"Yes," Miyuki replied without hesitation. "Cipher has the other. I don't know where it is, but this is the one I found. So I stole it and hid it here."

Jones stared at her, flabbergasted. "How… how does someone even steal a dreadnought?" she demanded, throwing her hands up. "That's not something you just do!"

Pierce raised a hand, gently grabbing Jones' arm to calm her. "Drop it, Commander," he said. "You could punch her until your arm falls off, but that's something you'll never find out."

Jones huffed but said nothing, clearly still processing the sheer audacity of what she had just heard. Meanwhile, the Jovian Dreadnought loomed ever larger on the display.

***

The narrow corridor was dark and ominous, the faint hum of electrical currents running through the walls the only sound accompanying Cipher's measured steps. Her polished boots clicked softly against the cold metallic floor as she moved down the passageway of her personal dungeon. The air was thick with a

389

mix of dampness and despair, the faint tang of rust lingering in the stale atmosphere.

On either side of the corridor, cells lined the walls, their occupants... were the arrested senators, their suits now tattered and their faces gaunt from months of captivity. Cipher was calm as she approached two specific cells, pausing between them. With a slow, deliberate motion, she placed a simple metal chair in the middle of the corridor and sat down. Her presence alone was enough to draw the attention of the prisoners within.

To her left, Commander Baptiste sat slumped against the wall of her cell. Her hair was unkempt, her face hollow with the weight of weeks, perhaps months, of captivity. She didn't look up as Cipher settled in. Whatever fire she had once held was long extinguished, replaced by the resigned silence of someone who had given up hope.

To Cipher's right, Ava Turing sat slumped on the floor of her cell, her back pressed against the cold wall. The CEO of Neura Tech's typically sharp, composed demeanor was gone, replaced by the hollow resignation of someone who had given up long ago. Her gaze was distant, unfocused, as though she no longer registered Cipher's presence. After 18 months in captivity, any embers of defiance or hope had long since been extinguished, leaving only a shell of the woman she once was.

Cipher leaned back in her chair, her hands resting lightly on her lap as her gaze flicked between the two women. She didn't speak at first, allowing the oppressive silence to stretch out, thick and heavy.

"You two have given me quite the dilemma," Cipher finally said, carrying an edge that made the air seem colder. "I must admit, I haven't quite decided what to do with either of you."

Ava didn't react, her hollow gaze fixed on the far wall of her cell. It was as if she hadn't even heard Cipher's words. Baptiste, on the other hand, shifted slightly.

"You've already won," Zoe said hoarsely. "Isn't that enough for you? Let us go. There's nothing left for you to gain by keeping us here."

Cipher's lips curled into a faint, humorless smile. "Let you go? Oh, Zoe, I think you misunderstand your position. This isn't about gaining anything. It's about ensuring I don't lose. You, with your rank and supposed resilience, are just a piece of the system I am tearing apart. And Ava? She's a shadow of the threat she once posed. You both represent relics of a structure I intend to dismantle, brick by brick."

Ava stirred slightly at the mention of her name but didn't lift her head. Cipher tilted her head, observing the broken CEO with mild curiosity.

"What's the matter, Ava?" Cipher taunted, her voice laced with mock concern. "No sharp retorts? No attempts at rebellion? You've been disappointingly quiet lately. Have you finally accepted your place here?"

For the first time, Ava's lips moved. "What's the point?"

Cipher's smile widened, though there was no warmth in it. "Exactly. What is the point? Resistance is futile. You were destined to end up here, like all who stand in my way."

Cipher shifted her attention back to Zoe. "And you? You still have that spark, that dangerous little ember of hope. Tell me, Zoe, what keeps you clinging to it? Surely you must see how pointless it is."

She didn't answer. The silence was answer enough for Cipher, who leaned back further in her chair, as if satisfied with the exchange.

"So here I sit," Cipher said, her tone almost conversational, "with two fascinating pieces of a puzzle. The question is… how best to play with them? Break them? Use them? Or perhaps simply discard them when I'm bored?"

A few moments of silence passed before Cipher stood abruptly, the chair screeching against the floor. She turned toward the exit. As she walked down the corridor, her cold, commanding presence lingered like a shadow.

A hand shot out from a nearby cell, gripping Cipher's arm with surprising strength. Prime Nguyen's gaunt face appeared behind the bars, her eyes burning with intensity.

"Why?" Nguyen rasped. "Why are you doing this?"

Cipher stopped. For a moment, she said nothing. Then, she stepped closer to the bars, leaning in until her face was inches from hers.

"Why?" Cipher repeated softly. "Don't blame me, Nguyen. I didn't create this mess. I simply.." Cipher looked around, as if scanning a list of words to find the right one, "stepped aside and let the inevitable happen. Your system was collapsing long before I arrived. All I've done is ensure the transition wasn't wasted."

Nguyen's grip tightened on her arm, trembling with frustration. "Stepped aside? You call orchestrating coups and imprisoning senators 'stepping aside'? You engineered this chaos, Cipher. Don't feign innocence."

Cipher's lips twitched into a faint smirk. "Engineered? You give me far too much credit. The cracks in your precious system were already there. I simply applied a little pressure, and watched how it crumbled."

She leaned in closer. "Face it, Nguyen. You and your ilk built this house of cards. I'm just the breeze that knocked it over."

Before she could respond, the sound of boots echoed down the corridor. Commander Kane appeared at the far end.

"Cipher," Kane said, stopping a respectful distance away. "Dr. Voss and Admiral Harker have urgent updates regarding Admiral Holt. They're waiting in the command center."

Cipher straightened, her smirk fading as she turned toward him. "Very well," she replied. She cast a final glance at Nguyen. Shifting to an almost mocking softness. "It seems duty calls."

Nguyen's grip tightened momentarily before slipping away as Cipher pulled back. Her eyes followed Kane, a flicker bitterness igniting in her eyes. "Kane," she rasped with disdain. "So, you're part of this too? A willing servant to her chaos?"

Kane glanced at her. "I serve the mission, not the person."

Cipher chuckled softly, her boots clicking against the floor as she began walking away. "Always so diplomatic, Commander," she said without turning back. "Come along. We don't want to keep them waiting."

As Cipher and Kane approached the exit, a faint, hoarse voice called out from the cell closest to the door.

"Water," the voice rasped weakly, barely audible. "Please… water."

Cipher paused mid-step, her head tilting slightly as she turned to look at the source. Hanging from the ceiling of the cell by his wrists and body stripped of clothing, was the man who had attacked her in the bar. His head hung low, his face gaunt and filthy, but the faint tremor of his voice reached her all the same. His toes barely touched the ground, just enough to keep him conscious but not enough to provide relief.

Kane shifted uncomfortably at Cipher's pause. "He's been here for three days. That I know of."

Cipher stepped closer and she stared at the broken man. Memories of that night flashed back—the cold tile floor of the restroom, the helplessness that had gripped her, the sneer on his face as he loomed over her. Rage bubbled up beneath her otherwise composed exterior, growing more and more by the second.

She grabbed a metal cup sitting by a nearby pail of water. The faint scrape of the cup against the metal pail echoed like a judgment. Kane watched her, uncertain of her intentions, but said nothing.

Cipher stepped unlocked the cell, the heavy iron door creaking as it swung open. The man lifted his head slightly at the sound, his sunken eyes locking onto her. For a moment, there was a flicker of recognition—then fear.

Without a word, Cipher dipped the cup into the pail and approached him, holding the water just out of reach. His cracked lips parted, his breath ragged with desperation.

"Thirsty?" Cipher asked, softly, almost tender and loving, but her words to wrought with hate. The man nodded weakly, a faint whimper escaping him. Cipher tilted the cup, allowing a thin stream of water to drip down in front of him—just enough to taunt him—before finally pressing the cup to his lips.

The man drank greedily, gulping the water as if it were the only thing tethering him to life. Cipher allowed him to drain the cup before stepping back, watching him. The faintest hint of a smile curled her lips.

Then, without warning, Cipher drove her fist hard into his stomach.

The man gagged, his body convulsing as he vomited the water he had just swallowed. It splattered onto the floor, mingling with the grime as he gasped for breath. Cipher stepped back, wiping her hand on her sleeve as she watched him with a cold satisfaction.

She got very close to the man's ear, her lips just centimeters away. "Did you think I'd forgotten?" she whispered. "Did you think you could take something from me and walk away unscathed? Look at you now."

The man coughed weakly, unable to respond. Cipher lingered for just a moment longer. Kane cleared his throat from the doorway.

"Cipher, Dr. Voss and Admiral Harker are waiting."

Cipher turned, smoothing herself back into the calculated calm as if nothing had happened. She cast one last glance back at the broken man. She spoke to him one last time, devoid of all emotion. "Enjoy the water. It's the last kindness you'll see."

She stepped out of the cell, her boots clicking sharply against the floor. Kane fell in step beside her as they walked out, the heavy door slamming shut behind them with a resounding finality.

***

The screen faded from black, transitioning to the vibrant logo of the Imperial Broadcasting Network. A solemn anthem played softly in the background as the image of two stars on top of each other dominated the screen. Moments later, the face of an impeccably dressed news anchor appeared.

"Good evening, citizens of the Empire," the anchor began. "Today marks the six-month anniversary of the glorious formation of the Centurian Empire, a milestone that signifies the beginning of a new era of prosperity and strength for all who call this empire their home."

The screen transitioned to a live feed of Emperor Jacobs standing on a grand balcony, overlooking a sea of cheering citizens. Clad in a regal uniform adorned with medals, Jacobs raised his hands, calling for silence. The crowd quickly hushed, their devotion palpable.

"Six months ago, we cast off the chains of Alliance oppression," Jacobs declared. "We took a bold step forward, creating a government that truly serves its people. Today, the Centurian Empire thrives, free from the corruption and stagnation of the so-called Alliance. Together, we have proven that a government for the people can be prosperous and strong."

The crowd erupted into applause as Jacobs paused, basking in their admiration. The camera cut back to the anchor, who continued the broadcast.

"While the Empire celebrates its achievements, it is imperative to remember that threats still linger. The enemies of the Empire remain at large, seeking to undermine our progress and destabilize our newfound freedom."

The screen shifted to display four photographs: Traci Yamato, Stephine Lopez, Jonathan Pierce, and Allison Jones. Each image was accompanied by red text labeling them as "Enemies of the Empire."

"These fugitives," the anchor said gravely, "have been charged with heinous crimes against the Centurian Empire, including espionage, kidnapping, and murder. Their most egregious act? The kidnapping and cold-blooded murder of the entire Senate of New Earth, carried out under orders from the Alliance Military Command."

The feed returned to Jacobs who was now speaking in softer tone. "I acted in the best interests of the people of New Earth and Centauri Prime when I exposed their plot. Their actions would have plunged us into chaos. It was only through decisive leadership that we were able to bring stability and hope to our people. This Empire stands as a beacon of justice and order because of our collective will to survive and thrive."

The crowd roared with approval, waving flags emblazoned with the Centurian crest. Jacobs continued, his voice rising above the noise. "Rest assured, these criminals will be brought to justice. They cannot run forever. We will not rest until they are held accountable for their atrocities against the Empire and its citizens."

The broadcast returned to the anchor. "The Emperor's words remind us of the vigilance required to preserve our great nation. As we celebrate this monumental occasion, let us also remember our duty to protect and uphold the values of the Empire. Together, we will endure, and together, we will prevail. Long live the Emperor. Long live the Empire."

The Imperial anthem swelled once more as the broadcast ended, the screen fading to black with the words, "Long live the Emperor. Long live the Empire." emblazoned in gold letters.